TIME OF THE PHEASANT

OTTO F. WALTER

TIME

OF THE

PHEASANT

Translated from the German
by Leila Vennewitz

Fromm International Publishing Corporation
NEW YORK

This translation incorporates authorized
revisions of the original text.

Grateful acknowledgment is made to
the Swiss Federal Department of Culture and
the Cantons of Bern and Solothurn
for their support of this work,
and to the Wheatland Foundation
for contributing to the translation
costs of this book.
Grateful acknowledgment is also made to
Pro Helvetia, The Swiss Council for the Arts,
for supporting this work.

The epigraph on page v is taken from *Faulkner in the University.*
Class Conferences at the University of Virginia 1957–1958.
Editors, F. L. Gwynn and J. L. Blotner. Vintage Books, New York.
Copyright 1959 by University of Virginia Press.

Designed by James Campbell

Manufactured in the United States of America

Printed on acid-free paper

First U.S. Edition 1991

Cover printed by Keith Press, Inc., Knoxville, TN
Printed and bound by R.R. Donnelley & Sons Co.,
Harrisonburg, VA

Library of Congress Cataloging-in-Publication Data   ′
Walter, Otto F., 1928–
[Zeit des Fasans,   English]
Time of the pheasant / Otto F. Walter ; translated from the German
by Leila Vennewitz. — 1st U.S. ed.
p.   cm.
Translation of: Zeit des Fasans.
ISBN 0-88064-129-0 (cloth: acid-free paper): $21.95
I. Title.
PT2685.A5Z313   1991
833′.914—dc20   91-3929

. . . time *is*, and if there's no such thing as *was*, then there is no such thing as *will be*.

WILLIAM FAULKNER

Translator's Acknowledgment

Throughout the work of this translation I have enjoyed the help, both expert and patient, of my husband William, for which I am deeply grateful.

L.V.

Contents

TIME OF THE PHEASANT

Time
of the
Land Appropriation

A s if a stage designer had conceived it for an old play, the night scenery
rose before them. The flight of steps flanked by terraces; at the top,
three more steps to the front door. The facade, lit only by scattered clusters
of light coming up from the town, rose massively into the darkness. One
of the windows on the second floor showed a light.

For a moment, the taxi could still be heard as it accelerated outside
the entrance gate on its way down to the town. Thomas and Lisbeth
walked slowly up the steps carrying their bags. At the front door, Lis
asked why he had never told her what a big house it was. Thom put
down the suitcase and rang the bell. He couldn't think of an answer. He
looked around. The tops of the two hickory oaks were lit up as if by
concealed spotlights. When the latch release buzzed, Thom, as he always
used to do, pushed open the heavy panel with his right shoulder. "Come
along."

In the hallway he groped for the switch on his right; three of the
four chandeliers lit up. Still the same dim light from the weak candelabra
bulbs; then the sound of a door being shut upstairs. As they advanced
into the hall, another light shone out above them in the gallery. Lis stood
beside him. Looking up, they saw the woman come down a few steps.
Before reaching the curve in the staircase, she stopped.

"Ciao, Gret," said Thom. And: "This is Lisbeth Bronnen." To Lis:
"My sister, Margaret, Mrs.—" He couldn't bring himself to utter the
name. "What's up, Gret?"

She continued to stand there, in her old-fashioned dress with the lace collar. "Gret, what's going on?" How much weight she had put on, suddenly a matron, at least since Thom's last visit. In fact she looked as if, in the performance in which Thom and Lisbeth seemed to have found themselves, she had assumed the role of Grandmother Helen. When Gret said, "Oh, it's you, is it? Why didn't you phone?" he was shocked at the sound of that now so familiar voice. Had she been drinking again?

She looked down at him as if he were responsible, though unwittingly, for some disaster, or even a crime. Fond as he was of her, this tendency of hers toward dramatization bothered him. They no longer even knew his addresses, she said. Ah well, she had probably been expecting Samuel. Was he supposed to feel guilty?

She proceeded to come all the way down. As she kissed him on the cheek, her breath smelled of red wine. They sat down in the pantry off the kitchen, where Gret had put out some bread and cheese, as well as a bottle of Fleurie. There was only a brief reference to each other's health, to the long train trip from Berlin. Also some mention of the uneasiness in town; word had somehow slipped out about the Winter Corporation's plans to cut back the work force by half in a large number of branch factories and subsidiaries. "Do you remember Uncle Ludwig's dream of an unmanned, fully automated plant? Samuel says this is now being put into effect, step by step. What's to be done?" Gret looked at them both as if they were experts.

"A sit-in!" said Thom with a laugh. "Why not? Seriously, what influence do we still have?" After all, they—Gret and he—had long since sold their last few remaining shares.

They ate, they drank. From the empty kitchen came the sound of the dripping faucet. Could Lisbeth and he stay for two nights? He would like to show Lisbeth this house, and the town too. Lis mentioned that she must be back at her editorial desk by mid-July. In these scant three weeks they were planning to go from here to France. To Burgundy, then farther south. Gret asked no questions, merely echoing: "Burgundy?" repeating the word as if her mind were suddenly elsewhere.

Later the three of them went upstairs, Thom carrying Lisbeth's suitcase. He heard the two women behind him talking about Gret's children. Barbara was nearly seventeen, Urs was twelve; they were already fast asleep. Upstairs Gret showed Lis to Thom's old room and switched on the light. "Here." And Thom could sleep in the Blue Room; that one was also made up. Then she left.

"Strange," Lis said in a low voice. "A strange woman." She smiled.

"Already she's separated us." Never mind, they really were tired after their journey. "Are you going to show me everything tomorrow?"

In the doorway she added, "What's this smell here? Kind of sweetish. As if the floorboards were rotting?" And: "Must feel odd, being a visitor like this in your own home."

Thom, already at the door of the Blue Room, turned back and went downstairs again. He wanted to finish the bottle of Beaujolais at his leisure. Gret must have turned off the light; hall and corridor were in darkness. So, as he used to do, he moved along in the dark. There, just ahead of him to the left, must be the massive black sideboard. He groped for its edge. Now the gilt frame of the Holy Family; now he could already touch the door to the Paneled Room.

Here, in the largest room in the house, he saw them all sitting in the light, at the near end of the long table placed across the width of the room. He wasn't really surprised. He had, it seemed to him, expected to meet them, Aunt Elsa and Uncle Theodor and his mother—yes, her too, and Uncle Ludwig and the rest of them, in those costumes of their day, all at the table, all looking at him; in the middle, Grandfather Elsazar and old Lilian too, all pale, solemn, in their satin dresses and cutaways and starched white shirt fronts. They looked, it was true, as they must have done after the disaster: characters, that's what they had probably been called in those days, but perhaps oddballs, to be more precise, powdered with dust from the plaster trickling down from the ceiling. The wall at the end was open. Billowing smoke curled over the ground beyond toward distant rocky cliffs. His father was there too. He raised his glass: Welcome, Thom!

A sudden fear gripped him. He quickly closed the door and went upstairs. In the bedroom he lingered for a moment at the window. Directly in front of him and above was one of the two hickory oaks, moonlight spilling through the branches in streaks, as if it were draining away.

He wondered whether Lis, next door, was already asleep. Not until Thom pulled up the quilt did he realize that he was lying in his mother's big bed. The moonlight began to fill the room, brighter now, moonlight mingled with the reflection coming up from the town, reddish, as if a distant farm were on fire.

*　*　*

It might really turn out to be quite pleasant: slowly you would surface from the confusion of your dreams, you would hear something like the sound of a flute, you would realize more and more clearly: I am here, where I grew up, everything is still there. And then feeling the cold water on your face. You go to the window, open it wide. In front of you the trees, beyond them in the sun the roofs of the town, high-rises among them. Breathe deeply, deeply in and out, and just below you, off to the right, the women already having breakfast at the round stone table, their voices, Lis and Gret. And then still that fluting or whistling sound. You would also discover, through the juniper branches, the two boys, perhaps twelve years old: the light mop of hair and that brown one, probably yourself, with your friend Rolf. They are sitting on the flagstones beside the flight of steps, directly below you. Now that thin, high sound made by a hammer struck lightly on a metal tube. You look more closely; they must have sawed out a piece of light metal tubing from a forgotten tent pole or from the frame of a cheap garden chair, then drilled holes and enlarged them, and fashioned a mouthpiece from wood and fitted it into one end. With a hammer the brown mop carefully flattens a dent, puts the tube to his lips, again three or four drawn-out sounds. Then the light-haired one joins in with his drum, softly, drumming with his sticks on the empty gasoline can between his knees. Yes, together they are playing a slow melody, perhaps one they have made up, playing just for themselves, absorbed, and as if astonished that from these bits of scrap and what they are doing with them should come music, their own awesome music. For a few seconds, something approaching happiness. Yes indeed, a day starting like this might actually turn out well. To walk downstairs through the house whistling; to be dazzled by the brightness outside; at last the hot coffee on the stone table, and at last that curiosity again: But tell me, Gret, about your lives, how are you? Yes, and how did it happen? And why: two days ago? Since when does this Bond Corporation from Minnesota hold the majority of shares? Why on earth do they want to shut down the foundry? Surely they can't be wanting to fully automate *everything*?

How did the conversation then turn to their mother's mother? Grandmother Lilian, the day after the events of October 1917—but, as noted, merely a family rumor—had been sitting in her Empire armchair beside the tiled stove in the big study in Mümlis, when her husband came home from the comb factory, in the middle of the morning, breathless with the news of the storming of the Winter Palace. At first all she said was, "Mais non!" But then she must have sensed that in faraway St. Petersburg something new of world-historical importance was beginning, for she added, "That does it!"

Alois, her manservant, is said to have stood in the open doorway, one-eyed, and long since subdued by Lilian, so she believed, to be her tool: to have stood there laughing, soundlessly and shamelessly, like someone who had long merely dreamed of revenge. And something else: two or three times he uttered a phrase rarely heard in this environment, much less in this situation: What a bunch! Probably because Thom's mother had always told this as if it had been an amusing recollection, he had for years regarded the connotation of the phrase as comical.

Why couldn't it have been like that: a permanent state of happiness for all, from one period in time to the next!

No permanence. War. Scenes of a struggle. For years, for decades, they haunted the house, became legends. That day in the study, remember? When did it start? It was already like that in 1936, wasn't it? And when my brother Ulrich came back from Berlin? . . . Legends.

Happiness is something it should be possible to describe.

So back to describing the celebration, describing that Sunday. And stopping for a moment in the corridor in front of the painting. The Holy Family. No sign now of the rip in the canvas. In the rather dim light you have to reach over the sideboard and carefully pass your fingertips over the paint to feel the tear that has been patched up from the back; perhaps feel that someone has taken a brush and tried to join the torn paint surfaces together again. The tear runs down from the Virgin's head and over to the left as far down as the foot of the manger. Charlott had once shown Thom the scar with a flashlight. Right along here, see?

Thom, when told about it, had had no trouble picturing the scene: the study, festively decorated with flowers on table and buffet. A happy coincidence had given rise to the celebration: at the very time when discreet preliminary discussions were being held about taking over the majority of shares of the Von Moos Company (Building and Textile Machinery) of Zurich by the Winter Corporation of Jammers, Paul Winter and Jenny von Moos announced their engagement. The mother of the future bridegroom, Helen Winter, together with the Von Moos parents, had issued invitations to a luncheon in the well-known resort of

Bad Lostorf, which happened at that time, though only briefly, to be controlled by the Winter Corporation. In addition to the immediate families involved, male in-laws by the names of Bircher, Rieter, Von Sury, and Hector Ammann, accompanied by their wives, had attended.

So, shortly before four o'clock the company had been driven up in seven black limousines to the steps in front of the Winter mansion to have tea. The guests lavished praise not only on the cakes but on Lilly Winter's vocal performance in the music room as she accompanied herself on the guitar. Text and melody had been especially written and composed by her for her brother-in-law and his bride-to-be.

Not until very much later, when Thom heard about the legendary quarrel and the rumors about politics, could he imagine what lay behind it. In a gradually more relaxed, indeed lighthearted, mood, the guests had gathered for a final glass in the study, where they sat or stood around chatting. And that was when Ulrich Winter, doubtless no longer quite sober, is said to have begun describing his trip to Berlin, having come home only a few days earlier from a visit there as a member of a delegation consisting of politicians and prominent businessmen.

Silence fell in the big room when, leaning against the mantelpiece, he began to tell them about the negotiations with Mr. Funk, Reich Minister of Economics. Yes, and then, on Monday evening at six, the delegation had had a private audience with the Führer. Even Funk, what an outstanding man! But then the Führer. Succinct, clear, no beating about the bush. The shrewd policy of courageous Switzerland: Adolf Hitler had no doubts whatever as to the strict policy of neutrality of that little country with its considerable economic capabilities. This neutrality, the Führer said, by no means excluded cordiality on both sides! Switzerland too—being, after all, part of the Aryan culture—would have to assume its share of obligations, now that the German Reich was turning with determination toward its historical task: the renewal of Europe. The way he stood there! Those eyes, as he looked at each one of us in turn! It was not the Führer's way to lay down the law for sovereign neighbor states—he smiled as he said this—but, gentlemen—and now he was suddenly the impassioned Reich Chancellor vibrating with energy, as we know him from his speeches: In this struggle, the call goes out to every, ev-e-ry man! This applies also to the Germanic peoples in the south with whom we feel united in a single common German culture! With a Gentlemen!, his arm raised in the Hitler salute, he dismissed us. Unforgettable! That magnetism—such charisma!

Ulrich Winter admitted that now, after that meeting, he was beginning to understand how a vanquished Germany, which until 1933 had done little more than lick its wounds, had been able to rise to new greatness in so short a time. The wild cheering that surged around Hitler was, he said, the expression of a nation's soul that had spent long enough vainly thirsting for self-respect and new tasks, new shores. This total mobilization of all the forces of the German people: only a strong, towering born leader of the caliber of Adolf Hitler had made that possible. Political decisions of the utmost consequence were being made there by *one* man—believe me, not like our country's democratic hot-air club, where each and every vote is blocked by a counter-vote. Only yesterday: six million unemployed. Today: no longer a single German without a job—after only three years of Hitler as Reich Chancellor! The wheels of the German economy are turning at full speed! Minister Funk reduced it to a concise formula: You know, he said, in the German Reich today everyone, every single person, knows what he is living for.

Ulrich Winter drank up his wine. Then, into the silence, a clear voice from the sofa: "Ulrich—for *what?*"

Ulrich looked at his wife in amazement. "Don't you understand? Quite apart from the fact that, finally, peace and order prevail again in Germany, in France we have the Leftist Popular Front running the country; in the East, Bolshevism is on the march westward in the name of world revolution; here in our own country Communists and intellectuals are doing their utmost to undermine Christianity, property laws, every aspect of authority." As a Catholic, as an industrialist, all he could say was, with Hitler's Greater Germany, *the* counterforce was at last emerging in Europe!

He smiled. "It is about time," he said, "that we—we Swiss, with our great industrial potential—recognize the writing on the wall of history and—need I say, without swallowing orders from the north!—that we recognize which side *our* bread, too, will be buttered on."

Would he, Mr. Von Sury interjected, be good enough to be a little more specific?

"Friends, is it really so difficult? We stand to gain! Because we'll use the German Reich as a protective power! And, in a word, as a market. As a model and a market!"

Uncle Ludwig laughed. "Very nice. Only, you know, Hitler—that means war, not tomorrow but the day after."

Ulrich Winter again: "We Swiss industrialists aren't afraid of any war. Remember how, in the 1914–18 war, our father supplied both sides, France and Germany, from the solid base of our neutrality? And didn't do so badly!" The men nodded. Only Mr. Rieter interjected, "But that can also lead to some kind of dependency, which we didn't want, did we?" Suddenly Grandmother Helen was heard to say, "This Adolf Hitler has been sent by Providence. He has admitted it himself, quite openly. So why should we worry? 'Man proposes, God . . .' " With a wise smile she raised her white hand.

Back to that wish, that things had remained this way, still peaceful. Describe happiness. And conjure up at least the study with the ancestral portraits on the wall, Theophil Winter, Elsazar Winter, and place the little oval portrait on the smoking table, the yellowing tinted photograph of Great-Grandmother Blanda in its narrow gilt frame, place it next to the lamp supported by the bronze figure of an ahistorical feminine form reaching toward the light. Describe how the cheerful Sunday afternoon gathering, having progressed from tea to Cointreau, say, or the sweetness of a discreetly parchment-colored Graves, lapsed into a comfortable silence, until Lilly Winter said, very quietly, "Did you actually say 'model'?"

"Yes. What about it?"

"For a moment I had to think of your friend Engelbert, Engelbert Dollfuss: shot two years ago, when he was chancellor of Austria, by Hitler's henchmen. I have to think of the concentration camps in Oranienburg, in Königswusterhausen, of the thirty thousand people arrested by the Storm Troopers in Berlin alone. Have you forgotten what that cabaret artist, Erika Mann, was telling us the other day at the Vontobels' in Zurich? Private prisons! And the torturing going on there! Oh, Ulrich! And why don't you read that book by Wolfgang Langhoff, *Rubber Truncheon?* Remember how shocked we all were? Concentration camps, torture, people being shot to death! Model? You never mentioned that before."

For a while Ulrich said nothing. As if sunk in thought, he gazed at the tall glass in his hand. In any case, we may assume that eventually he spoke, solemnly and like a man instructing his family in the ways of the world: "I needn't tell you what a terrible blow the murder of my friend Engelbert was to me. A shock!" But he had to admit that this trip to Berlin had changed his point of view on what was happening there. And he recited: The World War; the General Strike; Spartacus, the soldiers' and workers' councils, the revolutions! In their wake, the worldwide economic depression—our factories alone lost forty percent of their orders! Chaos, anarchy! Our own worthy liberal democracy could no longer cope with that onslaught. We might wake up tomorrow to find a Popular Front even in this country—look at Spain, at France! And now, in this hour of extreme peril, the answer to history's needs was emerging in this Christian part of the world, born in dire travail out of the profound depths of the people, humanity's primeval longing for unity, order, and peace: truly the sole conceivable bulwark against the forces of disintegration. To be sure, this birth of the New Order was not occurring without sacrifice, without pain. Had it not ever been thus in human history? The new was not to be achieved without the destruction of the old that we so cherish. History had rarely run a linear course; the law of renewal manifested itself like a volcano—in eruptions, instinctively, out of the archaic bubbling caldron of the suffering peoples' soul. Model?

He hesitated, we may assume, and drank a mouthful of wine.

Not by copying, but by drawing on our own traditions, men must now assume the leadership in this pigsty! Men capable of taking ruthless measures. We need a renewal of the political structure. Strict curtailment of parliamentary rights. A government with a strong hand, with a president vested with special powers to *lead*.

Mr. Rieter asked whether that didn't mean declaring a state of national emergency?

Ulrich Winter breathed heavily. Yet he was smiling as he crossed from the fireplace to the massive writing desk. He opened the middle drawer. When he turned around, still smiling, he was holding a small swastika pennant. "Exactly," he said. "A state of national emergency. A gift—from Minister Funk."

Describe what presumably happened. Reconstruction of possible history; a supposition. "A cross," Ulrich said. "If we disregard the colors, not unlike the Swiss cross."

Now Lilly Winter. She had risen from the sofa, but before she could say anything, Mr. Bircher muttered something from behind his cloud of cigarette smoke. "Friends, he's right, you know, new horizons are looming. I have no objection, but it is the degree, my dear Ulrich, the extent . . ." He fell silent.

Hector Ammann laughed. Anyway, it wouldn't hurt if in this country too the representatives of Jewish high finance, Messrs. Cohn, Rothschild, Breitkranz, and their cohorts, were shaken up a bit!

Ludwig Winter added, "Instead of swilling champagne in St. Moritz!"

Leaning against the table in front of the tall mirror, Lilly Winter said, "I simply don't know what to make of you anymore! It sounds as if the whole lot of you intend to join the National Front!" In a mere whisper, as if to herself, she said, "Crazy!" Then, turning to her husband almost imploringly: "Say something—surely you can't be serious?"

In her armchair Aunt Esther was toying with the letter opener from the desk. "But Lilly—you, a woman! They're discussing politics!"

Ulrich said drily, "Join the Front? No, Lilly," he laughed, "we'll be more discreet than that! Naturally I'm determined to see that the Frontists—and their numbers are growing!—get a sizable sum each month, on the quiet . . ."

Hector Ammann added, "As Count Schlieffen used to say: 'Give me a strong right wing!' eh?"

Exactly. Furthermore, they would have to work in a small committee here—Ulrich looked around the gathering—*en petit comité* toward the formation of what might be called a Patriotic Society, toward an alliance of influential personalities in politics and industry, to exert pressure on both major parties *and* on the government in Bern. "You are aware of my close contacts with the Federal Councillors Motta and Baumann."

Hector Ammann applauded. "And the first action of that alliance," he exclaimed, "must be to demand the immediate cessation of the anti-German hate propaganda in the Swiss press. We will demand that those editors in chief, Schurch of the *Bund*, Bretscher of the *Neue Zürcher Zeitung*, and Oeri of the *Basler Nachrichten*, be relieved of their posts. We'll bring pressure to bear!"

Was it like that? Was the germ cell of that group of Swiss industrialists, military officers, and politicians formed that Sunday afternoon at about 5:30 in the study of the Winter mansion, the group that demanded an "accommodation" of Swiss politics, a "new orientation" toward the goals of Hitler's Fascism? The group that was later to achieve fame with its "Petition of the Two Hundred"?

It could have been like that, and Ulrich Winter, now back in his place beside the mantelpiece, could have declared, "What Hector has just put forward is in line with the expectations expressed to me—confidentially, of course—by the German ambassador in Bern three weeks ago. Those fellows from the press go too far! The Reich Minister in Berlin put it—carefully!—this way: 'As long, gentlemen, as these smear campaigns against our Third Reich continue, not only in your Leftist newspapers but also in your conservative press, it will be difficult, indeed impossible, for our two countries to sign new trade agreements. You understand?' "

Yes, why couldn't it have been a time of peace, of continuing happiness for all? For a few moments now, Thom could picture his mother, her face flushed, forcing herself to remain calm. And saying, "No." And slowly, again as if only to herself: What she had suspected was bad enough, but what she was hearing now—beyond belief. Ulrich! In the face of this Greater Germany, this rising threat to the whole world, there was only one response, self-assertion, only the utmost resistance! Didn't they have allies, from Poland to France, from Hungary to Norway and even to England, to the United States?

Ulrich Winter was not to be shaken. He even smiled. "My wife, you know—she's only taken an interest in politics since Dollfuss's death. It affected her deeply—didn't it, Lilly? Only too often praiseworthy emotions—unfortunately—make for bad politics." And she must learn the meaning of the phrase: A well-considered step backward leads farther than two ill-considered steps forward. Here it was a matter of cool diplomatic deliberation, as we all know: a matter for men to decide.

Her lightly trembling hand to her chin, Lilly Winter left the room. Was it like that? And then, as Herminia knew, she was suddenly sitting at the big kitchen table, looking forlorn. And suddenly, with a sob, she had run upstairs.

At about 6:30 the limousines sped away down the drive.

Then Ulrich Winter, in hat and coat with his walking stick beside him, must have been driven off too, by Mr. Wenger, the chauffeur, while the parlormaid opened wide the library windows.

Legends? Yes, nothing more. Scraps in the memory of those still alive, vestiges of scraps of memory. Reconstruction, an attempt: that scene, too, when Ulrich Winter is said to have come home drunk at eleven at night. When, so they say, he stood in the hallway, still in hat and coat, and suddenly started screaming incoherently. First, it seems, he smashed the vase on the sideboard with his stick; then, with a second flailing blow to the sideboard, the walking stick itself. What was left of the stick in his hand, the broken-off handle, he flung away with a "Goddammit!" Fate, or whatever, intended that the handle should strike the painting over the sideboard, just where the smiling Virgin bent over the Child.

The artist who had restored the painting had done a good job. One had to look very closely to make out the tear that had been painted over.

After breakfast at the stone table, Thom had gone upstairs. At the writing desk in the Blue Room he then tried to type out at least a few of the notes he had composed in his head on the way here.

A few notes? That sounded harmless enough. At heart he had known for days that he would have to start all over again on his historical work, even on the outline, the draft. All over again!

After his conversation in Berlin with that retired Major General Ulrich Lyss, he had had to accept the fact that his work could not be limited solely to the evaluation of those military documents captured by German troops. To be sure, the documents and what they proved—that General Guisan, commander in chief of the Swiss Army, had personally and at enormous risk violated the fundamental principle of Switzerland's armed neutrality—were in themselves a historically remarkable event. Remarkable—for whom? For a moment he had a vision of Lisbeth in her living room on Schlüter-Strasse, Lis with the questioning look in her eyes: For whom, Thom?

After weeks of waiting, the conversation between the retired major general, now over eighty, and himself had finally taken place. For over three hours the old officer had readily answered Thom's questions, occasionally consulting the two files of private papers before him on the desk, looking for a date, a name perhaps, but otherwise recounting, from memory and with complete accuracy, piece by piece, the bizarre story of those documents and their significance for the German government of those days. The word "remarkable" had been uttered for the first time as soon as Thom had sat down across from the old gentleman. In a tone appropriate to an official interview, Lyss had asked Thom which aspect interested him, the purely military or the political. The political. Thom's letter, with a copy of the commission that Thom had been able to obtain from the Swiss National Foundation for Scientific Research, lay in front of him. "Remarkable," he said.

But then, suddenly: "Very well, my young friend, let's get down to business. We'll start with the discovery of the documents. At dawn on June 16, 1940, our armored units reached the town of La Charité-sur-Loire, one hundred and fifty kilometers west of Dijon. There, on a railway siding, a freight car filled with ministerial documents fell into their hands, documents left behind by retreating French troops. Among them were three wooden boxes full of documents concerning a secret pact between the army command of ostensibly neutral Switzerland and the top French military leaders. At the time," the old general continued, "I was in charge of the Foreign Armies section in the Supreme Army Command. The documents were passed on to me. Evaluating them kept me busy for weeks. Five of my staff members in Berlin worked on them for months: the translation itself posed difficulties, many of the terms being in code.

"One thing emerged clearly: it was an actual military pact between General Gamelin of France and your General Guisan. It provided in every detail for the entry of French divisions into Switzerland, as well as for their deployment on a line running between the Alps from the Canton of Zug to Brugg, Stein am Rhein, and Basel: this in the event of an attack by us Germans on your country. It represented a flagrant violation of the Swiss principle of neutrality by your supreme commander. One intriguing detail: We, that's to say, the potential military enemy, now knew of this secret alliance and thus held a trump card—according to international law, the discovery of the documents at La Charité would have justified a German attack on Switzerland. However, the matter was given 'top secret' status and strictly withheld from the public as well as from the Swiss government—until such time as we could have used it as a pretext for an invasion. On the other hand, our embassy in Bern discovered that your Swiss government had not been informed of the agreement by General Guisan. Remarkable, wouldn't you say?" The old general had looked at Thom with a twinkle.

Why did the old fellow have to be called Lyss of all things! Lis had shaken her head. But then: "Remarkable for whom, Thom? That's all past history. Why bother about it?"

Thom heard a gentle knock at the door. Turning around, he saw Lis standing in the doorway. She came closer. "Caught you!" she said, with a glance at the desk. "Red-handed!"

It was true: Thom had promised her not to do any work during this vacation. The only excuse he could think of was that at breakfast she had said she wanted to have a look at the grounds, at the washhouse, the stables, so he had thought, Just a few more notes, otherwise he would lose the thread. Gradually, he told her, he had come to see, after his talk with the old war-horse, that he wasn't going to be able to make do with a mere study of the documents discovered at La Charité; that could merely be his point of departure. At least as a rough sketch, at least tentatively, he wanted to—no, he had to—devise a more comprehensive framework for his subject than the one he had planned. And the subject must now be: The General's Politics. Do you see that, Lis?

She stood beside him, over him. Slowly, with a smile, she shook her head. Now she was the one who said, "Remarkable." In the doorway she looked back. Dreamer! She laughed as she left. In fifteen minutes down in the hall?

Once more he was sitting alone with his notes. Dreamer. She was probably right. Now, though, could he make her realize that what he had in mind was important, at least to himself as a historian, as a citizen of this little country? To her, as a German, what he was embarking on might seem of little interest. "I know, Lis, I know. The history of your country, taking only the last fifty years, is much more brutal than anything we have experienced here. And yet, try to understand! If I establish a link between the General's secret alliance and his speech to the officers of the Swiss Army assembled on the Rütli meadow, and, moreover, the concept of the 'Alpine redoubt,' doesn't that plainly reveal the politics of a stage-by-stage military coup? On the other hand, aren't I bound to back up this conservative, highly punctilious commander in chief of our own army? Should he have acted any differently in the face of our hesitant, vacillating government? But then again, hadn't he put the country at risk instead of defending its independence by every possible means according to his mandate? What had motivated him to overstep his authority vis-à-vis our democratically elected government and parliament? Is it permitted, in a democracy, for the highest officer in the military hierarchy, vested as he is with extraordinary powers—is it permitted for him to be more farsighted in terms of national politics and to act more uncompromisingly than the civilian government, even if this means violating the law to which he is subject? Where is the borderline? Have you any idea, Lis, how that interests me?"

The fifteen minutes must soon be up. The only words on the sheet of paper in the typewriter were: "The General's Politics. Sketches. Questions." That was less than a fifth of what he had meant to put down. Never mind. Thom stood up, went out into the gallery, and walked down the stairs. Yet all this time he had the old, bald head of the German general in his mind's eye, a smile playing over those gaunt features. "My young friend: General Guisan was gambling for high stakes! When I think of what means of pressure Berlin had in its grasp! Your high-handed general, long known to us as being anti-German, could have been forced by us to resign. He lived under this threat, he was well aware of it, and the Swiss government knew nothing. But now for a neat twist: The documents vanished without trace."

The old gentleman had suddenly laughed out loud. "Oh yes, your beautiful country had friends in the highest echelons of the Wehrmacht too. It happened this way: As you know, Hitler quite often made decisions on impulse, in an outburst of rage, decisions of far-reaching impact. Naturally he intended to gain control of Switzerland, with its Alpine passes, as a bridge to Italy. Men like Kaltenbrunner were pressing hard for an invasion of Switzerland. Operational plans had long been drawn up, sixteen divisions were earmarked. We knew that this victory too would be ours, but at the price of how much bloodshed? So although the discovery of the documents was reported to the Führer's headquarters as well as to Foreign Minister Ribbentrop, the report was couched in such general terms that its explosive content remained shrouded. Today I can tell you—yes, of course, by all means make public use of it—it was Canaris, Admiral Wilhelm Canaris, head of counterespionage, or, if you like, of the secret service of the Wehrmacht. He was the man I consulted. He advised—or rather, he ordered—me to have the evaluation of the documents proceed as meticulously as possible and with due recourse to the opinion of experts in international law. Without another word being said, I understood. The documents were, if nothing else, to lose their topicality. So I began returning the material with a constant flow of new instructions to the evaluation group. Shortly after the fall of France, Canaris telephoned me and casually mentioned that he had urgent reasons to inspect the documents personally. They were conveyed to him. And they have never been seen since. Later I met Canaris again at the Foreign Ministry, shortly before his arrest. He took me aside. All he said was, 'About La Charité—remember? I have meanwhile declared this top secret affair to be *so* top secret that no one—no one!—up there will find out what the documents really contain, unless he hears it from me.' I asked him, 'May I know the reason for this extraordinary measure?' Canaris gave me a serious look. 'William Tell is a very remarkable dramatic figure—don't you agree?' "

* * *

Here on the second floor, two steps from the door to the library, he already noticed the smell he remembered from the old days. As a boy of fourteen or seventeen, he used to spend afternoons in the library sitting in the armchair at the far end on the left, secluded and protected by the massive chairback and the armrests upholstered in slightly greasy, slightly worn tapestry material. Yes, there it was, that smell of rotting wood and floor wax and mildewed paper.

He pressed down the latch. Under his forward impetus he almost crashed into the heavy door with his forehead. The door did not give. And now Thom also remembered how even in those days the library door had always jammed in summer; the paint in the door frame would soften in the heat and stick. While pushing down the latch, one had to press against the door panel with one's right hip, and the door would fly open.

The glass-fronted bookcases against the dark red of the walls, as always. Cobwebs between the locks. He pushed the door wide open. What was lying there in jumbled heaps on the floor of the long room looked like the contents of old mailbags, stuffed full of city archives, that someone had lugged up here, twenty or thirty of them, and tipped out onto the floor. Thom went closer.

Open file folders; bundles of letters tied up with string; cash ledgers with gray marbled covers; contracts; cardboard boxes labeled in old-fashioned handwriting: large envelopes, prospectuses, business reports: a mountain of papers. That evening Thom was to hear from his sister Gret that old Boschung had actually turned up one day with his van, many years ago, rung the bell, and said that, since there had been no member of the Winter family on the board of directors for a long time, he had thought that this stuff was of no concern to the new people up there, and without waiting for her reaction he had proceeded to carry the bags through the hall and up the stairs.

"But isn't there a lot of our own stuff there too—private papers, letters, diaries?" And again Gret, as she looked across the table, "Don't forget that we finally cleared out Father's study, everything he left behind, including the political stuff, and everything of Uncle Ludwig's too. Aunt Esther said she couldn't stand the sight of it anymore." So, Gret said, she had moved it all, at least for the time being, into the library. Thom stood in front of this pile of ancient family and company papers, stepped forward, took a closer look. With the tip of his shoe he pushed a file folder aside. He squatted and randomly turned over a few envelopes and tied-up bundles of letters, picked up a photo album: his father as a soldier; as a lieutenant; as a captain—no, not now. A diary? He pulled the book from the heap; it was bound in green cloth and had a clasp and leather strap. He stood up. The clasp sprang open when he pushed back the button. He opened the cover and started turning the pages from the back, went on turning them—all blank. Then, on one of the first pages, he saw a few words in a strong, emphatic hand: *Lilly Winter, my sister-in-law, did not die a natural death. She was killed.* That was all.

For a while he just stood there; the word "killed" became blurred, reappeared, in Aunt Esther's impetuous handwriting, as sharp as if etched in glass, and it was some time before he began to grasp that this information concerning the death of the woman who had been his mother struck him like a riding whip slashing across his face, or like a man's fist punching him right in the chest. Very slowly he walked across to the old armchair and sat down. No. No—impossible! How could that be! In this heat there was now also a smell of turpentine or paint and wood and of the hundreds of books in their leather bindings, and he tried to recall that summer afternoon of August 19, 1961, when, in the Blue Room upstairs here, his mother had ceased to live—passed away as he, at least until today, had believed. He also noticed how rapidly he was breathing, rapidly out and in.

And then that voice. It was there again when he returned from town around five o'clock and knocked at the door of Aunt Esther's suite: the voice that was too deep, too resonant, for the slight five-foot-four figure, a voice that could change, abruptly and for no reason, it seemed to him, into the whinny of a yearling foal, when she told him—a boy of six or twelve or seventeen—the story of his parents and his ancestors in general, her version being mostly full of contempt and outright hatred. "You must know everything," she had told him often enough. Everything, yes, and perhaps the only thing she had kept back was what prompted her to tell him about such things and people of the past, or even to tell at all—as, moreover, she had been doing for years. For so many years that he became addicted to all those incredible stories that she repeated and unfolded and invented during those far-off afternoons, while he, the addict, had gone to her and sat on the stool by the open window to listen to her voice, her room smelling of a blend of something like sheep's wool and quince jelly and marjoram, and of the pears growing up along the espalier wires and hanging, already overripe, halfway into the room. She told her stories. Time stood still.

Frieda opened the door to him. Her face, more wrinkled than ever, lit up with a beaming smile. "Come in, come in! Aunt Esther's expecting you!" And in a whisper: "She tires easily. And—well, you know how it is." She led the way, nodding her little head.

The sun was slanting through the open window. Aunt Esther, in her wheelchair, swiftly turned her head, then leaned back again as she gracefully offered him her left cheek to be kissed. "My beautiful sorrel," she said. "I had to have him put away." Thom sat down on the old stool, facing her, the green diary on his lap. She said it as if the fact that she could no longer ride across the fields behind the foundry as she used to had nothing to do with her seventy-six years.

She looked at him with her small, lively eyes. "Our man of action," she said, as she always had, adding, "When are *you* going to earn some big money? In Berlin, eh?" Ha! She had been there in 1932 but had left again immediately. Dreadful place—everyone there lived much too fast. And always those parades and those Storm Troopers and that military music. While Frieda, following the old ritual, brought in the tray with the two glasses, one red, one green, and the sherry, she picked up the skein of wool from the basket beside her armrest and proceeded to wind a woolen ball, crisscrossing the wool back and forth around a wad of paper until the whole thing had grown to the size of a croquet ball. Then with her needle she began to stitch a twisting, colorful pattern all over the ball. Thom knew that she would finish by fastening the ends and instructing Frieda to give the ball "to the children out there," without asking whether there were still any five-year-olds out in the garden or anywhere nearby. Frieda would take the ball and unwind the wool in her room, so that when Aunt Esther asked for more wool for new balls there was always a supply available.

At some point he managed to interject, "Listen, Aunt," and "Just a moment—tell me, what about this diary?" She had just begun to tell him again how her grandfather and "your father's grandfather," Theophil Winter, when he was scarcely thirty, had already organized almost a brigade of two hundred and fifty horses and a hundred and sixty men and sixty swamp plows especially designed by himself, and had drained the whole marshy, swampy piece of land west of the town, on the right bank of the Aare, almost all the way to Schönenwerd, in less than six months, after which he had summarily appropriated one-half of the drained and fertile fallow land—which, covered with reeds as it was, hadn't really belonged to anybody—and presented one quarter to the town and another quarter to the men who had worked there so hard for him with the horses, as a reward—a gift, do you understand? and she laughed her little whinny—so that the town council had no choice but officially to make over the other twelve hundred hectares with the newly constructed ditches and water rights to him—when Thom finally managed to say, "But Aunt, listen," she looked down for the first time at the green diary he was holding out to her, open. She put the unfinished wool ball aside. She took the book from him, held it close to her eyes, and when she lowered it at first said only, "Yes, of course." She looked up at him. At the time, she said, she had thought that this story of his mother's death must be preserved somewhere, in detail, word for word, what had led up to it over the years and the whole history of the clan, that it must be written down and preserved so that no one could come along later and say he—she laughed—or she had known nothing about it. So she had bought the empty diary, and in it had written this first sentence and then the second one. But then she had thought of all the thousands and thousands of sentences that would have to follow and had said to herself, No, the few short years remaining to me are much too precious to waste on that. Thomas, now, he's a historian after all, that's his field, and yes, she'd had one more idea: One day, I'm sure, it will occur to Thomas that he will have to write all that down, you know, he'll start researching and writing on his own because he will feel that at some point he'll want to come to terms with this whole past. "You see," she exclaimed, "I get it out of my system by talking, but a clam like you, with your university background—the day will come when you will have to write it down."

Thom said something like, "But that's impossible! It can't be! Murder! Why? And if it's true, for heaven's sake, who was it?" But she merely went on, as if he had known about it all along, "I've also wondered, of course, whether actually it isn't enough for four or maybe five of us to know what happened and what led up to it. Why isn't it enough for us to preserve Lilly Winter's tragic death in our memories until we too are gone? The Aare certainly won't stop flowing toward the Rhine merely because the story of one more murder will have vanished from the face of the earth along with us."

"You mean it's true? And which four or five of us?"

She handed the almost empty diary back to him, picked up her half-finished woolen ball, and slowly began crisscrossing the yellow thread around it again.

"Aunt Esther, please listen to me now. Here you've just confirmed this monstrous thing, and instead of telling me why it happened and who was the man, or for all I know the woman, who did it, you're telling me there are people who know about it. And you've included me? Why? And who was it? You must tell me"—Thom felt he was about to lose control—"please tell me: Who killed my mother!" He was breathing heavily. And while still gazing at her, waiting in unbearable suspense for her answer, he began to grasp that for old Aunt Esther his visit and that whole grim chapter had come to an end. She looked past him through the open window across to the fir trees. She was smiling. It was not too much to believe that a faint look of triumph passed over her face, as if she were sitting at the card table, as in the old days, and holding all the trumps. She said, as if to herself, "Do you remember—my beautiful sorrel? He went lame. I had to have him put away."

Hopeless. Thom knew that at best he might get her back on the subject again tomorrow or the day after.

From Class to Class

MY MATERNAL GRANDFATHER? HIS NAME WAS JEREMIAS SCHAUB. AT thirteen he started work, at home, sitting at a long table with his brothers and sisters and sawing horn plates into large and small pieces twelve hours a day. These pieces were turned into combs in the little factory below. In the adjoining stable were three cows. At sixteen he was taught how to make ornamental combs, those big ones, you know, those big, fretted combs made of tortoiseshell. Designing and drawing, from patterns and freehand, sawing, stamping, polishing. In 1888 Jeremias, now twenty-five, started his own workshop. Ten years later he had six employees. In 1899 he traveled to London with his wife Lilian. There he met a former fellow worker, Erwin Imfanger, ornamental comb maker from the Solothurn area. He heard that Queen Victoria was old and ailing. He heard: When the Queen dies, high society in the United Kingdom will go into mourning for a year.

Tortoiseshell is the dried horny plate covering the shell of the hawksbill turtle. Usually brown, sometimes mottled with gray. Very rare: black tortoiseshell. My grandfather and his colleague began to calculate. The

Queen was over eighty, her heart condition serious. They founded Schaub and Imfanger Company Ltd., London. The firm started to buy up black tortoiseshell—so far not much in demand—from all over the world. They raised loans. In London and Mümlis, near Solothurn, black ornamental combs were produced in cheap overtime, large ones, some even trimmed with pearls and tiny diamonds. But the stockroom in London was filling up. The situation became acute. The loans became overdue. But then, on January 23, 1901, at Osborne, Queen Victoria awoke no more.

A year later my grandfather and his partner dissolved the firm, splitting the spoils fifty-fifty, a million Swiss francs each. Two years after that, Jeremias founded the Schaub Corporation, later to become Europe's largest producer of tortoiseshell combs.

He was soon employing some six hundred workers.

But unfortunately he could not enjoy his happy state as comb baron for long. When fine tortoiseshell shavings catch fire, there is an explosion. Forty-three workers, men and women, lost their lives. And scarcely was the factory rebuilt two years later than the 1914–18 war broke out, and after that, in the twenties, women began wearing their hair "bobbed." No one was buying large combs anymore. Sales and work force decreased by 80 percent. Jeremias Schaub managed to make the transition to the upcoming plastics, and now, beside pocket combs, he produced the necessary Bakelite in the molding plant next door. However, the prosperous times of the golden age were over, and with them the millions.

Nevertheless, Jeremias Schaub walked erect until he fell victim to a stroke. "God Save the Queen" remained his favorite tune.

Thom walked from the hall through the glass inner door and the porch out onto the wide, roofed terrace behind the house. Had everything back there, he wondered, remained as if the years between his childhood and this day after his return had been erased? As if yesterday he had been eleven and today he were forty-four, without a break, and everything from the old days were closer—at least now, as he walked along the terrace as far as the three steps down to the gravel path—than all his life since then? As if that childhood feeling had been preserved in him in a glass jar sealed with a piece of pig's bladder, the way his grandmother and Herminia used to preserve jams or mushrooms—until the seal split open today and the old emotions flooded him with the onslaught of a sultry afternoon heavy with the scent of wistaria?

No. True, there on the right was the old washhouse, behind and beside it the iron posts strung with chicken wire fencing off the poultry yard; a bit farther on, the entrance to the stables, the juniper bushes, and the water trough outside the washhouse, though the water seemed to have been reduced to a trickle: all that was unchanged. But suddenly he noticed: the ash tree, fifty meters from the house, just where the meadow with its fruit trees—as always, somewhat neglected—began to slope up to the fir copse—the ash tree was no longer there. Yes, the tree, which in its two-hundred-year-old strength and its tall beauty had filled the space behind the house with its gentle rustling—the tree had disappeared, and then Thom remembered that Gret had written to him, months ago, that the ash, its core long since rotted away, had burst apart one stormy night with a mighty crash.

It sounded, Gret had written, as if three lightning bolts had struck the loft simultaneously. It was only when she saw the red blaze of the fire through the gallery window that she realized the ash had been struck. Flames had leaped up from the huge stump; the firemen had been able to prevent the fire from spreading to the washhouse and the barn.

The ash: that had been Thom's tree. My tree. How odd that sounds. Slowly he walked down the steps and along the gravel path past the swing until he stood on the gravel area that had surrounded the ash. The wooden bench was still there; old Sepp or someone must have sanded down the weathered dark green paint and repainted the planks. Just behind it a low mound of earth about three meters across, already overgrown with grass and tiny lilies. Somebody with a chain saw had probably reduced the unburned remains of the ash stump to ankle height, then covered the flat surface with an antisprouting coating to prevent the growth of new shoots, and finally spread stones and earth over it. Nice to see that, at the very edge, one shoot had still managed to sprout a foot or more above the surface. There were seven leaves on it, ash leaves. He visualized the tree's root system spreading through an area about the same size below ground as the trunk and branches had occupied in the air. He and Gret and Charlott and his cousin Rolf had had to join hands for the four of them barely to encircle the trunk.

Thom started. Right behind him came Lis's quiet voice: "Hey—are you dreaming?" She stepped beside him, looked at him. She had been calling him from the house, she said.

He placed an arm around her shoulder. "There used to be a tree here. Let's go."

Together they turned toward the back of the house. What could he have told her? How he used to sit up in the ash tree where the trunk forked into three smaller ones, sit there between the three trunks that grew out of one, for many a long afternoon? He would unhook the rickety wooden ladder from the washhouse wall and use it to climb the four meters to his eyrie. Then he would haul up the ladder, hang it on a snag higher up, and knees drawn up, back and head against one of the trunks, simply be there, eyes half closed, sitting in his tree fortress. Up there neither his mother's habitually controlled voice, nor his grandmother, nor the whip brandished by his father when he was drunk, nor anybody or anything else could reach him, high up where sitting quietly and just breathing and listening and sometimes looking had been enough to make him feel sheltered in this leafy silence with its gentle rustling, in a dimension where the borderline between being safe and happy and dead became blurred.

They sat down on the top step leading up to the terrace, their backs to the house. Once while I was sitting in the tree I watched a kite dive into the poultry yard. For half an hour I had been hearing the kite trilling away in the air; shortly after that the predator had flown above me into the ash tree. Motionless, like the bird, I watched it in the tree as it watched the chickens from its high perch. The chickens were pecking and cackling around in the yard behind the washhouse, as usual suspecting nothing. Years before, in order to protect them against predators, the hired man had strung wires back and forth across the little yard about two meters above the ground. So then came a sudden cracking of branches high overhead, a flapping of wings, and the kite plunged down through the ash tree in a nose dive through the crisscrossed wires. Just above one of the chickens it stalled, wings outspread again, and dug its claws into the chicken. I yelled. I shouted for Sepp—I knew he was busy somewhere in the washhouse fixing up some weathered storm windows with fresh putty. In a moment Sepp was at the door and, alerted by the noise of the struggle, pushing open the lattice gate and rushing into the poultry yard, ripping out a cabbage stalk on the way, then dashing through the frenzied bevy of chickens toward the corner of the yard where the kite was in the process of killing the chicken by striking its head with its beak. Sepp, who must have been all of fifty, hit out at the marauder: it dropped its booty, spread its angled red-brown-and-white-speckled wings, and whirred upward, immediately becoming entangled in the wires. As it hung there trilling, Sepp hit out with the cabbage stalk. Now the predator swooped down on him, and for quite a while all that could be heard was the frantic beating of wings and Sepp's gasping and cursing. Shielding his face with one arm, Sepp flailed around with the cabbage stalk more than he managed to hit the enemy. Almost beside myself with excitement, I climbed down the ladder from my tree.

By the time I reached the lattice gate, Sepp was already standing beside it, his lacerated face covered with blood, a deep gash from the bird's beak just below his eye, but laughing—"Got him, here, see? I finished him off"—and he held up the bird by its claws.

My father had the bird stuffed. It stands on the tiled stove in the Paneled Room, its wings half spread as if starting out on a flight into eternity. Sepp needed medical treatment. He was given a day off and three bottles of wine plus an extra thirty francs; and when I watched him again in the washhouse, three days later, and later again, as with bandaged head he carried on with his puttying job, he would suddenly say, "You saw it, didn't you."

It was only late that night, over a glass of wine in the Paneled Room— Lis and Thom had come back from two hours in town at the Waadtländer Hall, where Thom had arranged to meet his old friend André Rupp— that Thom told Lis about his discovery in the library in Aunt Esther's diary. Lis sat facing him in the armchair. She looked at him, then said his name, said only, "Oh, Thom."

Conversations with André I

WERE THOMAS WINTER'S SMALL PRIVATE REBELLIONS AND SELF-ASSERTION maneuvers to mark him as a product of his class and its culture? Introducing André Rupp, as a figure that forced Thom to take a critical look at his social class as a historical force. To see history from below, too. André Rupp, mathematician, jazz buff, and anarchist, as Thom's mentor. It was from him that Thom, at the age of thirteen, learned the art of illegally catching trout in the wooded gorge above the town, by hand or by blasting. André, five years older than Thom: Is he the one who showed the fourteen-year-old the articles in *Der Morgen*, that pile of yellowed newspapers, in which during the thirties Thom's father had expressed enthusiasm for Franco and the heroes of the Alcazar? Who told Thom the meaning of anarchism, and why the Spanish Civil War was the great European dress rehearsal, and for what?

André, constantly being fired from his jobs as a high school teacher. How he disappears, then surfaces again, still with his Dostoevski and his Bakunin, from which he reads aloud to Thom. How finally, in the sixties, he lands a job as assistant bookkeeper with the Winter Corporation.

Invent those exciting late afternoons when André would take Thom along to the nearby Hupper clay pit, where he taught him how to shoot with a small-bore gun, then with a revolver, and finally with the short-barrel Biretta poaching gun. He taught Thom to attach detonators to cordite blasting charges and blow up tree stumps. André, who used to say, "You never know, you might find this useful some day." The first person who said to Thom, "You are needed." He explained the difference between Marx, Bakunin, and Proudhon. Invent Andy and talk about him, just as Thom, on his way to meet André Rupp at the Waadtländer Hall, is telling Lis about André, his mentor.

"When did you two arrive? How long can you stay, Thom?" Then, to Lis, "How about you?" And: "Are you still searching for the meaning of history, Thom?"

André laughed. The vertical creases either side of the strong nose, the curving ones around the mouth, had deepened; his hair, still worn short, had finally turned gray. Yet when the laughter stayed behind on his face, as now, some impish quality emanated from him.

"You'll join me in a glass of this Yvorne, won't you?"

"There seems to be quite a lot going on at the plant," Thom said. The smile disappeared.

"What's happening here—" André hesitated. Well, up to now and over the last twenty years, the process of automation had gone along quite comfortably, relatively speaking. But now it had suddenly turned into a dramatic revolutionizing of the entire production. Naturally, he had somehow realized long ago that a new age was approaching with the advent of information technology. But till now nobody had been that interested in it. The first shock had been for the people in administration, three years ago, when they had to take computer-training courses. And in these three years the administration staff had shrunk from two hundred to a hundred and forty.

Till now, said André, all this had proceeded at a fairly innocuous pace. But according to management's most recent decisions, that was a thing of the past. "How's the wine? Cheers."

Lis asked how these plans had become known.

André put on his impish expression again. Photocopies of the resolution had suddenly turned up in every department. "Don't ask me who made those copies and distributed them—incidentally, management has reported the matter to the police and offered a reward of ten thousand francs for information that will clear up the mystery.

"At any rate," André went on, "at present there are hundreds of people still working in each of the rolling mills, the steel mills, the foundry, the machine works. Just imagine all those workshops, some of which are enormous: before you know it, there won't be a soul in them. A few technicians will be sitting high up in the control cabins, punching in the programs and watching the play of changing colored lights. Down below the cranes, the conveyor belts, the rollers, the foundry molds, or the assembly arms will be moving soundlessly like giant octopuses from prehistoric times. Day and night they will go on producing—undemanding, uncomplaining slaves. A team of twelve specialists to attend to programming, inspection, and repair will be enough for each plant. And otherwise? We humans would only interfere with the work of the computers. No, another three or four years, and we, together with our fine expert knowledge, we humans in the Winter plants, will be redundant. Electronics will replace us and produce faster, more accurately, and in greater quantity. Last night some union people showed a movie about a fully automated Japanese machinery plant—I must say: fantastic!"

Thom said something about the end of mechanized manufacture.

André nodded. An era was coming to an end. What they were seeing here was a transition to electronically controlled production. We human beings were being swept into a void.

Thom and Lis hesitantly sipped their wine. And then Lis: Something she wasn't clear about—didn't this trend actually also mean a release from the drudgery of imposed labor?

André smoked. "Of course," he said, "it could. But that would mean fundamentally different structures—free of domination. My old, old question, Thom, eh? How to bring about such changes in the face of so much power and privilege at the top?"

"I can hear your voice," said Thom, "was it twenty or twenty-five years ago? As we walked along the path beside the Aare? And you read Kropotkin aloud to me, far into the night, told me about the anarchist communities of the watchmakers in the Jura, about Proudhon's federation principle, about the dream of the peaceable agricultural communes in Spain, about domination-free communal life in solidarity."

André looked across, the merry gleam once again in his eyes. "Nice to hear that; so you haven't forgotten?" And to Lis: "You know, I had plans for him, and today, of course, I blame myself for having been so naive. At the time it really looked as though he would one day be sitting up there among the directors. So I inoculated him with the sweet poison of the brotherly-sisterly society, the utopia of a humanized world. And, as usually happens with our plans, everything turned out differently. Thom has become a tunneler, a mineworker in the holes of historical research—which we know to be highly dubious! Cheers, Thom!"

"And never made it to the all-powerful industrialist," said Thom, "who selflessly hands over the Winter concern to a workers' cooperative! No economic basic democracy from the top! All the same, we won't entirely forget our dream even today, will we, Andy?"

Incidentally, he went on, until just recently he had completely ruled out the possibility of men and women workers in this country starting to fight for their rights again. "I still can't quite believe it."

André: "An act of desperation. What else?"

And Lis saying, That process he'd described—was there a chance— for the workers, that is—of halting it? After all, it was going on in every industry and everywhere, in Europe, the United States. And then the gigantic question: Must the attempt to halt it be the only, the correct solution? What will the work forces—what *can* they, actually—demand?

André nodded. That was now the nub of the matter. In every department seminar-like sessions were being held in an attempt to find answers to these questions. "I believe," he said, "I'll be able to tell you more about this in another two days."

In the Dovecote

ALL THINGS CONSIDERED, SEPP DID HAVE HIS OWN QUIET SPOT UP HERE. Nothing fancy, two by four meters, but nice and snug. Lying there on the mattress, he had only to raise his head a little from the pillow to be able to see through one of the pigeonholes and overlook the stable yard and the whole length of the avenue.

The population has been called upon to join in the demonstration against the closing of the foundry. No one has bothered to ask him. They knew why. He'd been there. Way back in 1932, when there was all that shooting. He'd been there. All those strikes and demos and pamphlets brought nothing but trouble. And in the end, when the dead and wounded lay around on the street, nobody wanted to be responsible, of course.

They didn't need to tell him a thing. He had known Mr. Oltramare personally. Mr. Ludwig, the boss's brother, had seen a lot of him back then. Schorsch Oltramare—where would you still find anyone today who could make speeches like he could, right up front on the stage? He'd been a personal friend of Mussolini's, and during those years, when he'd come back from Munich and Sepp sometimes had to pick him up at the station with the carriage, he'd always been ready with a good tip, and he'd told Sepp, "Another two or three years and it'll be our turn *here*! You'll see how we clean out this pigsty!"

Sepp had twice gone with Mr. Ulrich to meetings in the Hotel Schweizerhof ballroom, and Mr. Oltramare had stood up there on the stage and shouted, "If those Red ringleaders aren't arrested soon, we'll step in! We'll force the authorities! In a pinch the citizens of this town will know how to defend themselves, under our leadership, under the leadership of the National Union!"

The union was later called the National Front. Sepp had witnessed all that personally, sitting in the hall behind the boss and listening. And at the end they had all stood up and sung the "Horst Wessel" song. Although to this day Sepp didn't quite understand what was meant by "whom Red Front and reactionaries shot to death," and he hadn't known the words properly anyway, he had felt his eyes smarting at the line about "comrades marching with us in spirit."

These two-by-four meters were all he needed. Over the past year he had sealed all the cracks between the boards with tar and rags. Using the little wagon he had picked up some boards from the Walker sawmill, rejects, and jovial old Bärteli had said, "At seventy-five we both belong on the scrap heap." He'd taken the boards and nailed them tight all around, better safe than sorry, now the west wind could do its worst. From the double socket next to the stable door below, he had laid a cable and brought it up through the floorboards, then fastened the switch at a spot where, as he lay on the mattress, he had only to lift his right arm to turn on the light.

Sepp had been there. But now? As if there had never been that general strike, never been that November of '32. He could imagine what this would lead to. "First occupy, then negotiate." What were they thinking of? They were behaving just like Mr. Leuenberger and Mr. Koch and their cohorts all those years ago. Mr. Oltramare had wanted another meeting on November 9 in the Schweizerhof so he could publicly accuse those Bolshies. Three days earlier the Bolshies had demanded that the town council ban the meeting of the National Front. The demand was turned down, so then it was obvious what would happen. Rioting was in the air. The boss and Mr. Oltramare and Mr. Bertschi came twice in the late afternoon, in the boss's car—by that time Sepp was free of his old coachman's duties—and twice that afternoon and evening had sat in the Paneled Room. In those days Linda was still there in the kitchen; she was allowed to go in when the boss rang. Linda had told him: Linda, the boss had said, bring us a 1920 Bordeaux, but Linda had to ask Sepp where the better bottles were kept in the cellar, and the phone outside in the hall was in use half the evening.

Calls to the federal councillor personally, Linda had said, and to the canton government in Solothurn, and Mr. Oltramare had said on the phone—Sepp had heard that himself from the kitchen—"The local police forces are stretched beyond their limit, from now on I won't be responsible for anything! It's time you sent in the troops!"

And that's what I told them in court, too. What else could they have done, seeing that the Reds wanted to break up the meeting? What, I ask you? True, Sepp had been given a retractable steel blackjack by Mr. Oltramare's bodyguard, and when he heard that the troops had arrived and were marching through the town, sure enough he'd put it in his pocket and walked into town with the boss at five in the afternoon. But of course in court he hadn't mentioned any of that. And anyway, they hadn't asked about blackjacks, and by the time they reached the Schweizerhof the police had already begun to cordon everything off.

At the Schweizerhof, Sepp and the others had pushed the tables together, and the boss had treated them all to a schnapps and a beer, but by that time they could already hear the Reds making a racket outside on the station square beyond the police cordons. Sepp could hear them to this day: "Out with the Fascists! Out with the Fascists!"

At eight o'clock the police opened the doors to the meeting hall, and Sepp and the others took up positions at the door, letting in only those carrying National Union cards and wearing yellow rosettes. Finally the police allowed forty demonstrators in, then closed the doors.

But before Mr. Oltramare began to speak, Mr. Marthaler came to the back and said that demonstrators had broken through the cordon by the Old Bridge. He sent Sepp and twelve of the others over to the bridge.

On the square at the Old Bridge there was a great crush of people, everyone shouting at once. That Bolshie Leuenberger was standing on a beer barrel making a speech, but all Sepp could make out was that the bourgeoisie was corrupt; then came the news that the crowd had broken through the cordons on the station square. Sepp and the others forced their way through to where police were lined up, drawn swords in hand. Troops were said to be on their way.

Sepp had been shoved to the fringe of the crowd, alongside the Aare, when the catcalls and whistling began on the other side, where the 1st Company was marching down Frohburg-Strasse. The troops were not yet in sight; there was merely the yelling. Twenty meters to Sepp's right, people were cutting the ropes of the cordon, and with a great surge the crowd headed for the Schweizerhof. In the commotion some people fell, including a few policemen, and Sepp and the others were now holding their rubber truncheons and their blackjacks in their hands. When the judge asked Sepp whether he had hit the heads in front of him with his rubber truncheon, Sepp had said no. After all, he had no rubber truncheon.

Now the soldiers came marching across Station Bridge, but here the crowd was so dense that they were ordered to halt. The officers in front waded into the crowd with drawn swords, followed by a platoon advancing in single file against the demonstrators. Suddenly there was a wild melee, swords and rifles flew through the air, everyone was yelling, "Disarm them!" Meanwhile, by moving along outside the embankment railing, Sepp and the others had forced their way through until they were level with the railway station. They saw the platoon retreating in relatively good order.

"Send those baby-faced recruits home!" someone shouted. "They're just kids!" and Sepp had to admit that maybe it was a mistake for them to have been so young. How could they have had any military experience? The soldiers then set up their barricades near the municipal theater. Now some light machine guns were showing up in the front rank, and people were laughing at the retreat.

It was quite true, the sudden rat-a-tat of the machine guns gave Sepp a shock. To this day he could still see those muzzle flashes. Thirteen Reds were dead. Sixty severely wounded.

The crowd fled in panic toward the Schweizerhof. In the silence outside the theater, First Lieutenant Burnat called out to his men, "Helmets off! Smoking permitted."

Leuenberger was arrested that same night.

Sepp was there. He still had his steel blackjack, up in his loft in a trunk under the bed. If the boss were still alive! But nowadays they're striking again as if there had never been a November 9, yet a person only needed to have been there to know how it would end.

One thing Sepp could guarantee: When the shooting was over he would go and sit in the Waadtländer Hall. He would sit there and look at the others and sip his drink, then he would say: I told you so.

Saga of Origin I

ESTHER WINTER'S VERSION:

THE EARTH WAS A DESERT. THEN, AT THE BEGINNING OF TIME, THE primeval mother emerged from the foaming River Aare. Girdled with the snake, chanting the word "Dana," she danced on the floating shell. And she laid the moon egg, out of which fell all things. She pushed her hair back from her face and, with one foot on each of the two rocks on the river banks, gave birth downriver to the son she had conceived from herself. He was to become her lover and her hero. By their descendants she was named Dana.

Dana was the goddess of the sky, the earth, and the underworld; her gown glittered with stars, her head was adorned with the horns of the bull. Her weapon was the double axe of the waning and waxing moon. Her son was called Gwion, the rainmaker. With him she celebrated her wedding. But once every year she transformed him into a ram that she enticed into the Great Cave. There Dana felled the ram with the double axe. Then she mourned him. The earth mourned with her, and all life fell asleep. In the underworld she nourished the dead victim with honey and milk. So he was restored. At the sound of his singing she summoned him up to the earth. He stepped into the light. Life awakened. The earth blossomed and once again bore fruit.

A mingling, an intermingling. How to describe those days after Thomas's return on Wednesday, June 23, 1982? We may assume that Thom was in no position to perceive the impact either of the immediate events in town or, even less, of those beginning to affect him and his inner life.

Lis and he had spent the night together. When Thom woke up, he saw her face leaning over him. She was smiling. Propped on one elbow, she must have been leaning over him like that for quite a while. He could tell that Lis had probably been trying for some minutes to wake him by gently stroking his forehead with her hand.

"What in the world have you been dreaming about?" He had shouted, she said, called out, two or three times called for Gret, then hastily mumbled something incoherent into his pillow. "Do you remember?"

"Oh, I don't know—some nonsense or other."

Lis went on stroking his forehead and cheek with her fingertips. She sat up, clasped her knees. "I imagine you're going to stay here now for a while."

Thom looked up at the ceiling. The plaster and the crystal chains of the hanging lamp were hardly visible in the dim light showing through the drapes. Stay here. The way Lis had said that. Yes, he'd already thought about it yesterday but had immediately discarded the idea. Probably he had hoped that the decision would somehow be made for him during the day now waiting outside the window. Stay here. This history of an earlier time, everything that assailed him here, these images, confused thoughts, sounds, smells—it seemed inevitable that he would have to make his way through them alone. He had to stay here, had to allow them to come flooding out of the forgotten depths of memory. And it was always possible that beyond them he might also rediscover a piece of his own history.

"And you, Lis." Of course he would like her to stay too.

However, what she brought along to their breakfast coffee in the pantry next to the kitchen was the map of France, spreading it out where there was room at the end of the table. Should she go first to Dijon and then—here, see?—over to Burgundy? Or straight down to the sea— perhaps to Bandol? To Sanarys?

Lis was more familiar with the map than Thom had supposed. Yes, she'd rather go straight to the Midi—over here, around Nîmes? Or no, there: Saint-Rémy—must be beautiful. They sat down again. A little bus trip now and again, otherwise a bit of swimming, leisurely walks, reading; in the evenings a glass of wine at the café on the shady *Cours*. "I'll be all right. And I'll call you Sunday evening."

Shortly before noon Thom drove her to the station in Gret's little Fiat.

On the bridge, as he was moving into the right-hand lane, Lis said, "Do you think we'll ever learn, you and I—learn to spend our nights not merely as brother and sister? I wish now that we could."

And Thom: Did she mean whether he could learn to sleep with her as a man? "I don't know, Lis. I really don't know."

The train came in. "My own Touch-me-not," Lis whispered.

"I'll miss you, Lis. Very much."

From the open train window her last words: "But you'll write—every day—promise? Poste restante, Saint-Rémy."

On his way back—the traffic forced Thom to move at a crawl—he was already mentally formulating phrases to Lis while driving across the bridge. And how I miss you! At the same time the feeling: What's going on inside me is something I can't share, can't communicate. Not yet. I suppose the shock of this news of how my mother died is just beginning to hit me. As if a kind of protective barrier inside me had stood up for a while, and now that you've gone, it's collapsing. And an avalanche is sweeping me into the abyss. But never mind where: I want to make this journey or this plunge into the void. Whom or what will I find there? Stand by me, my love, and be sure that if I should arrive somewhere, I might even be changed. In my case, turning into a human being obviously takes an inordinately long time.

You'll hear from me, yes, certainly, tomorrow of course. Take care of yourself, do you hear? Meanwhile, my still brotherly arms enfold you from afar.

                                                    Your old Thom

Time
of
Roses

W hat for others were the good old days, for Aunt Esther was a glass of sherry. Usually she drank two glasses; on the rare days when she had three or more, she was as full of fun in Thom's company as Charlott, more talkative than Herminia ever was, and she could laugh like a flock of seagulls. She would laugh, "Why shouldn't we two, Thom, you dummox and I, why not raise the curtain and for once look and listen together at what's been coming and going on the world stage? What kind of human beings are strutting around there, have a look and remember who the leading lights are? Yet still are merely ridiculous. Benito Mussolini, of course, he was an exception, he was a man of genius."

Thom went over to the bookcase and brought back two volumes of *St. Sebastian's Almanac*. At age six or seven he had been allowed to take out two years at a time. Contained in the one hundred and seventy pages of the almanac was everything of importance that had happened in that particular year, in the world and in Switzerland—the most important people and events, illustrated.

"Which years are we going to look at today, Thom?"

Thom wasted no time deciding. This time he brought 1928 and 1933. Aunt Esther moved her wheelchair up to the table and set the brake while Thom was turning the pages. He ignored New Methods of Horticulture, Jokes & Jinks, Solothurn Cantonal Delegates; passed over the list of country fairs and markets in Switzerland for the year 1928, skimmed through the biography of Cardinal Achille Liénart, through Regional Costumes of Switzerland, and Obituaries; then he found Mussolini's photograph. World Affairs. What an impressive head! What a man! And an orator—inspired! "Italians! I promise you a future full of roses!" Or here, look, Aunt Esther, the man in shorts, with a mustache: Ferdinand Geier, Germany, the first German to win the Tour de France.

Thom stood beside her at the table as they looked at the pictures of the great personalities on the world stage, Aunt Esther explaining or reading aloud as they turned over the pages: the Pan-American Congress in Havana with the Non-Aggression Pact; the first regular radiotelephone service between Berlin and Buenos Aires; the revolt of the fishermen of St. Barbara; Salazar restores Portugal's chaotic finances; a smiling Alfred Hugenberg, chairman of the German National People's Party; the godless Bolsheviks setting fire to the church at Norogedonsk; Al Jolson actually singing in the sound film, *The Singing Fool*. The year 1933 was even more exciting. By reverse hybridization, the Munich Zoo succeeded in breeding the extinct aurochs. Or the burning of the Reichstag in Berlin. The picture showing Reich President von Hindenburg appointing Adolf Hitler as Reich Chancellor—that was one of Thom's favorites. Then the anti-Jewish riots; or Sir Oswald Mosley in England calling upon the Fascist Blackshirts to do battle. The anarchist disturbances in Spain; and the plebiscite and Reichstag election yielding 92 percent of votes for the National Socialist Party.

"Ah, Thom, how full of fear we were in those days, but how full of hope too. And what has happened? Now, eleven years later, in the fifth year of the war, the great German Reich has been reduced to ashes and rubble." Aunt Esther leaned back and closed her eyes.

Yes, and Switzerland? "That's enough for today," was all she said.

No question, it could have been a pleasant evening, sitting around the supper table with Gret and Samuel, with seventeen-year-old Barbara, and Urs, the "little one" as they still called him. Sitting there enjoying the calf liver and noodles, asking the occasional question as Samuel talked about the strike in the branch factory at Seveso. Samuel had recently been promoted to assistant manager in the engineering department at the works, in charge of the hydro section, specialist in turbines. His office handled coordination and planning between the main plant in Jammers and the branch factories.

Recently, said Samuel, he had been spending three or four days every month in Seveso, near Milan. Only this morning he had been having discussions until almost noon with the Italian work force. By the way, the drive home via Chiasso and the St. Gotthard had taken him less than four hours.

"I told them, 'You're crazy.' Seriously"—Samuel gave his good-natured laugh—" 'I'm telling you, they'll lock you out. The firm simply can't accept that. You're just forcing their hand—forcing it!' "

A faint blush crossed Barbara's face. "What choice do those men have but to strike?"

Samuel took another mouthful. He chewed. "Do you want us to get into an argument too?" For the past three days down there he had done nothing but discuss that very question, what choice was left for either side. "Come on, Barbara, let's change the subject. I need to relax."

For a few seconds both Barbara and Urs looked across the table at Thom. Barbara's expression verged on the indignant. She was about to retort, hesitated; Thom gave a barely discernible shrug. She got the message. Urs also went back to picking silently at his food.

Had Gret been aware of this minute, tacit agreement between her brother and the children? Was she ashamed for Samuel? Was she, like Barbara, furious with him? Yes, Thom was familiar with that expression on Gret's face, although Gret, in contrast to her mother years ago, had the somewhat puffy face of the secret drinker.

But in just that way, her expression grim, or rather, full of disgust and suppressed rage and plain resistance, stony resistance, the eyes directed downward at the edge of her plate, his mother had sat there, on that same chair around the corner of the table on her husband's right, and Thom, aged six or eight, had sat at the other end, beside Frieda, just where Urs, now twelve and no longer that little, was eating his noodles; had sat there conscious of the hatred radiating from his mother and beginning to fill the entire Paneled Room.

Two hours before supper, Thom had emerged from the sewing room into the gallery. He heard footsteps down in the hall, heard Father's voice, strangely low, a hoarse whisper. Looking from the landing over the banister, Thom could see his father, the thinning gray hair, the long raincoat, a slowly revolving figure in the dim light. Father was talking to himself, and now Thom could make out some words, without knowing who they were meant for: "I'll kill it, I'll kill that rat!"

He was holding a full bottle of wine by the neck, grasping it like a club, upside down at eye level, and moving it up and down in front of his face as he went on slowly revolving.

Even in those days Thom knew that wine or schnapps were somehow involved whenever, after a few quiet months, Father suddenly behaved strangely, as if preoccupied, his face lopsided, a smile on it, his eyes glassy and unfocused—strangely, or at least so that it was impossible to be sure he wouldn't suddenly start shouting or even whispering, in a vicious undertone when evil thoughts began to get the upper hand in his confused brain. But what Thom could not understand was the reason for this transformation, or the cause of it. So he trusted the explanation given him by Herminia in the kitchen. When his father had driven up drunk behind the house—so drunk that it took him a long time to get out of the black car—she had said, "He's been bitten again."

"Who by?" Thom had asked.

And Herminia in turn—and she may have only said it to stop him asking any further questions: "How do I know—by the rat."

Thom had continued to trust that, and when he heard his father whispering down in the hall and saw him swaying, it was quite clear to him that in such a condition his father would never manage to kill the rat. Even if there were a rat in the hall and Father threw the bottle at it, he didn't stand a chance of hitting it.

His father stopped revolving. Then, from around the corner of the gallery, Thom heard a subdued cough. He looked across. Not four meters away, leaning against one of the pillars, stood his mother, holding a handkerchief to her mouth. She must have been standing there the whole time, watching Father. She looked across at Thom, and he saw that the skin between her eyebrows was moist. In her eyes he read something like: Please, Thom, don't move: this is a matter between him and me—something like that. Then Father shouted, "Cold!" Swaying again, he swung back his arm and hurled the bottle against the flowers etched in the glass of the inner door. The bottle crashed through the glass and presumably landed against the corner pillar of the outer door. Thom heard the splinters rain down like hail in the porch, and no doubt the wine was now trickling down the walls in red streaks.

Missed it. Thom had known he would: his father had missed the rat. His mother came around to him and sent him off to Frieda in Aunt Esther's suite. So two hours later he was sitting beside Frieda in his place at the far end of the table, picking with his fork at the sliced liver and noodles. Each time he looked up he couldn't avoid seeing the lopsided smile on Father's face and the watery, glassy eyes, and his mother, sitting stony-faced beside her husband; as stony-faced then as Gret now, for these few seconds.

While Samuel was talking about the traffic jam outside Chiasso, Thom vividly recalled how he had been sent to bed that evening right after supper. Unable to fall asleep, he got out of bed several times, going to the door and opening it. The stillness in the house, the silence outside his room and downstairs in the darkness, scared him more than if someone had been shouting. When he heard Frieda coming up the stairs, he quickly got into bed and pretended to be asleep. She opened the door, approached the bed, listened to his regular breathing. She gently stroked his hair, then went away, putting out the light in the corridor and closing the door. As soon as he heard her closing the door to Aunt Esther's suite, he got out of bed and in his pajamas went up the stairs to the attic. In the darkroom that Uncle Ludwig had fixed up for his photography, he took the shotgun from the corner and slid a cartridge into the open breech, exactly as he had seen Uncle Ludwig do.

Then, carrying the gun, he walked softly down the stairs, past Charlott's and Gret's room, all the way down into the cellar. At the door to the main vault he switched on the light, then went to the back where the apples were stored, sat down, and waited, the shotgun across his knees, its safety catch off. He was ready. As soon as the rat showed up over by the stack of faintly gleaming empty bottles, he would take aim. He was prepared to shoot without warning. Although he had never been allowed to fire the shotgun, he knew that now, in view of his father's condition, he had to do it, and he wouldn't miss. So he sat there, waiting, waiting.

Sometime very early next morning, Gret was standing over him. "Here he is!" she had called up the stairs. All she said to him, quietly, was, "Come along, Thomi."

So he must have fallen asleep after all. Had the rat meanwhile crept out of its hole? He didn't think so. He was sure that, even in the light sleep into which he had briefly fallen, he would have heard the slightest sound.

He was still half-asleep as he climbed up the long cellar stairway ahead of Gret. At the top stood his mother. From her expression it was obvious that, although she didn't understand what he had done or had intended to do, she wasn't angry with him. She pulled him up the last step by the hand, and for two or three long, comforting seconds she held him close. Gret followed with the shotgun.

At this point Samuel asked, "How about it, Thom, shall we have our coffee in the other room?" He had brought home a very fine brandy from Milan, a Vecchia Romagna, he said. "I insist that you try it."

Sometimes she began with a phrase such as: Just imagine! Thom would look up from his stool past the dark-brown ankle-length skirt covering her knees, toward the glass cabinet beside the door. Inside, behind the reflecting glass doors, was the collection of china shepherdesses and poodles and vases and powderpuffs and flute players, or, on the lower shelf, the richly colored goblets of Murano glass that Aunt Esther had spent a lifetime collecting.

But at the same time he imagined, and saw in the cabinet, what she told him to imagine: How, for instance, Uncle Ludwig had one day burst into her suite shouting that the foal was there.

Then she proceeded to tell him about General Bourbaki. In 1870, during the Franco-Prussian War, he had broken through the German encirclement of the fortress of Metz with his Eastern Army. All those cannons. The fire visible at night from the heights of the Jura, the fire over in Alsace. The Bourbaki horses. The flags, the bayonets, the dead. And General Bourbaki being pushed toward the south. The waist-high snow. No supplies, provisions exhausted, and no remedy for the Turkish flu.

"Surely I've told you this before, Thom," and he would sit there imagining the Eastern Army and General Bourbaki being pushed farther and farther south, beyond Dôle, Besançon, and Belfort, and hundreds, hundreds lying in the snow, shot or frozen to death. What she wanted Thom to imagine, she described only to the point where her tone of voice and the events and people he was hearing about enabled him to form his own images. He saw them when he closed his eyes and still saw them when he kept them open: the remnants of the vanquished Eastern Army reflected in the glass cabinet. He heard the impact of the German mortars, saw the horses breaking through the snow and ice as they were led by the reins or bridle. He saw, he heard, the sound of the trumpets echoing over the snow-covered fields, and General Bourbaki giving orders for the white flag to be hoisted as a signal: Prepared to surrender. Yes, sometimes in late fall and winter, when darkness slanted across him early as he sat by the window, Thom even saw himself reflected in the glass cabinet.

"In a nutshell," Aunt Esther would often say. He knew then that for now she wanted to bring the story to an end, at least to the end of the Bourbaki story, not to that of Uncle Ludwig's breeding triumph, not that—"in short," she would say, then launch once more into her circuitous saga. About the Bourbaki army crossing the Swiss frontier at Les Verrières, and how the rifles, cannons, and even the muzzle-loaders and swords were tossed onto great heaps, and there they came, the defeated, half-starved, frozen, wounded, exhausted men, their blackened feet wrapped in rags, pulling their little horses behind them. At last the camp fires, at last the pigs roasting on spits and coffee containing so much absinthe that you could see the sugar dissolving at the bottom of the glass. The field hospitals, the melancholy songs from the Gironde and the Roussillon and Gérardmer, and still they died like flies. Eighty-eight thousand of the hundred and twenty thousand of the once-proud Eastern Army, officers and men, stood with their hundreds of little Bourbaki horses, ragged but spared, safe on Swiss soil.

No, that still wasn't the end. About the arrival of the Arabs too, six hundred Arabs and Moors forming a rearguard—Aunt Esther wasn't going to leave any of that out. When Thom said, "Yes, Aunt, but how about Uncle Ludwig's Spahi mare?" that was what she had been talking about all the time, she would say; the Arabs were known as Spahis, and they came with their pure-bred Arab horses through the snow over the frontier. He must try and imagine, six hundred men from Morocco and Arabia up there in Pontarlier in wintertime, and no more than seven or nine of their magnificent horses had survived. They were of noble blood, you see: they couldn't survive anything like that, except for those few mares and one stallion. The Arabs chanted their Allah il-Allah songs when in the weeks that followed more and more entire detachments of the Bourbaki army came down through the Jura mountains, via Biel toward Bern, or via Moutier and Balsthal over here to Jammers. Aunt Esther remembered how at night everyone had stood along Jura-Strasse holding jugs of tea. More and more new troops kept arriving, and when it sometimes occurred to Thom to ask, "But listen, Aunt, how old are you anyway? To have witnessed all that, in 1870 and '71, or even earlier, the freedom poles of 1832 and then again in 1848—you witnessed all that?" she would only say, "Just be glad that I'm still alive," and "One never asks a lady such a question." The steaming little horses were passing by again under the street lamps, and the wounded, ragged men, all of them disarmed, and the officers with blood-stained, red-white-and-blue sashes and the drums and the songs from Gérardmer. One night those Spahis came past, bowing in their brown burnooses to Aunt Esther when she poured them tea laced with absinthe.

Some of them remained for a while on the farms in the area. Over in the stables one detachment settled down for three nights on straw from the barn. She would rather skip that chapter, Aunt Esther said with a laugh. It was enough for two Frenchmen to remain behind when the others moved on. They were dead. And a few months later, here in town, the swelling bellies of three girls caused some talk.

But to cut a long story short. Or: When the war was over. "The Bourbaki soldiers gradually disappeared from the farms and the factory. What was left behind were the scrawny little horses, used for years by quite a few farmers to plow their fields. Also left behind at the rich miller's in Rickenbach, later also in our stables, was that magnificent Spahi stallion already mentioned. So, Thom—you see?—we are back with Uncle Ludwig and his experiment." Aunt Esther laughed, and went on crisscrossing her blue or yellow wool.

Her voice. Her dark Aunt Esther voice, and the way, as the late afternoon deepened into dusk, she retold what she had known and dreamed in her hundred and fifty years of life or was simply inventing on the spot. "That's how it was. But if you know nothing about General Bourbaki, you won't understand about Spahi stallions. And if you don't know what a superman is, how are you supposed to understand Uncle Ludwig's talk about elite and blood and race?"

Thom now made an effort to imagine 1933 and Uncle Ludwig working on his formula over there in his annex. Scientists must have proof. If someone claims that by crossing two superior races an upward leap in the development of the species can be achieved, it is of no use to him until he achieves demonstrable successes at least at the mammal level. Since Thom had his rabbit hutch up under the barn roof, a buck and five females and eleven offspring, he could form some idea, however vague, of what Aunt Esther meant when she spoke of the mammal level. And what was possible there would also be possible en masse on the human level, and then we wouldn't be stuck forever with this old defective race but would have a new race of supermen; Thom could see that too. Uncle Ludwig called it the Winter Formula.

Thom wasn't to ask her about details, she said. She had always been knowledgeable about horses, although less so about breeding them—she had really never concerned herself about that. But over there in Uncle Ludwig's laboratory she had seen with her own eyes genetic charts and great piles of calculations and test tubes and vials. Uncle Ludwig, she said, had corresponded with the most famous researchers of his time in Italy and Germany.

She then talked at length about the miller's son in Rickenbach, about how the Spahi horses died and the father of the present miller died too, but there was never a time when there wasn't a pure-blooded Spahi stallion, bred from generation to generation with Spahi mares.

Uncle Ludwig and the miller's son had also done a lot of other crossbreeding, Hanoverian stallion with Spahi mare, Icelandic mare with Spahi stallion, even Trakehners from East Prussia, English purebloods or simple Walloon blood mixed with Spahi blood, up and down all the mare pedigrees and the stallion lines, not without some success. Their main concern had been to study the optimal mixing of the genes of both blood lines. Aunt Esther remembered a foal that grew up to be a horse of such size and strength and queenly gait as had never been seen before. That mare would toss her head as she rolled her eyes; she had the velvet coat of a Freiberg gelding, and her hindquarters pranced on slender, purebloooded fetlocks. But when we tried to make her gallop in the paddock she would go around and around like an old circus horse, docile, sturdy. Neither as a mount nor as a carriage horse did she perform any better than our lame-assed Burgundians. We called her the dun mare, the Freiberg Spahi mare. But Uncle Ludwig and Sepp kept their eyes on her in the stable and tended her as if she were their bride.

Anyway, Uncle Ludwig also swapped experiences with a major cattle breeder from near Lucerne. One summer morning this cattle breeder came putt-putting up the avenue on one of the first tractors Aunt Esther had ever seen and stopped in front of the stables. The trailer was hauling a heavy box for transporting cattle. From up here, from the house, it was impossible to make out what Uncle Ludwig, Sepp, and the breeder from Willisau were pushing into the barn.

In the days before that August morning, Uncle Ludwig and Sepp had brought the dun mare into great heat with an ordinary Freiberg stallion. Now the two men were to be seen handling ropes and leather straps; next, they carried a sawhorse into the barn. Sepp brought the dun

mare from the stable and led her into the barn; then the barn door was
firmly closed.

An hour later Sepp emerged with the sweat-streaked mare, who was
now limping with one hind leg, hardly able to walk. Her hindquarters
were covered with blood. Then Uncle Ludwig and the cattle breeder also
came out, leading the bull by two ropes. All Aunt Esther could tell Thom
was that she had never seen such an enormous bull in her life, never
before and never since. They had wrapped leather straps around his horns.
He was led back into his box, and the ramp was tipped up into place.

The three men later emerged from the washhouse and put on their
shirts again. Then, still hot and exhausted, they sat down in their breeches
at the stone table outside. A bottle of the best white wine was uncorked,
glasses were raised, and before long they were singing, in the middle of
the afternoon. A few weeks later Uncle Ludwig said, "The dun mare's
in foal."

And so, when the three hundred and thirty days had passed, he
burst into Aunt Esther's room with the news that the dun mare had
foaled—a stallion had arrived. Aunt Esther, Thom's grandmother Helen,
and his father all had to go along with him; they stood beside the stall
watching the little foal trying shakily to get onto its thin legs beside its
big mother. Its coat was piebald, and it was Thom's grandmother who
suddenly said, "How very odd, Ludwig." And then: "Just look at those
hind legs—the hooves are cloven. The creature has goat hooves! Oh my
God!" She crossed herself.

Uncle Ludwig was beaming. "That was all carefully calculated.
Don't get excited. You'll have cause for amazement soon enough." He
named the foal Atar, father of the new breed.

The young stallion grew apace. In the reflecting panes of the cabinet,
in front of the porcelain objects and colored hair ribbons and the dangling
earrings from Bombay, Thom saw the two short, thick horns thrusting
forward above the young stallion's ears. The stallion's neck was thickset,
the chest broad; the forehead was heavy, the legs were sturdy, the croup
falling off sharply. And the stallion's shoulder level was nowhere near
that of the dun mare's. Uncle Ludwig had become somewhat taciturn.
And once, toward evening, Thom had heard the terrible sound of pounding hooves and a bull's roar coming from the stables. Right after that
Sepp could be seen dragging a blood-drenched Uncle Ludwig out through
the stable door. Atar had bitten him in the shoulder.

And two days later Atar killed the dun Spahi Freiberg mare. With his cleft hooves he smashed the stall to pieces: Sepp managed to scramble up the ladder to safety. Atar also wrecked the stable door and charged into the yard, where Aunt Esther had seen him: the stocky piebald, horned, his coat rough—no, shaggy, a bull-stallion or stallion-bull, you can take your pick, Thom. At first he stood there glowering in the sun, then snorted, bucked with all four feet in the air, reared up on his hind legs, roared, stood still, and Thom could see his eyes glowing red under the shaggy wings. Finally he galloped off down the avenue toward town. They say the police tried to stop the beast in the inner town, where it ran down a woman, leaving her unconscious on the ground, and an unemployed man who threw himself in its path was knocked down and trampled by the animal's front hooves. The police advanced with pistols; then, at the far end of the cattle market, they started shooting. All they achieved, said Aunt Esther, was that Atar broke through the police cordon, charged across the Old Bridge, and took off upriver along the Aare. Some people claim to have seen him swimming across the Aare in the Chessi gorge. From there he is said to have disappeared into the Born Forest.

Years later and to this day, there are woodcutters who can swear to having seen Atar, piebald, with horse's ears, a horse's head, with horns and cloven hooves; he had roared like a bull and his eyes had glowed red. "To this day?" Thom asked. Even as Aunt Esther slowly nodded and sucked in her lips, he foresaw that there would be many nights during his life when, as he started up from dreams, soaked in sweat, he would have to try and imagine how he could kill Atar.

Lis was right, there was a smell of rotting wood here. Nevertheless, the original classical building with its once-pale stucco, with bands and lintels of white Jura limestone in its well-proportioned south facade, had retained its cool style despite being weatherworn, as well as crowded by the hickory oaks and fir trees. This part of the house, more than a hundred and fifty years old, contained twelve rooms, the hall, the staircase, and the gallery.

Even on the east side, overlooking the stables, in spite of its present weatherbeaten aspect—the rusted gutter hung askew, the roof had collapsed, its holes patched up years ago with plastic sheets, and no one cared about the withered ivy tendrils or the honeysuckle that had crept along cracks in the walls up to the second-floor windows—with all this decay the intrinsically noble character of the architecture was still apparent from the east too.

However, Thom's grandfather Elsazar had already added on to the rear of the building, along its whole length: the mezzanine terrace with the addition of cellar steps for his wine trade, and above that two bedrooms and the sewing room: to the west—what then became known as the west wing—a two-story structure that architecturally destroyed two-thirds of the facade, built, moreover, of brick that had begun to show in large patches through the peeling stucco.

After Elsazar's death, further disfiguring additions were undertaken by Aunt Esther and Uncle Ludwig. An inheritance dispute had been settled by Thom's father, Ulrich, letting his sister have the west wing and allowing his brother Ludwig to build onto the already disfigured north side. Uncle Ludwig took immediate advantage of this, and the result was a three-story building that rose two meters higher than the eaves: kitchen on the first floor; laboratory for Uncle Ludwig's scientific experiments on the second; and bedroom plus studio, equipped with large window and glass roof, on the third floor.

Nor was that all. In the early thirties there was further construction; Aunt Esther found that the sloping roof on her west wing did not harmonize with the original building. She had always wished for a tower room, so an additional room, accessible by a spiral staircase, was built on top of the west wing. Without concern for unity of style, she had it crowned by a four-sided steeple, reminiscent of the patrician houses of the eighteenth century, topped by a weathercock, which, it was said, for the first few years turned merrily into the wind. The tower room was not used for long. Aunt Esther traveled with her Englishman to Thailand; after her return three years later, a bad knee prevented her from using the spiral staircase. The tower room became a storage place for Grandmother Helen's furniture, in which no one had shown any interest.

Thom was fourteen when his father died in 1952. Much later he heard that, on Uncle Theodor's legal advice, he and his two sisters had had to refuse the paternal legacy. Apart from the house—instead of the original twelve rooms it now contained twenty-one—Father had left more than two hundred thousand francs in debts. It was not until seven years later, after Mother's death, that Gret, Charlott, and Thom had taken up their inheritance.

Charlott and he had been in favor of selling the house. Although it was still, or again, heavily mortgaged, its market value was estimated— in those days!—at half a million Swiss francs.

The four of them had been sitting outdoors in the shade at the stone table, drinking coffee: Charlott, Gret, Uncle Theodor, and Thom, some weeks after the funeral. "Are you out of your minds?" In her excitement Gret upset a cup; brown stains formed on Charlott's light-colored dress. She would *never* agree to that!

He could clearly see Gret's face again, in those days still slender, under her brown hair, which she wore up, and the dark flush spreading into her face from her neck—quite clearly for a few seconds, as he lay smoking on the bed early in the afternoon. In the ceiling plaster above him were the water stains, four or five of them overlapping; toward the door and one of the valances they took on the color of coffee. In the chandelier overhead three or four bulbs had been unscrewed and not replaced, and where the fixture was attached to the ceiling wide cracks showed in the crumbling plaster. The valance over the window facing the stables hung down in the middle like the frilly hem of a Biedermeier gown.

Then, with his legal skills, Uncle Theodor had acted as mediator. Thom, Charlott, and Gret came to terms on his proposal: Charlott and Thom let Gret and her husband Samuel have the property—always minus the west wing and Uncle Ludwig's addition—at the extremely favorable valuation of three hundred thousand francs, which meant that within three years they would each receive the sum of one hundred thousand from Gret. Should the owner of the property ever sell it, Thom and Charlott would in turn each be entitled to one-third of the value in excess of three hundred thousand francs.

Thus Thom's, like Charlott's, inheritance—including some gold coins, a few shares, and their mother's earrings—amounted to roughly a hundred and thirty thousand francs. Now for the first time it was possible for him to continue his studies in peace. True, this whole legacy business was a bit odd. Family? Clan? The voice of blood? By what coincidence in the endless chain of coincidences in the lives of his ancestors had he been born a Winter? Incidentally, in the intervening twenty or so years, all the money, apart from the three gold coins, had somehow melted away.

Might Gret be prepared today to sell the house? Aunt Esther was living with Frieda in the two first-floor rooms of the west wing, and the annex with the studio had been closed off since Uncle Ludwig's death; furthermore, the attic room, ceded to Sepp for his lifetime by Thomas's father, had to be subtracted. But that still left at least fourteen rooms for Gret, Samuel, the two children, and old Herminia—she too with lifetime privileges. Was it any wonder that Gret had simply closed off two rooms on the first floor and three up here—shutters closed, white sheets over the furniture? Those rooms were never aired more than twice a year.

As he gazed up at the water stains on the ceiling, Thom could imagine what conditions were like in the attic above him. A year and a half ago, on his last visit, he had examined the hole in the ceiling out in the gallery. Probably a burst pipe, and the plumber, after replacing part of the piping, had stood the broken pipe, black with rust, in a corner, swept the plaster debris into a heap, and left. Since then no one had done anything about it.

"What do you expect?" Samuel had asked, letting his fist fall comfortably onto the arm of his chair. This was Gret's house. And she wanted everything to stay the way it was, refusing to see the minute changes taking place every day. A brick is split by frost, a beam turns gray, all the gutters are rusting through, fungus is growing in the floorboards, and the walls, inside and out, are sweating saltpeter. Look at the beams in the washhouse, or the shingles up in the roof. Oak borers and mildew. What did Thom imagine?

Samuel as a do-it-yourself home repairman? All he cared about was for the few inhabited rooms to be kept more or less in shape, and there were still enough rugs to cover the damage in the parquet floors. Not to worry, he said, this shack would stand up to the storms for another few years. After all, he had had an oil furnace installed in the old building, with hot-water heating; he had drawn and calculated the plans for this himself, unfortunately just before the oil crisis.

"Let's not worry about it, Thom," he had said, raising his brandy glass, "what will fall, will fall."

Yes, he was right. Even here on the south side there was a feeling of dampness. Rotting wood: that faint, sweetish smell, in the middle of summer.

Passages I

AND THAT HE SOMETIMES WISHED TO BE BACK AGAIN IN THOSE AFTERNOONS or evenings of the dead past. Hadn't the rustling of his ash tree been life, and the quivering of the sun drops in the branches or the grass? To be afraid and long for somewhere or someone and for moments of happiness? To be there. Just to be there. There on the steps to the back veranda in the afternoon, hearing Frieda's voice from the kitchen through the open window, "Kept to her bed again for three days now," and sensing that up there at the back of the house, in the Blue Room on the second floor, his mother had been lying in semidarkness again for three days looking up at the crystal chains of the chandelier, while

Sepp had brought out the chopping block and driven the hatchet down into it so that the wooden handle stood up at an angle, before Thom saw him going around the washhouse into the poultry yard. Sepp reached in among the fluttering, cackling fowl and grabbed the one he may have had his eye on for the past week: a medium-sized guinea hen, speckled blue and gray like a seashell, that he had promised Herminia to kill, together with two other birds, for the holiday tomorrow and

Thom merely sat there blinking and watching, and was startled when he remembered Charlott, Charlott's voice upstairs in his room, whispering—Charlott had tiptoed into the room in the dark and had sat down on the edge of the bed, said, "Are you asleep?", and the shock it was to his soul when Charlott had said, "You know, we're engaged now, secretly of course," and when he had finally asked, "What does it feel like?" she had whispered, "I'm so happy it hurts," before flitting out of the room again, and he had felt more alone than he had for a long time

Thom was aware that something in him suddenly began to think, "It's my fault she's now been lying up there again for three days, that migraine, my fault that she and Father this never-ending war and Father's drinking and that he had begun to drink again, although that's over now and Father can laugh again if, yet she's now been lying up there again for three days—", slowly began to think, although he couldn't have said how at age thirteen he could possibly be to blame for this quarrel, almost a duel, between his parents, but now Sepp again, coming out of the poultry yard beside the wash-house, in his left hand the frantically fluttering guinea hen; still carrying it, entered the washhouse, for some unknown reason, but immediately reappeared in the doorway, squinting into the sun, before walking toward his chopping block, quite casually and yet as if he were a kind of high priest approaching a blood sacrifice of which only he knew to whom it must be offered, so when he was thus, still with the cackling struggling guinea hen

but how should Thom not have been afraid, let alone have followed the path of that longing, since he felt as if tied down, condemned to sit here as if shackled, never to move, and the rustling coming down from his ash tree and the smell of afternoon or, wafting down from the orchard, the smell of rain-soaked hay, because now the sun, because now its ribbons of light glinted across it—as if shackled to her and at the same time to him, to them both, for after all they loved him and children must love their parents for ever and ever—and again this longing for that island of Aulis, but he mustn't even escape in dreams across the sea, lying in bed again for three days migraine in semidarkness, hadn't she, since it was all his fault, sent him into exile to that convent school behind walls in the mountains and written him in her large hand "I hold you very close Your Mother" those lying words "I hold you close," so that he only

while over there, just beyond the shadow of the washhouse, Sepp standing in the sun talked soothingly to his guinea hen, but the flapping, "nice and easy now put down your head, that's right, nice and easy on the block," but the hatchet flashed in the sun, and "goddammit" said Sepp, till his left hand grasped the bird so that he could get a good swing at it and down came the blade, down, since

how else than watching, how else could Thom have thought of her again, sensed her lying up there in the big house behind him, since at that very moment the guinea hen's head, and Sepp just beginning to let the blood spurt from the severed body into the tin basin beside the chopping block, how else than when watching and having to laugh, to laugh in horror as the guinea hen, headless, suddenly fluttered up and, without its head, fluttered up and away, rose in a great arc over the washhouse into the sun and disappeared behind it and suddenly there was Herminia and that was Frieda, both laughing loudly across to Sepp from the kitchen window, laughing, while Thom found he couldn't go on thinking what he had begun to think, "kept to her bed for three days" and "I'm so happy it hurts" and always somehow in some incomprehensible way having been to blame and feeling what being alive was and longing

In Those Days

WHAT FOLLOWS IS ALSO VOUCHED FOR BY STILL-LIVING WITNESSES. AT least some of the material should be recorded here so that it will not be lost. Recorded as a draft for a commemorative story, a story belonging to Max Strub, then an employee of the Swiss Federal Railway repair shop in Jammers.

1933. It is known that, after the National Socialists had seized power in the German Reich, some twenty extreme Rightist "national movements of renewal" sprouted from fertile soil in Switzerland. Most of the groups called themselves "Front," "New Front," "National Front," and so on, and originated mainly among small tradesmen and students. Their fascist programs—invariably anti-Bolshevist and anti-Semitic—demanded the abolition of parliaments as well as the establishment of a "new people's community" in an authoritarian state. Until the mid-thirties, they found a sympathetic ear among the middle classes, which had not yet recovered from the shock of the nationwide general strike of 1918, and also, for obvious reasons, among the Catholic population with its authoritarian structure.

On May 20, 1933, the National Front, Jammers Branch, made its first public appearance with a rally in the local auditorium. More than two thousand people, their curiosity aroused by posters and newspaper advertisements, crowded into the hall. Fifty uniformed security guards had arrived in two buses from Basel. Wearing dark trousers, white shirts with black ties, and party armbands showing a spiked cudgel aslant the Swiss cross, they stood in two rows guarding the entrance. Inside the hall, on the stage, some chairs were lined up for the newly organized Nazis of Jammers: Messrs. Sutter, electrician; Hänggi, stationer; Meier-Ennemoser, stationer; Lüthy, dentist; Huffschmied, insurance agent; Burger, jeweler, and others. After some introductory remarks by Mr. Emil Sutter, the president, the first of the two speakers was welcomed with applause: Colonel Sonderegger (Ret.), well known as the com-

manding officer of the military units that had fired machine guns into
the crowd of strikers in Zurich during the general strike of 1918. The
short, slight militarist spoke at length about the dangers of pacifism and
Bolshevism; he demanded the New People's Community as a nonpar-
liamentary government by the people: the government must have legis-
lative and executive powers simultaneously. In particular, he demanded
stiffer penalties for putschists and revolutionaries, together with protection
from strikers' terrorist acts against those willing to work, the sifting and
screening of foreigners living in Switzerland and revised regulations concerning Jews: specifically, all Eastern Jews were to be categorically denied
the right of residence in Switzerland. Freedom of speech and of the press
would have to be limited.

The second speaker was Robert Tobler, a lawyer, recently appointed
Zurich Regional Leader of his "Front," National Leader of the National
Front, later the sole Frontist member of the Federal Parliament in Bern
until 1939. He in turn inveighed—although, modeling himself on Nazi
speakers in Germany, in far more scathing terms—against socialism as
the "red plague," against liberalism, and against "hot-air parliamentar-
ism." All that must be smashed to pieces. In a fanatical voice he repeated
the central tenets of the Frontist program. He concluded his speech with
the old battle cry of the Swiss mercenaries: "Out with them!" The two
hundred or so Nazis in the hall now also roared, "Out with them!" The
townspeople applauded.

Material: A voice from the hall demands a discussion. Surprisingly,
the demand is refused. Sutter: "Here there will be no discussion. Here
there are only commands!"

Now someone starts singing the national anthem. Gradually the
singing spreads through the hall, with all the spectators on their feet,
including those in the balcony.

Draft: At this solemn moment Max Strub (repair shop employee and
brother of Herminia's brother-in-law Isidor Strub) advances to the railing
and starts singing the "Internationale" at the top of his voice: "Arise ye
wretched of the earth . . ." He doesn't get very far with his song. The
uniformed security guards grab him, drag him out into the upper lobby,
and beat him up, then force him down the stairs as they batter him with
their steel blackjacks. In the lower lobby the police intervene. Strub, his
head, arms, and back bloody from the beatings, staggers out into the
lighted street. In the hall the singing continues.

Material: Draft of a story, of a commemorative story; for Comrade Max Strub.

But with that, my dear, faraway Lis, this day was not yet over. You know that I like my brother-in-law Samuel. When he sits his massive body down in the capacious leather armchair beside my father's—and probably my grandfather's—tiled stove, leaning back his head with the heavy spectacles, his great paws on the two carved lion's heads, and stretches out his crossed slippered feet and says, "Come, Thomas, sit down. You'll have a drink, won't you?" and leans forward to pour some of his vaunted brandy as he asks, "How's your research coming along?"—then once again I feel wrapped in the comfortable security familiar to me from other evenings with Samuel.

In answering his question I also mentioned the working title. Samuel pondered. *"The General's Politics?* Why don't you take a topical historical subject for a change?" he said. "How about *Trends Toward the Erosion of Paternal Authority?"* He laughed. "You know that I know what I'm talking about." And he went on to tell me how Barbara would wearily decline to listen whenever he ventured to warn her of her tendency to take a negative view of everything. And it was scandalous what Barbara brought home from her high-school discussion group as to the origins of so-called patriarchy. And even the youngest, Urs, calmly walks in the door on Saturday nights at one A.M. instead of at ten. In response to his father's question, he would merely ask back, "Why, exactly?"

Then we started talking again about my work. Eventually we arrived at the question that constantly preoccupies me: To what extent was the past really past? Did we actually have to imagine time merely as something linear, something following a line from the darkness of prehistory up to this day? What if time, understood in this way, were nothing but an auxiliary construction of our imaginative powers and, in a dimension transcending thought, perhaps be what some physicists are now conjecturing: an immeasurably vast space, the Now being the swinging star of our consciousness within it—a star figuratively speaking, of course—and the Present comprising in this time/space our entire past history together with our consciousness of today and of the future as one? Why aren't we satisfied with the natural cycles, like those of the sun and moon, as

determined by the magnetic fields and poles in the universe as well as
in the minutest living organisms? Do we, does our consciousness, need
the division of time into twenty-four-hour periods if we are not to succumb
to madness? Or is it the clock itself that represents our alienation from
nature?

You know how it is, Lis. Over an old brandy one soon finds oneself
indulging in profundities. When Samuel smiles, his nostrils move; for a
few seconds he looked no more than twenty-five. He raised his glass to
me. In the ensuing silence I felt as if I could hear his brain working.
No, he said, that was too much for him. That would be tantamount to
a synchronicity of all happening that he didn't care to contemplate.

You remember how two days ago we talked about the moon; that,
although we can perceive it as a sickle, then as a half moon, or as a
shining disk, we can never grasp the whole of it: the gigantic sphere in
space that it actually is. I told him about that too. Time as a sphere? As
a cyclical event and state of being? I told him how the idea of synchronicity, or in other words, the constant Present of past and future, renders
my existence as a historian far more thrilling than in the days when I
used only the old auxiliary construction in thinking of the measurement
of time.

Probably a mistake on my part not to have explained to Samuel why
for me this is not merely a case of playing detached intellectual games.
However, he is more perceptive than one might suppose. He may have
noticed how intensely I am now—at least since yesterday, here in the
house and also in town—experiencing that very synchronicity, or at any
rate the presence of the past in my Present. I want to tell you, I must
tell you, all about this as soon as we see each other. When? As you see,
I'm not reconciled to your departure. While I write here in the Blue
Room, you must be on the night express from Geneva to Avignon. Are
you reading? Are you looking out the compartment window into the
night, and when you turn your head a little do you suddenly catch sight
of yourself, close up, in front of the passing lights in the distance? Catch
sight of your face looking out into the night?

I fear that a handsome young Frenchman has sat down across from
you, reads the *Nouvel Observateur* for a while, then, his manner very
reserved, very deliberate, offers you a light. A little later he is bold enough
to ask about what you are reading. I know him. An intern at the Infirmerie
de Saint-Georges in Besançon. Or a young lawyer who has just completed

his training stint at the civil court of Annecy. In his light-colored zippered sports jacket he may look like a member of Bourg-en-Bresse's top handball team, but, as you are quick to notice, that's deceptive. A faint shadow of grief on the pale face with the horn-rimmed glasses. He is seeking peace of mind. He is still suffering sérieusement from the breakup with his fiancée. His aunt in Paris—she's a friend of the four-star General Bouvard—has advised him to relax for a few weeks in her summer home on the Ardèche. In speaking he often says: Premièrement, deuxièmement. Perfect manners. Did you know that the sons of the French bourgeoisie still live absolutely in the strict male role of their grandfathers? There can be much charm to that. The little summer place on the Ardèche: nothing special, a big old mill, although furnished with impeccable taste. Wonderful, the sound of rushing water at night through the open window, the rustling of the ancient elm trees. Wouldn't you care to keep him company there as his guest for a few days or longer?—Watch out, Lis! I'm a jealous person. In another two hours, before you get to Montélimar, you'll have to decide whether you want to step off the train with him into the dawn.

I feel as though I were only now gradually arriving here. And as if I were continually being flooded with simultaneous experiences. Whether I go across to the washhouse or stand outside in the gallery looking at one of Uncle Ludwig's dramatic paintings of storm-tossed coastal land-scapes; whether I walk down the cellar stairs or sit in the shade at the stone table drinking coffee: again and again everything appears to me to exist in a space consisting of time. Almost a bit eerie. There I sit down below in the shade, reading the newspaper, and simultaneously I truly am for a few moments the little fellow of so long ago, cradled in arms; the hum of a woman's voice, very close, can be heard, can be felt in the minute vibration of the warm body carrying me across the room. Light engulfs me, light skin meets my little groping hand. That hum lulling me to sleep. Feeling of being one and secure, I am being stroked, being kissed, there are red and green patterns, and I don't know whether they are the flowers on my mother's yellow marocain dress, yes, and now with me on her arm she stops in front of the high sideboard, in front of the slender white alabaster vase.

She gently flicks the nail of her index finger against the vase. A wondrous bell-like sound floats up and echoes through the room and me and my mother. I am sailing through this earliest of my memories, sailing down and through, now I *am* that tiny creature, until I bring myself back, back here into this room where I am sitting at my mother's desk and writing to you about my mother, at 12:30 at night.

Later Samuel and I moved on to Samuel's heavy Bordeaux, and Gret joined us in a glass. When she came in, I was afraid that the terrible stoniness of her whole being into which she had locked herself only an hour and a half ago at supper would now, as she approached us, explode against Samuel in unconcealed rage. Instead, Gret smiled gently as she stopped beside Samuel, her right hand on the back of his chair. As if nothing had happened, she said—shapeless and fat, to be sure, as she has now become, but then that can also have a certain dignity—said that under the glass bell in the kitchen there was still some nice ripe Gruyère cheese—wouldn't we like some, to go with the wine? And on her return from the kitchen with the platter: Had Samuel shown me his pictures of their vacation on the schooner they had chartered? Starting from Sicily along the coast to Marseille, with stopovers on Sardinia and Corsica, wonderful, I must see those pictures. They were then shown to me, one by one, with a running commentary by both of them, and it's years since I've seen Gret so animated.

I was also struck by the way Samuel neither avoided nor deliberately touched on the open secret of Gret's alcoholism. He went across to the sideboard and came back with a brandy snifter and a large red-wine glass, both for Gret. All he said was that a couple of days ago, in Seveso, he had brought on rather a nasty bout of gastritis with the brandy. He said it very nicely—just some advice, a tip—and left the decision to Gret. So she picked up the little straw cradle containing the bottle of Bordeaux and poured herself a glass. "Your health, Thomas, and yours, Samuel dear."

No doubt the evening would have ended like that, pleasantly harmonious. And no doubt I wouldn't have asked that question, that ill-fated, to me so vital, question, had not Gret, understandably enough, asked me how long I planned to stay this time, adding, in a sisterly tone, that of course she would be happy if I stayed on for quite a while. The house was too big anyway. Incidentally, she even went on into the silence, it was a pity that young woman, Lis Bronnen, had had to leave so soon; she had liked your quiet, frank manner and your Thuringian accent.

And then I found myself telling them. As late as yesterday morning I hadn't imagined staying more than three or four days. But then upstairs in the library, in the big pile of papers, I had come across Aunt Esther's diary—Gret must remember, the green one with the lock. And in it I had found that entry. I asked both Gret and Samuel whether what our aunt had written in it wasn't just plain nonsense, although the two sentences had really shaken me. What did they both think about it?

About what?

Then I quoted the actual words.

Now came a suppressed shriek from Gret. She clapped her hands over her face; her whole body was shaken by sobs. Slowly she stood up. Slowly, as if oblivious, she walked past me to the door leading to the corridor. There she stopped; with bowed head she finally, finally, said, "Thom." And again: "Thom, if you have ever had a spark of feeling for me—you must promise me never to say another word about it—we did swear—do you promise, never again? Not a word, Thom? Please. Do you hear?" Word for word, slowly, in a whisper. Then she left.

I raised my glass to my lips, but couldn't drink. When I looked at Samuel he was staring, his cheek propped on one hand, at the meandering pattern of the carpet. Then he rose. Still without looking at me, he hitched up his trousers and muttered something to the effect that she probably needed him now, and "Goodnight." I sat there alone.

I emptied my glass and the bottle—yes, that is the word: lost in a jumble of overlapping, tangled questions. What a good thing you are there so I can at least write to you about it from here and how it all happened. How I miss you, dearest Lis, now, here. Although I fear I lack the words to tell you this.

Later: It is five in the morning, above the trees the first rosy streaks are showing in the sky. As I said, Samuel stood up too. His spectacles reflected the light from the standard lamp, so I couldn't tell whether he was looking at me or at the white vase on the sideboard. Now I remember him saying something like: "You two with your ancient stories! Why stir them up, Thom, let them be. Let them rot with the past"—something like that. The past! As if we hadn't been discussing it. No. You, Lis, knew it before I did, and Aunt Esther knew it before either of us when she prophesied that I had no choice: I would have to find my painful way through these stories.

The General's Politics I

THOM HAD NOW DECIDED TO WORK AT HIS DRAFT FOR AN HOUR EVERY day, in the morning if possible. He sat at the desk in the Blue Room. One of the two windows facing south was open. He jotted down:

What is myth? What is reality? What actually happened in Switzerland between 1936 and, say, 1945, and how to interpret it? Replace the word "myth" by "legend"?

Following the introduction, the *background* will have to be examined in a first chapter.

(A) The field of tension between social politics and economic politics (devaluation of the Swiss franc in 1936, etc.).

(B) Which economic and political forces, parties, groupings—i.e., interests—interacted with each other? In addition to the positions taken by "classic" adversaries in class and other conflicts, describe the role of clerico-fascistoid trends, e.g., in Federal Councillor Motta's circles, and the overtly fascist forces of the National Front groupings. Then: Gotthard League; Popular League; "Petition of the Two Hundred"; differences within the army command; position of the Swiss Communist Party, the Swiss Socialist Party. Banning of the Front and the Communist Party.

(c) How could the legend of the Swiss determination "to defend the Swiss community of fate" arise? How much of that was reality?

(d) What was the level of armaments among the individual branches of the Swiss Army at the beginning of World War II?

Said to have been meager. Antiquated. Where can I find exact information on this? Phone my friend P. K.; as a military historian he should have access to documents. Also the figures: stores; army budgets in the years beginning 1935.

(e) On August 30, 1939, the Federal Parliament issued the following declaration intended to clarify (yet again) the country's domestic and foreign policy: "The Swiss Federation reaffirms its inflexible determination to maintain its neutrality under all circumstances and vis-à-vis all powers." And further: "that it will preserve and maintain the inviolability of its territory and its neutrality (. . .) with every means at its disposal."

(f) Reawakening of a mythologizing concept of one's native land as part of the measures taken to increase self-awareness/self-assertion. The 1939 national exhibition in Zurich an instrument for the above. "Blood and soil" mentality, Swiss version. Native versus foreign (seen as "alien"). How did the notion of a "spiritual defense of the country" arise? How and by what institutions was it launched and effectively spread by propaganda?

The attempt from above, at that point, in that historical situation, to eradicate social contradictions. In the face of a common danger, the class nature of society is publicly cast aside in favor of a "truce."

However, in all fairness the opposite aspect of the circumstances here negatively depicted must also be looked at: the "truce" as an alliance between bourgeoisie and social democracy, an alliance without which no defensive front against the common threat would have been possible.

(g) Fascism as background: make it clear that we are not looking merely at an Italian, Spanish, or National Socialist German phenomenon. Fascism as a manifestation of—Christian!—European history, the origins of which are to be sought in the crisis of liberalism at the end of the nineteenth century; point to the broad palette of European fascisms in their various national versions, also in the Swiss variation of a definitely antisocialist, authoritarian, corporative image of society to be found chiefly in the upper bourgeoisie of industry and trade. Offer at least for debate the proposition: In domestic/foreign crises, capitalist and liberal/democratic societies are by nature in danger of slipping into totalitarianism—more precisely, into fascist structures.

(h) On August 30, 1939, Parliament resolved to invest the Federal Council (government)—"in this time of danger"—with special powers. Of which constitutionally guaranteed rights were the Swiss people and the cantons deprived by this resolution? A detailed depiction of the origin and workings of this "special powers regime" is outside the scope of this work. However, there appears to have been what amounts to a "self-divestment of power on the part of people and parliament" clearly going beyond analogous resolutions at that time in England (e.g., re censorship). Here too an element of putsch, of violation of the constitution in favor of authoritarian leadership prerogatives of the Federal Government? (Why is there such an obvious lack of a thorough study of this significant, dark chapter of recent Swiss history?)

Saga of Origin II

DANA TAUGHT HER SON AND SPOUSE THE ART OF RAINMAKING. SHE ALSO lent him the vessel of abundance. It never became empty. When Gwion filled it with mead or wine, he and Dana's sons and daughters could go on drinking from it until they were all in the throes of a sacred intoxication. Thus they became singers and poets like Gwion. He learned the art of making the living weep and the dead laugh by playing his harp. He hunted the white stag, and often he lay on Dana's couch and, as he sang, surrendered to the sacred intoxication. His club was so huge that seven men were needed to carry it. When he was intoxicated he would twirl it around in the forest of hollow oak trees. Thus Gwion also created thunder.

And so Gwion was the glory of his spouse Dana. On his return from the underworld early in the year, he was required to perform three deeds to prove himself once again worthy of his spouse. He fought the Great Bear of the mountains and vanquished it. He solved the riddle of the Sphinx. And he captured the hind with the golden antlers, Dana herself aiding him in the form of the invisible huntress with the golden bow. Now for another year he was allowed to return to Dana's couch.

Your mother Lilly. Don't forget that she is by birth a Schaub. A daughter of that comb baron from the Gulden valley. I don't suppose I need tell you again how he made his money so quickly. The nouveaux riches are crooks, remember that, Thomi. Easy come, easy go. The year 1911, when the comb factory blew up in that explosion, you know about that, and forty-three loyal workers died. No, don't ask me how it could have happened, let's leave that nasty old story about the insurance buried with the dead, and as to what disappeared later from the office ledgers—don't ask me. In any event, the baron managed once again to put up a new building, and once again he drove a carriage-and-six to his summer residence in Lucerne, but by now it was wartime, and from then on those Schaubs lived beyond their means. The advent of bobbed hair put an end both to high life and to large tortoiseshell combs.

Her Aunt Esther voice, a little too deep, always slightly breathless. Her way of repeating her stories in a kind of singsong, and only occasionally was Thom startled when she gave a short laugh or suddenly fell silent, and for a long while, without his noticing, her eyes had been on him. That was how she sat sometimes, holding her small fist to her mouth so he knew that it had suddenly occurred to Aunt Esther how things, or what she was telling him, could have turned out quite differently, and worse, without giving much thought to whether he, aged maybe thirteen, understood what she was saying.

Most of the time he had simply sat there on his stool, his back to the wall, his eyes closed. Through the open window beside and above him he could hear the chirping of the starlings, or from time to time the shrill cry of the kite; he had smelled the heat, breathed in the sweet scent of the overripe espalier pears, and punctuating Aunt Esther's words there was the hard, bright sound coming up from the croquet lawn when it was Gret's turn in the game with her friends and Cousin Rolf. With the hard ash-wood mallet she would hit the ball to make it pass through five iron hoops at one stroke, and Gret would give a shriek of exultation—or had it been Charlott? Both his sisters often had the same excited girls' voices, and then Aunt Esther suddenly asking, "Are you asleep?"

Had he really been thirteen then? How could he have been asleep, and she would resume her story. Do you know, and then. And at that time. But your father. Again her hands were winding the wool into bright-colored balls. How could he have been asleep, seeing that she was talking about his mother? And seeing that she, Aunt Esther, did everything she could to make him want to hear more and more of her stories which, he sensed—and this made his toes curl up in his sandals—also had to do with himself.

He really didn't care whether she was tampering with the truth or exaggerating, that she was weaving whole strings of lies into her net, and when she said, "Go ahead, tell your mother, and she'll say, 'Your aunt has always been a liar, your aunt is lying, she wants to poison you with her gossip,'" she would laugh, utter her "Pah!" and "Go ahead, send your mother to me if she wants to hear the truth. The truth is that the whole trouble came into this house with Lilly. My dear brother Ulrich has always been a capable, highly intelligent fellow, only where women were concerned he was a perfect fool. It had to be that power-hungry daughter of a nouveau-riche gambler whom he saw fit to bring into the family after poor Hortense died," and with that Aunt Esther would launch once again into the story that Thom loved so much to hear.

The story of how in 1912 his father had become a military pilot. At that time there was no air force in Switzerland, so the government had been looking for a few daring officers. No wonder they chanced upon Thom's father and a few other cavalry officers. They needed men who feared neither breaking their necks nor the Evil One. The government sent telegrams ordering this handful of officers to Bern, and with them also came seven or ten airmen and pilots, all there were in Switzerland at that time—you know, those amateur mechanics and aviation pioneers, who were circus artists too, rounded up from half the world, they came with their Blériot or Fokker or Wright monoplanes, patched up and patched again after their ten or fifty crashes, flying them in or, if they happened to be temporarily out of commission again, hauling them, from wherever they could be reached as they performed their stunts at circuses and in the clouds. Their country was calling.

There was a smell of war in the air. And only a few months later, during an emergency landing in the Gulden valley—the site of the villa and, down by the river, the factory—back there in Mümlis, Thom's father, Ulrich, had met that girl Lilly Schaub of the comb factory Schaub & Cie. Thom knew how it had happened, had heard the story also from his father: that he, Father, and Oskar Bider, the aviation pioneer who that very year had been the first person to fly over the Pyrenees and, shortly after, the Alps—Thom knew that the two men had orders to fly from Bern to Basel over the Jura Mountains. They happened to run into violent gusts of a westerly wind over the Gulden valley. The machine circled, failed to make it over the Passwang Pass, lost altitude, and only three hundred meters above the ground Thom's father yanked back the control stick and managed to pull the plane out of its spin. Next he tried to regain altitude by circling out of the trough of the valley, then made three or four attempts to fly over the Breiten ridge into the Langenbruck valley. But at that point the engine began to stutter, and Thom's father heard the aviation pioneer in the observer's seat behind him shouting in his ear, "Emergency landing!" A few minutes later Father steered the Blériot in a glide toward the schoolhouse in Mümlis and landed it neatly in the meadow behind the school.

For more than half an hour, people from the bakery, the inns, the butcher's, the school, the housewives from their homes and the police and the men and women employed in the workshops and sheds of the comb factory, and the local farmers had all been waving at the two fellows in the sky; now they ran, ran in their hundreds, to the meadow behind the schoolhouse.

They applauded when the heroes of the air in their short leather jackets climbed out of their wire and canvas crate. Thom's grandfather Jeremias stepped forward to welcome the pioneers in the name of the population. It was an honor for him to welcome them to the Gulden valley, and if they had no objection he would like to invite them as guests in his house. He introduced his twelve-year-old daughter. Lilly blushed as she stepped forward.

At this point Aunt Esther invariably had to laugh. She shot a glance at Thom. "Twelve! She was just a child the first time she saw my brother. But even then she must have already made up her mind: That pilot, that Ulrich Winter and no other!

"Five years later, when Ulrich married his French girl—we were all shocked, and all I can say is, poor Hortense was as beautiful as she was crafty—on that early summer morning in June, with the war still on, seventeen-year-old Lilly took the dogcart and drove over here from Mümlis and, wearing her quite unsuitable chiffon dress, stationed herself in front of everyone else on the steps outside St. Sebastian's Church. There she stood as the bridal couple walked up the steps—I can see it as if it were yesterday. Only a few minutes later she pushed her way through the crowd again and was standing at the very front in the north side chapel, where, with a set face, she never took her eyes off my brother and his bride. That's how it was, Thom. You know what a woman's eyes are capable of. So Ulrich and Hortense remained childless, and why his wife soon began to mope, was always sick, and died twelve years later is something no doctor ever found out. Yet Ulrich had called in one specialist from Innsbruck and another from Lyon.

"But less than eight months after her premature death, Ulrich received a letter, an invitation to a party signed by the comb baron, now over sixty. And who do you think, Thom, had added underneath in her tiny handwriting: 'In my heart a rose bush. The years are passing by. The roses bloom, even in winter'? You see? Three years later the wedding took place, a gala affair at the Hotel Schweizerhof in Lucerne. Now Lilly had what she wanted. The trouble could begin."

*   *   *

Munich, September 29, 1928

Dear Ulrich, beloved brother,

What a lively city this Munich is, bubbling over with contrasts! Generosity is the word that first occurs to me if I am to characterize the people I meet. Generous is certainly the word for the layout of the city, with its parks, the architecture of the villas and the palace, its avenues and squares. Here distinction is not concealed, as with us in Switzerland: it is proudly displayed. Again I am struck by the fact that every third person I meet, whether industrialist or banker, has no compunction about having his "von" and "zu" form part of his name—quaint, no doubt about it. But I am inclined to regret that in our democratic zeal we Swiss abolished aristocratic titles a hundred years ago. How much genuine culture has that cost us!

Just imagine, I even had to have my friend Hugo von Scholz teach me the correct way to kiss a lady's hand! And I still feel awkward when the chauffeur—with your consent, I have hired a proper, fully trained "gentleman's chauffeur"—when at every opportunity this Bavarian colossus smartly clicks his heels together as if we were in the artillery!

I must admit that, when I stroll through the inner city and look at the people, I always have the feeling that a monarch has given the day off to his subjects, his servants, his many thousands of foresters and head foresters, together with their wives and children. Having traveled here from all over the beautiful state of Bavaria, they are happily spending that day in the city.

At the same time I am conscious of a new wind blowing here. Both the brief Communist republic and Versailles are ghosts of a distant past. Life, Ulrich, has carried the day!

Your note has left me puzzled and anxious. Father in bed? Elsazar W. even for a single day of his life not in command on the captain's bridge? The man is eighty-six years old! At that age even a minor attack of vertigo can herald the approach of the Dark Angel. With all due respect to the skill of our dear Doctor Muralt, I do most solemnly beg you to lose no time in calling in two first-class cardiologists. The heart, Ulrich, the heart!

So yet another relapse in the condition of your lovely Hortense?

Only the day before leaving I took the liberty of asking her point-blank the reason for her silence. She even smiled: "Je suis fatiguée, toujours fatiguée, c'est mon tempérament mélancolique—c'est tout." Of course, as a Frenchwoman she will always feel somewhat of a stranger in our house. Add to that her homesickness! But I believe that, more often than we suspect, such emotional states have their origin in an inadequate functioning of the liver. Her chronic lack of appetite would also seem to indicate that. Well, I know that in your tender care you do everything possible for your wife. No doubt a certain apathy is part of her constitution; she and all of us will have to live with that.

Now briefly to business. The enclosed report will, I trust, make it clear that within a short time I have been able to awaken our branch from its profound sleep. Scarcely a day goes by without my being able to establish new contacts, particularly now that I have been accepted in Count Gerö's circle—he is a Von Wichow. Some of the most cultivated industrialists of South Germany meet in his salon. Two evenings ago Heinrich Brüning was a guest; in an informal address at dinner, the Count openly welcomed Brüning as the future Reich Chancellor. I am convinced that before long these contacts of mine will show concrete results in orders for our plants.

To revert to our good discussion about strategies for the Winter concern. Need I say that I am one hundred percent in favor of your intention to speed up the refurbishing of our mechanical equipment on the one hand, and to improve efficiency on the other. The constant systematic review of our technical installations must be continued. And as for improving efficiency, I advise you to go far beyond anything Father has undertaken in this respect. Our motto must be: We will install more machinery per square meter of space than any other factory in the world! Every unused centimeter of space represents an increase in production costs. Every worker is to have the exact amount of space needed to do his job—but not one single centimeter more!

At the same time, every movement, every stage in the work process, even every hand motion and every step made by the worker must be measured with a stopwatch and adjusted with maximum care to the optimal functioning of the mechanization. In turn, in collaboration with the foremen, every machine must be examined: Which of its functions can be cut down or speeded up? For example: Are two workers absolutely essential to its operation, or are 1.8 enough?

You see the *direction*! It represents progress. This is the path we must take through the decades that lie ahead. What perspectives are opening up!

I feel that we are on the historic threshold of an age of the independent machine! Do you realize what that actually means? No longer will the machine be an instrument of the worker, his extended arm; the machine itself will be the worker, and human labor will consist only in providing the machine with whatever is necessary for the performance of its work. Mechanics and electrification must and always will be ever more closely integrated.

Ulrich, we have already reached the point where we are entitled to dream of totally unmanned factories, free of people! From a negative point of view: people will become redundant in production! Seen positively, however, what it actually means is that man will be liberated from millennia of drudgery. He will be free to indulge in his godlike games: in the cultic dance!

This last part of my letter is, as you will have guessed, a distillation of the philosophical treatise I intend to devote to that great subject, "The Machine." I shall keep you abreast of the progress in my work by sending you copies of essential passages.

My very best wishes to you and all your loved ones.

Yours,
Ludwig

It was probably no coincidence that today I decided to have a look at the condition of the rooms in the cellar after all this time. Over my morning coffee it occurred to me that the last time I had been down there was some twenty years ago when, shortly before Mother's death, I spent a few weeks of my university vacation at home. Sepp and I—yes, that must have been it—had picked a few baskets of early ripening apples in the meadow and carried them down the steep outside stairs into the cellar. In the floor of the covered terrace at the back of the house there is a rectangular patch, about ten by two and a half meters, covered not by red brick but by heavy oak planks, now long since dark gray. Oddly enough, my grandfather Elsazar had dealt on the side in wine he imported in two- and three-hectoliter barrels on horse-drawn wagons from Burgundy across the Jura Mountains. In order to store those barrels, he had this cellar entrance built directly from the terrace. Three iron rings for the pulleys are still there in the east wall; when the oak planks are removed one by one, the second plank reveals the first step down with the two heavy iron wheels that carried the steel cables for lowering the barrels. Did Sepp, I wondered, still uncover the outside stairs for a few days in the fall? And stack the planks around the opening to prevent anyone falling in, even in the dark?

That must have been more than twenty years ago. Now I walked through the glass inner door into the back porch and opened the door to the inside cellar stairs, those leading down from the house, not from the terrace. There it was again, that smell in the dimness, that blend of sour must, and potatoes sprouting in the damp, and wine and slightly rancid butter and vinegar; there they were again, the stone steps disappearing one by one down into the darkness. And inside, to the right of the door, the storeroom under the stairs leading up to the second floor was still there, with the protective wooden balustrade on the side next to the cellar steps, the two old bicycles, the cupboard with the bottling jars, the (now empty) butter cask with the white stone on top that even in those days had looked like a skull shimmering back there in the dim light. The marten trap still hung on its nail; astride the wooden balustrade still hung the two slightly mildewed saddles that for so many years no one had slung onto a horse's back.

No, no coincidence. Yet I still don't understand why, today of all days, scarcely an hour ago, I felt this vague urge to have a look around down there. Something of the fear that creeps up on us when as children we go down alone, for the first time, into the rooms below the house, overcame me—fear, expectation, pride of discovery; they are there when we pull open the oak door at the bottom of the stairs and stand above the last three steps, facing the first huge vault, always making sure of an escape route behind—yes, I was conscious of something of all these sensations even now, as well as of the quickened pulse in my throat. Then I walked down those last few steps.

It might have been better if I hadn't. In that way I could have spared myself the necessity of sitting here at the little oak desk, the blank sheet of white paper before me, the ballpoint in my hand but not moving, and I wouldn't have to try—hopelessly—to write the first sentence about what happened to me down there; to commit it to paper in order gradually to unload that shock, to make it stand in front of me, accessible to my attempt to apply my methodology (or what is left of it at this moment) to get at the root of it, that to me still inexplicable root.

I am no longer used to the silence in this house, especially up here. Nine thirty in the morning: Samuel long since at the office, at one of those meetings at which the firm's executives are trying in their wily way to defuse the protest. Urs and Barbara at school, Herminia probably busy in the linen room or in the Paneled Room; Gret apparently never stirs before ten anyway. Silent, yes. The Blue Room in front of me, with the high, unmade bed next to the closet with its mirrored door; the water stains on the ceiling; the flowered wallpaper and those faded, sagging drapes. However, they still work; on getting up, I had drawn back one curtain just enough to let in the summer light from outside. Within me there is still something like shock or shocked amazement.

The unshaded light bulb high above just enabled me to make out the storage shelves for fruit on the left and the shoulder-high barrels at the far end. As I walked, I stumbled over the rotting boards laid possibly a hundred years ago over the earth floor, which, though firmly trodden, was always damp and slippery. When I stood still, I could hear water dripping in the dark every three seconds. A sickening feeling in my stomach as I continued to the left and pushed open the door to the next vault. Groping along the doorpost, I found the switch and turned it. The room remained dark. The only light, filtered through cobwebs, came through the shaft of one of the two small windows high up; outside the other window, I knew, were hydrangea bushes—so dense that, when my eyes became adjusted, it took me a while to make out a pale green shimmer.

I stepped forward into the vault. A little scratching sound brought me up short. A low rumbling, as if a roof slat were rolling down a beam onto the ground; then the silence again. Another drop, quite distinct now: the water was dripping into a puddle. Again I tried to separate the smells—wine vinegar, rotting wood, plus the merest trace of carrion, probably from a dead bat. Was it fear that made me so tense, so tensely alert, my senses so acutely receptive in this damp, cool atmosphere? To my left, high above me, I sensed the presence of the arching vault through which the steep outer stairs led up behind the wall.

And now it happened: as I walked, I suddenly slipped on the muddy floor, stumbled, and stepped onto an iron barrel hoop. The hoop flipped under my weight and struck me just above my right knee so violently that I staggered and fell sideways to the ground.

While I was still falling, and my left hand, then my hip, and then even my knee landed in the slippery mud, I seemed to be walking, walking as if weightless through doors; walking through long cellar passages, three, four, and more rooms, a series of vaults behind, even below, each other. In the space of a few seconds, I assume, and while getting up—muddy from head to toe—onto my knees, I traveled through this vast cavernous system down there; and even now, half an hour later—meanwhile I have had a shower and changed—I feel as if I had been expecting in each cellar vault in turn to encounter some frightful mythological monster— a winged cave creature, a giant lizard, the horse Atar with the cloven hoofs, a vulture with a snake's body—on one of the steps I was climbing. What may not, in one reality, have lasted more than ten seconds, I experienced as a never-ending anticipation of some horror. The fact that it did not materialize—no beast, no human, no bird—was no consolation. Where is the difference? The things for which they are images are there, are down there, so as fast as I could I finally ran up the inside stairs.

Are my nerves overwrought?

But on no account am I going to give up my search. I intend to know the truth.

Leafing through the Festschrift I

—THUS THE WORD *INDUSTRIA* STANDS FOR MAN'S CEASELESSLY FORWARD-looking activity. To look back is to him a waste of time. Man knows that, unless he advances with the times, they will overtake him. To the man of industry, the historical is equated with the obsolete.

In stealing the fire, Prometheus lifted us, the human race, from the status of a nature-bound people to that of a practical people of culture.

—here, too, the historical background shall serve merely to explain how what you see today evolved from the struggles with nature and its forces, how the steps in the unswerving course of progress

—no longer under an obligation toward family history, to describe the force of the individual, but to depict the birth and growth of a mighty interplay of forces, historical and personal, mechanical and financial.

How much do they mean, those deeds of the historical figures of a past era, in terms of the overall development of our country, when we compare them with the revolutionary transformation wrought by the emergence of the Winter concern and its industries?

And yet: It needed far-sighted men with the leadership qualities and dynamism of a Theophil Winter, an Elsazar Winter, to make possible something that less than 175 years ago few people could even imagine. And with a personality such as Ulrich Winter at the helm, the Winter concern, although now for many years a public corporation, may today look with confidence into the future.

Thom was sometimes allowed to choose a story. A nice story, he said. One that goes on and on.

Aunt Esther leaned back in her armchair. She smiled while Thom lifted the globe from the table onto the floor. And where shall the story take place?

Thom twirled the globe on its wooden base. It squeaked a little, sounding like the twittering of the starlings through the open window from the garden. There was a smell of autumn, or of rain in the spring and impetuous human life. Where shall it take place?

Here, he said, in Berlin, but only for a bit. And there's Bombay: here too. And in Rome. And on a frontier. And especially where the word "Switzerland" is written on the globe, and here under the letter *w* of Switzerland is our house. Thom had to go quite close to the globe to see the tiny country. The heart of Europe. The country from which the rivers flowed north and south. The country that, as he knew, was a Tom Thumb among the giants.

Here, he said. And already knew, even before Aunt Esther asked him who he wanted to appear in this story, that he would name his mother and Great-Grandfather Theophil; his father; Charlott; Uncle Ludwig and the anarchist Luigi Luccheni; but also Aunt Esther herself and our general and the joke about the Jews, the horse Atar, and above all the war. He would also name Mussolini. Perhaps the River Aare, perhaps love. And the words—yes, those too. And the wheel of history. And himself. A long story, he said. One about us.

Aunt Esther kept her eyes closed. "Very well," she said. "But you'll have to invent some of it yourself!"

Time
of
Discipline

Ah, those far-off summer afternoons, the two of them sitting outside at the stone table on the terrace, and Aunt Esther exclaiming, "How does someone hope to become the head and heart of our world-renowned Winter Corporation if he can't spell corporation? How does this stripling of almost eleven hope to sit in the boss's chair one day and guide the affairs of our company when he doesn't even know how to spell it, and doesn't know the story of either his great-grandfather or his grandfather?" And, she went on, if she were to tell how in the summer of 1912 she was driven with her Uncle Edi and his stupid wife Emilie to Paris in an open Peugeot, and how they had taken lodgings in Burgundy, in Vézelay, and dined with Monsieur Apollinaire, she would have to discover that this scion of the Winter family had never even heard of Apollinaire, let alone read a single line by this the greatest poet of our century! "Bird-brain!" she said—no, coughed; "Sit up straight!"

Thom had leaned back and slid down so far on the wooden bench in the corner that he could brace his sandals against the stout wooden pillar of the stone table. Looking under the table, he could see Aunt Esther's shoes and part of her artificial leg on the other side and, just above the tabletop, Aunt Esther's narrow face with the lively eyes. He sat up. He took the exercise book she had pushed across the white stone tabletop and put it in his leather satchel. Did he really want to become the head and heart of the renowned concern? Actually, he had been thinking of being something more like a farmer. But for Aunt Esther, everything had already been decided. It was time he learned, she would often say, to wish to do what he had to do. She leaned forward, and the sunshine reflected from the white part in her hair as she lifted the teacup from the table. She drank, her little finger pointing upward. In the silence Thom could hear the humming of the bees in the juniper bush above him as they cooked up their honey.

"How am I supposed to tell such a lazybones about Monsieur Apollinaire when he forgets everything? Can you remember what Mr. Apollinaire said to Uncle Edi, Aunt Emilie, and me as we left? Can you, or have you already forgotten it all?"

Again Thom slid slowly down on the green bench. " 'The clouds are wandering,' that's what he said," said Thom.

"You see? All down the drain! Guillaume Apollinaire pointed with his silver cane to the morning firmament and said, 'The clouds, the shining, wandering clouds. No one can grasp them, they change eternally, they come, they go. Happiness? It is like the clouds.' Then Monsieur Apollinaire threw his white silk scarf around his neck, kissed my hand, and, accompanied by his friends Francis Picabia and Marcel Duchamp, walked off to his big open Bugatti. I can still see him, trailing a cloud of dust behind him as he drove across the wheatfields of Burgundy and, getting smaller and smaller, disappeared over the horizon."

Aunt Esther coughed as she lit her cigarillo. "I won't tell you about that business with my tea salon in Bombay. But don't forget: Five- and six-star generals were among my customers. I won't tell you about my honeymoon in Burma. Nor about what happened on my night crossing on the *Andrea Doria* from Naples to Tangiers. If everything goes in one ear and out the other, you won't be told about the wonderful stroke of fate that caused me to meet my fiancé and future husband George Rhowland."

Thom was aware he was lying as he said that he knew what had happened. And he had asked his mother about the stroke of fate, and she had told him everything.

Aunt Esther smoked. She could see the day coming, she said, when Thom would have to learn to distinguish between those who lived in an aura of lies and those who lived in the truth. Smoke rings floated from her lips into the air. They quickly expanded, caught the sunlight, and drifted away.

And his aunt again, saying, "As for my sister-in-law. As for that person, Thom, who happens to be your mother, you couldn't choose her, after all, that's no reproach." As for her, the former Miss Schaub, she, Aunt Esther, had promised her brother Ulrich never to say another word to Thom about this relative by marriage. One of the bitterest lessons she had learned in her long, long life on this earth was that the truth often, too often, must remain hidden. Aunt Esther picked up her wide-brimmed blue straw hat with the blue ribbon around it and put it on. Without removing the cigarillo from the corner of her mouth, she lifted her face and said in a loud voice, "But the truth will out! For the day will come when the battlements of the lie will crumble, and the truth will triumph over its foes!" Aunt Esther raised her clenched fist. Thom knew that the fist as well as the raised voice were meant for his mother, who was probably busy up there behind the facade in her Blue Room, sitting at her desk over her long columns of figures. A cold shiver ran over him, and he had a feeling that Aunt Esther would now no longer hesitate to tell him a new and even greater truth than before about her time in Burma or Bombay. He knew that, in order to learn the greater truth, he must not make too frequent use of his lie that his mother had told him everything. It was a barely pardonable sin; besides, Aunt Esther might become suspicious.

"Would you like some more tea?" he asked quickly before she began, and refilled her cup. "Sugar?"

"Where did this whippersnapper suddenly learn manners?" She sipped her tea. "As a woman of twenty-seven, still wealthy as I then was, I started out on a trip around the world. I wanted to see Australia, China, the Malay Archipelago, Johannesburg and New York and Rio and Greenland, and planned to be away for eight months. I had booked a very nice cabin on the *Andrea Doria* for the first leg from Naples to Cape Town. So I traveled by wagon-lit from Rome to Naples.

"You're right, Thom, of course I had been in London six months earlier. And I don't mind admitting to a little liaison with an officer in His Majesty's Navy. And you can take this as true too, that he was called George, like my second husband. Coincidences *do* occur, Thom. But it is one of those deliberate lies spread in this household that my father made enquiries about this George through business friends in London, and that, as a result, he forbade me to have anything to do with such a drunkard and rake, and that only then did I arrange to meet George in Rome—secretly, because my father had threatened to disinherit me. All trumped up," she said, "slander invented by people here in this house, relatives by marriage with an eye to their own personal power.

"The truth is very different. I want you to know it. I want you to preserve it and pass it on beyond the death of those who never rest in their ludicrous attempt to turn your aunt's existence into a hell. Behind this are some substantial interests, let me tell you. The truth is that I had a dream. In the wagon-lit between Jammers and Rome I dreamed I saw Saint George conquering the dragon with his spear. And the truth is that on Saint George's Day, on November 3, I went on board the *Andrea Doria*, first to my cabin, then to the upper deck to watch the ceremonies marking the departure of the ship. While we were all, myself included, waving a final goodbye to the noisy crowd on the dock at Naples, a man stood beside me. He saluted, took off his cap and, holding it to his chest, said, 'My name is George Rhowland, captain in the 19th Guards Regiment of the Seventh Royal British Colonial Army.'

"I wonder if you can imagine the thoughts that went through my head. My Saint George's dream, then Saint George's Day—and now? Providence. There is no other word for it. I felt that here a Being more powerful than any of us had intervened. Is it any wonder that when, four weeks later, George stood up at a candlelit dinner—the *Andrea Doria* was already en route from Cape Town to Bombay—when he, George, stood up and said, always in English of course, 'Madam, will you do me the honor of becoming my wife?'—is it any wonder that I blushingly said yes? George escorted me out.

"There we stood at the railing on the upper deck, above us the firmament with its myriads of stars. George pointed out the Southern Cross. The vast Indian Ocean lay all about us, breathing quietly. There we stood, in a close embrace."

Thom knew what would come now—the landing in Bombay, the wedding in Bombay, the train journey through eastern India, days, nights, days; the ambushing of the train, and George defending Aunt Esther's honor with drawn sword. Next would come the days and weeks when the bearers carried Aunt Esther in a litter through the swamps and jungles of Bangladesh, then the crocodiles, the pythons, and the monsoon.

George Rhowland, now Aunt Esther's husband, had to be back at his frontier post on January 10. Downriver by cutter via Chittagong to Rangoon, then on and on via Pegu to Moulmein and from there to the defense of the British Crown territories all the way to the border of the Kingdom of the Thai. Aunt Esther was now so engrossed in all her experiences with George that Thom could safely lie down on the opposite bench without fear of disturbing her. He pushed his satchel along the bench and lay down carefully on his back, the satchel under his head.

There he lay, listening to her voice, fighting with her and George and George's soldiers against the attacks of the Thai rebels on the British Crown, lay there listening, above him the juniper blossoms and the industrious bees, and above them all the vast expanse of sky with the clouds, those shining clouds of Apollinaire's. What a beautiful name! A name that he, Thom, wanted to preserve forever as the sound of happiness. Preserve like Bombay, as the sound of bombs. There he lay, and Aunt Esther might suddenly start to weep a little, because there are tongues, irresponsible tongues, that are not ashamed to maintain that her George had gone off with all her money and all her jewelry to the land of the Thais, that he had abandoned the United Kingdom and his men and Aunt Esther in the bush beyond Moulmein and had simply failed to return from a reconnaissance raid, because, they say, he had been fed up with the glory of His Royal Majesty and with Aunt Esther and married life in the jungle.

No, her George had been a gentleman from head to toe, a colonial officer for whom honor ranked above all else, she said and exclaimed, while the white clouds of happiness sailed across the Indian Ocean, clouds like royal yachts and crocodiles and flags of the British Empire along the river dividing life and death.

"Of course," she cried, and over the edge of the stone tabletop Thom could, without moving, see her small fist raised above her blue summer hat, "of course he drank sherry, what else does a gentleman drink who guards the rights of God, King, and Empire at a frontier post, what else does he drink if he doesn't want to die from the sting of a tsetse fly or the bite of a python? Anyone casting a slur on his memory as that of a drunkard and a rake is insulting an officer who fought for His Majesty until one of those Thai Mongols treacherously murdered him. And if his body was never found, what does that prove except that those Mongols are without honor? So devoid of honor that they threw their wounded enemies into their filthy rivers as fodder for their wretched crocodiles?

"Anyway," Aunt Esther wondered aloud, after a silence that was no doubt devoted to George's memory, "why is there in this house, Thom, why is there on this terrace of the house kept occupied by slanderous people, why is there no sherry?" At the frontier post, it must be said, Aunt Esther had only to clap her hands softly for the Thai boy to appear instantly with sherry and ice. What was Thom here for? Would he now please run upstairs immediately to Frieda and ask her for the bottle of sherry and the Green Glass? "The green one, please!" she called out as

Thom, in the role of a Thai servant, hurried upstairs and returned with bottle and glass on a silver tray.

Holding the bottle with both hands and reaching past the blue straw hat, he filled the Green Glass, then put the bottle back on the tray. He sat down again on the bench. Aunt Esther took a sip; for a moment she had her bird face, then she quickly tossed back her sherry. He got up again and refilled the glass. Aunt Esther was absorbed in her silence, and probably on her way back to Bombay from the eastern frontiers of the British Commonwealth. High up in the hickory oak, a blackbird was singing. Even the noise of the car passing by on the street below the box hedge did not distract her. Herminia used to say: When the blackbird sings, rain's on the way.

And the bombs?

"What in the world made you think of *that*? Such nonsense! Bombay: the word means Big Bay."

But then what did bay mean?

"Doesn't this birdbrain even know that a bay is a gulf in the ocean? Can you believe it! It's high time you studied the globe!" Aunt Esther tipped the Green Glass back, into her throat, then lit another cigarillo. "Bom-bay," she said.

Thom thought about that. He had no real picture of a gulf in the ocean either, but he didn't follow that up; suddenly that other mysterious word came to his mind again, Frieda's word. He had never known Aunt Esther's Frieda to be anything but quiet and pleasant, but the other day she had come out of Aunt Esther's suite very red in the face. Without a word she had gone to the kitchen where Thom and Herminia were and paced restlessly about, then suddenly burst into tears and said, "What's stopping her! Why doesn't she go back to Bombay!"

Frieda had then suddenly taken fright, and when she barely whispered, "To her brothel!" her eyes above the hand clapped to her mouth had turned into huge, terror-stricken marbles. Since then all he knew was that there was something utterly mysterious and scary about this word. But what? What? He swallowed and said, as if he were merely asking about the Green Glass, "Aunt Esther, what's a brothel?"

Above the sherry glass at her lips, Aunt Esther's eyes now also widened until they were like marbles. Slowly she put down the Green Glass on the stone table. She whispered, as she leaned her head in the straw hat against the chair back, and as the hat fell over her face and she ripped it off and tossed it on the floor, leaning her head once more against the chair back, she whispered, her eyes closed, "Oh, infamy!" Again Thom gathered that it was all about the truth, the Almighty, the enemies who would be crushed, and about the fact that Aunt Esther would never allow—"never, do you hear?"—would never allow Thom's childlike soul to become yet another sacrifice in this house, for the sole purpose of hurting *her*. "Six-star, in fact: seven-star generals, Thom," she said. But no! Not another word! "This"—and now she was shouting up at the facade behind her—"is not yet the end, I swear!" After a short pause, she said—no, she commanded, "I wish to be taken around to the rear of the house."

Thom pushed her carefully over the flagstones, brought her her crutch, and helped her out of the wheelchair; as she climbed the three steps to the rear terrace, Aunt Esther leaned heavily on his shoulder with her left hand. Frieda was waiting for Aunt Esther in the doorway.

Thom returned to the stone table and continued to sit there for a while. Now he told himself the story of how Aunt Esther, after her husband's heroic death, had returned to Bombay via Rangoon with only two Thai servants; briefly he relived with her the experience of being ambushed by bandits in the swamps when she had had to surrender all her possessions, including her jewelry, to save her own life and that of the servants. In Bombay, in order to avoid starvation and to save up enough money for the journey home, the widow Esther Rhowland-Winter had had to open a tea salon for the six- and seven-star generals, which, after all, was quite understandable.

On looking for the blackbird in the hickory oak, he saw the clouds. Apollinaire, he thought; he picked up his satchel and went into the house, this time up the front steps. Inside, in the dark corridor, he suddenly remembered that there was also the story about the gypsy, and that that story was also connected with Aunt Esther's trip around the world. Why hadn't he asked right away for that one too? Never mind, it was really quite a different story.

In any event, years later, in the library, he happened to come across that sentence about the clouds, not word for word but almost; he found it in a little volume of Charles Baudelaire's prose poems. He had felt a brief pang. Apollinaire: it was such a beautiful name. Oh well, Baudelaire sounded beautiful too, and what difference did it make to the truth that happiness was where the wandering clouds caught the light?

*　*　*

Thom was writing today, and unusually fast. Although he was trying to put his upwelling memories into some kind of order, sometimes even into a convincing sequence, he was aware of writing under a compulsion, that his writing had taken on a positively manic dimension. It was to this mania or compulsion that he now wanted to yield in two or three hours of writing, without considering where it was leading him, or why. He soon noticed that into his actual experiences he was weaving elements that lifted him onto a plane of what was probably pure invention—a plane of images and even people, situations, thoughts, feelings that he had never known or thought or felt. Strange, where this ballpoint pen could take you if you surrendered control to it—apparently to a place where memory, the editing of memory, assumptions, imagination, speculation, lies, truth, and dreams all became one.

In the Dovecote

Not that Sepp was really that interested in soccer. But why shouldn't he watch the cup game tonight? Not in the Waadtländer Hall, that was always too noisy and the set was so high up in the corner that you couldn't see the ball anyway. And he wouldn't put it past Köbu to start talking again about the game between Germany and Switzerland in 1938. No, Sepp would rather go and sit in the pantry, close to the screen, where he could at least watch those soccer artists of Real Madrid performing their tricks and see the ball moving. Lugano, that team hadn't a chance anyway. Besides, in the pantry you could go to sleep if you felt like it. Herminia could always be relied upon to arrive in time with her "All right, Sepp, it's getting late."

In 1938 things had been a bit different. There had been only the voice from the loudspeakers, no picture, you had to imagine the crowded stadium in Paris and all those Swiss with their shouts of "Hopp Schwiz!", and Walaschek's cannonball into the Greater German goal was also something you had to imagine for yourself, and how they carried Georges Aeby off the field on a stretcher! Karl Rappan: there was a coach who knew what he wanted. He had fielded the same winning team as against England, when Trello literally shot down the English goalie to achieve that two to one. There was—Sepp felt confident he could remember them all—Huber of course, in goal. Then Minelli, Lehmann, Springer, and then someone from the Zurich Grasshoppers on the national team, never mind the name, anyway then the forwards—Loertsche, Amado, Walaschek, Bickel of course, Bickel, he was the greatest, and Trello Abegglen, then, oh yes, Aeby from Servette. There you are. No one could tell him anything. Hadn't Sepp himself been shooting goals on the company team, a defense man at that time, in the late twenties when there was still a Winter Corporation team?

How quiet it was again up here. Sepp was tempted to take off his shirt. But then he might fall asleep; he'd better keep it on. Such heat, so early in the year! What would it be like in August?

He shouldn't have said that about a bullet in the head. Not that. To be frank, that fellow could count himself lucky not to have run into Sepp in the weeks following. Sepp would have stuck his switchblade right into his guts, that's for sure. He was a lathe operator by the name of Rubitschon, from Olten, but he'd always been with the other two so Sepp had never caught him alone. With the other fellow, the heating mechanic, and that tall one, from Zofingen, a foundry worker. Bastards.

The day before, the city had already attached the loudspeakers to the chestnut trees on Bastian-Platz. Of course Sepp had gone there too; he had just as much right to listen to that game as everyone else, didn't he? Late afternoon, and the square was already filled with people; of course the Germans also had Austrians on their team. The coach—hadn't his name been Herberger? One of them was called Stroh, and then there was a Goldbrunner or some such name, and then that blond fellow known as the Dribble King, but they'd been playing for less than half an hour when the score was already two nil for Greater Germany. The radio commentator had said, "Greater Germany—Switzerland: this is more than a game, this is the victorious German Goliath versus the Swiss David, this is the game of the century!" Frankly, when Loertscher, that asshole, kicked the ball into his own goal, bringing the score to two nil, a silence fell over Bastian-Platz, and all those tens of thousands could only swallow with dry throats. For him too, for Sepp, it had also been grim, and those fellows should have known that he hadn't had anything more to do with the Front for a long time.

But scarcely had the Germans kicked off again when that fellow Rubitschon stood beside Sepp and said to the others, "He's another one of those. What'll we do with him?" By now the other two were also standing behind and beside him, and the foundry worker said, "If we lose this game, it'll be your turn, you Frontist swine!" and Rubitschon pushed Sepp with his elbow and asked which way he would like it, but Sepp only said, "Watch out, or you'll be sorry," whereupon Rubitschon said, "How about a bullet in the head—all right?" Then they pushed off.

He shouldn't have said that. Not that. But then, what should Sepp have done? One against three. All he could do was wait till he got him alone. Anyway, from now on he would take his switchblade with him whenever he went into town at night. And so when Walaschek shot that cannonball into the Greater German goal, two to one, loud cheering broke out, and the commentator in the chestnut trees shouted, "Where there's life, there's hope!" But almost the next moment Georges Aeby was carried off on a stretcher, and a woman's voice yelled across the whole square, "Beat his brains out!" For a moment Sepp wasn't sure whether she meant him or the Greater German Dribble King.

Now things really got going. From the trees came the shouts of the people in Paris, "Hopp Schwiz!", and it wasn't only the Swiss there, this was the game of the century that had now turned into a battle, a battle for freedom, a battle against Hitler, and even Sepp joined in when the thousands around him shouted "Hopp Schwiz!" louder and louder, almost drowning out the voice from the loudspeakers. Ten rampant red jerseys were assaulting the Greater German fortress; then Amado kicked across to the center, and Bickel smashed the round leather over the heads of the Greater German defense spot on between the goalposts. Two two. Sheer delirium. The loudspeaker voice cracked: "The Greater German colossus is groggy! All hell has broken loose!" The voice was drowned out, then our three great A's immediately attacked. Aeby, a white bandage around his injured head, came onto the field again and spurted off— Aeby to Amado, Amado to Trello Abegglen, one merciless attack after another culminating in Trello's header. The giant German goalie was defeated, three two, and even Sepp had to admit that there were tears in his eyes. "Yes, my fellow countrymen at home, the stadium is boiling over here! This is the battle of Sempach, the battle at Morgarten! Our eleven red jerseys with the white Swiss cross! Our sons of William Tell!"

Then suddenly the silence. You could have heard a pin drop. The impossible—the commentator was screaming now, stammering, howling. Had the Germans managed to even up the score after all? Victory! The impossible, the miracle! *Four* two! *Four* two! Trello: he's done it again! What a resurrection! The old Rütli oath, the old Rütli spirit, had risen again! In every village, in every town, in the farthest mountain valley, people were dancing and singing. In Paris and London, Stockholm, even in Rome: the rejoicing knew no bounds. On Bastian-Platz too, the thousands were hugging each other. On Helvetia's mountains, bonfires were blazing.

To be sure, no one hugged him, Sepp. In a way he preferred that; after all, he could laugh without being hugged. That this lathe operator, this Rubitschon and his "How about a bullet in the head?" hadn't been forgotten in all this turmoil and yelling, went without saying. Rubitschon could count himself lucky that in the weeks following, when Sepp was roaming the streets looking for him, he didn't run straight into Sepp's switchblade. Sepp would have done him in, that's for sure.

Sepp had never cared too much for singing. But now, on the square under the trees, the commentator from the loudspeakers gradually became audible again as he described the two teams on the field—the annihilated German team, and the victorious red jerseys now standing at attention because the white Swiss cross on a blood-red field was being hoisted— and the band struck up the national anthem and they were now all standing there joining in, it was the old anthem, the real one, "Hail to thee, Helvetia," when it came to the words, "Standing firm like rocks of old, Facing perils ever bold," Sepp had to admit that even he was humming along.

Through the window he looked into the oak trees. The leaves shone in the sun as if oiled. Beyond and below, the sea of roofs, the high-rises among them. Seventy or eighty thousand people working there, at home, in offices, in workshops, at wickets, behind counters. A few pensioners, a few hundred unemployed strolling aimlessly about, and passing them, people in cars, all on their way somewhere, to buy something, to deliver or pick up something. Or the ones in the factories who had plunged into the battle and must now be gradually beginning to feel how little chance they had of winning it.

Quite a privilege, to be able to afford to spend the morning groping around in the cave system of past, long past times in search of—well, what, really? Down there on the drive, the grass, the weeds had come to resemble a carpet. Hardly a trace of gravel left. The faintly discernible tracks were the tire marks of Samuel's Volvo.

Thom sat down again. The circle of possible culprits. Wasn't it absurd to be struggling, with the cool, analytical mind he always admired when watching police detectives on television, to get to the bottom of that terrible entry of his rather foolish Aunt Esther? He wrote down: Who could have had what motive?

"We four or five people." Who? Who? By "we" Aunt Esther must have meant to include herself. And who else? Had her "we," summarily and mistakenly, also included himself, Thom? Who else did she mean? Who, for God's sake? Gret? Samuel? Had that diary entry been an indirect, ambiguous accusation against herself? Or Frieda, that kind-hearted soul, who wouldn't hurt a fly? Sepp? Herminia? Or perhaps even Doctor Muralt? Charlott?

He took a fresh sheet of paper from the drawer and wrote down all those names, one below the other. For a moment he saw clearly that he must now systematically try to analyze the relationships between all these people and his mother. But immediately his recollection of Charlott wiped away all clarity—of Charlott's face as she stood in the doorway to his room, dry-eyed, distraught, and whispering, "She's already dead!" He must have been stunned by the news, almost insensible for days on end as if under heavy sedation. Gret, Samuel, and André too told him later that he had done nothing but sit in a daze, staring at the pattern of the carpet, barely reacting when spoken to. Later on, that time seemed to him like some distant illness, a time spent in feverish dreams that he couldn't remember. We are condemned to love our parents. He had a feeling he had only recently encountered those words. In talking to Lis?

Start again. Should he first try to establish whether Doctor Muralt had been in the house that evening while Mother was still alive? That nice old doctor, the Winters' family physician as far back as Grandmother Helen's days when Thom's father was still a child? How gently Doctor Muralt had always cured Thom or Gret or Charlott of their injured shoulders and sprained ankles, their influenzas and measles. Even a slight sore throat was enough for him to say, "We'll have to keep you in bed for three days, then we'll see." He would look very stern, yet Thom knew that Doctor Muralt was well aware how much Thom relished being occasionally let off school for a few days on doctor's orders, and being entitled as a patient to Mother's undivided attention at home. The doctor a culprit? What if Doctor Muralt had deliberately given a fast-acting overdose of some medication or other to terminate what he knew would be a long period of suffering for Mother, who was already drifting into the twilight zone of death?

And what if Aunt Esther, aged thirty-five or so and before she had plunged into the escapade with her George, had had a liaison, as it used to be called, with Doctor Muralt? And if he had then, after his wife's death, married some other woman, and Aunt Esther had hated him ever since? And her diary entry was intended now, after all these years, to strike at her faithless beloved?

But how to track down such material, such obscure stories, at this late date?

Again Thom ran over the list. What was there about Sepp? It occurred to Thom that he had hardly seen the old man since he arrived. Even now, Sepp and Herminia still had their supper, usually together, in the pantry. True, two days ago, in the washhouse, Sepp had clearly been pleased to see Thom again. What a strange figure, that handyman: tall, always a little stooped, with his long arms, his bald head; taciturn, smelling permanently of chewing tobacco; when he laughed, which was seldom, his mustache quivered. No, he hardly needed words to communicate, unless he was talking to himself in the washhouse. For over fifty years he had belonged to the place—not to the family, like Frieda or Herminia, but to the house, to the washhouse, to the barn. That was his preserve. And from there he observed, in fact kept under careful scrutiny, whatever was happening in house and grounds. In the old days, when Mother told him to do something he would stand there mutely, staring straight ahead, and to Thom it had always seemed as if he could hear Sepp's brain working. Then after a while he would leave. Usually he had carried out the order, but always as if with mental reservations; sometimes he ignored it.

Sepp must be well over seventy. Had he hated Mother? One thing was certain: Sepp's total devotion to Thom's father. The two men, while always respecting the social barriers, were cronies, linked by a bond of common male interests. For Father, Sepp was—well, what had he been? In the mid-twenties he had joined the household as coachman, stable hand, and manservant, at a time when the directors of Winter's already had two black limousines at their disposal. Nevertheless, until well into the thirties Father used to have Sepp drive him by horse and carriage to the office and back every day.

The stables, and the workshop at the far end of the washhouse, had remained Sepp's domain. And what had also remained was Sepp's role whenever Father was in the throes of one of his drinking bouts. Then Sepp was Father's bodyguard, his valet, drinking crony, and confidant in one: sturdy, cunning, and loyal.

Thom's mother had made repeated attempts to lock up the wine and schnapps. When he was about seven, Thom had stood in the pantry doorway watching Father trying to lever himself out of his armchair. Finally Father was on his feet, swaying. When he started moving toward the sideboard, the empty bottle fell off the little serving trolley. Thom saw his mother's wide, staring eyes. She too had risen. She too was watching Father as he slowly crossed the room, supporting himself on chair backs and the edge of the table. She must have known what would happen next.

Father's drinking bouts occurred only every few months. Invariably, in the course of a few days, he would go on drinking until he reached the point of wanting literally to wipe out what remained of his consciousness. By that time wine was no longer adequate. Two bottles of potent schnapps was what he needed at that moment. The bottles of transparent schnapps, with their handwritten labels, stood in a long row on the bottom shelf of the sideboard.

Leaning against the doorpost, Thom watched his father aiming for them. Beyond the dining table he could see there was no key in the door of the sideboard. Father was now standing with his back to the room, bracing himself with both hands on the chest-high sideboard. Slowly he turned his head toward Mother. He mumbled something incoherently. Thom could feel his heart throbbing in his throat. He heard his mother's voice, loud and clear, say no. And: "That's enough for today, dear!"

When she stood like that, erect, her chin slightly uptilted, her nostrils quivering, a faint color rising from her neck to her face, and her voice not loud but clearly enunciating each word, everyone knew that it was she who was laying down the law. Even Father hadn't a chance.

From the right, Sepp appeared beside the tiled stove. Father feebly hammered away with both fists at the sideboard. Sepp paused, he sniffed, suddenly looked across at Thom, and said, "You there, beat it!" Thom was petrified with fright. Sepp walked around the dining table, passing slowly behind Father, and said, "The boss needs it, I guess—" Stretching out his hand he said to Mother, "The key." Father half turned his face; there were tears on it. His mumbling died away. And into the silence

Sepp said, "Come on, come on, let's have it!" No "Mrs. Winter," no "please." "Let's have it."

For two or three seconds Mother and Sepp faced each other silently, but with the small round table between them. Still Sepp's outstretched hand. Mother slowly turned her face away, toward the stove, then reached into the pocket below her belt and gave Sepp the key. Thom ran through the pantry into the kitchen.

A little later, pressed against Herminia's hip, he saw Sepp coming along the corridor with Father. Sepp had placed one of Father's arms over his shoulder so that, holding him by the wrist, he could half carry, half lead him. On Father's face was the lopsided smile that Thom knew. In their free left hands Sepp and Father were each carrying one of the transparent bottles. Thus they shuffled their way past him toward the stairs, and up.

The General's Politics II

IN THE SECOND CHAPTER HE WOULD HAVE TO DESCRIBE THE INSTITUTION of commander in chief and his legal powers. (The CC is the only person in Switzerland authorized to bear the title of "General," and that only in times of emergency, during the mobilization of the army, the "active service." He is elected by parliament.)

1. Describe that election of August 30, 1939, in Bern.

2. The operative sentence of the federal government's instructions to the General: "You have a mandate, by deploying all appropriate military means, to maintain the independence of the country and to preserve the intactness of the territory."

3. Extraordinary powers of the General, with the right to delegate them to subordinate military authorities: carrying out house searches; the right to ban public assemblies and demonstrations; surveillance of postal, telephone, and telegraphic communications; power to arrest suspicious persons; imposing of death sentences by court-martial in precisely defined cases such as treason, mutiny, or desertion. Plus participation in the area of press censorship, etc.

4. His personality. Biographical data (on hand).

5. Pursue the following questions: How was it possible that, unlike General Wille during World War I, Henri Guisan, son of a Vaudois country doctor, rapidly gained the respect, not to say veneration, of the population on both the right and the left, as a unifying symbolic exponent of a national will toward self-preservation? How did he manage apparently to combine authority with popularity? Quote contemporary evidence (press). His "chivalrous nature" is mentioned; his "attractive naturalness of manner and cordial spontaneity in conversation"; he "personified the square-dealing Swiss soul," although with his "upright character" he was not an "exponent of creative thinking." "A man of quiet distinction," he had "possessed an infallible sense of the needs of the common man." His position "above party quarrels gradually became inviolate." His "effect had been that of an apparition from another world"; "when the events of the war underwent a heated acceleration, he calmly found words that delved into the very depths of the Swiss soul. The Swiss nation then took notice and gained a feeling of national unity" (E. Bonjour, *History etc.*, Vol. IV).

6. Sketch the General's political world view: Guisan's reactionary ideas directed toward a corporate republic à la Mussolini. Sources: speeches. His reports to the government. The General's concluding report to parliament in 1948 (?). Personal testimony. Colonel Bernard Barbey's report. Also look up J. R. von Salis, Hans-Ulrich Jost, Jakob Tanner. (Return to this point in the chapter on the Rütli accord.)

7. In which field of force within the army did the General operate?

Describe the conspiracy of the Officers' League (founded in Lucerne on July 21, 1940, by officers Ernst, Hausamann, and Waibel, initially joined by 34 other senior cadres).

The members were determined:

(a) to oppose all tendencies toward capitulation; if necessary, the General would have to be coerced into issuing battle orders to the army;

(b) if necessary, to arrest the government (federal council) should it be inclined to declare capitulation. Appropriate measures were pre-pared—always without the General's knowledge—in every detail;

(c) to continue the struggle even after an—anticipated—military defeat as the core of a partisan organization by guerrilla warfare—if possible, in cooperation with the General but, if necessary, either without or against him.

This Officers' League was closely allied to the "Gotthard League"

(Prof. Theophil Spoerri), which, advertising in 74 newspapers, called upon "all living forces" inside and outside the parties to cooperate in "unconditional combat-readiness."

Close links also with that other civilian resistance organization: Action of National Resistance.

Describe the arrest of the conspirators. How, although found guilty of attempted mutiny and sentenced, they were received by the General and told by him that "in his heart he was close to them." The prison sentences were correspondingly mild.

8. Describe the other, pro-German opposition in the (professional) officers' corps. Leading figures of this (numerically smaller) wing: Colonel Gustav Däniker as well as Colonel Corps-Commander Ulrich Wille. Däniker: declared opponent of the General and his politics. Openly supported pro-Nazi-German positions. Maintained close relations with the leaders of the National Movement of Switzerland (2,000 supporters), a formerly banned Frontist party, resurrected in 1940, favoring Switzerland's joining the "New Order in Europe." Dismissed from the army in 1942 by the General. Quote Werner Rings, *Switzerland in the War* (*Schweiz im Krieg*).

Wille: Son of General U. W. (supreme commander during World War I). Criticizes the General as a personal rival, also in the name of Swiss industrial interests. Discreetly suggests to the German ambassador in Bern (who claims to have "heard" of the document discovery in La Charité) that he exert pressure on the Swiss government to dismiss Guisan on grounds of infringement of neutrality. Carl Otto Köcher, German ambassador in Bern, refuses (Köcher to the Foreign Office, October 3, 1940). After the defeat of France, Wille repeatedly tries to influence members of the government to consider demobilizing the Swiss Army. In July 1941, in a memorandum to Federal President Wetter, Wille demands that Swiss policy, including economic policy, be made to conform to the Third Reich (details: E. Bonjour, Vol. IV, pp. 424 ff.).

"(. . .) without the Wille nimbus he would have had to pay dearly for his agitation against General Guisan and his extreme Nazi sympathies (. . .). Whereas the lumpen proletarian Ernst S. was sentenced to death and shot (as a traitor) for supplying a few grenades to the Germans, Colonel Corps-Commander Wille went scot-free" (Meienberg, *The World as Will and Delusion*).

Included in this faction were also ultrareactionary figures such as Eugen Bircher, divisionary colonel and co-founder of what was first the

Aargau, then the Swiss, Patriotic Coalition, as well as of the Alliance for People and Homeland with close ties to the Fronts (other senior officers were also members of the Alliance). Among other things, Bircher tried to build up a Swiss militia along the lines of Rüdiger Count Starhemberg's Austrian home guards. In an "emergency" they were to be deployed against "attempts at Bolshevization" by Social Democrats. These activities, mainly in the canton of Aargau, never went beyond the initial stages.

                                                      Saint-Rémy, June 27, 1982

Dear Thom,

How I miss you!

Today, on my long hike up into the Alpilles, I discovered a lake—artificial, but beautifully situated in silent pine woods. Yellow broom all around it, still in flower. Swimming prohibited—too bad. On the way there, and later while I was sitting on the rickety landing stage in the sun, I was always talking to you.

What do we know about each other?

The hotel—the big old place on the *Cours* shown on the enclosed card—has a covered terrace at the rear. That is our dining room. From there two steps lead down into the spacious grounds, with their old plane trees. Inside the building—and it reminds me a little of your sister's house—everything is a bit run down, the lobby with its TV set, hand-cranked phonograph from the forties, and worn brocade armchairs, fake Empire no doubt—delightful; the owners also from another era. The food is good. My little room is at the back, very quiet; at night I can hear the trees rustling.

How much nicer it would be if you were here too! Sometimes, for a few seconds, you are so close to me that I feel I could put my arms around you. I smell you, hear you, hear your breath beside my ear on the pillow, feel the little bristly hairs around your mouth caressing my eyebrows and cheek. I wonder how you've been, what you've been doing, these two days?

On the train, incidentally, between Geneva and Montélimar, a sixty-year-old salesman traveling in canned soups—also spices and ketchup—told me his life story. He had been in the Foreign Legion, always in some war or other, the last time in Dien Bien Phu. I will tell you all about him. When, Thom, when?

No, I certainly don't mean to pressure you. As for this news about your mother's death, I am still literally speechless. Have you tried again to talk to Aunt Esther? I suppose she isn't the most reliable of witnesses. What do I know, what do you know, about the fantasies of an eighty-year-old woman? Then again I think: Why shouldn't a clan like yours, for instance, repeat the comic tragedies of the classical Greek era? Reenact? Suffer again and again?

Oh, Thom. What strange people you Swiss—or rather, you Winters—are. Take just the house! As seen here from the *Cours*—it is 9:30 P.M., by now quite a variety of people are sitting in wicker chairs around me in front of Silvio's bar, and at this very moment the colored lights strung along the wire above me have been switched on in the dusk—seen from here, those two days in your house seem to me—what shall I say, unreal? Weird? Nightmarish? At times as I moved about the house, I had a feeling of moving through totally dissimilar zones. Whether downstairs in the passage, in the hall, then on the stairs, again in the gallery, in your room or mine, I seemed to be constantly entering new fields of highly dissimilar tensions. I felt it almost physically. They don't emanate from underground streams or electrical conduits! You're smiling, I know. But really, Thom, I could feel them—energies emanating from human passions that could never come to rest; some psychic substances are in the air there, and when I moved through those fields I couldn't help picking them up, just as we can physically pick up vibrations of music. They are there, overlapping, intermingling.

Your reticence when you're together. Your cordiality—to me they seem strange, in a way. I know, of course, that we Germans usually like to talk, and talk a lot. You people are more reticent. What are you keeping back, Thom? That silence often made even you seem like a stranger to me.

I really don't know—did I dream it, or did it actually happen? Your waking up beside me, smoothing both hands down over your face as if to wipe away whatever was oppressing you. In answer to my question, "Were you dreaming?" you said, "Yes, some nonsense." But then you did say, "I was walking through old, half-ruined vaults. Whenever I came to a door and opened it in the hope of getting outside I always found myself in yet another cellar room. Again only the light shafts, barred, high up in the wall. I had to go on, up steps, down steps, into one new, unfamiliar vault system after another. As if a distant magnet were pulling me along. Yes, it was really a kind of suction."

You said it as if you meant: a curse. You said it sadly, the inescapable nature of the suction or curse was in your tone of voice. "I found myself in—" you said.

In thinking about this today, Thom, beside that little lake in the Alpilles, it struck me: I refuse to believe in curses. And even if they purport to be of mythological origin: please, Thom, you must believe that even myths, they too, are fathomable; their prophecies, even in the guise of an inescapable destiny, can be voided. That would still leave enough room for the unfathomable.

I imagine you walking about the house, pondering, probing around in your memories as you search. How much that is unsaid, unclarified, unlived—even in your own life—is tied down in that house until you have uncovered or voiced it and written it down. I am afraid for you. Old stories can, when we descend into them, become part of the present, they can wound and change us. Can they also destroy us? Don't be too bold!

How I wish you were sitting here telling me about what you have discovered on your journey through your family history! And what emotions this has aroused in you.

The old concierge in this hotel gave me a room with a wonderfully wide bed, of course. Tactless—don't you agree?

Your Lis

What happened in the past? Lis had asked, had asked again.

At his request, Herminia told Thom what had to be bought in town. He made a list. Just before five he took the bus into town, intending to meet André at six.

Your life, Lis had said. What do I know about you?

Here on the bus—Thom and the two elderly women in front of him were the only passengers—the sweat poured off him in the heat. With some difficulty, leaning away from the seat back, he stripped his light linen jacket off his shoulders and arms, then unbuttoned his shirt down to his belt.

Her softly rounded, open Lis face. Her laughing eyes, when she was thinking hard, would suddenly give him a severe and slightly frowning look. "Born in 1938, professional historian, jobs in journalism, archives— what else? Surely that can't be all?"

Through the window Thom looked down on the roofs of the cars slowly passing the bus. At the intersection the bus stopped; people crossed the street on the green light and disappeared in front of the bus. Lis again, again her voice. Lis had sat up in bed. Without looking down on him she had said, as if to herself, "To live with a father, with such grandfathers in your past—as an only son and as the grandson of such captains of industry," she laughed: such big-game hunters—she could imagine that was pretty strenuous.

Thom hadn't really felt like penetrating the jungle of explanations, of baring his memories and feelings, into which Lis seemed to want to entice him. Strenuous? "I suppose so," he murmured. Did they, Lis and he, right at this moment when he was scarcely awake and just beginning to look forward to his breakfast coffee, to that quiet half hour with Lis at the kitchen table in her Berlin apartment, and to his first cigarette— did they have to begin, this very minute, to tackle such life-and-death problems? Hadn't he finally succeeded—and at the cost of so much effort!—in leaving behind him all those expectations implanted in him by his family background? Hadn't he succeeded in taking his own path away from the career that had been mapped out for him? He got out of bed with a yawn that he knew to be not quite genuine. Lis would drop the subject, he hoped. He began to dress.

The lighted name of the next stop, Elsazar-Winter-Platz, appeared above the driver's head. Thom walked to the door. It opened with a hiss, and he got off. In the supermarket, the hum of the air-conditioning; in fact, pushing his cart along the aisle, shopping list in hand, he actually began to feel a bit chilly. As he took down a bag of coffee, a woman beside him said, "Well, isn't it—aren't you Thomas Winter? How are you?"

"That's right," he said, glancing at her and the little girl of about four standing obediently beside her and looking up at him—Huwiler, wasn't that her name? Or had been twenty years ago when, the object of his secret admiration, she had served him in the little tobacco shop on the right near the old bridge—"Miss Huwiler?" She nodded and smiled at him. "And how are you?"

He hurried away, pushing his cart in the direction of the cashier. And was aware of the questions flashing through his mind as he stood there waiting: What was this fear? Familiar to him when he walked through town, here, at home—the fear of meeting people he had once known who might ask him: What are you doing these days? A foolish fear, certainly, but there it was, and he even felt relieved to find that the cashier handing him his change didn't know him.

Later, at the breakfast table, while he stood pouring Lis some coffee, she had looked up at him. "Why are you so evasive? I would think that such superfathers often do become a problem for sons, and for daughters too. If your father had been, let's say, a foundry worker, you would probably have had to cope with the burden of a so-called socially inferior background. In moving up socially to the level of historian, you might even have had a vague feeling of guilt. And it can also be the other way around—those rich, widely respected men of action like your ancestors—tell me, Thom: Is it possible that, comparing yourself with them, you might at times feel something of a failure?"

Carrying a grocery bag in each hand, he walked at a leisurely pace along Weissenstein-Strasse toward the Old Town. Stopping for the red light at the intersection, he was conscious of being eyed by the tall man beside him. Thom glanced at him. The man looked amazed, then broke into a wide grin. "Thomas! How super! I can't believe it!" The man, his expression, his lively gestures as he talked—all radiated some hectic quality. "Of course! And how've you been?" Thom racked his brain for the name. As they crossed the street side by side, he remembered: they had played soccer together on the junior team. "Of course, Jürg," he said. Even though he would have liked to go his own way after crossing to the other side, he knew there was no escape. They turned into the pedestrian zone, Jürg talking, talking. At the first sidewalk café they sat down in the shade. What Jürgen needed now was "one on the rocks." Yes, there was something hectic emanating from this fellow Jürg. The waitress brought the two martinis.

"And now let's hear about you, Thom! Didn't you go on to university someplace? Are you married? I'll bet you're a big shot by now!"

And kids?

Thom raised his glass, and they drank to each other. Yes, why shouldn't he tell this fellow Jürg at least a few of the things he'd been doing? How, in the fall of '58, he had first attended Fribourg University, then on to Basel, after his mother's death. "And then I finished up, in '65, with a thesis on 'Peasant Revolts in the Canton of Solothurn.' "

Jürg nodded. "Super," he said. "Wild." Had he been listening?

It was only now that Thom began to notice the twitching in the left corner of Jürg's mouth. And that Jürg was speaking in an undertone, like a conspirator. He had leaned forward and was talking on and on with flailing gestures: he was a section head, high tech, right? Awesome. Controller. Jürg had nine girls working under him in ITS (he pronounced the letters in English)—"that's also one of your Winter subsidiaries."

"Hold it!" said Thom. "Hold it! Surely you know that my father lost his fortune speculating and was also up to his neck in debts as a guarantor"—but this fellow Jürg thought that was terrific, super, and anyway, hybrid circuits, right? awesome these miniaturizations, mini-mini-circuits, and he had two kids and out toward Kestenholz a house with a pool, and, as he'd said, mini-circuits, he and his ladies were a semiautonomous unit, just wild, mini-mini, for medical technology and the military, really super, they worked in sterile rooms so that not so much as a speck of dust and everything handled only with tweezers and microscope or display screen superaccurate, of course, but flexible, flexible hours, we're flexible—Jürg shot out his wrist—at six, you see, the parking meter, he still had ten minutes, three of his ladies were from Vietnam, they're super, those Asians have precision in their blood, you know, terrific, and he'd always been, you know, this interaction of mechanics and optics and high tech, just wild, gross, but you look super, Thom, I'll bet you're a big shot, come on come on, let's hear about it, and Jürg ordered two more on the rocks and threw down a bill; Thom also found the drink refreshing.

So he began again: After university he'd done this and that, substitute teaching in Zurich, history in high schools, but Jürg found it gross that sales just in the last eight months, you know, by thirty-six percent again, simply super, he was now getting six two and he couldn't deny, that light, that greenish artificial light and windowless sterile rooms and all day long that face mask mini-circuits supersensitive poled onto the semiconductor plates, and Jürg and his ladies never know whether it's snowing outside or the sun is shining, it's amazing, but everything is flexible, superflexibilized so that like now in the middle of the afternoon he's free to stroll around town "and how many kids did you say, Thom?"

Jürg sent him a feverish look. Was he on dope? Wild, he said, leaning forward again, and in a pinch Thom would have told him briefly about Maria too: neither of them had wanted children, they were living on Fortuna-Gasse at the time, so that was that. Then at some point Maria had left him anyway. So he was free-lancing, working for *The People* for about a year, then was a contributor to a history of the Winter Corporation, from the earliest days through the founding of the company up to 1945, a bit romanticized, mind you, a well-paying job, before he moved in with Susann in Basel in 1972.

Jürg's hand around the glass trembled. "Of course," he said, "as section head a sandwich position, right? super, and with fresh air too much dust and dirt would come in onto the disks, wild, he and his ladies were a crack team as far as speed, they were dealing with chemical and photochemical processes plus conventional mechanical ones, hybrid circuits, mini-mini, you know, a terrific job six two: but listen, Thom, what've you been doing all this time? Super I'll bet and three kids," Jürg's gaze wavered, the twitching at the corner of his mouth increased.

Yes, well, and Thom began to speak about the time in Basel. Not about Susann, though. Susann, always in charge of her life: that would require a whole separate chapter—anyway, he'd landed a part-time position in the state archives where his main job was collating historical material. He had also written a paper, "Social Policy of the Bourgeoisie in the Nineteenth Century." Until 1975 he had also been lecturing at the university, "but I also needed time for myself, you know," while Jürg again shot his wristwatch up to his eyes, "we're flexible," he said, everything was flexibilized, a minute and a half to go and a fantastic team spirit with his ladies, great girls, in a conspiratorial tone he whispered he would confide his secret to Thom, human touch, gross, awesome, and in the fall a trek through southern India, simply super, "here's my card, control assistant. Super, Thom, to talk to you again, and don't forget, if you guys on the board—where are you located now, New York or someplace?—need a high-tech adviser, give me a buzz and say hello to the family," Jürg knocked over the glass, jumped when it shattered on the ground. Then he had himself under control again, Jürg Buser, high-tech controller, his face feverish, twitching, awesome wild superaccurate sandwich position "we're flexible and bye-bye and take care and," "yes, Jürg, you too."

Thom's gaze followed Jürg as he hurried off. High tech. He shook his head, wondering. Then, strolling beside the Aare, he was once again on his way to the Waadtländer Hall; the two bags were getting heavy. Yes, today he wouldn't even have minded being asked a lot of questions. In fact, while he walked along in the shade of the chestnut trees—on the river a flock of seagulls was circling low over the water, around, so it seemed, their own reflection, their own screeching—now he would even have enjoyed telling the people here, at least some of them, at least those among them who, as they passed, looked at him as if they knew him: tell them, that's right, I'm scared of you now that I'm back. I don't like the way you look at me. I don't like having to imagine, just even imagine, that you're using a yardstick to determine the distance between my ancestors and me, their partially paralyzed descendant. True, with the name I bear, as an ordinary and not especially successful historian and prober of the past, it isn't easy to walk through your town; for a hundred years, men of this name have ruled the town and the environs and yourselves more or less gently; you have raised your hats to them, the big-game hunters, and let yourselves be fooled into believing that when the Winter Corporation prospers you prosper too. Measure me, go ahead and measure me against them. Power? Such as my grandfather and even my father possessed over you? Certainly not that. Career? On the modest side. The man you're looking at is nothing more than one of you, but with a university degree, yes, like several hundred others enjoying that privilege hereabouts, the only difference being that he has trouble taking on a secure, permanent, subordinate job with a secure income and an old-age pension. Because, you see, he is a rather unstable person and spirit, always moving around. I hear the question, I see it written on your faces. Lis has asked it: "Are you a failure?" No, Lis was kind, the way she put it was: "Do you feel like a failure?"—in Berlin, through the steam from the breakfast coffee on the table. That's not the point, you people; not anymore, or hardly anymore. Above all, not merely in terms of career, of comparing and being compared with my forefathers. Let's leave them, the big shots and the captains of industry, with their strong and less strong sides, let's leave them in the peace of the Eternal Cycle. The point, my friends, is that I—how can I explain it to you, or to you, Lis—that I often, as for instance now, here, at the kitchen table in your cheerful apartment in Berlin, feel rather as if I were in a boat, anchored by a chain. Yes, maybe that's a suitable image: I am sitting in my boat, the oar is shipped, I raise the sails, a breeze springs up, the sails begin to fill, the boat slowly gets under way, and then a shudder goes through the dinghy, I have to hold on, the mast sways, and I know: once again I've sailed my boat on its long chain over the anchor out into the lake, but now the chain has uncoiled to its full length, it's been stretched to the limit, now it yanks the boat and me back again. Once again I failed to get up enough speed. Once again the mass of my accelerating boat wasn't enough to tear the anchor out of the muddy lake bottom. People, do you understand? And you, Lis? Do you understand? It must be a specially designed anchor—by whom or by what I don't know—that has been sunk fantastically deep into this damned slimy bottom and secured down there seventeen times over. Why so deep? Why can't I get free of it? Something like that. Psychically speaking, partially paralyzed.

Have I made myself clear?

But I shall try again, with the next stiff breeze! As a last resort I may get myself a blowtorch and cut the chain. Don't worry! And I'll be free to sail away, as far as I like and as far as you like, Lis. Patience, just a little more patience—our sail will be terrific, a super sail, gross, a smash hit, the greatest!

When Thom walked around to the back of the Waadtländer Hall, into the little garden with its wisteria-covered walls, André was already sitting there. He greeted Thom with a laugh. "How come you look so determined?" he asked. "Don't tell me you're spoiling for a fight?"

Conversations with André II

TOGETHER, THOM AND ANDRÉ RUPP HAD STOOD ON BASTIAN-PLATZ UNDER the overcast, darkening sky; together with the other roughly four thousand people in the demonstration, they had listened to the messages of support and the speeches. They had left just before the end and walked to the nearby bus stop, then taken the bus for the next four stops.

What was the good of all that talk? The anger, the disappointment, the feeling of the employees that the firm—*their* enterprise—had duped them, had become quite palpable, even audible. Hadn't they informed management of their willingness to negotiate? Hadn't they even, in a show of solidarity, signaled their readiness to agree to a restructuring and even automation in reasonable stages? Weren't they willing to accept a reduction in the work force of 10 percent a year, and for the transition period of five years even a wage cut? And their demand that the remaining work load be distributed among the existing workers—this demand for a phased reduction of working hours in stages down to a thirty-hour week:

wasn't that an additional proposal aimed at avoiding the planned mass dismissals?

Our struggle represents a precedent. What is prescribed for us today will be the fate of all tomorrow! (The voice in the loudspeakers that had been attached to the chestnut trees around the square cracked with emotion.) I say to you: all working people—every temporary female worker, every engineer, every laborer, every typist or bookkeeper, be it in the chemical, textile, watchmaking, or machinery industry!

Thom looked around. The faces seemed unfamiliar. That elderly man over on the right, yes, he knew him. The man nodded at Thom. A little ahead of him, a young man turned around, nodded, then whispered to the women beside him; all three turned their faces toward Thom and looked at him, then began talking again, obviously about him.

While Father was still alive, Thom had often been at the steel plant. As a little boy of six he had stood in the foundry beside the huge furnaces and marveled at the hoarse breathing of the blowers, or at the way the lava stream of molten iron shot through the gates into the molds. Or later, he had often spent half the afternoon in the company garage, watching Mr. Wenger, his father's chauffeur (whom, like Father, he was allowed to call Markus) standing at the work bench near the open garage door regrinding valves, or linings being replaced, gaskets changed. Markus or one of his mechanics would fashion axles at the lathe for the pedal car that the seven-year-old Thom was trying to put together. At fourteen or fifteen, when his father's secretary would pour him a cup of tea, or when, as if nothing had changed since Father's death, he would go over to the drafting office to pick up a drawing pad or a roll of graph paper, he began to notice that he was observed very attentively and greeted with special politeness. This was when he realized that what his mother and Aunt Esther had tried to explain to him for years was also taken for granted by the employees at the works. Clearly for them, too, he was more than just one of the Winters. He was also the only son and, in direct succession to the founder of the firm, the only male descendant of his generation, hence the heir apparent; obviously the people here at the works also assumed that he would one day be heading the Winter Corporation. Thom turned his head slightly. André, standing motionless beside him, was looking straight ahead at the speakers' platform. Hadn't he too, in those days, seen Thom as the successor in whom he had deliberately tried to inculcate his egalitarian ideals?

Here at the gathering it was obvious that most people didn't know

him. And if they did, and recognized him, the only interest he still held
for them was as someone who at one time had failed to live up to his
obligations; if interesting at all, then only as a member of the Winter
clan, and hence as a survivor of a bygone era of the company. Those
who did nod to him were people he recognized too, former schoolmates,
comrades from his army days, men whom, at some time, somewhere in
town, he had actually met, perhaps over a glass of beer at the Waadtländer
Hall.

So, just before the meeting ended, Thom and André took the bus
back to the Hammer stop. They walked up the last four hundred meters
to the house. When Thom said, "And how will it end?" André asked,
as if he hadn't understood, "What do you mean exactly?" then filled his
pipe and stopped to light it. His gaunt features showed up sharply in the
flare from his lighter. The cloud of smoke drifted into the light from the
street lamp overhead and away into the darkness.

Thom again: "How about coming in for a drink?"

"I don't know." His eyes were invisible in the shadow. A smile
creased one corner of his mouth. Did Thom know when he, André, had
last been inside that house?

Thom shrugged. André laughed. "Thirty years ago. Let's go."

As they walked on, he reverted to Thom's question. How will it
end? In any event, it might be assumed that what was happening back
there was perhaps the last great labor struggle in history.

And while he went on talking—no, he could see no solution; theoretically, perhaps, one could visualize socially acceptable developments—for a few seconds Thom could see his father on that late, twilit
October evening. Thom, then fourteen, had been walking up the steps
to the house when the front door opened just as he reached the top. A
figure stumbled out, and behind, in the doorway, his father stood sil-
houetted against the light. The young man on the steps paused, half
turned, and muttered something like, "My apologies, sir," but Father,
still outlined against the light from the hallway, said, "Here. Your jacket,
Mr. Rupp!" and tossed the jacket into André's face. Thom instinctively
ducked, as if it had been aimed at him, and stepped aside.

What was needed, André said, was union pressure on a worldwide
basis. International coordination. Pressure on governments to force them
into multinational agreements. Agreements on the gradual phasing-in of
automation, as well as agreements on taxation for each type of automated
equipment.

"All very well," said Thom. "In thirty years maybe. But now? What do you suggest?"

Father's voice. His chief-executive voice. Thom always knew, when it sounded like that—not loud at all, a bit hoarse and leaning on the words—that it might at any moment turn into the roar he so much dreaded. He had moved still farther away from the steps to the edge of the fan of light coming through the door. "My daughter is seventeen! If I ever catch you again with her—if I ever see you again in the grounds or in the house, Mr. Rupp, you'll pay for it!" Now Father was roaring. "Clear out—for good, you young lecher, you!" Father turned away and slammed the front door.

"But it won't be a controlled, soft landing for all when we move into the post-mechanical, post-industrial society. For that," André said, as they walked on, "apart from great understanding on the part of all concerned, new structures would have to be developed along with guaranteed space for creative communal living in a work-free, or more precisely, profit-free existence. No. There'll be chaos again, in endlessly painful struggles between higher up and lower down, and as always, again and again at the expense of the weaker ones. They'll go under."

They reached the entrance to the grounds. As they walked up the gravel driveway, they were swallowed by the inky darkness under the trees. At least the front door was lit by the old lamp.

"You know," said André, "what really makes me mad: imagine the potential productivity in automation! Release from labor imposed by others! Prosperity for all, here and in the Third World—all those things could be financed! But that's exactly what won't happen. Exploitation will continue, into eternity!"

Thom momentarily lost the thread of André's strategic reasoning. At that time he had gone around the house and entered by the back door. He had found Gret sitting bare-legged, in her slip, at the kitchen table, sobbing violently. "He slapped me! Slapped me!" She burst into loud sobs again. Herminia said, "First drink your milk, then into bed with you, my girl—if you like, in my room. Up there you can sob your heart out. Here, drink up!"

But Gret again: *She* had betrayed her, Mother had, it was Mother!

Thom hadn't quite understood what was going on. He heard their parents' heated voices coming from the Paneled Room. Then Charlott had suddenly appeared in the door to the pantry. Leaning against the door jamb, she said to Gret, "You two really are stupid! At your age, smooching right here in the house!" She, she said, she and René, before René had his own room, had always gone off into the loft, climbing up from the back over the woodpile. She laughed.

"You just be quiet." Herminia was indignantly wielding her spoon in the salad bowl. "The devil only knows where you'll end up!"

Charlott laughed again. "What happens now if you have a baby?"

When Thom looked across at Gret, he saw her tear-soaked face light up. "I have a lover," she whispered. "I have a lover!"

That feverish look in her eyes! Those whispered words! He ran off, into the hall and up the stairs. In his room he threw himself face down on the bed. He couldn't understand himself why he was suddenly sobbing, sobbing.

At the foot of the three steps up to the front door, André paused. "No, not thirty years ago, twenty-nine. Do you know how long that is?"

They went inside. The light was on in the passage too. The grandfather clock pointed to nine; Thom guessed it must be 10:30. Gret and Samuel must have already gone to their rooms. To the right, a brighter light came through the open kitchen door. There was no one in the kitchen. Beyond that, in the pantry, he saw the pale blue material of the blouse covering Barbara's shoulder. "Hi there!" he said. "Still working?"

Barbara came through the kitchen. "You startled me!" Now she was smiling.

Turning around, Thom saw André standing a few feet away in the passage, looking at the picture on the opposite wall as the light from the kitchen fell on it. Did André know his niece? Barbara Glur. And to Barbara: André Rupp was an old friend of his.

André had turned around. He held out his hand, hesitated, and let it fall. Thom, standing beside Barbara, saw the astonishment crossing André's face. André said something like: "Her daughter—is it possible?" And again, in a whisper: "Is it possible?"

Barbara smiled. Then: "What is it, Uncle?"

André shook hands with her. "Twenty-nine years," he said, slowly shaking his head. "As if they had never been. Incredible! Forgive me." He laughed. "At my age one gets a bit strange. Think nothing of it!"

Still with a slightly absent-minded air, he took his glasses from his breast pocket and put them on to peer at the drawing in the passage. "A remarkable picture"—did Thom know who it was by?

As Thom stepped up to him, he noticed that the shadow of his head fell upon the picture in its black frame. He moved to one side so that in the dimly lit passage the light from the kitchen could fall past him onto the picture. He looked at it across André's shoulder. Of course he knew it. But only now did he realize that it had been familiar to him since childhood as a pale patch on the wall with figures sketched on it, as familiar as the black chest below it and the brass candlestick standing on the faded dark-red cloth on the chest—familiar, yes, but what was actually drawn on it, the outlines and the shadings, and by whom—if he'd ever known, he'd forgotten.

The picture, no more than forty by thirty centimeters, showed, as Thom now noticed, three scenes, all mere charcoal sketches—studies, they might have been called, maybe the artist's preliminary designs for three larger works. In the upper right corner, what looked like a Greek hero, his sword at his side, embracing a woman, who was likewise clearly modeled on classical Greek figures, a diadem on her brow.

To the left, in the middle, the same or a similar female figure, her billowing gown uplifted by the storm. And at the bottom, on the left, again the hero, again the woman, larger this time, standing close together. In front of and slightly below them, turned away from them in profile, a second woman, her hair coiled on her head, a forbidding expression on her face. With his right hand the hero is pointing the sword at the second woman. The younger woman has placed her hand on the hero's fist grasping the sword. It is not clear whether she wants to restrain him from making the deadly thrust or, on the contrary, is guiding his hand.

André peered through his glasses at the writing on the bottom of the picture. He could make out the scribbled word: Electra I–III. In the bottom right corner, the initials: L. W. 1938.

Uncle Ludwig. Of course. This was the same kind of pseudoclassical drama Thom had always liked in the three cliff landscapes, done in oils, upstairs in the gallery. "My uncle," Thom said, "considered himself an inspired painter. I believe he did spend a year in Munich at the academy. And all his life could never decide between his weird sciences and his art."

As they walked back along the passage to the Paneled Room, André told Thom that he could well remember Ludwig Winter, in his leather helmet, his racing goggles on his forehead, careening through town in his convertible coupé. Often, too, he would trot on horseback through the traffic. There was an extravagant air about him. "Well," André laughed, "I suppose you Winters, at least your father's generation, have hardly ever conformed to the usual discreet, modest behavior of the upper classes in this country." As a young man he had admired Ludwig Winter. Let me see—wasn't his enthusiasm for the Nazis such that in the thirties he went to Munich?

Yes, Uncle Ludwig had taken charge of a branch office there. "Ah well," said Thom, "that was a long time ago. Come and sit down."

Seated in the armchair, André relit his pipe. Electra? He reflected. Was she the woman who guided the sword of her brother Orestes? Then the second woman must be Clytemnestra. The first sketch might be of the brother and sister, before the deed, embracing after a long separation. And finally, in the sketch in the middle, Electra on the cliff, implacable in her hatred.

How did Uncle Ludwig happen upon these remote mythological motifs? Electra—the concept is, at a guess, three thousand years old, originating from the era when Queen Clytemnestra attempted to reverse the victory of the young patriarchate over the matriarchal culture—you remember: her murder of Agamemnon, the homecoming conqueror, in his bath? Strange, Thom was thinking: physics and astrophysics and hormone research, the invention of rapid-firing cannons and, in addition, painting and fascism and mythology—all of it in Uncle Ludwig's head, all in *one* human heart? Quite a bizarre brew! What could he have been searching for? What image of which truth?

André had left. Thom locked the front door, picked up his wine glass, refilled it, drank a mouthful, and carefully carried the glass out of the Paneled Room. With his free left hand he switched off the light and closed the door. The two grocery bags! Now he remembered—he had set them down on the chair beside him in the little garden of the Waadt-länder Hall. Idiot! Would they still be there? All he could do was phone first thing in the morning. And go and pick them up. He could already see Herminia's face, eyebrows raised as she shook her head. Typically Thom! Head in the clouds again? Embarrassing. He slowly crossed the hall and went up the stairs. In the Blue Room he sat down at the desk.

Dearest Lis! Do you still want to know everything? He began to describe the evening. The demonstration. The demands of the work force. The hardening of the conflict. André's resigned analysis. Did you know that it wasn't until the eighteenth century that idleness was declared to be a vice and work a virtue? Shouldn't we rejoice that automation is relieving us of that damned drudgery?

Then the bus ride, the walk up here with André. How André had said: Thirty years. And Uncle Ludwig's sketches in the hallway. Or Andy, from his armchair into the silence: "You had come home from boarding school for your vacation. I was at the university in Zurich, but during that semester vacation I was spending the mornings working at home for myself, and the afternoons at the plant. The morning after the row with your father—remember?—you rang the bell at our front door, and my mother asked you in. I can still see your slight figure standing there. You must have rehearsed that very formal sentence: 'I have come here at the request of my sister Gret.' You handed me the letter. I went up to my room for the letter I had written Gret during the night and gave it to you to take back. In those first weeks of separation, you were the bearer of our love letters. So, in spite of the difference in our ages, we gradually became friends."

As you know, Lis—you did meet him briefly—my friend André is a strange person. When he occasionally lapses into silence and then resumes speaking, you can almost be sure that, on continuing the conversation at some new point, he only *seems* to be changing the subject. Half an hour later you realize that he has stayed on the same topic all the time.

André went on: "A few weeks later Gret wrote that she would be going to a boarding school near Lausanne to learn French." From there came two more sad letters. Since then he had lost all contact with her. He looked across at me. "Do you know how she is?"

What could I have told him? That here in the house we politely keep out of each other's way? That, like Father, she has become an alcoholic, shy, unapproachable? That she seems to get along well with her two children, and that her relationship with her husband appears to fluctuate constantly between affection and hatred? Is Gret happy? She doesn't give that impression.

"Those Winter women!" said André. He had a feeling they were all self-willed, strong, and determined to be independent at almost any price—Gret, Charlott, old Esther. Or take Thom's mother—even that dynamic industrialist she married had, at least as far as he could tell, come off second best with her. All of them had the peasant woman's assertiveness, yet at the same time an almost irrepressible desire—or compulsion?—to flout conventions or, if need be, to topple them, almost as if in this clan a streak of the primordial matriarchate were surviving in a patriarchal culture.

A strange thought, isn't it? Patriarchate, matriarchate: whatever made him think of looking at our family history from that angle? Granted that the women in this family have always been self-confident, strong, also slightly eccentric—I wouldn't hesitate to include even Grandmother Helen—yet among those characteristics I would really find it difficult to discover any vestiges of some mythical primordial culture. We historians have our doubts anyway as to the alleged primordial matriarchate.

André laughed. "Of course!" he said. His lenses sparkled as if he were having fun at our expense.

From a scholarly and historical point of view, I told him, none of that has any firm basis. How did he, as an anarchist, come to concern himself with these theories? To me that all seemed pretty insubstantial.

"Do you remember Fourier, the early socialist with his claim that the degree of feminine emancipation was the natural measure of progress in general? Four or five years ago you and I argued about this. I followed up the thought, came across Bachofen's *Maternal Law*, Erich Neumann's *Great Mother*, and Gerda Weiler's book, *The Dispossessed Myth*, and that led me to the research undertaken by contemporary women historians. Eight thousand years of matriarchate: as the supremacy"—André smiled—"of a principle in accordance with Nature. For an anarchist like myself: heady stuff!" He stood up. "Too big a subject for tonight. See you soon."

Outside in the passage he went up to Uncle Ludwig's picture again. "That's right, you know, those three figures lived during just during that brief, crucial era of the downfall of the matriarchal culture. Would Ludwig have known about those associations?" André turned back to me. "I'm only a mathematician," he said. "Long live historical research, Mr. Historian!" and off he went.

You can see, my very dearest, that the webs in which I am becoming entangled here are growing more and more intricate. So now it's the primordial zones of our universal culture? I feel absolutely lost without you. As for that history, I can see I'll have to sound out my old friend André a little more carefully next time I see him.

But you, how about you now? What a relief to have your letter confirming your safe arrival in Saint-Rémy, that you've settled in and are breathing the relaxing air of Provence! That nice old hotel on the postcard you enclosed! I admire the way you manage, all on your own, to explore such a beautiful spot in a foreign land. Your words have been following me throughout the day—the evening of our arrival here, you were sitting on the bed saying that letting go was an essential part of loving. I asked you to explain, and you said: Didn't that mean accepting as true everything that flows ceaselessly back and forth between us, down to the minutest emotional and mental reflexes, even in our dream images and our decisions? And also knowing that our life histories, yours and mine, are always present in that flow, endlessly interwoven in ever-changing patterns? Sometimes, you said, you felt that those life histories of ours predetermined whether we were right for each other or not. Is it our life histories, intermingled with what may be a still more powerful universal history—our cultural and political history—that cause us to live the way we do or don't?

Yes, that haunted me today. Letting go. Accepting as true. And yet, the word "predetermined"—something in me rises up against that. It would mean that like some celestial bodies, we would, subject to our law, have to sail through our existence on preordained orbits, or that like jellyfish, we could react only within the narrow band allowed us by our life history. The idea makes me rebellious. Where, in a life so strictly circumscribed, would there be any room for my development and yours, for coming together, for love and its dynamic? For change—through insight, and equally, through the madness of passion? Letting go? Instead of holding on? Your phrase describes something I wish I could do.

Ah yes, our mutual reticence here in the house. What are we keeping back? I believe that, because of your entirely different background, what strikes you is something typical of our kind in our dealings with one another. When I am with Germans I am often amazed at how much they talk, especially how much they verbalize, where we communicate by silence, by minute gestures, by a scarcely perceptible movement at the corner of the mouth. There are people who define our Swiss trait of nonverbalism as "understatement." That's a misinterpretation. I can only assume that in us, at least among German-speaking Swiss, there is an old experience at work that makes us skeptical of speech as a means of communication. A lack of confidence toward language, toward speech. Despite our close linguistic ties with you, our life is based on a different historical experience; within the German language we live a different culture from yours, we Swiss being a very small minority in constant danger of having to roll up like hedgehogs in order to survive.

Did I hear you laugh? Were you thinking, That's all very well—rebuttal by theory? Fine. To some extent, at least, I'll admit that. But don't worry: as to your question about what we're keeping back, here in this house—yes, I'll go on trying to track that down, you know that. And back to something more general again: our reticence also has to do with our, my, aversion to conflict. We are, that's to say I am, very good at that, as you know. I swallow provocation. I turn aside, keep clear, avoid confrontation, while you Germans often seek it out in an overbearing and, to me, irritating manner. Believe me, in that respect I am merely typical of the inhabitants of the land of Helvetia.

The church bells in town are already striking one. Just two more things: What you noticed about the electrically charged fields here, on the staircase, in the hall, in the rooms—"energies radiating from human passions that could never come to rest"—irks me. No doubt you, a newcomer, more attentive than we, more sensitive, feel the presence of these currents. Have I become so inured to them over time that my antennae react less strongly? Now I am aware of them again, as intensely as when I was a child.

My search here. I am groping around in a daily expanding maze. Conjectures flare up, then immediately sputter out; stories leap to my mind, evoke other stories, still more stories; memory sweeps me through time. More and more I feel myself to be less a seeker after truth than a man pursued. Where is it to be found, Lis, tell me where I can find this truth about my mother's death? In the pile of papers in the library? In Aunt Esther's stories? In Gret's closed, fear-marked face? In Samuel's silence? In the looks exchanged between Frieda or Herminia or old Sepp as they communicate over my head, as it were—unintelligibly to me—about things from which I feel excluded? Now I am firmly hooked. I feel as if I had long since lost my way in my childhood home, in a house that grows bigger, more uncanny, more fantastic by the hour, and when I walk up and down the stairs and along the passages and through the rooms and the cellars, the reverberating echo of my footsteps makes me realize how futile would be the return to the way in or the way out.

It is good to feel you so close to me as I read and reread your letter. I thank you for being there for me.

Sleep deeply, and sweet dreams.

Your old
Thom

*   *   *

As if a bang on the door or even a shot had awakened him, Thom started up out of sleep. Only as he sat up in bed did he realize where he was: in the Blue Room. A morning breeze was stirring the torn curtain at the open window. From the town came the subdued sound of the deep-throated bells of the cathedral. Six in the morning?

He lay back. Probably a gust of wind had blown a window shut. The noise had been enough to rouse him from sleep into still confused wakefulness. No matter how he tried to catch a few fragments, at least a few dream images, in his memory, he didn't succeed. Yet he felt as if he, or at least that part of him that he could only call his soul, had made a long journey through war-ravaged zones, like an owl with eyes that can see in the dark gliding soundlessly mile after mile through the night. The banging of the window had been enough: the journey was abruptly over; in the space of one tiny second, his consciousness had crossed the frontier from sleep and dream into the waking state.

No, he couldn't remember. Bombed-out buildings, rubble overgrown with tall hollyhocks, and yes: hadn't Father been calling him? Even these few shreds of dream dissolved.

And only now did the feeling return: that he had lost his way in his search—lost his way in a town once familiar to him, a town inhabited by people whose language he didn't know. Whenever he asked after a street, a square, a name, the faces of people crumpled in dismay; fear was reflected in their eyes, as if he were the author of a disaster, the prophet of a plague. And yet he was quite sure: behind at least one of these faces, behind one of these unfamiliar facades in this endless series of streets through which he was prowling, the answer was to be found.

There seemed little chance of drifting back into sleep. The wheels of speculation had already begun to turn in his head again. Once more he was confronted by those two sentences in Aunt Esther's diary. Once more an attempt to dismiss the whole thing as a figment of Aunt Esther's imagination.

Try again: "Lilly Winter, my sister-in-law, did not die a natural death. She was killed"—couldn't that also mean, for instance, as bizarre as it may sound, that days or even weeks before her death she was administered poison by some fiendish person, and that was what she died of that August evening?

Or another possibility: somebody in the house could no longer bear watching Mother's protracted dying and out of pity had speeded up her death—mercy killing, wasn't that what they called it? Illegal, of course, nevertheless an act of compassion. But in that case would Aunt Esther have written those terse, accusing words: "She was killed"?

Variations played a hundred times in his head! For a few moments, when they surfaced, a glimmer of hope that a new idea, or at least some fresh light on the problem, might be bringing him closer to a solution. Followed immediately by the feeling of being adrift, or, more precisely perhaps, at a complete dead end. And worse still: gradually he had become an element, puzzling even to himself, of the overall puzzle into which his foolhardy search had landed him. Even the thought—yet another variation!—that Aunt Esther had meant her two sentences figuratively, for dramatic effect, as one might say that a person had been killed by an excessive burden of duties or by the many demands of those around him: even this hope immediately collapsed again.

He buried his head in his pillow. Sleep eluded him.

Passages II

AND AGAIN THE SPARROW HAWK, NOT IN SIGHT ONLY ITS DISTANT TRILLING, and just to lie there hidden behind the hazel bush next to the clump of anemones in the mossy grass

calm down keep calm face in the grass smell the moss and resin in the air and the earth, smell of the earth, forehead resting on both arms keep calm and hearing the hawk and still that panting and Charlott's "Blood! I'm bleeding!" with her tear-stained face

calm down still that pounding in there and

no! don't think about it don't: "that's the sign" and "you're almost a woman now," no stop! stop! but that's the blood sign and again Charlott again in the gallery, she's sitting on the stairs her cotton skirt pulled up over one knee, and the blood running down her thigh "I'm bleeding" her tear-stained face, drip, drip and Charlott almost vanishing in a blur, and her face the terror the terror in it, drip, and to feel she is almost but calm down keep calm

must be the hawk the sparrow hawk they trill like that smell the earth and here in the hiding place the bumblebee suddenly in the hazel bush anemones and through the tears think about the mossy meadow think hard of that and of the barn owl down there in the barn where the broken bricks under the roof in the barn high up think of the owl up there in the gable

"It's blood" don't think about it think of something else, of the daisies salvia buttercups out there in the mossy grass and ribwort, hawks trilling as they circle over the tops of fir trees but then this tiresome bumblebee go away go away, "you're almost a young woman now" and

but again Mother from her Blue Room "what's going on there Ohmygod, child" through the gallery, keep calm, what *is* that, why woman why blood? that sign, that blood sign, what do women have where the thighs deep inside where it's forbidden, forbidden to look, why woman why blood "Oh do stop child" and "you're almost a young woman now," but think of something else something else think of the daisies when they bloom again out there and this bumblebee go away, or the barn owl down there and suddenly it blinks its eyes and glides off into the dusk, think of something else, that blood

and again the thighs "I'm bleeding!" and the innermost deep inside forbidden, drip, the tear-stained face still in a kind of haze, the gasping, the trilling and when Mother goes off with Charlott to the bathroom calm down now "you're not hurt, child! Calm down!" that terror and why and lying there still panting and smelling, smelling the moss, and why and why almost a woman and what do they have where deep inside forbidden and why woman why blood?

Pamphlet

THE WORK FORCES OF THE WINTER CORPORATION IN JAMMERS, SCHWEI-zerhalle, Winterthur, Liestal, Lucerne, Lausanne, and Seveso/Milan state and resolve:

1. In 1976 the number of employees in the parent firm and branches amounted to 17,800. In the six years since then, our numbers have been reduced, due mainly to layoffs, by 8,100 to 9,700 employees. During the same period the sales of the Winter Corporation increased by 12 percent (adjusted to 1976 francs).

2. Decades of neglect and errors in management have driven our

plants into a crisis that has now lasted three years. The costs are being borne by us, the work forces, thousands of whom have had to sacrifice their financial existence.

3. Only three days ago the Board of Directors officially announced that the process of restructuring had been essentially completed; further layoffs were not to be expected. Today we know that as long ago as June 6, 1982, the Board resolved (subject to approval by the shareholders at the General Meeting) as follows: (i) the share capital is to be increased from 100 million to 200 million; (ii) all production processes (with the exception of administration, the engineering department, and special production) are gradually to be automated up to a level of 80 percent; the appropriate expert proposals have been accepted; (iii) the foundry in Jammers is to be permanently closed; (iv) a consequence of these resolutions: reduction of personnel from 9,700 to 2,900. In the words of the Board's resolution: "The elimination of these 6,800 work places must be deemed acceptable in order to maintain the competitiveness of our enterprise."

4. The extent to which the work forces have contributed to the prosperity of the Winter Corporation in the nearly 180 years of its history is well known. We welcome the introduction of new technologies, although this must not occur regardless of cost. Our delegation has therefore declared our willingness to negotiate and offered the benefit of our expertise. The offer was rejected yesterday at 5 P.M. This rejection constitutes a gross violation of existing overall labor contracts, which are based on good faith, trust, and so-called partnership. The Board has specifically violated its obligation to maintain labor peace.

5. The work forces have resolved: A strike will be called against all plants of the Winter Corporation commencing Monday, June 28, 1982, at 6 A.M.

6. Until further notice this strike will continue until noon on Wednesday, June 30, 1982. Its objective is to force management to negotiate all outstanding issues.

7. Militant measures of a more far-reaching nature are being prepared.

Jammers, June 23, 1982
The assembled work forces of the Winter Corporation.

*　*　*

Aunt Esther leaned back in her chair. Once again through the open window came the strong scent of the espalier pears, and from the croquet lawn the click of wood hitting wood. There was a smell of autumn, of long Aunt Esther life, and then again of marjoram and old times, of falling leaves. Aunt Esther kept her eyes closed. Or she closed only one eye, looking down at Thom with the other. "It may be, Thom, that I even liked her—liked her at first, at least that—what would you call it— crazy part of her, or shall I say the really childish or downright intemperate part of her: at first. You may well be surprised. After all, how would you, at age ten—"

"Twelve, Aunt Esther."

"—very well then, twelve, know how she suddenly changed, turned hard, hard or stern and pious, going on about her Heavenly Mother all of a sudden, so that the very sight of her makes one feel positively uncomfortable? I can't explain it, nor can your father, believe me! Yes, intemperate, that's the word. She wanted all of him, wanted him all the time. She could dance in the Paneled Room for a whole hour, all by herself, or she would spend half the morning at the piano singing in what I must say was her quite lovely contralto voice, or accompanying herself on the guitar. Or she would telephone your father in the middle of the morning, have him called to the phone out of a meeting, as if the house were on fire, she would stand out there at the telephone, and then all she would actually say was, 'Ueli, I love you.' Or she would call him up and laugh, 'Have you seen the hazel catkins? They're there, they're suddenly there today outside! Let's take the horses and ride along the Aare to meet the spring—I mean it, Ulrich: drop all that silly business stuff! Do come!' "

Yes, and then? Thom's voice was breathless: how could the things his aunt was telling him about his mother fail to rivet his attention?

"Then, ten minutes later, she would be standing in the hall in her riding breeches, shouting, shouting through the house, 'All right, then I'll go by myself!'

"But that wasn't all. I can see her," Aunt Esther went on, "Sepp had already saddled the horse she had in those days, a gift from my brother, a graceful Trakehnian mare, then she would come back in through the front door, toss away her whip, wrench off her boots, then suddenly sit sobbing on the stairs, sobbing although she was over thirty, and calling out in a voice that reverberated throughout the house, 'Am I so impossible in this house? To want to go for a ride with my darling and lie in the sun somewhere beside the river, because spring is on its way—are such things forbidden? Am I married to a man of flesh and soul or to the Winter Corporation?' That's how she sat there, loudly bemoaning her fate. Or she would fall silent. And sit there for hours in her stockinged feet, her fist held to her mouth, chewing her knuckles raw, and refusing to utter a single word, until I couldn't take it anymore and went up to her and said, 'My girl, I think that's enough. Now you're going to drink a glass of sherry and start growing up.' "

To Thom it seemed that in telling her story Aunt Esther had forgotten that he was her audience and that she was talking about his mother. She spoke as if for the sheer sake of the story, and when she started asking those questions he knew she didn't expect an answer, at least not from him. How had it happened that this intemperate woman, with her crazy moods, this woman whom it was still possible to like, could turn into a stubborn, rigid bigot who could think of nothing but imploring her Mother of God to give her the strength to tyrannize herself and this household? "At some point," said Aunt Esther, "she must have sensed that she did not conform to the laws that do, after all, govern this house. At some point—it must have been between Charlott's birth and her mother Lilian's death—your mother developed into the person she now is. One must really wonder what happened to the woman she was.

"She must"—and Aunt Esther said it as if to herself—"she must have buried her within herself."

Time
of
Honor

"All this didn't happen at random, Thom, or at just any time. It was here, here in the house, here in the town, in this country of yours; it was in 1936, the world was seething like the ocean when a volcano beneath it is about to erupt and push up a new mountain, yes, and the wheel of history was turning, turning. Some were carried to the top"—she laughed—"while the others were crushed by the wheel. Not just any time. Let me list what was happening at that time all over the world, and you will be amazed at the way your aunt—who, God knows, is no longer young—has preserved her memory, nothing has been lost."

She laughed, and Thom saw the wheel of history lifting up some people and rolling over others, while she told him how it was when Wilhelm Gustloff, the leader of the National Socialist Party of Switzerland, was murdered in Davos; when Silone's novel *Bread and Wine* was published; when the Berlin-Rome axis was consolidated by a formal treaty; when Bernd Rosenmeyer won the Grand Prix of Germany on the Nürburg Ring in a Mercedes; when Konrad Zuse developed a giant calculator with 2,200 electrical circuits; when the Popular Front in Spain won the election and General Francisco Franco started the civil war with a putsch; when, after the republican revolt in Greece, General Metaxas seized power by a putsch; when Franklin Roosevelt was reelected President of the United States; when Clark Gable and Spencer Tracy rocked the world in the movie *San Francisco*; when the B.B.C. broadcast the first television program; when the poet Federico García Lorca was shot in Spain; when the Swiss currency was devalued by 30 percent; when Josephine Baker sang "J'ai deux amours" at the Olympia in Paris; when the *Queen Mary*, powered by Winter steam turbines, won the Blue Ribbon by crossing the Atlantic in 95 hours and 57 minutes—

"—you see what I mean, Thom? And how everything is connected with everything else?

"And then in June, June 1936, they were suddenly standing out there in front of the house, hundreds of them standing in the driveway and at the foot of the steps, the striking metalworkers of the Winter plants. By that time it was eight in the evening, and they were yelling and shouting, 'Ulrich Winter, come out!' Your father was sitting in the study with his managerial staff, and outside a strike leader mounted the steps; silence fell. He gave a speech about the crisis, and the hard times, but now the plants were working to capacity again; overtime again, and double shifts: exports had increased in the first six months of the year by thirty percent or two hundred million francs; prices for our products in the domestic market had risen by forty percent—the devaluation, you know? 'But wages,' he shouted, and I was standing upstairs at the open window behind the curtain: wages were still at the 1933 level! And so it went on. They yelled and applauded, and that hulking fellow shouted, 'We demand'—in that tone, you know?—'we demand an increase of five *Rappen* in hourly wages, and piecework pay must be increased by seven percent: in support of these demands we are on strike for an unlimited period!'

"At that very moment your father went outside and paused in the doorway. The crowd became silent. Then he walked slowly down the steps toward the thousand strikers. You know how he can stand there, how he can speak, clearly and to the point—a true master! At the edge of the terrace he halted: He could fully appreciate the concerns of his valued fellow workers, he told them. However, the crisis had struck at the very substance of the firm. The high credits required for investments. Did they want to fight world competition with obsolete machinery? He gave them figures, spoke of his responsibility for the company as a whole, and—surprise—declared: Their wishes would be granted—not right away, and not all at once, but as a start they could reckon with a two *Rappen* increase beginning October 1 and a three percent increase in piecework pay. He would personally vouch for that. The remainder would have to be discussed at next week's board meeting. But right now: down in the town the company was going to treat them to thirty-two barrels of free beer, 'and now let's call it a day.' Tomorrow morning sleeves would be rolled up again! A few catcalls and whistles, some arguing back and forth, and five minutes later the last of them left the grounds."

The wheel of history. Not just any time. A volcano. And how everything was connected with everything else. Aunt Esther stopped speaking. A few weeks later there was a strike after all. But that was another story.

When Thom went into the Paneled Room for lunch, he found Gret already sitting there. He would have to make do with her today, she said. He knew that somewhat pained smile on Gret's face. She could do that: smile and frown at the same time. No, his sister didn't look happy as she sat in front of her bowl of salad.

Samuel was in Zurich today, she said, Urs had gone on a school outing to visit a farm in the Bucheggberg area, and Barbara was having lunch at her friend's house.

Before Thom could respond, old Herminia brought in the main course and a small dish of creamed horseradish and placed them on the table.

Boiled beef? Gret looked at Herminia. "We haven't had that for a long time," she said.

Creamed horseradish. Herminia's round old peasant's face beamed. She knew how much Thomas liked that.

What a memory! Thom thanked her as she went through the pantry door. And Gret, smiling: "She doesn't remember *my* favorites—but never mind. I'm fond of her."

It was a long time, Thom said as he ate, since the two of them had had a meal together alone. Twenty years? What a pleasant change! And into the silence: How was she managing with the house, with herself—Thom hesitated—with Samuel?

Gret refilled her wine glass. "*This* is my consolation, you know that."

Consolation?

How wearily she smiled. He knew, she supposed, that alcohol at least gave her the illusion—for a while—of being alive. It enabled her from time to time to emerge a little from her solitude. And yes, perhaps the most important thing was that it formed a kind of crash-barrier around her, a flexible, cushioning protective zone against the pressure, including the pressure from within herself.

That inner pressure—might she want to tell him something about that?

"Oh, Thom." She took a sip. Over the rim of the glass her eyes were strangely fixed on him. Nice of him to ask, to be interested. "Please do it again," she said.

Even the subjunctive wasn't enough to persuade Gret to reveal more about herself. She might have added, after a lengthy pause, that she was glad he was there, "here amid all this decay." And: What did he say to the workers' demands? Now that she had read the newspaper report on the demonstration last night, she grasped what the men's concerns were all about. Maybe they weren't quite that much in the wrong after all. And she asked, "You've seen André?"

"Yes, we were sitting here till well after midnight"—Thom nodded toward the armchair over by the tiled stove. Thirty years, Andy had said, since the last time he was here. "He inquired after you and asked to be remembered to you."

Gret stopped eating for a moment. She picked up her glass. "And Andy, how is he?" After a brief pause, perhaps merely to hide her agitation: Could Thom spare a few minutes after lunch to go up into the attic with her? There were still two or three boxes of his up there—clothes, books. She'd appreciate his having a look at them and telling her, sometime in the next few days, what could be thrown out and what was to be given away.

A little later, Thom preceded Gret up the steep stairs from the gallery to the attic. In the sparse light from the two bulbs hanging from the beam overhead, past Uncle Ludwig's darkroom and past the wardrobes, they crossed the red-tiled floor of the big room strung with old clotheslines to where the garment bags were hanging, and where, under the sloping roof, boxes and sleds, ski poles, old books, the threadbare yellow sofa, and a broken television set were piled up. Even Thom's brown teddy bear with its red leather collar was still lying there, face down.

As they stood looking at the pile of junk, Gret told him that Samuel had promised Urs a Ping-Pong table that he could set up here in the attic. And anyway she would be glad to get rid of the stuff, but, as she'd said, there was no hurry.

Squatting down on his heels, Thom heard Gret call out from the door to the stairs: She would put on some water for coffee downstairs—see him in a few minutes?

Books. Schoolbooks. Exercise books. The only thing Thom pulled out of the pile was the old world atlas. He didn't feel like going through all those physics and Latin and French textbooks, all those blue exercise books full of his writing—sentences, figures, sentences. No, throw them out! Sepp was welcome to burn them. Even the contents of the garment bags hanging on nails under the sloping roof received only a cursory inspection. He did take out his old winter overcoat, the gray checked woolen one: otherwise he was not in the mood to wallow in memories of the person he had been twenty or forty years ago. With a sense of distaste he zipped up the bag.

On his way back to the door he paused in front of the massive wardrobe that stood against the inside wall. As a boy of ten or twelve he had often opened the double doors to look at the uniforms, the officer's boots, the three old rifles stashed away at the back. He had fingered the gold buttons, each with the Swiss cross encircled by tiny edelweiss leaves, the gold braid on the stiff collars with their three stars, or the wide gold band in front where the collars could be closed with the little metal hooks and eyes. When he had put on one of the stiff officer's caps, his father's or grandfather's, it had slipped down over both his ears; he had smelled the sweetish odor of sweat, of sweat and camphor balls.

At the door he switched off the light, but hardly had he walked down the first three stairs when he stopped again. The creaking of the stairs—yes, he remembered that.

Here, on the fifth step from the top, here in the dark and listening, he had, as a thirteen-year-old, spent what must have been one of the worst minutes of his life.

"For his own good"—it was with those words that the misery had begun. Or maybe earlier, three or four days before? Yes, it had been that night: Thom, lying asleep on his side, had felt someone crawling under the covers behind him. He had sat bolt upright, about to run across breathlessly in the dark to Herminia's room. But then he had heard that whispering in his ear—it was Charlott: "Can you hear it?" Her arms went round him, she pressed herself against him. He could feel her trembling. "Can you hear it?"

Yes, Father's strident voice from the Blue Room. Thom opened his mouth to hear better, but they couldn't make out any words. They jumped when the door across the passage was yanked open.

Father screaming now in the passage—something like "insane" or "insanity." Then, quite distinctly: "From now on I'm going to sleep over there!" Once again a door, it must be the door to the guest room on the other side beyond the Blue Room. The door was slammed shut. Shortly after that, Father came out again. Shouting curses, he walked along the gallery and down the stairs.

Charlott, softly: "Now he's starting again, you'll see. In an hour he'll be drunk."

In the black silence Thom could feel only Charlott's breath on his neck. The trembling stopped. His eyelids closed.

But again he was being shaken. "Thom!" Charlott must have sat up in the dark. From outside they could hear someone crashing around, right after that an oath, then that howl Thom knew so well. It sounded as if Father had stepped into a leg trap on the stairs, as if the iron teeth of the trap had snapped shut and he couldn't free his foot. They listened. He howled, drawing out the first syllable, something like "Lii-lyy!" Frantically Thom tried to think what he could do. Once again—as he had a few months ago—turn on the light, go out into the gallery and walk down the stairs, and Father would be sitting on the stairs, staring at him with glassy eyes? Thom would say, "Come, Father," would bend down, once again place Father's arm over his shoulder and try to help his father onto his feet so that he could pull himself up by the banisters while supporting himself on Thom's neck? Last time none of that had worked; Father had been too heavy. But now, with Charlott's help, would they be able to manage?

Behind and above him Charlott said softly, "Maybe I should go out there now. Maybe I should go to him and give him a shove, then he'll fall down the stairs, then he'll be dead." She said, "Like an animal." She was whispering, and Thom could feel the heat of her body through her nightgown.

She mustn't do that, Thom told her, and he couldn't understand why Charlott whispered, "Don't worry, I won't go." Now he couldn't go either, so they went on listening—incoherent words, sounds of stumbling about, sometimes that same drawn-out moan when Father was calling for Lilly, and again sleep and again waking up and again.

Why did it always start like that? Why could Father be relaxed, cheerful, for months at a time, and they would run to meet him when he drove his red Fiat past the foot of the outdoor steps? Why was an argument with Mother all it took to know that Father had once more crossed the borderline and was beyond reach, either with words or eyes or by touch, beyond everything that Thom might have been able to comprehend?

It was only when Father was totally exhausted by the alcohol, the pills, the falling about, and the frenzied nights that the time came when they all tiptoed about the house and closed every door very gently. At last he's sleeping it off. After eight or twelve days, by which time everybody else was exhausted too, came that sleep lasting two or three days and nights from which Father would awake, clear-eyed again, and ask, "What happened?"

Once, on his way home from school at five in the afternoon, Thom, while walking up the avenue and past the barn, had seen Father upstairs at the library window. Seen the flushed face, and Father trying to open the window. Thom waved, hesitated; Father didn't notice him. Then Father flung open the window and proceeded to throw out first one empty bottle, then two more, wine bottles, throwing them down into the big lilac bush beyond the terrace. He disappeared from sight. During the night he lurched and stumbled through the house, where they were all lying in bed in their rooms, staring into the darkness, Mother and Charlott, Gret, Thom, as well as Aunt Esther and Frieda, Sepp, Herminia.

Next day, in the late afternoon, Father, his face all lopsided, walked past the kitchen as he headed for the front door, his broad-brimmed hat set jauntily on the back of his head. Under the long coat the red cuffs of his pajama legs were visible. Thus attired, and with only a slight stagger, he walked out of the house. From the inside door Thom and Herminia watched him get into his car and drive off. Turning around, Thom found his mother standing behind him. She was white in the face. "Good God!" she said, said it twice in an undertone.

And then in the kitchen: "He is quite capable of driving out to the villages, Kappel, Kestenholz. And stopping off for a drink here and there, and the innkeepers know Mr. Winter and must treat him with respect." Eventually, she said, he would pile up his car and kill himself or others.

At that point she went out to the phone in the passage to speak to the innkeepers in the villages. A little later—Thom and Charlott were having supper with Sepp in the pantry—Herminia went to the door to the passage and listened. "She's talking all this time to the doctor," she said, "the one in Basel, at the clinic. It's serious now."

Sepp first said, "If anyone needs it, he does." He went on eating, took one more sip, then stood up. In the kitchen door he turned and said, "She knows. She knows what can drive a man to that," then left.

When Mother summoned them all to the Paneled Room, it struck Thom as soon as he walked through the door that she was sitting in Father's armchair, sitting there for the first time, and she told them that two men from the clinic would be coming to take Father away. From the door Gret asked, "You mean this evening?" Mother nodded, and asked them to go across to Aunt Esther and stay there "until it's all over." She hoped they understood that she had had to make that call to Basel. She no longer had any choice. "For his own good," she said.

Until it's all over. Thom went along with them, and they sat at the little round table in Aunt Esther's suite. Aunt Esther asked whether they would like to hear the story about Uncle Ludwig's rocket car. Nobody spoke. Frieda placed the colored tin of Willisau cookies on the table. Or the story of the attempted assassination? Or maybe the one about the strike, and how the men had gathered on the grounds in front of the house? Herminia said, "How about a game of dominoes?"

After a while they could hear Father's Fiat driving up. Through a crack in the door Thom peered out under Frieda's elbow into the passage. Three unfamiliar male voices, then Mother, and Frieda reporting back over his head into Aunt Esther's room: "They're bringing him." They could hear the three men driving away in another car. Father was laughing his slow, loud laugh. Now he was singing, almost unintelligibly but Thom knew the song: "Once again the roses bloom—ro-o-oses red!", just that refrain, over and over again; he was still singing when Sepp suddenly appeared, dragging Father past with one arm around Sepp's shoulder. They could be heard stumbling up the stairs. Frieda closed the door, and Thom was thinking, as he smelled that odor of camphor balls, quince jelly, and marjoram: "Until it's all over," and: "For his own good."

Once more at the round table, once more the waiting. The dominoes had to be put down so that only the halves with matching numbers of dots are laid together. The winner is the person who has played all his pieces first. Until it's all over.

Gret said, "Just a moment—can you hear that? Now. There it is again!"

No question, up in the gallery furniture was being moved around. Gret jumped up, ran through Frieda's room, and opened the door to the passage a crack. Yes, furniture was being pushed around upstairs. Once again the roses bloom. Gret covered both ears with her hands, crying out, "I won't listen, I won't listen, even if you pay me a thousand francs"—

and ran out of the room. The front door slammed shut. "It's your turn, Thom," Herminia said.

Within a few minutes the car from the clinic arrived. When the doorbell rang, they all stood up. They could hear Mother talking to the men. When Thom walked away from the table, Charlott and Herminia followed him. He heard Aunt Esther call out after him, "You stay here until it's all over!" but Charlott and he left the room. In the dim lamplight they turned to the left into the hall, where Mother and the two men in their dark coats were standing with their backs to them. Mother called up, in a voice that shook a little, "Ulrich? Ulrich, two gentlemen from Basel would like to speak to you."

Father laughed. In a loud voice he said, "Sepp, what do you say now?" Then he sang his rose refrain again, broke off, shouted, "My ass, d'you hear?"

Suddenly the gallery was flooded with light, and there was the sound of crockery clinking. Was Sepp emptying out the cabinet that contained the precious blue-and-white Dutch dinner service? Now Thom saw that Father and Sepp had moved the black oak sideboard to the head of the stairs. Piled on top were two or three of the massive Renaissance armchairs with their legs facing the stairs. He understood. Father and Sepp had set up a barricade.

Father's red face appeared above the gallery balustrade; in his raised right hand he was holding one of the heavy Dutch plates. He was laughing as he brandished the plate in the air. "For the gentlemen from Basel!" He hurled the plate down over the balustrade. Just missing Mother and the two men, the plate smashed on the red tiles of the hall floor. All three, as well as Charlott and Thom, retreated into the passage. Charlott said, "I'll go to him, Mother!"

"You stay where you are!" Mother—Thom had hardly ever seen her shake with rage before—grabbed Charlott by the arm and pulled her back. "You'll leave this instant with Thom—off with you both to Aunt Esther's!"

But then Father's voice again. "Thom!" he called, and still louder: "Thom! Come up here! We need another hand!" Charlott suddenly received a slap from Mother and ran howling into the kitchen. One of the men from Basel turned around. "Are you Thom? All right, get out! And close the door after you, d'you hear?"

What right did that man have to give orders here? Thom was suddenly aware that his teeth were chattering with rage as he followed Charlott into the kitchen. He did not close the door. Charlott and Herminia were sitting at the table, both sobbing. Herminia put her fat arm around Charlott. "Stop trembling, child! You're trembling so!"

Thom heard Gret's voice from below: Coffee was ready and waiting. Here he was, still sitting on the fifth step of the attic stairs, in the semi-darkness, allowing the images of that evening—was it thirty years ago?—to form in his mind's eye, together with all the terror he was now reliving, as if it were happening now. As if it were happening now, on this quiet afternoon.

Images: Another plate from above, crashing onto the tiles. Fragments all the way to the kitchen door, where Thom, looking past Herminia, could see Mother. As if quite calm, she stood leaning against the right-hand wall, her hands in front of her face. Against the passage wall on the left the men were now standing one behind the other, taking off their overcoats. Each of them proceeded to wrap his coat around his left arm.

Images: Where the passage joins the hall, the staircase goes up to the left, rising in a curve to the landing, and from there up to the gallery. The gallery balustrade runs around three sides of the hall and staircase. Up there all is quiet. The men advance to the corner and raise their thickly padded arms like shields above their heads. Now they dash up the stairs. The heavy dish painted with blue-and-white windmills crashes against the wall above them. Spinning plates strike them, strike the balustrade, explode. Nevertheless they get to the top, but there, faced with the barricade, they can't get through. From a position of safety and peering past Herminia's shoulder, Thom sees Sepp appear above the barricade, holding one of the wooden chairs over his head. Father's voice, as if he were not drunk: "Go on! Hit them!" The men duck and escape down the stairs. One of them is limping. The other, grimacing comically, is holding his right arm as they take cover again.

From above, Father and Sepp, laughing. "Go ahead, gentlemen! That was just the beginning! Once again the roses bloom . . ." And right after that: "Thom, come up here! D'you hear me? I need you!"

Images: Thom walked slowly around Herminia and toward the hall. Father needed him. Without looking at Mother, he stopped. In a low voice she said, "You stay here."

With trembling knees he walked up the stairs, step by step. Not a sound, except for a creak from the oak sideboard as Sepp pulled it back to allow Thom to pass. Thom slipped quickly through. "Well done, lad! Come along!"

Placing a finger to his lips, Father pushed Thom toward the door of the attic stairs. That smell of wine as Father bent over him and whispered. No, this time Father didn't shout. "The revolver," he said. "Up there in the big cupboard, remember? And the cartridge magazine— get going!"

As Thom climbed the attic stairs he had a momentary mental picture of the magazine. He knew it. One day, when Father and Sepp had been shooting at a target in the quarry, Sepp had shown him how to refill a magazine, one cartridge after the other; each had to be pressed in hard enough for the spring to be pushed down. The most difficult part was pushing the last, the sixth, cartridge into the magazine opening.

Thom found the revolver in the cupboard right away, beside the boots and the riding whip. He opened the leather case, removed the revolver, then took out the full magazine from its narrow compartment. He glanced briefly up at the wasps' nest attached to the beam in the corner, but in that uncertain light he couldn't tell whether the wasps were still inside that white globe. Then back down the attic stairs.

Yes, and here, on this very stair, he had paused. He was panting, yet he could hear the silence from below. Then again, very loud, that voice: "Thom! What's keeping you?" That made him sit down. For his own good. Until it's all over. Ro-o-oses red. He placed the revolver beside him on the stair, then held the magazine in his fingers between his knees. Suddenly he knew that much, very much, depended on him now. He called out, "Coming!" He knew it was wrong to shoot at people except in a war; otherwise one became a murderer. If he took the revolver to Father now, *he* would be guilty, or share in the guilt, if Father became a murderer. Again he called out, "I'm coming!" but his throat was so tight they probably couldn't hear him down there. Father shouted something, then clearly: "Anyone who comes up here will be shot!"

Thom swallowed. Now he must stand up and go down the stairs. Or mustn't he? Simply go on sitting there in the dark, on the fifth stair? Until it's all over?

While he could hear the men renewing their assault on the staircase, and again the cursing and smashing and crashing about as if a hand-to-hand fight were going on at the barricade, Thom began to press the cartridges one by one out of the magazine until the empty spring plate reached the top. Some of the cartridges rolled down the stairs. Thom pushed the empty magazine into its slot in the handle of the revolver and pressed it down until the spring caught. Then he ran down the stairs.

From one corner of the gallery, Sepp was spinning plate after plate toward the attackers, who were trying to push back the armchairs and sideboard with their shoulders. Father was slashing away with a chairleg at the protective overcoats. When struck from behind by a plate, one of the men cried out. Looking through the uprights of the balustrade, Thom saw the two men retreat down the stairs. He went over to Father and handed him the revolver. Father swayed, the revolver in his raised fist. "This is my house! I'll kill anyone who comes up the stairs—is that clear?"

No one answered. Father again: "You sons of bitches, I know where you want to take me. And I'll never get out of there again, I know all about that. Clear out!"

Images: Then footsteps were heard below. Slowly, as if sunk in a dream, Mother came through the hall. Came step by step up the stairs. Thom could see the part in her hair. Father stood there, beside the pillar, the weapon in his right hand against his thigh. He whispered something, took a few steps back, staggering slightly: "She's crazy." Sepp approached the barricade from the other side.

Mother, almost at the top, had stopped. "I have to talk to you," she said. "Ulrich, do you hear me?"

Father was leaning against the wall beside Uncle Ludwig's seascape. Thom watched intently. He saw Father release the safety catch with his thumb and raise the revolver. "I told you I would," he said, and Thom was the only one who knew where the cartridges were.

"Sepp, would you please remove all this stuff now?" Mother said.

The image: That lopsided smile crossed Father's face, his right cheek twitched, he was still holding out the revolver at chest-level. Sepp also looked at Father; then Thom saw Sepp wipe the sweat off his face with his sleeve. He began to remove the armchairs from the top of the sideboard. When the barricade had been pushed aside, Mother went up to Father and put her arms around him. The revolver fell to the floor. Then Father, his face on Mother's shoulder, walked down the stairs with her. Thom followed slowly. Yes, Father was sobbing. A little later, his head bowed, he sat on the black stool in the passage while one of the men from Basel, the one with the white bandage around his head, knelt down and pushed the long hypodermic needle through the pajama leg into Father's thigh.

Mother was crying, now at last she was crying. She went into the Paneled Room and closed the door behind her. At first, Thom, Sepp,

Charlott, and Herminia stayed together to watch the two men help Father on with his coat, then lead him out through the front door.

As the gleaming black car started and drove off, Sepp and Thom stood alone in the doorway watching the two red taillights disappear down the drive. Sepp put his hand on Thom's shoulder. "Goddammit," he said. He said it twice.

Conversations with André III

WHAT A STRANGE FELLOW! THEY HAD KNOWN EACH OTHER FOR SUCH A long time, had climbed up through the wooded ravine along narrow rock ledges bordering the stream, as far as the shady pool in the rushing water, and André had shown Thom how—No Fishing!—to lie on your stomach on the overhanging flat rocks and, spreading all ten fingers, cut off the escape of the rainbow trout from under the rocks; then, as the fish remained there seemingly transfixed, you could tentatively touch them, then grab them and lift them out with both hands—three or four trout in less than an hour.

And those evenings in fall when they had wandered along the banks of the Aare or, each with a bottle of beer in his rucksack, up through the forest. They had sat on the wall of the old ruined castle, gazing into the moonlit night and down onto the carpet of city lights as it gradually sank into the darkness; they had drunk beer, had smoked and argued about Van Gogh, about Le Corbusier and his Notre Dame du Haut chapel in Ronchamps, about Picasso, Charlie Parker. At some time or other André had begun to talk about Prince Kropotkin, about Bakunin, about Malatesta and Proudhon, about the anarchist circles of the watch-industry homeworkers in the Jura Mountains, about the self-governing communes and factories of the anarchists in Catalonia. Again and again André had elaborated on his dream of the undominated society, had lectured him on the brute force behind the liberal facade of those in power and behind Stalin's concept of socialism. André's sweet anarchy, so closely approaching the communes of the early Christians: What had become of it?

"What has become of it, Andy?" Thom had to admit that he knew of no better dream than that one, the dream of an anarchist autonomy in brotherly love. Once again, in late afternoon, after taking the bus up to the Fahris Pass, they had wandered over to the ruins and, as in the old days, sat down on the partially restored castle wall and gazed out over the countryside.

Over the countryside? Thom got a shock when, in the clear air of that summer day, the heat no longer quite so scorching, he tried to take in the view below. Yes, the old encircling walls were still visible, and the three bridges over the Aare, the Winter cement plant, the foundry, the rolling mill, and the squat old buildings of the living quarters beyond, but how much had been added over the last fifteen years! Had Jammers really grown so much that you could scarcely make out where it came to an end? Where a town had once stood in the open countryside, now a freeway network surrounded it with a huge tangle of over- and under-passes, access roads, and expressways, while spreading out beyond were the great factory halls, office buildings, tennis courts, sports arenas, and apartment blocks, then again whole sections built over with factories and railroad sidings: all beautifully symmetrical, it must be said, laid out with wide avenues—high-rises, apartment and office silos, and beyond, in the haze, as if rising from a sea of concrete, the cooling tower.

André, busy as usual with his pipe, said, "Sweet anarchy? Oh, Thom." He gave a dry laugh. "It is a dormouse, sleeping, hibernating. The question is whether the time will come when we can make it spring to life again. It is sleeping: in me, in you too, I suppose, and in many others—also, incidentally, in quite a few of those involved in our strike at the Winter plants down there."

"How is it coming along?"

André seemed not to have heard the question. Pointing down at the town he said, "Every day we can witness a minute part of that rampant destruction, or we hear about it; we read, we see on television, how it is spreading. It makes me sick, just as it does all the others—but still, in order to round out this picture of our home town, I want, just once more, once more! —oh, never mind."

They fell silent. Then Thom again: "You wanted to round out the picture. Don't forget that over the past ten years I've never spent more than two or three days here, and then only as a visitor."

"Do you really want me to reel it all off again? What's going on here is happening everywhere, with variations. The trees, the forests— the very lungs of our cities—are also dying at the Wannsee in Berlin. In the soil there is the heavy metal cadmium. The River Aare, the lakes and streams—it's war, against humans, animals, against nature, the expression and basis of all living things. Add to that the proliferation of cables, the pollution of this world by forty or more TV programs aimed at universal stultification of the people. Add to that the corresponding destruction of the power of critical thought, the silent liquidation of democracy. Or should we mention the isolation of the individual, the silent rapture of children in front of the computer? Or should we talk of the arms race, even here in Switzerland?"

André refilled his pipe. Had he calmed down a bit? "Just look over there—if you stretch out your arm, about a hand's breadth to the left of the cooling tower—the Born Forest. They're drilling there now, that's where radioactive nuclear waste is to be stored and guarded for the next ten thousand years.

"Over there, that speck of green, where the metropolitan areas of Jammers and Zurich meet, they're building the national storage site for designated waste from the chemical industry. Or over there, on the right, the Fahris valley, seemingly still so pristine—they're building the road to the high moorland beyond the first Jura range: for the newly developed target area for armored vehicles. Shall I go on? A month ago two local physicists took some measurements: first, of the proportion of poisonous particles released into the air by traffic and oil burners down on the plain, then of the radioactivity in the center of town seven kilometers from the nuclear power plant. The two men started out by being interested in establishing those figures merely for their own purposes. Both figures were way above the permitted limits. Then the news leaked out that three filters in the power plant's cooling system had broken down. The authorities—you know what they're like—hastened to assure the public that there was no danger. And when questions were asked in parliament about the extent of the danger if the two poisonous doses combined to act upon the human organism, not one of the experts was qualified to give an answer."

The shadows of a few single clouds drifted across the wide plain, as if dragging pale veils of sunlight behind them. Beyond the tips of their shoes as they sat on the old wall, dangling their legs into the void, they could see the thinning tops of the beech trees. In the forest below a hawk trilled, followed by silence again, or, to be more exact, the steady, subdued roar of many thousands of motors operating in factories and offices, on streets and on rails.

André held out his pipe at eye level. Thom might have imagined he was writing the word in the air as he said, "Progress." It sounded like a title for the broad landscape. "Or shall we call it growth?"

Then, after a pause, another of André's abrupt changes of subject, of which it was never clear whether they were meant to push aside what had just been said, or whether he was trying to approach his subject from a new angle, one that only seemed to be remote. "Funny," he said, "since our conversation about your uncle's sketches in your old home— remember? Electra I to III—I've been reading Gustav Schwab's *Myths of Classical Antiquity* before going to bed—you know, those legends about the Atridae. And I've also been dipping into Robert Graves' *Greek Myths* for the sources and interpretations of the various episodes. Quite a turbulent clan history!" He smiled.

"Oh, of course," said Thom, "Electra, Orestes, Aegisthus, and all those characters." Charlott had often read him the chapter on Orestes' banishment to Aulis and his liberation by means of the garment embroidered with wild animals—he'd been twelve or fourteen at the time. What made André choose to read that stuff, just now? "You the diehard preacher of enlightenment and the materialistic interpretation of history— now you're wallowing in myths about the worlds of the gods, about destiny ruled by blind fate? What's the idea?"

"No, not as an escape from the destruction we can so comfortably look down upon from here. Not as a return to the belief in an imposed destiny. Nor as a psychologizing of the myths in order to rescue them from fascism, as Thomas Mann tried to do. You know, it's really fantastic the way those ancient myths tell of the entire spectrum of human potential in all its contradictions." What he was after, he went on, was to try to gain fresh insight into them—that was it, to look at them out of the context of their time, in other words materialistically. And to relate them to what was happening all around today.

Thom shrugged. He did not, at the moment, feel particularly inclined to discuss ancient Greeks and their passions. "I'm sorry," he said, "but that view down there—I simply cannot absorb that shock so quickly. Your word 'progress'—it reminds me of my Uncle Ludwig."

André looked at Thom. "I once heard him give a speech—some jubilee celebration of the Winter Corporation's. We had had to assemble in the courtyard between the administration building and the foundry, the works band played the 'Winter March,' and the high point was that speech by Ludwig Winter. I can still see him. I can hear his voice cracking with enthusiasm for what lay ahead of us, now that the war was over, in the way of permanent progress, permanent growth, and prosperity for all. He really was a kind of ideologist-in-chief of Winter Corporation policy. Wild! A wild mixture! The way he kept invoking 'our native land,' as if we of this country were a nation. They love to do that, the spokesmen for big business—whenever they want to subject the rest of us to their goals. 'Native land! Progress! Freedom! Less government!'—what they mean is 'might is right,' the right of the economically more powerful and their managers to do as they like with this native land and all of us to serve their own interests. Behind their concept of freedom is the image of an economically oriented, supposedly rational person and—male— affluent citizen who has only one goal: profit. Native land? To the likes of them, the idea would long since have become a matter of indifference, if it weren't so easy to misuse it to mobilize feelings of solidarity."

Thom was still observing the scene below. Only a few plumes of smoke were to be seen, the big one over to the left slanting up from the cooling tower, or the familiar plume from the cement plant. The poison content and radiation levels remained invisible. "A kind of bottom line," he said. "The bottom line of destruction, of 'devastation,' the obverse of the coin 'progress.' "

And André again: "I'm even willing to assume that Ludwig Winter believed in the delusion he was preaching with his 'progress.' In this kind of thinking he was, like most of his generation, also of our generation— and this, mind you, applies to those of the right as well as of the left— a product of the nineteenth century. The aftereffects of this can still be felt, in practice, in production, almost unimpaired—to this day, to this very day."

André paused. "No, it's not just a matter of slip-ups, not just the result of accidents. This aggressiveness toward living things is rooted in the principles of our industrial society. Its production methods, the mentality and the value system behind and within it, turn this society into a deadly threat to itself—to all of us.

"All right—the bottom line. Of what, in this case? Are we to make the rabid belief in progress responsible, or the belief that every question has a technical and technological answer? The bottom line of what else? In terms of politics, I would say: the bottom line of the French Revolution, whose aim was mature *citoyens* in a state of equality and fraternity. Today, after two hundred years, the bottom line proves that the Great Revolution was a failure. In terms of political economics: the bottom line of capitalism? Measured by the bottom line of its enterprises, it continues to flourish, constantly changing, cyclically and merrily. Measured by its ideals, by the belief in progress, by the costs to society, and by the level of this concentrated destruction here, I can only conclude: a failure."

From somewhere came the noise of a plane. Thom squinted up into the sky. The white clouds were still drifting through the blue air. At last, far over toward the west, he saw the vapor trail and the dot of the plane pulling it in its wake. The noise came from directly overhead; the plane was flying far ahead of it.

"But where, André," said Thom, "does this aggressiveness originate? Who can still profit from this violence and its thrust if the foundations of the lives of all of us, including the politicians, the managers, and their bosses, are gradually dying?"

To him, said André, the whole thing looked more and more like one final great auction. The best items had been knocked down long ago, and much too cheaply. Now the mob of dealers and collectors was scrambling for the last green areas, the last resources, the last as-yet-unexploited square meters of homeland: they were all being put under the hammer. "Seriously, Thom, let me repeat: you're right—if we don't know the causes of this aggressive mania, how can we do anything about it?"

"Still that enlightenment thing, André? Still analyzing, still the old search for insight into what is happening to us?"

André's eyes flashed as he looked at Thom. "What else? And you can add: thinking in alternatives."

And Thom: "Actually, as an explanation for this bottom line I'm satisfied with the old observation: we happen to be an aggressive, selfish species. The internal rudder that should be steering us toward humanitarian behavior, toward dignity and reverence for our own kind and for nature, is not working, not in us humans."

André chewed on his pipe. He couldn't accept that. "Man as man's predator? This mania for destruction seen as human nature? No. That idea would sit nicely with all those who refused to admit that we have to change our thinking." He insisted: "We are capable not solely of perpetual war, not solely of greed, selfishness, domination. We also have the gift of humanitarian behavior, of sharing, of living at peace with one another and with nature." Yes, he insisted: "Both dispositions in us human creatures, both potentials in us, could be developed—one at the expense of the other. Whether it is the possessive, warlike potential of human existence that prevails as the dominant type, or the disposition toward solidarity—that will be decided by our culture, by the values and norms by which we learn to live."

"Tell me, how long ago was it that you first tried to convince me of that?" Thom asked with a grin. "I was your disciple for many years, but over this point I couldn't go along with you, remember? Sounds wonderful, sounds enticing—as wonderful as it did then. Only I'm afraid, André, you're repeating yourself. There comes a time when we must add to our knowledge—some new aspect or other, based on experience, should penetrate our consciousness as well as our theoretical thinking— the experience of the complexity of all these phenomena, for instance."

Was André annoyed, was he hurt? He was silent; he knocked out his pipe. Thom climbed down again onto the ground behind the wall. "How about making a move toward that restaurant back there?" he said.

"A new aspect? Yes, of course. Or a very old one? I'm repeating myself, but that doesn't mean I'm not about to see these things in, shall we say, the light of what is—for me, anyway—a new dimension."

Leaning forward, Thom rested his elbows on the wall. Once again the wide terrain was spread out before him. Once again he heard himself muttering the word "appalling." "Violence," he said. "Its destructive effect is obviously accelerating from year to year. The end is predictable."

André was still sitting on the wall. "Don't take it amiss, but I must trouble you again, my historian friend, with my ancient Greeks. What is suppressed in your scholarly field, what is scarcely dealt with in your classical literature, is precisely what is beginning to fascinate me in these legends. I am coming more and more to see that these legends bear the imprint of the great historical upheaval of their time, of the defeat of the old matriarchal systems by the new warlike social order of patriarchy. Now that I am reading the myths of the Atridae from *this* aspect, I can observe, step by step as it were, how at least remnants of the history of that war of annihilation are mirrored in those myths. The ancient agrarian peoples had no system of writing as we know it. The legends are told and retold, and eventually written down, by men—expropriated, ma-triarchal myths, censored, refashioned."

Thom pondered. "André, seriously: What are you getting at? We have agreed that the destruction spread out at our feet represents a bottom line. Of what? Now you're telling me about the historical transition— something I do know about, by the way—from matriarchal to patriarchal cultures four or five thousand years ago."

"A bottom line," André nodded. "That's what I'm saying. Above all else, it seems to me, what we see and don't see down there is a bottom line of the white man's four-thousand-year-old culture. In a nutshell, and to use an extreme metaphor: at that time the matriarchal culture, with its principles of communal property and peaceful intercourse among human beings and with nature, was killed by a kind of collective matricide by males, wiped out by the principles of domination, exploitation, divisiveness, and war. This new value system, founded on private property and lifelong monogamy, the central motor in all our social systems since that time, has now, today, led once again to what amounts, figuratively speaking, to matricide, by which I mean, to the murder of all living things, of nature."

For a few seconds Thom could hear his own breathing—in, out, in. "But that's—" and he broke off. Then: "Never mind, I'm afraid I'm becoming cynical."

The subdued roar from below became briefly audible again. And there seemed to be a high-pitched hum in the air. "I did say matricide figuratively speaking. The legend of the matricidal Orestes was made into a play by Aeschylus in 450 B.C., when the defeat of matriarchal society already lay far back in the past. Aeschylus transposed it to the time of the Trojan War. King Agamemnon returns as conqueror. Clytemnestra, the queen, has meanwhile been wielding power in Mycenae. She kills the returning conqueror of Troy in his bath. Historically speaking, she refuses to hand back the regained female power to the male. But that doesn't help her much, for already the next man has grown to maturity—Orestes, the son she had banished. True, if we interpret his murder of his mother from a purely psychological point of view, it is the revenge of the son on the murderess of his father. In historical terms, however, this deed is the revenge of the representative of the new patriarchal order on a woman who dared to insist on the old female rights. The murder illustrates—not only, but also—the fact that male domination, when threatened by a woman, does not shrink even from crime. Unlike us, the Greeks were skilled in the art of interpreting mythical figures not merely as exponents and victims of private conflicts, but also as the protagonists of historical forces."

"This much I've grasped from your long lecture: that the causes of aggressiveness—no doubt numerous—are to be found not in the French Revolution, nor in capitalism, nor even in human nature. You place its origins in the beginnings of what you call the white man's culture. But where, if you'll forgive the naive question, did this warlike, exploitative attitude come from, how did it find its way into patriarchy—into, if I have understood you correctly, this culture or nonculture of ours that is staging the battle down there?"

"I know," said André, "I know. That is precisely the question. I'd like to learn more about it too. For the moment, just this, as a conjecture: At the core of all aggressiveness lies fear, the unconscious fear, innate mainly in males, of what men perceive as feminine—fear of all that is flowing, chaotic, fear of untamable nature. The fear of extinction, of death." André was silent for a while. "Ah, Thom," he sighed, "there's another vast subject. Shall we go?"

Passages III

BUT EVEN WITHOUT THE PIGEONS—THEY HAVE LONG SINCE BEEN SHOT, plucked, eaten, buried—even without them, to lie there, to surrender to the feeling that there are these two things: one, that maybe he could now once again see a cobweb, glittering with tiny dewdrops, in the branches of his tree, his giant ash tree behind the house, now felled by lightning, to see it artfully stretched and woven just above him, just above him in the branches, simply to see it, to gaze at it in untroubled curiosity; the other, that simultaneously and without the pigeons, without the cooing of the pigeons that used to sit lazily outside the open window under the dome of the sky, on the finely carved limestone pedestals that did not, or only seemed to, support the roof out there—that feeling was present too, that he was moving around in the house or in a room of the decaying house or maybe only inside himself around a cell or at least around some innermost zone or circle on the floor—a circle or cell that he was forbidden to enter, never mind by whom—two things that really had nothing to do with one another but were simultaneously present in this single feeling, in contradiction to, or rather independent of, each other: that possibility of seeing the spider's handiwork, and this prohibition.

The pigeons had been there all year; from time to time they had plummeted a short distance from their sheltered stations as they stood or sat on the pedestals, caught themselves as they fell and, with a clatter of their white or dove-gray iridescent wings, suddenly taken off, obeying some mysterious law of their own, to form a flock without Thom ever having understood how they communicated, a flock that, still clattering and whirring, rose faster and faster between the two hickory oaks into the sky and vanished in the sun. Seconds later, their wings now probably scorched, they were to be seen far out over the roofs of the town, disappearing into a street, reappearing—still in a flock so dense that their beating wings must surely touch—like a squadron of dive bombers by the fir copse, plummeting, flying past the south front of the house or away over the roof before landing above the stable on the beam outside their dovecote, approaching it from below as if they had merely wanted to show off their flying skills and now they all, all of them at once, had had enough. And soon after, they were once again squatting lethargically out there on their stone pedestals above the upper-story windows, cooing and blinking down at Thom with one sleepy round eye as he leaned out of his window to look up.

In those days, when Thom was seven or ten or fourteen, he had never bothered to wonder whether their cooing and periodic wing-flapping and flying were merely part of his afternoons, or whether it was they that enticed him to spend half an hour or more lying on his bed, in a kind of half-sleep, letting images pass behind his closed eyes: cobwebs in the branches of his ash tree or the grain resembling a procession of ants along a weathered beam of the woodshed—a kind of self-concocted movie in which he could make the images and scenes whirl about in quick succession or let them unfold with infinite slowness, until the spider reappeared in its dark funnel, venturing out into the light and climbing to the top of its web, where it hurried back and forth spinning new threads into the web, threads it pulled along behind that clumsy body on its thin legs, yes, or

until Thom's cousin Tildi from Milan, leaning against the wall over there in the library, cupped her hand around one mound on her breast so that her yellow blouse tautened over the curve, and she said, "See?", then began with a fingertip of the other hand to circle around the center of the mound, half turning toward the window, saying, "See, my heart?", and she took Thom's hand and guided his finger around the tiny hillock on the mound, around and around so that, amazed and bewildered, he could feel and even see the little hillock becoming firmer and more distinct under the yellow blouse, "my heart, see?" Tildi was whispering, over there in the library and simultaneously here as he lay half asleep in the cooing of the pigeons, and neither over there nor here could understand something tautening in his pants with a pleasant sense of pain, while Tildi undid two buttons of her blouse and placed Thom's hand under the blouse on the warm mound of her breast and whispered, "my heart?" and was taken aback when Thom suddenly said, "No!" and ran out of the library as if bedeviled and no no!—out through the hallway and up onto the meadow

but now to lie here in the afternoon even without the pigeons and their cooing outside the window and simply surrender to the images as they rose up from the past, surrender to this feeling that he might now once again be able, as in the past, just to see and gaze at the cobweb or feel Tildi's breast or Lis naked over him, kissing him, and at the same time this feeling that the forbidden zone, that closed area inside him, would open up for him only when he accepted the miniature scenes and images of now and over there and in the past, just as they were, undistorted by the meanings he had learned to give them, no: naked, just as they were, and without the pigeons and their flying together in a flock, only when he could let them form inside him in such a way that they could reveal their essence, their own mysterious essence, without his immediately covering them up again with what he knew or sensed or presumed to know about them—no no: lie there; wait, feel, gaze, and maybe sense that in all that wasted time he might somehow have come a shade closer to the essence of the spider and its web, even without the pigeons, and to that forbidden center that must be there somewhere in the house or inside him.

In Those Days

THIS CHAPTER SHOULD BE DEDICATED TO THE WOMAN WHO PROBABLY DID more for the survival of the occupants of the house during the summer of 1940 than, say, Major of the Artillery Ulrich Winter, assigned to a regimental staff in the upper Frick valley; more than Private 1st Class Sepp in the Freiberg area; and perhaps even more than General Guisan when he addressed the officers on the Rütli meadow that same year.

It should turn out something like a monument to Herminia Zingg, cook in the Winter household.

However: the great, the overall story of those days? Stage it as an opera using literary means? Design an epic sequence of dramatic scenes as if on a wide screen? Colors, smells, moods; the choruses of opposing voices in Switzerland's upper class; bring on the speakers who are being constantly drowned out by the war?

On May 10, 1940, Herminia was riding into town on her bicycle, her big leather satchel behind her on the carrier. She was planning to buy bread, meat, cooking fat, and sugar on ration cards, as well as beans for planting in her vegetable garden, "Schreiber's Grandresista" wax beans; they were rust-resistant and gave a good yield even in light soil. At Straub the butcher's she had a place in the yard where she could leave her bicycle. As she came out onto the street, she heard someone shouting, "Extra!" Herminia was hoping for three pork chops at the butcher's. She joined the line waiting at the door, almost all of them women, with three old men among them.

"The Reich Government has given the German troops orders to secure the neutrality of Belgium and Holland with all available military means of the Reich."

Invasion. Surprise attack. Four thousand parachutists storm the airfields. Sixteen cities bombed. So after Denmark and Norway it is now the turn of those countries—also small countries, also neutral, like Switzerland.

Describe the fury in Switzerland: the fear. Quote the reaction of the press, headlines such as: Infamous Act of Violence! Outrageous New Violation of International Law! Breach of Faith and Brute Force! Ruthless Cruelty of Germany's Lust for Conquest! Outbreak of Barbarism!

There should be mention of the despair, and of how, in kitchens and living rooms, at tables over a glass of beer, on streets, in factories, on trains, the one increasingly ominous question was ever present: When will it be our turn? Military resistance: doesn't that amount to suicide?

The center of Rotterdam bombed by the German Luftwaffe—25,000 dead. One million French and British troops marching into Belgium.

Would the Allies succeed in stopping the German Wehrmacht? If so, would the Supreme Command of the Wehrmacht order its troops to break through Switzerland in order to attack the rear of the French Maginot army from the south?

Herminia walking down Frohburg-Strasse with her satchel. Have you heard? Did you hear the news? What do you say? Really? General mobilization? Is it true? Large concentrations of German troop units north of Schaffhausen as far as Basel. Preparations for a German attack.

We've already packed our bags, how about you? Yes, but where to go?

Those who can't keep silent are harming our country! Reports casting doubt on the determination to resist on the part of the federal council and the army command are fabrications of enemy propaganda.

Bridges and mountain passes prepared for demolition.

Members of local militias to report with their arms at.

At Niggli's seed store Herminia bought the wax-bean seeds, three little packets, then went to pick up her bicycle from behind the butcher shop. After a brief stop at the co-op on Wengi-Strasse, her spoils behind her on the carrier, she rode home.

May 12, 1940: Herminia had been up and around since six A.M. The house was full of the military; they had arrived at 1:30 A.M., a whole staff company, weary infantrymen. They were sleeping in the attic, in every available room, sleeping wrapped in their blankets, in the gallery, in the stables across the way. The washhouse was now the staff kitchen, the woodshed had become the guardhouse; a command platoon had taken over the vaulted front cellar; despatch riders turned up, riding their bicycles along the avenue. From the corporal in the washhouse Herminia got herself a pot of tea, plus, after some back and forth, six cans of meat. These she hid in the linen closet in the Paneled Room, pushing them behind the tablecloths on the bottom shelf. Just in case. People have to eat, even in wartime.

Did Herminia know what was happening at that very time? That a Swiss fighter squadron under the command of Hans Thurnheer encountered a German bomber in the air space between Brugg and Basel? That the German crew opened fire? That Thurnheer's squadron immediately attacked and shot the Heinkel down in flames?

Army field order. All fighting troops to be notified immediately: Riflemen, whether overtaken or encircled, will fight in their positions until all ammunition is exhausted . . . Machine gunners, cannoneers, and artillerymen will destroy their weapons before seizure by the enemy. Then each man will resort to cold steel: as long as he still has one cartridge or his bayonet, he will not surrender. Signed: General Guisan.

At 7:30 the alarm was sounded from the stables and throughout the house. Sirens wailed over the town. At 8:40 A.M. Infantry Battalion 123 marched off in the direction of Bärenwil-Langenbruck. The kitchen corporal was the only one to say goodbye to Herminia. He brought her a pound of bacon wrapped in paper. "Just in case: Put that away safely! And ciao, Herminia, and take care," and: "Yes, you too. And when the

war is over I'll come and see you and we'll go dancing together. Ciao!"
Herminia in the doorway. She waved. He had called her Herminia.

In a series of portrayals, add one more description to the thousand
descriptions of the war. The capitulation of the Belgian Army. The pocket
of Dunkirk. Death; the staring eyes of men torn to shreds by grenades.
Italy enters the war, Switzerland is surrounded, encircled by Axis powers.
Over a million French, British, Dutch soldiers captured, wounded, killed.

How did the days pass?

How to describe the waiting in Switzerland, in that extraordinary
island of peace: the waiting, waiting? Press censorship. How much of the
historical truth was it permissible to report, transmit, listen to, read?
What did the population know, in May and June 1940, of the acts of
sabotage committed in Switzerland against airfields and munitions factories by specially trained German units? What did it know of the Reich
Government's demand that Switzerland immediately hand over to the
Wehrmacht all war matériel ordered by the Western powers? Censorship.
The people of Switzerland were not aware, or at least not yet sufficiently
so, of how dependent their country had become for its supplies on the
will of the rulers in the Third Reich; they knew nothing of the secret
trade negotiations in Berlin between Greater Germany and Switzerland
in which raw materials, especially coal, were being stubbornly wrestled
for. Four hundred fifty thousand men of the Swiss Army were standing
combat-ready, largely in the north of the country. At all tactically important sites there was continued feverish construction of emplacements,
tank traps, bunkers.

May 13, 3 P.M.: the telephone rang in the passage at the Winter
residence. Ulrich Winter, calling his wife "from the front": Reconnaissance units had reported that bridge-building preparations were under
way along the Rhine. In the border zone to the rear, German troops
units were being steadily reinforced. "This is the final deployment," the
major said. "We expect the attack to take place tomorrow night. You
must take the children and Aunt Esther to Morges, to Stephanie's, tomorrow morning at the latest. My cousin is expecting you."

Lilly Winter merely said she would think about it.

"You must, Lilly!"

"Well, then: May God protect you!" With that she hung up. Going
into the kitchen, she still seemed quite calm as she told Herminia and
Charlott about the call. Yet it was unusual for her to sit down beside
Herminia at the kitchen table. You must! he had told her. And a little

later she said, "You two, Charlott and Gret, go and pack your bags. You will be leaving with Aunt Esther, today, on the seven o'clock train." Charlott's protests were of no avail. "And what about you?"

She would stay, of course, with Thom. Herminia must decide for herself whether or not she wanted to leave with them.

Shortly after six a taxi came for Aunt Esther and the two girls. The man urged them to hurry; down in the town there was panic, he said—anyone who could was getting out. Anyway, the better-off ones had already left. "Come on, come on, get in."

When Lilly Winter returned from seeing them off and stood in the doorway to the kitchen, Herminia noticed her pallor. "So," said Mrs. Winter, "just the two of us, and Thom, we're the last ones here." From the Paneled Room she brought two glasses and an open bottle of wine. "I suggest we start by drinking to that." Herminia beamed and wiped her hands on her apron. "Your health!" Ten minutes later Lilly Winter was back in the Paneled Room, twirling the radio knob as she searched for the voice of the Royal Air Force announcer. When the telephone rang again, Herminia lifted the receiver. The local commander informed her that an artillery unit would arrive at eleven that night: two heavy-mortar platoons plus the battery command were to be billeted at the Winter house, forty horses in the stables and barn.

"Please see to it, Mrs. Winter, that everything is prepared by ten thirty tonight." Saying that she would pass on the message, Herminia hung up.

The attack on Switzerland by Wehrmacht units, expected for two A.M. on May 15, did not materialize. Had the preparations in southern Germany been staged as a vast deceptive maneuver in order to tie down important sections of the French Army in the south? At that very same time the tank battles were thundering away on the plains of northern France. Casualties. Casualties.

When Herminia entered the Paneled Room the radio had been switched off. Lilly Winter, her back to the room, was standing beside the tiled stove that reached almost to the ceiling. She groaned. She did not notice Herminia. She screamed. With both fists she hammered against the pale green tiles; Herminia could make out "War! Are they human? Those men! I can't—I can't—I can't—" She sobbed. Lilly Winter collapsed, sobbing, into the leather armchair. When Herminia went up to her, she could see, she could feel, the woman's whole body trembling. With a swift turn Lilly Winter buried her tear-streaked face in

Herminia's apron. Herminia stroked her hair, over and over again. "It's just that you feel so helpless," she said. Haltingly, Mrs. Winter told her about the advance of the German tanks; they were already on their way to Paris! Herminia then took her upstairs to the Blue Room. When, at eleven o'clock sharp, the commanding officer of the mortar battery appeared at the front door and wished to discuss the billeting with Mrs. Winter, Herminia replied, "I am in charge here. There is room for twenty men in the house; the rest will be quartered in the barn. Come with me."

Lilly Winter was ill for four whole weeks. She scarcely spoke, scarcely ate, merely lay on her bed looking up at the crystal beads of the chandelier. The drapes had to remain closed.

Back to describing the panorama in an epic sweep. On June 1 twelve German bombers penetrate Swiss air space. Four Swiss pursuit planes— Messerschmidt 109s—order the formation to land, to no avail. Two bombers are shot down. No Swiss losses. June 2: A Heinkel bomber shot down over Yverdon on Lac de Neuchâtel. June 4: New air battles over the Jura. Reich Marshal Göring orders a punitive expedition against Switzerland: 32 German attack bombers enter Swiss air space and begin circling over northern Romandie. First three, then ten Swiss pursuit planes keep them under surveillance. In the ensuing air battle two German bombers are shot down, whereupon the formation leaves Swiss territory. One Swiss pilot, wounded by three bullets through the lungs, manages to land his badly perforated machine. The other Swiss pursuit planes, some of them damaged, return to their bases. A provocation. Protest notes in the sharpest terms arrive in Bern from Berlin. From now on the Swiss pursuit patrols are kept on a short leash, like overzealous watchdogs, by the Supreme Command of the Army. Any more planes shot down might form the pretext for a German attack. Next, Switzerland kowtows before the wielders of power: The Bern government formally apologizes for the shooting down of a total of ten German machines within four weeks and undertakes to compensate Germany for all losses resulting from the air battles. Nevertheless, Hitler cuts off the supply of coal to Switzerland, thereby paralyzing important sections of the Swiss economy.

On June 18, 1940, Lilly Winter, in her blue housecoat, made her first appearance again in the kitchen. Yes, of course: she was hungry now. Was there any cheese in the larder, any bread? Herminia gave her a brief rundown of what had happened in the meantime. Told her the boy was well, still asleep. That she had told the major she must have seven men; she and these men had planted a potato patch in front of the house. In the cellar were three kilos of beef in brine, next to them five pig's trotters in sterile glass jars, everything in the dark back there in the second cellar. Oh, and she had also pressed twenty kilos of sauerkraut, layered with juniper berries, into stoneware crocks. And so on. She had had to make it clear to the military that in this house hobnailed boots were left in the porch. And up there in the French Jura, in the Ajoie, French troops and two Polish divisions, altogether 42,000 men, had fled before the German tanks into Switzerland, 2,000 vehicles, 6,000 horses. That was yesterday. The day before yesterday the French government had asked Germany for an armistice.

"And Paris?"

Herminia gave a shrug. "Occupied," she said.

At the table Lilly Winter stopped eating. For a long time she was silent. Then: Might she ask Herminia from now on to call her Lilly?

Herminia turned on the water in the sink. "Sure, that's all right," she said. And soon after: "I have to go now, those wax beans back there near the raspberries need hilling—they're already a couple of inches high, you know. But someone should take Thom's bottle to him now, ma'am."

Something like a monument: to Herminia.

Saga of Origin III

THE ORACLE OF THE DANA HAD BIDDEN BRAN, THE YOUNGEST SON OF THE primeval mother: Follow the River Duna through the Jura Mountains, and you will come upon the cave beast, and the cow grazing in the wild. Follow it. Where it goes to slake its thirst and lies down, there you will find your sister. In the evening and in the morning, found the city with her.

Bran, armed only with a spear, set out and followed the Duna, which today is called the Dünnern, through the gorges of the Jura Mountains. On the evening of the third day he caught sight of the Great Cave. He approached it, whereupon Gwion reared up in front of it. Menacingly he swung his club. Bran challenged him to do battle. After a terrible struggle Bran pierced Gwion's breast. Taking the vessel of plenty and the club with him, he continued on his way beside the river. When darkness fell from the sky he lay down for the night.

On awakening, he saw the white cow in the rising sun. It was grazing. He followed it through the swamps for a day and a night. Where the waters of the Duna and the Aare mingle, the cow went to slake its thirst, then led him up onto a hill. There, under a great ash tree, sat his sister, Europa by name, combing her blond hair. She was singing. Her singing was sweet, and when night came Bran lay with her.

At the place where this happened Europa and Bran founded the city. They called it Jah-mer, which is Celtic for "Leap over the water," or Jammers to this day.

The thought struck him: Of course, throughout those long years, whenever he had come for a visit he had been intensely aware of the house, its atmosphere as well as various details. It had always been a renewal of familiarity.

But now when he walked around the house and, for instance, from the terrace glimpsed beyond the sparse fir trees what had once been the white garden furniture, the graceful, curving, now rusted wrought-iron chairs and table (it must be the table with the hole in the middle for the sun umbrella), he didn't feel merely, Oh, of course, they're still there, it's just that nobody's repainted them as he and Charlott used to do: no, this time, and since the revelation about his mother's death, his senses had become acutely alert.

While strolling along the flagged terrace on the west side below Aunt Esther's suite, crossing the graveled patch behind the house over to the grave mound of his ash tree, then continuing slowly under the trees— the two apple trees still covered with delicate pink blossoms—he wondered how long it was since he had seen Charlott, at least for more than half an hour. Two years? Three? How was she getting along with Alain, that composer whom Thom liked, a rather short fellow, and in her executive job high up in the office tower where she headed a large branch of the department store chain whose name Thom could never remember? Yes, Charlott was the only one of the three who in their mother's eyes had made a success of her career.

Gret had responded to his question about Charlott with a shrug.

Once in a while, she had said, Charlott would phone. He knew, didn't he, that no matter whether one asked Charlott about herself or Alain or about her job or their home or their recent trip to Kenya, her response would invariably be, "Oh, just fine." Fleetingly, Thom saw Charlott and himself on the covered terrace, trying to remove the rust from the garden chairs with steel brushes before giving them a fresh coat of white paint. Charlott, two years older than Gret—she must have been about sixteen then—Father always called her "our whirlwind." This in turn had to do with the puppy brought home by Father the previous year and given the name "Whirl." A nice-looking mongrel, perhaps from a Bergamasco sire but with a jolly Great Dane's face, and this Whirl attached himself, as if forever, to Charlott. So it was she who fed him, she who fixed up his basket in the hall with a jute sack, which she had stuffed with straw and sewn up, and an old cushion. When she went off to school, he would trot along with her down the avenue past the barn. At the end of the avenue, where it meets the road, he would sit down at her command and follow her with his eyes, swiveling his head, until with a wave she disappeared into the bus. Then, but only then, he would trot back to the house.

When Whirl was still no larger than a young boxer, Aunt Esther had already called him an impossible dog. He grew apace. Within a few months he was the size of a Great Dane and went on growing until, on his long legs and with his heavy body and powerful head, his brindled coat, he stood level with Thom's chest. And now he began to distort his face with rage, began, as soon as one of the grown-ups approached to within three feet of him, to drop suddenly into a defensive, straddle-legged crouch, snarl, and bare his fangs.

Thom stood still and looked across to the washhouse. Where the poultry yard had once been, grass now grew; the sorrel blossoms on their tall stalks reached as high as the roof; in fact, they touched the rusty gutters. He could also make out the half-concealed roof of the woodshed. It occurred to Thom that over there, propped against the wall, would still be the gravestone with the name "Apollonia Moll" chiseled into the once white, now weathered limestone, surrounded or guarded by stinging nettles, if Thom remembered correctly. Apollonia had been one of Grandmother Helen's sisters; at the age of nineteen, as Frieda had once told Thom in a whisper, she had severed an artery in her neck with a knife owing to an unhappy love affair. Because she had committed su-

icide, she had been buried not in hallowed ground but outside the church-
yard wall, in the place where unbaptized babies, destined for Purgatory,
were buried.

Thom walked on up through the mossy grass of the meadow. Ah,
yes, Charlott: for an instant he saw his sister's merry, animated face before
him. Unlike Thom and Gret, Charlott had dark hair; in those days her
bangs had almost hidden her brown, slightly almond eyes.

And whenever she came through the front door her dog Whirl, with
a howl of delight, would hurl himself so violently at her that, staggering,
she had to hug him so as not to fall down. And he would stand like that,
his front paws on her shoulders, his tail wagging frantically, until Charlott
could finally calm him down by stroking him and saying in a caressing
voice, "That's all right, Whirl, you're a good, good boy." Thom could
remember how he had once come upon Charlott over by the summerhouse beyond the swing: Whirl was lying in the grass with Charlott's
head resting in the angle between his neck and the paw he had placed
over her shoulder from behind; above her hair Whirl's raised head, with
its fierce mastiff's face, was keeping watch, while Charlott was holding
one of her books. Whirl usually ignored Thom; now he barked at him
with bared teeth. Stupid dog! Without looking up from behind her book,
Charlott said, "Just go away. Then he'll be quiet."

The postman began leaving the mail, at a safe distance from the
house, on the driveway under the low-hanging branches of the cedar
tree. He said he wouldn't deliver the mail to the front door until that
"monster of a dog" was put in a pen, so for a time it was Charlott who
brought the mail up to the house. But then Whirl attacked the man who
had come to read the meter. He leaped straight at the man in the porch,
knocked him to the floor, and bit him in the arm. Now Mother had had
enough. Sepp would have to shoot Whirl, she said at lunch. Human
lives are more important. Charlott burst into tears and ran out the door
and upstairs. After some tough negotiations, Mother, Charlott, and Father agreed on two conditions: that Whirl would definitely be kept in a
pen to be built by Sepp, and that starting from the very next day he would
have to wear a muzzle.

Sepp built a pen by erecting a six-foot chainlink fence attached to
sturdy wooden posts rammed into the ground, leaving an opening in the
wall of the woodshed. The next morning Whirl had disappeared; the
muzzle was hanging in shreds high up in the fence. Around noon Whirl
attacked Sepp as he was chopping wood behind the shed. The dog's claws

raked Sepp's back, leaving it covered with blood. Then Whirl appeared in the hallway in time for Charlott's return from school; he proudly brought in a dead goose, its long bloody neck clamped between his jaws. A gift for Charlott.

It was she who then kept insisting that from now on Whirl would not misbehave anymore, she was quite sure, she would see to it. Nevertheless, shortly after midday Whirl was led away by a man in a leather coat. Charlott did not cry, did not rail at anybody. She sat on the steps: for a whole hour she sat there without a word; and when Mother asked her—by then it must have been almost four o'clock—whether she and Thom were now, as agreed, going to take the garden furniture out of the washhouse and start scrubbing it, she came along, although perhaps a little too calmly.

As Thom opened the wooden gate in the fir copse and walked along the road that led in a curve through the quiet Bellevue district, he once again saw himself working away with a steel brush at the wrought iron, the smell of ammonia in his nostrils, and from time to time looking at Charlott beside him. Charlott was scrubbing grimly, in her face the determination to go to any lengths. When Thom asked her what she was going to do now, all she said was, "You'll see."

Dusk still came down early from the meadow. Thom, whose back and hands were aching, was glad when Charlott said that would do for today. After moving the garden chairs into a corner, they went to the kitchen to wash their hands. Thom saw Charlott put on a sweater as she walked across to the washhouse. Then she wheeled out her bicycle and rode off in the direction of the barn and presumably down the avenue toward town.

She did not appear for supper. No one mentioned her absence. While Gret was talking about school, the fingers of Mother's left hand were drumming, almost imperceptibly, on the tablecloth. Father arrived, too late as usual. He sat reading in his armchair, while Mother in her place by the window worked at her embroidery, the drapes drawn shut behind him. Thom, Frieda, and Herminia played dominoes in the pantry; at ten Thom was sent off to bed. Although he had intended to wait for Charlott, he couldn't fight off sleep for long.

"Thom, it's only me! Wake up!" Yes, that was Charlott whispering. Instantly Thom was wide awake. He sat up. His groping left hand felt Charlott's sweater. The wool was damp. Her hair felt damp too. He asked if it was raining.

"Oh no, just the dew." Now Thom could see the gray dawn creeping like a snake from the windowsill into the room. He could also make out Charlott's shadowy figure as she sat down on his bed. For a few seconds he could even see her eyes; they were shining feverishly. Thom listened.

Charlott had first ridden to Ruth's; there, at the Schenkers', she had had supper; then, around ten, she had ridden on into the Old Town, along Gold-Gasse, over to Bastian-Platz, across the Old Bridge to the railway station, back across the Wengi Bridge into the Old Town again, then once more Bastian-Platz, all the time expecting to catch sight of Whirl. As the hammers in the Bastian Tower struck midnight, the town fell silent. "It died away in a silence," Charlott said.

"How you talk," said Thom. Nobody had ever told him what happened down in the town between midnight and five in the morning. "Did anyone hang themselves?"

Charlott had not heard his question. "Terrible," she said, "and beautiful."

And Thom again: "And the prostitutes? Did any prostitutes pass you?"

Charlott had left her bicycle somewhere and sat on the wall, first in one place, then another. Each time she heard footsteps, she hid. Her voice sounded feverish.

"And murderers? Did you see any murderers? Were there any Luddites there? Or Atar? Come on, tell me!"

He sensed that she was smiling in the dark as if in a dream. "The moon drifted away from the roof of the Old Bridge." Thom pressed his hands over his ears. "Its silvery garlands are flowing right across the Aare, and wisps of mist are beginning to dance on the water." She was whispering, Charlott was whispering. She was breathing fast.

Thom wanted to know whether there had been any shooting.

"But did you know that the moon can giggle? When the three white rats ran up the embankment, I could hear it. Then a man dressed in black leather came by on a motorbike; when he saw me disappear behind the wall, he made a U-turn and drove up to me. 'Here we go, bride,' he said. He said 'bride,' you know?"

"Was he in disguise?"

"He's a molder, works at the foundry, and just imagine, he wanted me to kiss him!"

"And did you?"

Charlott shivered; Thom sensed a shudder running through her.

"Not yet. 'Come with me, bride,' he said, 'we'll drive all night, and by morning we'll be in Venice. Or in Rome, if you'd rather.' "

"Fantastic," said Thom. "And what happened then?"

"Not so loud!" Her voice dropped even lower as she told him how she climbed down the embankment, moving farther and farther away from him. To the motorcyclist all she said was, "I can walk on water. By full moon, and because I'm a virgin and believe in Jesus Christ."

The man on the motorbike had laughed, she said. " 'A bride who's nuts!' " he called out. " 'Come back up! I'm not going to fish you out of the water!' " And that was when she had seen the elves again, out on the middle of the river. She had prayed to Jesus Christ, and then she had slowly walked, step by step, onto the Aare. She had heard the fellow with the motorbike shout, "Come back, you crazy girl!" but she had walked on, through the ring of dancing elves with their veils of mist, on and on right across to the other shore.

"When I reached it, the man in black was there again. 'That's enough now!' he shouted." But just then she had heard barking from up on the Old Bridge. She had quickly climbed the iron steps, and on reaching the top found Whirl on the point of lunging at the man with the motorbike. " 'Call this beast off!' he said." But at that moment Whirl hugged her, and now they had come home together. "He's been injured," she said. "He can hardly walk. He's been beaten. His front paw, his neck, his back," and she had taken him into the washhouse, put disinfectant powder on his wounds, and covered him up. He had run all the way back in that condition, all the way from Zofingen. Charlott coughed. The dawn painted crosses on the closet doors, mother-of-pearl gray. Perhaps Charlott really was ill. Thom placed his hand on her forehead. "So hot," he said. "What will happen if you die?"

"Just a touch of fever," she said. "But that won't change anything." She stood up, and pulled on the cord at the window, drawing back the drapes far enough for Thom to see from his bed the branches of the hickory oak reaching up into the rosy sky.

"Do you see the moon?"

"Is it setting?" Thom couldn't see it from where he was.

Charlott gave a feverish laugh. "The moon is a chopped-off head." She laughed again. "Now it's rolling through the smoke from the blast furnaces—look at its angry red face!" She left the room. When Thom got up and went to the window, there was no moon in sight. Pale clouds, tinged with pink. The long veils of the mist elves hung down from the two hickory oaks. Still muzzy with sleep, he closed the drapes and, shivering, groped his way back into his warm bed.

Then suddenly Charlott was there again. He could hear her pulling off her sweater, her shoes, her skirt. "Move over a bit." Thom propped himself on one elbow; Charlott lay down in his bed with her back to him. With his right hand he pulled up the quilt and covered her. Under the sheet she took his hand, drew it up over her hip, and laid it on her breast. "Hold me tight, Thom," she said. Yes, she was cold. She was shivering, and Thom was suddenly almost petrified to feel her heart beating under the swelling of her breast. "Whirl is dead," Charlott whispered. Thom still scarcely dared to breathe.

"He laid his head in my lap, and I sang him to sleep. I knew he was done for." Then she had thrust the knife into his chest. "You know, that big hunting knife from the workshop. He leaped up, looked at me, then collapsed and lay still."

Thom was holding Charlott in his right arm; he had pushed the left one under his pillow. "And now?"

"Now no one will ever be able to take him away. And now no one will ever beat him again."

Thom could say nothing. And Charlott: "Will you help me bury him up there by the fir copse?"

He had a brief vision of Charlott walking through the dancers on the waters of the Aare. And he could see the moon too. Charlott's moon, rolling across the sky. "I will," he replied.

From Class to Class

AT A LEISURELY PACE THOM STROLLED THROUGH THE BELLEVUE DISTRICT. Do nothing but walk about here, hearing voices from behind the shrubs in the gardens, mostly women chatting as they sat together in the shade on this sultry afternoon. Children's shrill cries coming from swimming pools. In the hedges and bushes, now no longer flowering, beetles and bumblebees humming; the scent of rhododendrons or dahlias wafting by. For a moment Thom visualized his gloomy, one-bedroom apartment on Niebur-Strasse in Berlin; from its windows all he could see above the houses across the street was a narrow strip of sky. Even so, that was where he had experienced it: being among people again. In the building, on the street, in the subway, at the corner store: wherever he went, the opportunity for normal conversation. To be sure, there were times when that thronging familiarity got on his nerves, and many a time he would breathe a sigh of relief as he shut the apartment door behind him and wearily put on the kettle for tea. With so much human proximity, it was only natural that he should also feel like a stranger, like a foreigner in Berlin among strangers.

He had come down in the world, no question; a straggler of the mighty clan which until thirty or forty years ago had provided jobs for the inhabitants for miles around, but had also taken jobs away from them—depending on circumstances, or what was at stake. Yes, today Thom couldn't help being glad that his former professor in Basel had wangled that research grant for him.

This idyll of single and duplex houses appeared to exist, in its discreet affluence, its tranquillity and orderliness, remote from the destruction to be contemplated from the castle ruins. Or perhaps it wasn't like that after all, perhaps the man mowing his lawn behind the hedge was an insurance expert who had been fired, his executive function rationalized out of existence by the latest management analysis, and now he was tyrannizing himself and his entire family merely because since his dismissal he had become silent, had simply stopped speaking? Perhaps here too, at the very back of some built-in closets, lay those leather cases or shoeboxes containing, wrapped in dolls' clothes for camouflage, the hypodermic needles for the addiction of the lady of the house or of her seventeen-year-old daughter? And perhaps in the mind of that Herculean old man, who was carefully trimming his cedar hedge from the sidewalk, those sentences were again taking shape, sentences that had been forming and reforming every few days for years, words that he planned, now at last, now tonight, or certainly tomorrow morning, to leave behind in a note: "If there were as much perfidy in animals as in you, my dear, you would be an animal. After fifty years of marriage I am setting myself free with this bullet. May it penetrate your heart too"—words of that kind, and he would know that tomorrow and the day after and, if God should grant him the time, even a year from now, his mind would still be carefully honing them until they finally became the weapon that could really kill.

When Thom was less than five meters away from him, the white-haired giant looked up. He paused, lowered his long shears, and raised his eyebrows. "Isn't it—?" he said. "By God, isn't it Mr. Winter—Mr.

Thomas?" Standing erect, with an almost threatening air, he looked down at Thom. "If I may say so—"

Thom thought for a moment. "Do we know each other?"

The giant laughed. "I'm Karl Berger. I knew you'd turn up some day!"

His paw was sweaty. "Let's go in." Thom, somewhat hesitatingly, followed him. The front door stood open. Through the hallway and a room crammed with old furniture, Mr. Berger preceded him into the garden. A wide lawn, a fountain, flowering shrubs; beyond them, the high-rises of the city, and, farther still, a clear view of the Born Forest with the huge quarries of the cement plant. The peaks of the Alps far away in the distance could be only imagined in the haze. Berger gestured toward some garden chairs at a round table. They sat across from each other, each with his glass of beer. "Your health."

The man immediately began talking. His bushy eyebrows, his forehead, his big face—his expression switched so rapidly from serious to merry to almost ferocious that Thom could at first only watch the play of his features in fascination.

"Your historical work at that time. Your article in the local *New Year's Gazette*." Then the giant began to speak about the *Festschrift*, 1969, that was it, for the jubilee celebrations Thom had been commissioned by the management to write that account of the company's history from its founding up to the end of the war—yes, Thom nodded. What did this big fellow want of him?

"You know, I'd just been promoted to assistant manager in accounting." His face worked. He gave a sudden laugh. "I've just turned seventy-nine—I don't look it, do I?"

Thom expressed dutiful amazement. The erratic and slightly fanatical manner in which the old man was talking away at him was beginning to annoy him. "What is it you want?"

The giant leaned back in his chair. He certainly didn't look his age; and an accountant? A lifetime spent over figures at a desk? He looked more like a skilled worker or someone who started out as a truck driver and eventually had his own small haulage company. "The truth, Thomas Winter! You, as an educated man, are about to learn it—on one condition: that you publish it in the year following my death! That event"— he laughed immoderately—"can't be that far off! So, what do you say? Your promise in return for my truth—is it a deal?"

But how, then, asked Thom, could he be sure of what was the truth?

"Don't worry!" Again that laugh. He would provide Mr. Thomas with all the documents, everything neatly photocopied. Did he remember his Uncle Paul Winter? "Hold on a minute!" the old man cried. "What nonsense, you're much too young! Paul Winter died in the fall of 1939."

Oh yes, in the past Thom had occasionally heard about this uncle. He recalled a photo of the four of them: his father, Uncle Ludwig, Aunt Esther, and that tall, spare Uncle Paul with a small mustache and wearing a hat. Hadn't he lived somewhere near Zurich?

"For a while he was in charge of the Winterthur plant. The last few years before his death—cancer, devoured by cancer!—he had, as a member of the board, spent two days a week here at head office. Capable, quiet, a hard worker. The only trouble was, his imagination tended to run away with him. Do you want to hear his story? In anything concerning the Corporation, you see, I'm an expert!"

Way back in 1918, the old man said, he had joined the commercial department as an apprentice. Those were tough days. Thom's grandfather Elsazar used to have all the gates of all nine plants locked every morning at seven. Latecomers stayed outside; they found the lost time recorded on their pay slips. Anyone needing to relieve himself had to pick up the key from the section boss—and for no more than four minutes, mind you! Periodically Elsazar Winter would check out the taverns in the Old Town or the bars behind the railway station and even farther. If he saw an employee from the plant still there at eleven P.M., he would send him home. Drunk at night means poor work next morning. That's the way it was. Kindly but patronizing, that was him. Every morning he would go through one of the plants, and he would always ask the men, "Show me what you're working at now. Do you need better tools? Any problem with the flow? With supplies? Isn't your material too porous?" Yes, he knew how to handle the men. If necessary, he would take over the milling machine and demonstrate a faster way to exchange the rough pieces. Anyone who didn't like it could quit.

Thom swallowed some of his beer. "I know," he said. "There are plenty of funny and not so funny stories about him. But where does Uncle Paul come in?"

It had all begun when Paul and his brother Ludwig made a trip to Argentina in May 1936, the idea being to find out how the Corporation could extend its market over there. The giant stood up and moved away. When he came back he placed a box of cigars on the table. Thom declined with thanks.

"Anyway, the two brothers returned from Buenos Aires—your Uncle Ludwig, by the way, minus half an ear. A dancer, it was said, had bitten it off. Well, whatever: they brought back two nice fat orders—one just for plain milled shafts, but still for 1.3 million Swiss francs. The second order was for fittings—you know, those big, heavy pressure gauges for turbine conduits and steam boilers, worth some five million francs. A lot of money in those days, and that was to be just the beginning.

"Well, the deliveries left six months later for Lisbon, where they were shipped to their destination. The bills were paid with surprising promptness. You're wondering about the point of all this?" White-haired Karl Berger puffed out his cheeks and exhaled a splendid cloud of boiler steam. And immediately drew on his cigar again, as if savoring the truth he had promised to divulge, one last time, alone, to the full. "What happened, you see, was that a second order, or, if you like, the third, arrived from Buenos Aires, again for milled steel shafts. But the other follow-up order, the one for those profitable fittings, never came. Paul Winter, normally not much given to talk, went around cursing in our office. Telegrams were sent off to Argentina, to a certain Carlos Belmondo—oh yes, I made a careful note of all the details at the time— by then I was assistant treasurer. Paolo—among ourselves we never called him anything but Paolo—made another trip to Lisbon, on November 11, 1937. When he came back and I asked him about the outcome, he said in his tight-lipped way, 'Wait and see.' "

What was the old man driving at? Thom watched him shifting his cigar from one corner of his mouth to the other, balancing it with his lips, his teeth, his tongue, watched him contort his mouth as he chewed on the stump. "Now look here, Mr. Berger!"

Wait and see! Again the man laughed. And was off again: How he had suddenly become suspicious. A feeling, no more than a feeling. No question, he had always got along famously with his boss, Mr. Bader, the treasurer, fa-mous-ly! Many a time they played Skat together after work. And it was this Mr. Bader whom he had heard, at ten o'clock one night, having a discussion with Thom's Uncle Paolo in his office, their voices beyond the door strangely low. As he'd said: a feeling. Instinct, and perhaps a bit of fun too, in the beginning, but gradually he, Berger, became more and more doggedly convinced and turned hunter, detective if you like! He had spent months searching, making notes, observing; made copies, put two and two together, then at some expense obtained information on this Carlos Belmondo through a bank as well as the Swiss

Embassy in Buenos Aires—always, of course, in such a way that his good friend and boss Alfred Bader was never aware of this tracking process. Gradually the little chips became a mosaic.

"To make a long story short," the giant laughed again, this time more to himself, "Señor Belmondo and Paolo Winter, together with my friend Alfred Bader, the treasurer, had had a small company registered in Lisbon. It was to this company that the second delivery of cheap milled shafts was forwarded. This tiny export firm then had the shafts carefully packed in a lot of straw in large wooden crates; that's how they were loaded onto a Portuguese freighter. On behalf of the captain and owner, the little company insured the freighter, and it also insured the freight— again with Lloyds of London; but—and this was the whole point—not as ordinary milled shafts but as high-priced fittings, for a total of 5.4 million hard Swiss francs.

"As planned, the freighter with its crew of twelve put out to sea. As planned, the freighter caught fire northeast of the Azores and, as planned, sank with the milled shafts. Still as planned, eight of the crew managed to reach shore, but, not as planned, the remaining four seamen lost their lives in the 'disaster.' A slip-up in the planning? A case of bungled arson? Lloyds started legal proceedings. There was no evidence of any irregularity in the execution of the order; no trial took place. Lloyds paid up: first the captain for his sunken, presumably overinsured, vessel, then the firm in Lisbon the insured amount of 5.4 million for freight lost at sea. I had gone to Lisbon personally—on my vacation, needless to say. I was now holding all the trump cards and could prove that this freight had consisted exclusively of milled steel shafts.

"Do you get the picture?" the old man asked. Again he blew out his clouds of steam into the sultry air. Then, he went on, he had asked Thom's father for a few minutes of his time. Upstairs in his plush executive office, Ulrich Winter was sitting behind his desk; he put down his horn-rimmed glasses and wearily leaned back. "Keep it short, Berger," he said.

So Berger the giant proceeded to lay down his cards—one at a time: Proof Number One, Proof Number Two, and so on. Thom could picture his father getting up, cigarette dangling from his lips, hands in his wide pockets, coming around the desk and starting to walk slowly up and down on the magnificent blue and red carpet. "Let's just get this straight," said Ulrich Winter quietly. "The shipment of milled shafts was paid for promptly, so the Winter Corporation suffered no loss. Further: it is

obvious that criminal offenses were committed by my brother as well as
by the treasurer of our company."

Thom's father returned to his chair. Placing his elbows on the desk,
he rested his forehead for a few seconds in his hands. "Four, did you
say? Four seamen?"

Berger replied, "That's the truth."

And Thom's father again: "Berger, you can't expect me to institute
criminal proceedings against my brother, or even to countenance them.
I thought I knew him. What do you want? What is the price of your
truth?"

So what did Berger want? Only three things. "Look, I'm thirty-four.
My friend and superior Alfred Bader turned fifty this summer. It will be
years before his job becomes vacant. What I want is to be appointed, a
year from today, treasurer of the Corporation, irrevocably for thirty-three
years. Coinciding with my appointment, Mr. Bader is to retire—on
medical advice, no problem. And in addition I have in mind that you
personally will transfer twelve common shares of the company to me
annually—you personally, Mr. Winter, as a gift and as a reward for my
silence or, if you prefer, for my services. I would expect you to hand me
the shares personally every year on New Year's Eve."

Thom's father reflected. "Didn't you, Berger, come to us as the son
of one of our unskilled laborers—how many years ago? Nineteen?" Ulrich
Winter rose. "That," he said, "is what I would call a successful career.
My compliments."

"He must have known even then," Berger said, "that from that day
forward nothing could be done in the company without my consent."
He shook with silent laughter. "And it wasn't long before people spoke
of me as the Gray Eminence.

"So that's it, then." The giant rose to his full height, frowning. "We
are agreed on the publication of the facts of this case, are we not? Together
with the other little examples I have preserved here in the file—published
in such a way that at least all the inhabitants of the city and region of
Jammers are given the opportunity to read the truth. Any problems? You
write better than I do."

On the way to the front door, Thom heard Berger saying something
behind him about instructions he had left with his lawyer: If Thom should
fail to publish this material within the year following Berger's death, the
lawyer would make the file available to three well-known journalists of

the opposition. His laugh resounded through the house again. Just in case.

At the front door Thom turned almost reluctantly. Berger looked down at him. "You don't resemble your father. But now, that expression, that mixture of courtesy and contempt—that's how he shook hands with me, all those years ago in his office."

Leafing through the Festschrift II

TO THE NATURE-WORSHIPPING EIGHTEENTH CENTURY, SWITZERLAND MUST have seemed the ideal embodiment of all nature

When a traveler from the north, inspired by Haller's poem about the Alps, approached the Jura

at the base of those heights the rolling landscape with its forests, hills, and shining rivers

a mighty overture to the vast natural spectacle of the Alps. Everything a devotee of Rousseau could dream of, here it

intoxicating symphony: romantic valleys, tranquil and bosky, glades and cliffs, picturesque meadows, mountain and plain, watered by a sparkling network of streams and rivers

and one of those was once the cradle of the Winter enterprise! At the foot of a steep limestone cliff overhanging the Aare, it stood on a flowery meadow at the edge of the forest.

Where in 1800—today many thousands are working day in day out at the twelve plants, auxiliary plants, subsidiaries, and branches, in production, planning, administration, and sales, spread throughout our land.

After returning from town, Thom walked around the house, strolling along the flagstones on the west side toward the rear; he felt like making himself a sandwich in the kitchen. Still that silence, that sultry heat, now, at five, five thirty in the afternoon. Not a leaf, not a blossom stirred among the espalier pears along the house wall. The blackbirds, and the sparrows too, had retreated into the scent of the lilac or the wistaria. They too were probably waiting for the thunderstorm. Already the clouds were massing behind the fir trees on the Gütsch hill. But the flagstones, the house wall, the branches overhead, were still dappled; the patches of sunlight barely trembled.

Just before reaching the level of one upper window, he suddenly heard Aunt Esther's voice. Unmistakable. "What do you imagine?" she exclaimed. The question was not directed at him. It came from the open window above him on the right, from the suite where Aunt Esther was no doubt sitting in her wheelchair winding a ball of wool and telling Thom's nephew Urs—it was sure to be he—about life "in the old days" or "in my time" or "when your great-grandfather said to me." Thom paused. He had to smile at the thought of the eleven-year-old boy in there, sitting on the stool by the window, turned half toward his great-aunt and half toward the glass-fronted cabinet, and saying, "Tell me, Aunt, how old are you?" She ignored the question, and although her voice was not yet trembling it did crack slightly as she exclaimed, "Heavens, child, surely I must have told you how Theophil Winter, your great-grandfather, drained the swamps and appropriated some of the land for himself and gave some of it away?" She laughed. "And how he negotiated the water rights, and how he began to raft timber from the highlands down the Aare and the Emme and soon down the Thur too? He was one of those versatile men, you see, and then in 1802 when he married the Stamm girl, the daughter of that rich miller in Hägendorf, he could afford to lend people money, at a nice rate of interest to be sure. And it was in those same early years of the last century that he began to prospect for ore, in Welschenrohr, Matzendorf, Herbetswil, and even farther down into the Delsberg basin, successfully, like others before him; he drilled horizontally into the bog iron ore seams where they rise from the valley floor into the sides of the mountains, digging his way through hupper and molasse and dogger, through keuper and bauxite, and on striking quartz sand he knew that in this area the search for bog iron ore should be left to the competition. He often laughed when he told me how the first shaft in Matzendorf collapsed and buried him with five of his men. Three bodies were recovered; Theophil and the other two managed to dig themselves out on their own. If you want to know what your great-grandfather—what am I saying, your great-great-grandfather, you're already another generation, aren't you—what he had to cope with, firedamp in the galleries and hand pumps and the earliest steam pumps, flooding in the shafts and the water power for the rock drills, then read his diary of 1812. Those were real men, you see?" she cried, "and do you know what was the only thing he still needed to really get going—do you know or don't you?"

Thom couldn't make out his nephew's murmured reply. He walked on, past the arched colored-glass window, along the terrace and into the house. As he took the loaf of bread from the cupboard and cut himself two slices on the old bread board, he could picture Aunt Esther at this moment probably puffing out the smoke of her cigarillo and telling Urs about the blast furnace, describing in great detail that first blast furnace with which his great-grandfather Theophil had laid the cornerstone of the Winter enterprise. "That was no mere child's play. People who lend money have enemies. And a man who wants to fight his way to the top needs more than brains, courage, and fists—he also needs strong nerves, strong enough to wait for the right moment, and then pounce, do you understand?

"Now at City Hall in Solothurn there were a few gentlemen who were far from pleased to see this Theophil Winter wanting to branch out into the foundry business as well. They refused Theophil what he needed, refused to grant him a permit for the blast furnace"—Aunt Esther used the French word, *concession*, and when she described the way the great- or great-great-grandfather had been none too scrupulous in going after what he needed, she laughed and snorted, so that Thom, and now more than thirty years later Urs, couldn't help laughing too. "For Theophil Winter was as smart as they come, so when the chips were down he simply went to a man called Glutz, at that time the owner of the only blast furnace in those valleys, and—through a straw man, of course— loaned him two thousand *livres suisses* for an extension of his furnace, and when that stupid fellow was in the throes of his extension, Theophil abruptly turned off the money faucet! And who was it, Thom," Aunt Esther cried, "who was it, Urs, who promptly came to the rescue and generously offered to help Glutz in his hour of need? Just listen! Theophil lent him the same two thousand *livres* that he had demanded be returned via the straw man, only that Glutz didn't know it was the same money. And only that Theophil had fifty-one percent of that blast furnace in Gänsebrunnen transferred to himself—at first as security, later perma- nently. This gave Theophil his *concession*; now the gentlemen in Solo- thurn could protest as much as they liked: he ignored it all and stayed.

None too scrupulous, to be sure, and a bit of a prankster too, why not? How else do you imagine he could have acted? With velvet gloves? And that was only the beginning."

Thom spread some soft cheese on the bread and poured himself a glass of wine. Had Herminia lain down for a nap in this thundery heat and not yet woken up? And Gret? Frieda? Perhaps they had gone into town. There was no sound, either, coming through the open kitchen window from the washhouse, where Sepp was usually pottering about at this time of day. Or had he retreated into his dovecote again?

And Aunt Esther? Was she still talking away in her suite, her wheelchair half turned toward the open window, behind the three doors between her room and himself, Thom, here at the kitchen table? Or had she, she too, even she, nodded off mid-sentence in this sultry heat, for a few seconds or longer, and Urs had to wake her if he wanted to hear more about those heroes who were his forebears: about Theophil and later about his son Elsazar, heroes before whom he could only sit and marvel, overwhelmed and at the same time avid, avid for their bold stories, genuine or embellished and tripled and unscrupulous poker moves in the power game that was unfolding with such force when she embarked on her narration? Or had Urs let her go on dozing and waited, waited, until he eventually got up and quietly left the room? Even then Aunt Esther's voice would pursue him for quite a while, through the house and through the garden; even when he sat on the Gütsch hill in the shade of the fir trees and tried, without much enthusiasm, to concentrate on his history or physics textbook, his great-great-grandfather Theophil's battle for wood for the furnaces would be there, his battle for coal, his battle for rafting rights in the Freiburg region or the Emmental valley; and her voice would be there, telling him about new blast furnaces in the Klus, at Olten, at Grenchen and Jammers, and about the ore, and in 1812 the first forge and the printed cotton factory and the hydraulic power of the River Emme—more and more new steelworks, new hammer mills, already three ore concentrators, two new forges: Frischfeuer, Gänsbrunnen, Ramiswil, Matzendorf, and constant research and calculation, development and more research, already two tons of castings a day to fill increasing demand for barrel-hoop iron from France and even England. Then in 1828 the first foundry, with Theophil Winter always out front, setting up the first rolling mill in Jammers and the fourth steam hammer, importing two hundred and fifty tons of pig iron from Rhein-Preussen because the mines in the Jura didn't yield enough, until the newly invented use of forced air in smelting improved the yield sufficiently.

But then the *récession*, then again the battles for new blast furnaces, in Winterthur, Lucerne, Schaffhausen, in 1846 the one in Choindez. Then the wrought-iron boilers and first turbines with that tremendous increase in hydraulic power; more than eleven hundred tons of rolled steel, steel rods, and nail iron, fish iron and sheets, then the takeover of the Courrendlin steelworks.

"Now the stream of people from rural areas had begun. In 1848 the news of your great- or great-great-grandfather's death traveled throughout our country, and thousands mourned. But then, compared to him, what do you think his son Elsazar was like?" Aunt Esther's eyes glowed as if they were watching the molten iron shooting in a red lava stream from the furnace gate. So back to the stream of people from the rural areas, how that stream became a flood, coming down from the upland farms and from the schoolhouses and villages and workers' barracks at 6:30 in the morning into the Winter foundries, forges, rolling mills, smelting works, into the hammer mills, the welding plants, and more and more and ever more into: machinery! The flood of the skilled and unskilled, of the old, of women and men, of children, into the fifteen-hour working day, into the Industrial Revolution.

"Do you want to hear what happened in 1832 and how we danced around the freedom poles?" Aunt Esther blew the smoke from her cigarillo toward the open window. "Or what led up to the wrecking of the machines?"

Somewhere upstairs a door was slammed. Thom stood up. Little dust devils were skipping along the gravel beyond the terrace. A rustling in the fir trees; the air suddenly darkened in the kitchen and even outside. The sound of the first heavy hailstones striking the corrugated iron roof over the woodpile; the storm was even driving the hail in under the roof of the terrace. As Thom closed the window, he could see Urs running down from the Gütsch into the shelter of the terrace.

When Thom turned around, Gret was standing in the kitchen door, once again wearing her old-fashioned long dress with the lace collar, obese, as if bloated, on her face the lopsided smile: "Oh, it's you. Now do you see what's going on here?"

Thom sat down again. "Would you like a sandwich too?" She stood at the table, swaying slightly, then picked up his full glass and drank down the wine. As she padded on into the pantry, she laughed softly and said, "Winter is early this year." Thom remembered the little family joke from the old days. He heard her move on into the Paneled Room but couldn't make out what she was muttering—partly because of the rain, still mixed with hail, lashing down outside the windows.

In the Dovecote

Sepp wouldn't have minded getting married, but should he have been satisfied with the first person to come along? Sometimes he had replied to personal ads: Vigorous fifty-year-old, or later: Vigorous sixty-year-old, if you really are a warm-hearted woman, mid-forties, in good health, and yearning for love, he and that person could arrange to meet. Sunday afternoon at four. Am tall, of robust build, and—Sepp had often written—kind-hearted and financially secure—Herminia had advised him to include that. A red carnation in his buttonhole.

But the experiences he'd had at the station buffet! Really rich! The ones who, you could tell from a mile off, were has-beens or shrews, or their hats had a veil reaching down to the chin to hide the gaps in their teeth, and actually those weren't the worst. Some looked kind of flustered. Or they just pretended to be nice, and when they mentioned their dear departed and their life as a widow, they would wipe away a tear with a dainty little handkerchief. But actually all they wanted from a man was his money. Those were the worst of all, the weepy ones. A good thing Sepp had an eye, or better still an ear, for those: when the voice was suddenly lowered and, with a greedy edge to it, asked, "And how about that financial security, Mr. Kull?" or, "I take it there's a nice little bank account behind that, am I right? Enough to fly to Mallorca and back?" and they would laugh again. Anyway, Sepp hated never knowing whether they were after the money or love.

All things considered, Lina would have been the best.

A good thing Sepp had made a list of his six points and always glanced through it before going to the station buffet wearing his carnation.

1. warm-hearted
2. good health
3. cheerful temperament

4. no yakkety-yak
5. thrifty
6. nicely plump

Warm-hearted, that she was. And Lina had had a good job at the Progress Café, with two evenings a week off. Why the devil did she have to go to America? Strictly speaking, Sepp and Lina might have been considered engaged. Though not with rings. At first, after spending that evening at the Hammer, they had met every second or third evening, in 1935. Later on, after a couple of years, not quite as often, but still every two weeks or so: Lina was kept busy in the Progress kitchen, and Sepp naturally hadn't wanted to abandon his buddies at the Waadtländer Hall. Actually, that had suited him quite nicely. But then, in the spring of '39, Lina had shown him that letter from her aunt and said, "You know what, Sepp? I'm going to America!" She had meant to stay only a year, and at first she had written him a letter every month. California, then Texas: Sepp and Herminia had looked them up on Miss Winter's globe. Boston. Lina had become the chef's right hand. And she had kept on about the drama school. At first Sepp had always replied, while he was on active service; his corporal, Kattiger—he was from Schönenwerd—had usually helped him a bit when it came to descriptions. Then, when Lina wrote about a certain William, Sepp got the message. "I believe my heart beats for him."

Lina would have done better to stay here.

Dear Sepp, William and I got married, very quietly, on Whit Saturday. I hope you will be just a little glad for me, even if you feel upset by this news. This is to tell you we are now living in Winesburg, Ohio, at 23 Sherwood Anderson Street. I am taking a typing course. I want to help William build up his career. He is taking a training course in washing machines, as a traveling salesman for the Stormy Company. Those machines, with tumble driers, are the best. Starting October 1, he will get a share of the profits. Here at the hotel I'm already helping out at the front desk. That's much more fun, of course, than being stuck all the time in the kitchen. I'm sure you'll realize that nothing's going to come of the drama school now. End of a dream. But such is life, right?

William has a great big Chevrolet, a company car, off-white. He was allowed to choose the color. A real gent.

Isn't the war in Europe and the Far East ever going to stop? William was lucky, he wasn't drafted because of his back. Weekend before last we chugged along in the Chevvy all the way to South Carolina and back.

But now we've started saving up again, our goal in life is a coin laundry. And two kids.

I still don't understand why things turned out the way they did with us two. Everything was really going fine, and those Sunday outings. And then suddenly, without our noticing, love was no longer there.

There's one thing I'd like to know. That Easter Monday, when you pushed that slip of paper under my door with "You're a ninny" on it, did you know how much it hurt me? Or did you mean it affectionately? Write and tell me how you are. Still in the army? I hope you'll soon find someone too. After all, you're not that old.

Love
Lina

And d'you want to know something else? Sometimes when I think of the Sälischlössli restaurant, my eyes begin to smart.

Nowadays Lina wrote only at Christmastime, a card from Lucerne. And Sepp had stopped even sending cards. Or maybe he might write the occasional one.

Anyway, forgetting about Lina now, Sepp could be glad he had kept to his six-point list. What good would a wife have been who might have had a cheerful disposition but threw money out the window? Or was warm-hearted but sick? Sure, there were times when he would rather be a little less lonesome. But then here in the house he was doing all right, even though Gret did let everything go to wrack and ruin. And in a pinch, he still had the pistol from the father of his late boss.

The General's Politics III

(A) THE STRATEGIC CONCEPT AT THE OUTBREAK OF WORLD WAR II. "Contingency North": Military concentrations facing North and East and, for reasons of neutrality, also West in the Jura. Operational plans?

(b) The significance of the secret alliance between General Guisan and General Gamelin, commander in chief of the French Army, as substantiated by the documents discovered at La Charité-sur-Loire.

As a preliminary: after reading (this morning) Georg Kreis's "On the Trail of La Charité," 1976, the suspicion that Major-General Lyss might have played up or overestimated this affair of the discovery from the German point of view—what reasons would he have had? Or: Kreis is playing it down? (Reasons?) From documents presently available, it seems that all I can do is follow my own assessment, which amounts to roughly a middle course between the two extremes.

1. Clarify: The legal quality of the secret military alliance with the French generals. (To what extent and in what situation was it operationally binding on both parties [also on both states] in military terms and those of international law?)

2. How the alliance came about, and what were the functions of the participating officers: the French Lieutenant-General Garteiser, the Swiss Colonel Gonard, and Major Bernard Barbey. Initial negotiations as early as mid-1939. Head of the French team: commander of the 8th Army General Besson on behalf of General Georges, member of the Supreme War Council of France. For the Swiss: General Guisan. General Besson, as commander of Army Group 3, reported directly to the supreme commander of the French Army, General Gamelin.

3. Compare the testimony of these French officers appearing before the parliamentary investigation committee in 1946/47 in Paris with documents I have on hand.

4. What military actions did the agreement provide for and at what exact juncture?

In particular: In spring 1940 five divisions stood ready in the Vesoul/Besançon area to march as agreed into Switzerland in order to support the Swiss Army in its resistance to the (anticipated) German attack. Additional units would have been brought up. Which ones? Precise march routes? Concentration and deployment areas? Emplacements of Swiss and French artillery? Chain of command? Weapons, e.g., strength of armored-vehicle units? What provisions were made for a retreat?

5. From the angle of the General's mandate (to protect the sovereignty and inviolability of the country):

How expedient was the secret alliance? No doubt it would have provided a significant reinforcement of the defense potential against a German attack; on the other hand, it might have delivered up the northwest of Switzerland to military control by a foreign power. Inviolability of the country? Ref.: Policy of the lesser evil.

Important: What (political) price might Switzerland have had to pay for this military support?

6. From the angle of the principle of neutrality: Switzerland's conception of neutrality. This requires a strictly equal arm's-length stance vis-à-vis all parties to a conflict.

Theoretically speaking, then, Guisan would have had to negotiate— if at all!—analogous alliances with France and with the German Reich covering the eventuality of war. Although he did negotiate formally with both parties, including the German Reich, he concluded an agreement with France only. In line with his defense strategy, his agreement with the Supreme Command of the French Armed Forces was without a doubt directed against an attack by Nazi Germany.

By the same token: The agreement represented a violation of the principle of equal treatment, a violation of the principle of neutrality.

Interim assessment: On the one hand, with the alliance with France General Guisan provided the rulers of the German Reich with a (doubtless welcome) pretext for an eventual military invasion of Switzerland. (Replace "pretext" by "argument"? Or by an "alibi" barely tenable in terms of international law?) By his action, he placed his country in additional jeopardy. The speculation that the German government might have advanced other arguments for an attack has little bearing on the circumstances.

On the other hand, with the agreement Guisan increased the military effectiveness of Switzerland's defense potential against the expected German attack. Thus, in line with his mandate, he organized additional "appropriate means" to protect the inviolability of Swiss territory.

On the other hand, again: The General presented France, a foreign power, with an opportunity to occupy northwest Switzerland as far east as the line Zug–Brugg–Stein am Rhein, which can be seen as a breach of his mandate.

At this point, examine the crucial question of the General's authority to conclude a military agreement. If the concluding of such an alliance lay within the scope of Guisan's authority, why did he conceal the agreement from the government, the ultimate authority? Secret diplomacy is hardly a sufficient explanation here. Obviously Guisan was aware of the risks involved in overstepping his authority as well as of the irregularity of his procedure. The logical inference is that he wished to bear sole responsibility for his action.

Quote E. Bonjour here: "One hesitates to imagine how badly things might have turned out if Guisan's projected case of Swiss-French cooperation had actually occurred" (Vol. V, p. 35 ff.). Comment: Certainly no worse than in the case of a German attack. . . .

Apparently the General overestimated the French forces and underestimated German military power. Nevertheless, even he could not have doubted the victory of German forces in the event of a German attack. He followed the doctrine: "To jack up the price for an aggressor as high as possible."

In closing *this* chapter on the General's politics, make the point: By concluding the secret alliance with France, the General put our country at great risk. The fact of the discovery of the documents at La Charité-sur-Loire—nullifying as it did their secret nature—speaks against his action. The question of whether it would have been expedient in a strategic and military sense can, scientifically speaking, remain hypothetical. As a non-strategist I must say it would not.

As a citizen of the body politic of Switzerland I must judge the alliance to be the expression of a (to say the least) high-handed and hence dangerous policy of the General's in our semidirect democracy.

P.S. Brief conversation with André on this subject. A. laughed. In the fifties, he said, he would still have welcomed the agreement, had he happened to hear of it. Today? "For years now I have favored the outlawing of all attempts at resolving conflicts by warlike action. By their very nature, generals cannot but pursue wrong politics."

Sheer coincidence that Thom opened the big wall closet in the Blue Room. He had just come in to see whether he had closed the windows properly at noon and had stood for a moment at one of the south windows looking out into the thunderstorm. The rain was still coming down in such dense sheets that the roofs and high-rises had disappeared behind the gray curtains of water being driven past from the west. Then Thom had gone to the door to turn on the light; he had stood there for a moment, wondering whether he should write to Lis or sit down in the armchair and get around to reading today's paper. His eyes fell on the blue doors of the closet beside the bed. He walked over to it.

On opening both doors he was greeted at eye level by that statue. The statue of the Madonna. Thom was taken aback. There it stood, completely unchanged, as if forty or twenty years had not passed, as if he hadn't long ago become a quite different person. There it stood, as if time were no more than a foolish invention.

Madonna and Child. The Mother of God with the serious smile on her young girl's face, sitting there, enveloped in the flowing folds of her blue gown, on the cushion supported by the two horns of the bull. Or was it the crescent moon, with its upward-curving points one on either side of the Virgin's head? A faint smell of camphor; it had obviously kept the moths away. Yes, unchanged and as if not even touched by dust, that twelve-inch figure, with Jesus cradled in her arm, sat before him, just as it had always done in the far corner of the room on the little table, probably an example of fin-de-siècle mass production, plaster, both faces brightly painted. Behind them the silver-plated aureole, as a backing: it was still there, and in it, for a second, Thom once again glimpsed the reflection of the two candles. As a boy of four or seven he had been allowed to light them when his mother knelt down at the prie-dieu facing the statuette and, together with himself, Gret, and Charlott, began to recite those fervent invocations of the Litany of Loreto—Thou Mother most pure, Thou Mother undefiled, pray for us! Thou seat of wisdom, Thou Queen of patriarchs, Thou Queen conceived without original sin, pray for us!—that, or the tenfold "Hail Mary, Mother of God, full of grace," those ten Ave Marias that together form one of the decades of the Glorious Rosary. Thom, kneeling beside his sisters on the carpet in front of their mother's prie-dieu, had kept looking into the face of our Lord and Savior's Mother as she gazed solemnly at her little Son's foot. But for a long time her eyes never turned toward Thom, much as he tried—perhaps while singing "Stella maris, hail unto Thee"—to attract her attention. From whom, if not from her, the Holy Mother of God, refuge of sinners, Queen of martyrs and Mother most chaste, could he hope for strength and grace and forgiveness for his sinful, unclean heart? Who, if not she, gate of Heaven, Queen of the seas and Virgin of all virgins—Thou tower of ivory, Thou ark of the covenant, Thou most chaste, inviolate, immaculately conceived mirror of justice and purest, thrice purest and singular vessel of devotion!—who, rather than she, could plead for mercy for him, Thom, before the throne of Christ, who had risen in the body from the dead to sit on the right hand of God the Father and judge not only the dead but all those who, like Thom, were still living?

Again and again the voice of his mother, as she knelt behind him on the prie-dieu's crimson cushion, had intoned one more Ave Maria and then another, for the children and mothers perishing that night in the war's hail of bombs, for our soldiers in the field and guarding the frontier, and yet another Hail Mary for Father, that he might at last find the strength to abandon his path of sin. Sometimes his mother's clear, dark voice would begin to tremble when, with two or three decades, she moved into the second, additional recital of the Litany of Loreto; this time he and his sisters had to pray with her that the most pure and mighty Virgin and Queen of prophets would vouchsafe her, Thom's mother, strength, the strength she needed, to snatch Father from the gates of Hell that were threatening to swallow him up. Give me the strength, O Thou Holy Mother of God! Like his mother, Thom, trembling from the shivers creeping down his spine, would burst into tears. Charlott and Gret often wept too, as did Frieda and Herminia kneeling at the very back of the room, and so once again they would all sing together, fervently and much too loud, "Morning star, hail unto Thee!" with the cry, "O Mary, help us!"

Then, on two or three occasions, it actually did happen, the thing Thom had so ardently implored: the Madonna had raised her head, very slightly, and smiled at him. He saw the Mother of God, together with her divine, immaculately conceived child, and with the red cushion, the crescent moon, and the aureole, begin to float up into the air. The walls vanished, and Thom watched, marveling, as she, blessed among women and carrying the blessed fruit of her womb, floated away over the tops of the fir trees and the roofs of Jammers, up into the firmament. Thom had to close his eyes in bliss, for she was bathed in the light of the Holy Ghost and of the myriad stars of the Almighty. Now he knew that his prayer and their joint prayers, for Father and again and again for purity, had been answered, at least for the next few nights and days.

True, the statuette there in the closet in front of him looked much smaller, much more modest than the memory of it that had now resurfaced after so many years. What did he know of the woman who had given birth to him? Of his mother's fears, her longings?

Yes, there were these shreds of memory, these fading pictures, blurring at the edges—his mother as the bright, soft, warm creature who used to carry him across the room to the white alabaster vase; who, kissing him and humming a little song, would whirl around on the terrace with him in her arms; the woman who carried him, barely two years old, up to the meadow and through the flowers; who suddenly, on hearing a cry from Gret, set him down in the grass and ran off. Or how, with measured steps, she descended the staircase from the gallery into the hall, in her long gown of blue lace with the big round collar and the satin sash, a few small blue blossoms nestling in her hair. Her radiant smile: Aren't I beautiful? And how she placed her beaver fur cape around her shoulders and, urged on by Father, formal in black jacket and striped trousers, preceded him through the front door to vanish into the dusk beyond. Or again, when she walked up the stairs from the hall, while Father and Sepp and he, Thom, ensconced behind the barricade and the gallery balustrade, helplessly watched her approach.

Thom took the blue notebook from the shelf beside the Madonna, and while he lay on the bed, propped on one elbow so he could read, the images of his mother seemed to him like miniature scrambled scenes from a badly lighted film, images that flashed into his brain, flared up for a moment, overlapped one another, and were gone. What color had his mother's eyes been? Greenish blue? Bluish brown? Even that he couldn't have said with certainty.

Lying on the bed, one knee drawn up, he opened the notebook. Unmistakably Gret's handwriting; some sentences, as well as whole paragraphs, scribbled with a ballpoint, others in pencil, certain words underlined. The title on the first page consisted merely of the word "Notes," followed by: "Our mother's perfervid Madonna cult was above all an impassioned purity cult." The word "purity" had been underlined twice.

"Mother must have been terrified of anything instinctual, especially anything sexual."

"Jammers, April 12, 1976. A visit today from my friend Margot Keller. Margot tells me that she and a woman friend, a theologian, are studying representations of the Virgin Mary for a possible connection between the Madonna and the mother goddess who, under a variety of names, was the primordial mother in all matriarchal cultures—the goddess who was 'in the beginning,' who on her own gave birth to all other deities and eventually humans as well; known by the Sumerians as Inanna, by the Babylonians as Istar, by the Egyptians as Isis and Nut, by the Celts as Dana. To the Greeks she was Demeter or Gaia."

Next, Gret had written that she had shown Margot their mother's statuette of the Madonna. Margot had been thrilled. Even in this sentimentalized representation, deriving from the nineteenth-century religious spirit—Margot said it had been copied from Dürer's "Life of the Virgin Mary"—the attribute of the ancient goddess was present, that is, the moon, or more precisely, the moon as female. According to Margot, this link between Madonna and moon turns up everywhere in portrayals of the Virgin Mary throughout the centuries, just as in ancient beliefs the mother goddesses and the moon were intimately connected—the moon representing procreation, fertility, decline, and in turn new life.

Thom read the paragraph again. He turned pages, compared dates. It seemed that in the mid-seventies there had been a period in which Gret must have made strenuous efforts to come to terms with her long-dead mother. Did Thom have any right to read the notes? Ought he to ask Gret? He went on turning the pages; after a dozen or so, the notes came to an end. The rest of the book was blank, the last entry dated September 19, 1977.

Flicking back, he happened to see the underlined question: "Did my mother have any inkling of a possible connection between her immaculate Virgin Mary and the earth goddess Gaia? I received some new material from Margot today. Exciting. It contains more about the continuing, hidden influence of the universal matriarchal experience on Christian culture, about its unconscious persistence in Marian worship. Margot calls Mary a 'goddess who has known better days, remote from earthly concerns, offered by the patriarchal church as a substitute.' Nevertheless, this image represents a continuation of the tradition of woman's primordial power in the world. Had Mother, as she prayed for support in her struggles against lust and impurity, also been entreating the Madonna to restore that ancient strength, the strength to bring her husband and her clan under her own influence? Did she really try to gain power over the Winter Corporation? What a strange wish for a woman! A woman's revenge in a patriarchate? Did she sense that such power might enable her to break out of the prison of the white man's culture? What do I know about her? She's been dead fifteen years. I'll never find out. The worst of it is, I notice that the longer I live the less I can distinguish between my personal experiences with her and what I have heard about her from others—especially from Aunt Esther. What actually did happen back then in 1952, that August night in the bathroom, after Father fell and broke his arm?

"For years now, no one in the house has been inclined to remember it—except Aunt Esther with her wicked tongue. What if things had turned out differently? In that case, would whatever it was that happened nine years later at Mother's sickbed have lost its justification? Been to no purpose? I daren't think about it!"

Thom turned over onto his back. With his hands clasped behind his head, he gazed up at the chandelier. The light of the weak bulb was reflected in the broken crystal chains surrounding it.

Here in this very bed his mother, near death, had lain just as he now lay. On the left, Gret, here—Thom could have reached out and touched his sister's cheek when he thought of how lovingly Gret had tried to persuade their mother to sip some tea; "it's soothing, you must get some sleep, you know." To the right, Thom saw himself pulling up the stool and sitting down beside the bed across from Gret—for the blink of an eyelid he saw himself lying here near death, with a terribly pale, pointed face, with *her* face, in which only the sunken eyes moved, only the eyes, to see who was still keeping her—or now him—company, knowing as she, or he, did that the coming night would probably be the last. O Maria, help us all. Barely audible, that whisper; the lips did not move.

Hadn't there been another person here in Mother's room? For a moment Thom could smell the extinguished candles on the little Madonna altar over in the corner. He had sat—how had it been?—on the right of Mother's bed, Gret on the other side, half rising as she tried, by slipping her right arm under the pillow and gently lifting it, to push another pillow underneath. Thom had stood up and, to help Gret change the pillows, leaned over Mother's face and raised her head, holding it carefully with both hands behind her ears, while the dying woman's two bright eyes stared up at him. What had there been in that look? Fear, reproach, or a question?

But then, across the room, half hidden in the shadows, to the right of the door and at an angle to the desk—yes, Aunt Esther had been sitting there in her wheelchair, watching, not speaking, not moving. She had been there, observed every movement, registered every breath, as if merely waiting for the breathing to cease.

Yes, and who else? Had anybody else been present? He had then gone across to his room. Had he tried to sleep? Is it possible that the culprit, man or woman, had entered the room in the hour after he left it? Of course, that must have been what happened—but who? Who? Once again he felt Charlott's presence as she stood in the doorway to his room, whispering that their mother was already dead.

Time
of
Blood

"But first," Aunt Esther would often say, "ten minutes of wisdom. Do you see what a whippersnapper like you has in his head? If you ever want to belong to this country's elite, Thom, if you ever want to win one of those radio contests, or if you want to achieve even half of what your forefathers did, you have no choice but to replace the straw in your head with knowledge." It sounded as if she were shouting the words out into the afternoon. "Knowledge is the first step toward wisdom. Give me the book."

She opened it again at the chronological tables but scarcely looked at them. "Have you learned the years '38 and '39 by heart? Tell me: Why did Austria want to 'go home to the Reich'? What did Neville Chamberlain declare before flying home in 1938 from the Munich conference? When exactly did Germany and Italy conclude the so-called 'steel pact'? Which film with Zarah Leander touched the hearts of women and men in Switzerland at that time? What did General Franco demand when, having won the civil war, he proclaimed himself state president of Spain? Why did Adolf Hitler found the protectorate of Bohemia and Moravia on Czechoslovakian territory? What is the title of the book by James Joyce published in Paris that same year? Who was the physicist who demonstrated what has now become the practical utilization of atomic power? And who was elected the new pope? Who were the men who stood on the Parade-Platz in Jammers singing 'Wenn wir fahren gegen Engeland'? How many kilometers of autobahn in the German Reich had been completed by then? Which world-famous psychiatrist died in London that year? Which neighboring country was invaded by German troops on September 1, 1939? And the general mobilization of the Swiss Army—when exactly was that ordered? Which of her songs did Billie Holiday record in September 1939 in New York, and who was the composer? Why were the six hundred Swiss who fought for the republic in Spain convicted in Switzerland? To how many months of imprisonment were they sentenced by our courts-martial?

"You see?" she exclaimed. "You can't answer even half! Now you take this book to bed with you tonight, read everything three times, and before you fall asleep put it under your pillow opened at the chart for 1938. And don't show your face to me again until you know it all by heart. Sound knowledge," she said, "is the first step. And what about the second step toward wisdom—what about that?"

Thom said, "Suppose I draw a line from General Guisan to the German invasion of Poland."

And she: "Wherever did you pick up *that* nonsense?"

"From you, Aunt," Thom said. Sometimes she became furious when he spoke the truth, but when she was in a good mood she laughed. "Be off with you."

And when, pausing in the doorway, he asked whether tomorrow she would tell him the story about Duce Mussolini and the hand grenade in her purse, she laughed again, laughed and said, "Only if you've learned everything by heart. Everything, understand?" And she called after him, "And where, Thom, did your father, when he was a major in the artillery, defend our country in September 1939?"

Before supper André Rupp telephoned: Would Thom like to share a bottle of wine with him at the Waadtländer Hall? "Fine then, eight thirty."

They sat in the far corner on the left and immediately began talking about the strike again. The day after tomorrow, July 1, was the date set for the new round of negotiations between the two delegations. André expected management to reject all demands outright.

"And then? What happens next?"

André looked at Thom over the rim of his glass. Then for the time being everything would remain stalled. Arbitration? "No doubt we will increase our efforts to persuade workers in other plants to go out on a sympathy strike." Who had the greater staying power? Hard to say. "You know, this sitting around, these daily rallies, the waiting—that's hard on the nerves." The fact that the workers at Jura-Metall in Solothurn had joined, and—as of today—those of the Breitenstein Corporation in Olten too, that was encouraging. But what would happen in ten, twenty days? In two months? Needless to say, management was doing its utmost to create disunity among the workers. André sipped his wine. "And then the danger of the union leaders going behind our backs—we'll have to wait and see, Thom. But how about you? What are you doing with yourself these days?" He was still puzzled as to why Thom hadn't left with Lis. There was a smile on André's face. "Have you two had a quarrel?"

"No, not that." And Thom began—to his own surprise—to tell him, hesitantly at first, about his visit to the library; about the green diary; about his vain attempts to find out anything definite from Aunt Esther and Gret.

André tamped down the tobacco in his pipe, then sucked the match flame two or three times into the bowl and blew the smoke past Thom. "Assuming that someone did kill your mother—what do you propose to do about it, today, twenty years later? Interrogate all those who were in the house at the time? Look for a motive? If you ask me, Thom—that won't bring your mother back, and even if you do succeed in clearing up the mystery, what then? Do you want to play the role of avenger? Seriously: How would that help you or anyone else?"

"To understand, at least to understand," Thom replied.

When André murmured the word "madness," it was not clear whether he meant Thom's search or the deed. Even so, for Thom just to be able to speak out here, at last talk to someone again about this— yes: madness; the sense of being liberated, briefly, while he told André how, back in 1961, he had sat beside his mother's sickbed and helped Gret push a fresh pillow under the invalid's head. On the right, back in the corner by the table with the Madonna statuette, Aunt Esther in her wheelchair, looking on silently—no, there had been no one else present.

André was thinking. The room had meanwhile filled up, and for a moment the noise of voices drowned out what André was saying. People from out of town had arrived and were celebrating with their striking fellow workers.

A woman jumped up, she must have been about forty, and called out something. She stood there, with upraised hand, her face flushed and twitching; again she asked for silence. She got nowhere. Even her two table companions, who loudly demanded that she be heard, gave up as a new crowd of customers pushed their way in from the door, waving and shouting vociferous greetings. The woman looked around. Then, suddenly making up her mind, she approached the corner table where they were both sitting and, as she came up, said through her sobs that it didn't matter how she had found out, did it, please would André also say it made no difference whatever how she had found out? Sitting down beside André on the corner bench, she gripped his arm with her right hand.

André gave a pained smile. Now would she kindly tell him what all this was about? "Come on, Monique, what's up?"

Thom realized that the glitter in her eyes, half-covered as they were by strands of hair, were tears of rage. "They've been roaring drunk since noon!" She drew avidly on her cigarette.

"You're probably right about that. But go on."

"The police," she said. Her information was absolutely reliable. The police were already in conference rehearsing their deployment. There was even a model of the plant site in the control room. This evening in Aarau they would be negotiating with the cantons of Bern, Aargau, and Zurich about reinforcements for the police, also about coordinating the possible eviction of strikers from the branch plants. At the same time a military staff had been set up to prepare for the troop deployment. "Andy, say something—" Pushing back her hair she looked at him, then at Thom and again at André.

André picked up his glass and offered it to Monique. Absentmindedly she set it down in front of her. "Every day there are phone calls back and forth between management and police. There's talk of live ammunition. People will be killed! And you two are sitting here getting plastered! As for you"—she broke off, looking at Thom. "Where did he spring from, anyway?"

André laughed. "Don't worry. A friend of mine—his name's Thomas. Thomas Winter."

She stared at Thom. "Well, I'll be—!" She whispered, "Thom?" Then she told him her name: Monique Jeheb.

No, Thom hadn't recognized her. "How long has it been? Twenty years?" They reached out past André and shook hands across the table. "What are you up to these days?" "How about you?" Monique was working in the same data-processing department as André.

André: "You're right, things are really bad. And the worst part is that it's not the first time they're making preparations to shoot at people—right here in Jammers—not the first time, and not the second. Three times in this century, Monique, even in Jammers, demonstrators or strikers have been fired on. And each time people got killed. And, just by the way, three times the management of Winter's had been among those pulling the strings." André looked at Thom. "I'm sorry, but you're aware of all that."

For a few moments there was only the din from the crowded tables. Was Thom aware? Well, yes, occasionally in the distant past, it seemed to him, he had heard about the strikes and demonstrations, about police and shooting and people getting killed, had heard from André too, long ago when they used to take those evening walks beside the Aare as far as Aarburg or Büren—surely a lifetime ago? Those clashes of which he had heard talk or rumors—certainly he knew about them, had heard about them in his student days too, of course. But he'd never let those events really touch him. Those murky stories in which Father had also been involved: apparently Thom had relegated them in his memory to the repository of Aunt Esther's stories, the place where the family history had long since mingled with legends of dim antiquity, with memories of legendary heroes, of martyrs and demons.

Behind her strands of hair Monique momentarily closed her eyes. That twitching in her face. But just because it had happened more than once in the past—the shootings, the killings—surely that didn't mean today's police preparations were any less menacing? André nodded as he drew on his pipe and carefully tamped down the glowing tobacco in the bowl—no, it was just that what had happened before might explain the seeming indifference of those at the other tables.

Did André mean, asked Thom, that those people probably suspected what Monique had been trying to tell them? That at least now, tonight, they didn't want anything to spoil their fun?

André shrugged. Maybe. But how come they'd known each other that long—where had they met?

Monique began to smile. "Is the big swing behind the house still there? Until I was twelve or fifteen my mother used to take me along when she went to visit Aunt Herminia at the Winters'—Herminia, not a real aunt, I just called her that, Aunt Herminia—"

Yes, André knew her, he still saw her sometimes, stout and amiable as ever, pulling her shopping cart behind her as she walked along in town.

"And the summerhouse," Thom said, "do you remember? And how we used to climb over the woodpile up into the loft? We would lie there in the hay, munching the bits of cake we had squirreled away in your canvas bag."

And as if he were sitting or standing beside himself, he listened to himself talking, listened to Monique. The noise from the bar seemed louder than ever, subsiding, then mounting again as Thom talked, his eyes on Monique and André, or listened to her telling André about her mother, and how in 1934 her mother and two of her socialist comrades had avoided arrest in Heidelberg by all three going to Lörrach, where Robert Kehrli, a carpenter and a socialist, had owned an allotment garden right at the border. From there he would help people on the run, members of the German Resistance, to get across the border at night. They were also brought in illegally across the Rhine, then handed on from Basel or Schaffhausen or Lake Constance to "safe houses" all over Switzerland, wherever the network reached. Even at that time, anyone in this country taking in illegals, which also meant hiding them, risked stiff fines; later, in 1936/37, imprisonment too. This Robert Kehrli, incidentally, the man who helped hundreds of people and saved the lives of many of them, was arrested while crossing the border. After being convicted by the People's Court in Berlin, he spent five years in solitary confinement in Dachau and Ludwigsburg. Gratitude, recognition, let alone a monument to the antifascist heroes in their native land of Switzerland? Not on your life!

These old stories, these eternal old stories! Thom had a feeling that he attracted them. Or that his presence here, at home, was enough to trigger them. While Monique went on talking, the thought flashed through his mind: Must he now work his way yet again through the thicket of the past and its stories? Something like despair overcame him. The futility of it all!

André's bitter smile. "After all, Hitler, and everything that went with him, did guarantee war against the Leftist revolution, against the Bolsheviks and anarchists, so that many of those in power in our country were not particularly worried about him. On the contrary. And the order books continued to fill up."

Monique: "So my mother and her two companions turned up illegally here in Jammers. For a time they were hidden by one of the Winter foremen and his wife, Mrs. Strub, who was a sister of Herminia's, who in turn had been cook in your family for scarcely six months.

"A few days later Kehrli and his people brought seven more illegals across the border and then five more. Strub's home, even including the cellar, couldn't take them all, so Margot and Isidor Strub consulted with Herminia. The upshot was that the Germans—three women and twelve men—were given shelter in three rooms in the stables of the Winter villa, provided with straw and blankets, and fed by Herminia, her sister, and four or five other people here in town. Sepp is said to have tolerated the billeting in the barn without protest.

"And you know," Monique laughed, "Herminia used to go twice a day to the stables and try to teach the refugees enough Swiss German so that, if they should ever have to move around in public on their own and want to order a glass of beer or a cup of coffee, they wouldn't immediately stand out as Germans."

While Monique went on talking, Thom could picture his father coming home late one evening, getting out of his car, and glimpsing the light of a lamp in one of the stable windows. He walked across, listened, heard voices inside, flung open the door, switched on the light. There they lay in their blankets, on the straw, a few of the men sitting on crates and playing cards in the shaded light of the stable lantern. Ulrich Winter was not easily disconcerted, but now he gaped, and his amazement grew as he persisted in his interrogation until he found out where they came from and why, why here, and who had put them up in the stables.

Then he yelled. He ordered them to pack up their stuff and get out, "right now." A minute later he was up at the house, standing in the hall—still in his hat and coat—calling up through the gallery for Herminia, for Sepp, for his wife. "Herminia sobbed out her confession. You must realize she was about twenty-five at the time, no more; there she stood, in tears.

" 'Communists!' he shouted. 'Or Jews, or both! And right here, in my stables!'

"But these people were refugees, he was told. Across the border in Germany they were threatened by concentration camp or even a firing squad.

" 'Atrocity propaganda!' Even if that were true, there were probably good reasons for it. 'And you, Lilly,' he asked, 'did you know about those people in the stables?'

"Herminia hastened to say that she had told Mrs. Winter nothing. Thom's mother spoke very calmly, as she always did when his father was in a rage. It was true, she said, Herminia really had told her nothing, but yes, she had known about it. Even about that night three weeks ago when those people moved in.

" 'Are you all pretending to have gone mad? Here we are, still negotiating for contracts worth millions, the company is finally out of the red—and you three? What do you think will happen if the delegation from Berlin now negotiating in Switzerland hears that the head of Winter's is harboring Communists and Jews? Herminia, go and pack your things and—out with you!' And to Thom's mother, 'You and I will have a word later!' whereupon he walked back to the stables again, this time accompanied by Sepp."

By now the Waadtländer Hall was half empty, and Thom became aware of the quietness. He knew that the story didn't end here. The strange thing was that as Monique went on telling it, he wished he could have tuned out. There she was again, his mother, unbending, saintly. "Thom, it is our duty to set an example! A Christian duty!" There she was, the woman who unswervingly, yes, relentlessly pursued her own path, she who had borne him and brought him up and, with her implacable virtue of brotherly love, her vaunted humility, had consistently awed, tyrannized, and humiliated the whole household. Weakness? She had never permitted any in herself, or only when she had one of her migraines. Then she would lie mutely on her bed, or kneel before the candlelit Madonna, tearfully beseeching her to give her strength. Strength and, if need be, ruthlessness, even toward herself. And steadfastness, that above all!

Yes, that had been another of Mother's great performances. Without a word the refugees had calmly gathered up their belongings, dressed, and folded the blankets, while Ulrich Winter paced up and down in front of the stables. Sepp had lighted two lanterns outside.

"Then she made her appearance. With her beaver cape around her shoulders, and carrying her suitcase, Lilly Winter stepped into the cone of light, stopped, looked over at her husband, and said, as if remarking on the chill of this November night, 'You know, I've been thinking—it will be best if I go with them.' Then, in her boots, she strode up to the stable door where she said in a loud voice, 'Good evening! I will accompany you. I am sure we will find something. I am Mrs. Winter.' She leaned against the door and waited." Thom was tempted to get up from the table and leave. Monique was radiant, as if recounting a miracle. "Fantastic, Andy, isn't it?" André nodded.

"And then what happened?"

"Her husband must have stared at her. He must have made a couple of false starts before saying, 'You will kindly come back to the house with me, immediately.' She turned her face, merely looked at him.

"And he, suddenly so that everyone could hear: 'For Christ's sake, who's supposed to give orders around here, anyway?'

" 'Orders?' she said. 'Why, you, Ulrich!' "

Thom closed his eyes. "Monique, don't go on." Wearily he said, "You've made a saint out of her. With all her wonderful, appealing, patronizing charity, she could also, when occasion required, be utterly unscrupulous."

"Thom," said André, "why not let her go on? She must have heard the story from her mother, who was there after all. I'd really like to know what happened."

"It's possible, of course"—Monique looked across—"that the people there exaggerated the role of your mother that night in 1934. All I know is that their eyes shone, yes, my mother's too, when she described how your father passed his hand across his brow and walked off into the darkness toward the house.

"And she, Mrs. Winter, gave instructions, not orders, for the people to creep back into their straw at least for that night. And after wishing everyone good-night, she took Herminia straight back into the house."

"Yes, Monique, I know, and no doubt she slept in her boots on the chaise longue upstairs in the drawing room. And once again will have savored her power."

He stood up. "What's the matter?" Monique said. "After all, it meant that my mother and her companions were able to stay on another three whole weeks in a safe place—doesn't that count for something? Stay there before they moved on and went into hiding, in Bern or Zurich, or crossed the border into France. My mother stayed on at the Winters' for another six months, as a kind of kitchen help and maid, before meeting the man, Viktor Jeheb, who then became my father."

Thom turned to leave. "Take care," he said.

                                                        Jammers, June 29, 1982

Dear Lis,

Since I wrote this salutation, five minutes have passed. Not wanting to start by complaining that there's been no letter from you today, I have been sitting here looking for an opening sentence that would convey to you only the happiness I feel whenever I think of you, during the daytime too.

Meanwhile, something totally ridiculous has happened. You can tell from my handwriting that I'm still trembling. I was seized by an unaccountable fit of fury. Till a few minutes ago I was calm; I was still looking forward to this conversation—albeit pretty much of a mono-logue—with you, still wondering how to begin, and I suddenly remem-bered my mother's Madonna statuette that I had rediscovered this evening in the closet across the room. It reminded me—as gradually everything in this house does—of my childhood, of the countless evening prayers I had to recite before it with Mother and my sisters. So now, as I was about to start this letter, I suddenly sensed its presence. Don't think I'm crazy, but I had a downright physical sense of its being there, behind the closet door, and its very existence was enough for me to feel, as I sat here, an onrush, a torrent, of all those smells and fragmented images and words, of figures from the past, especially that of my mother, of the contradictory feelings that Mother and all the others aroused in me.

Lis, try to understand: Throughout the past two days, and again today, I have been finding myself more and more caught up in this vortex, or rather in this chaos of fragments issuing from a memory ma-chine that, it seems, I can no longer slow down, even now when I want to talk to you. After a few unsuccessful attempts at concentrating on my letter, I got up, still hardly more than annoyed, went over to the closet—quite aware, incidentally, of the somewhat childish nature of my action—took out the foot-high plaster Madonna and Child and brass aureole, and carried the statuette out into the gallery, intending to place it on the high sideboard. While I was still walking, and before I reached the sideboard, that fury exploded in me. Three more steps, and I was at the gallery balustrade. With both hands I lifted the Madonna over my head and—perhaps you'll laugh, perhaps you'll be shocked—hurled it over the balustrade down into the hall. It shattered on the tiles down there in the dark. Breathing heavily, I returned to the desk. And at the moment I have no desire to fathom what went on in me. I want to write now. Write to you.

Enough of that. How odd: here I am, normally a fairly active person, spending my days in idleness, doing an occasional bit of work at this desk or going for a short ramble. And this evening I also met Andy in the Waadtländer Hall and told him about my search. He doesn't see much point to it. He's right! An hour ago, on my way home, I was tempted to send you a telegram: Am dropping everything here taking early train to Saint-Rémy. Long live life! The sun! Your lovesick Thom.

It's probably true. As I entered the house I thought, What am I doing amid all this decay, this gloomy silence? All living things were by now fast asleep—except for my taciturn brother-in-law, whom I discovered in his study, to the left of the front door, absorbed in his papers. Do you know what he is doing—secretly, so it seems? He is drawing plans, calculations litter his desk, my sudden appearance obviously embarrassed him: he is figuring out the cost of a complete renovation of the house. The additions, even the tower, are to be demolished, and everything is to be restored to its original state. He hastened to assure me that he was still toying with these ideas, that everything was still at the preplanning stage. Still, a bit nutty, the whole idea, wouldn't you say? Ah well, everyone to his own obsession!

My own obviously consists in my inability, in spite of all my longing for you, to detach myself from the spell of history to which I have succumbed here. It consists, in this particular case, in my being obsessed, obsessed with the idea of wanting to know. André asked, "How will the truth help you?" I could only say, "I want to understand; at least to understand."

My catastrophic error: As recently as five days ago, after the first shock, I was convinced that with a good nose, my powers of recollection, a knowledge of human nature, and my talent for piecing together, I would have no trouble in quickly hitting upon the truth. Today? I am paralyzed. Literally not a glimmer of truth.

One day when I was six years old my playmates and I ventured out of the house late one morning to go down into the Old Town. Between the buildings on the Outer Ring I suddenly saw, quite close, the Winter smokestacks. So, instead of searching all by myself, in that heat, for the wearisome way back, I headed for the plant, hoping to get a ride home with Father in his car. After half an hour I finally reached the plant, saw Father's black Citroën—or was it the red Fiat?—in the garage, and in my short pants rode up in the elevator to the management floor. Here Miss Hoffmann, eager as ever to be helpful, right away brought me some apple juice. Yes, Father was there, though at the moment over in the rolling mill. Did I wish to wait? I decided to go and look for him. How surprised he would be to see me—You came to the plant all on your own? You found me here all on your own?

In those days the administration building was attached to the foundry. After finally managing to pull open the connecting steel door, I found myself on the observation platform high up in the foundry hall. The mixture of heat and noise almost bowled me over, but the explorer's pride and my eagerness for this test of courage outweighed the temptation to run back. Far below were the three furnaces, one of them spewing out a red-hot stream of molten iron. Just beneath me, hoppers hanging from rails and filled with ore rumbled past. In some trepidation I walked down the steep iron stairs to the grating of the lower platform, and from there down onto the concrete floor. And off I marched, my heart in my mouth, my hands over my ears, straight ahead to the narrow lane, barely six feet wide, between all those noisy flywheels, wheezing bellows, transmission belts, ventilation ducts, and hammering pistons, past the foundry workers in their black mechanic's overalls and with goggles on their sooty faces. I gave a start when one of them grabbed me by the shoulder, when another one bent down and shouted something that, even without my hands over my ears, I couldn't understand, with all that screeching, hissing, and hammering around me.

Then I began to run, paused at the next crossing, turned right; somewhere ahead must surely be the yard with the loading ramp, and from there it was no distance to the rolling mill. On I ran, then turning left, past the huge furnace, past blinking lights, across the tracks for transporting coal, but hadn't I just been here, or was it over there? I ran, and the combination of terror and heat, plus the dust, brought a rush of tears to my eyes. I ran, I wanted to get out into the open, that was all, outside. I trotted, I raced, doubled back as far as the next crossing, past pounding cooling-water pumps, past glowing slag buckets, ran on, halted, I knew I'd been here before, under that huge, noisily vibrating feeding hopper. Back again, back toward the blinking lights, toward the sooty men and past them.

Don't ask me, Lis, how long this went on. I found myself in another building; the noise had suddenly ceased. Endless piles of strangely contorted tubes and turbines surrounded me; here all was quiet, not a soul in sight, I felt as if beleaguered by horribly misshapen giant lizards in a dark purgatory. The floor a puddle, with the black oak supporting beams growing out of its black water. A blow on my forehead, a stab of pain, put an end to my flight through the world of machines. I fell down.

When I came to, my father's face was bending over me, his little mustache, his searching eyes above the conspicuous dark pouches. I was lying on the sofa in his office, a gash on the left side of my forehead.

I suppose part of growing up is that, when you come to after a fainting spell, you don't find a father leaning over you whom you can hug. And you, my darling, are too far away. Why, I wonder, did I want to tell you this story from my childhood? Anyway, there must be a reason why I thought of it twice today. No, I am not running, I am walking about, with a feeling of going around in a circle. Then again I find myself standing at a point where seven or ten or more paths lead away from me, and I am incapable of deciding which direction to take. Yes, as if mentally paralyzed. At the moment, all I know is that if I give up now I shall have suffered a lifelong defeat by this compulsion, by this need to search for the answer to the question that is spurring me on. I know you understand.

My recollection of that flight through the machinery halls has re-awakened a picture in me, a different, more terrible one that—and I'm sure this is no coincidence—has begun haunting my dreams again. It has pursued me since I was fifteen. A part-time worker was cleaning one of the cogwheels, and in order to start the chain running over the wheels he switched on the motor. In doing so he caught his arm in the mechanism of chain and cogwheels, couldn't free himself, was dragged back to the flywheel, seized by the wheel—that twenty-three-foot wheel—and lifted up; he hung on with his right hand and his legs, thus revolving with the wheel, his screams unheard in the din of the hall, up and down, up again, was swung around three times, four times, until, with only one arm, one leg, the rest of his bones broken, he fell from the giant wheel and lay on the floor.

As I pictured that man being swung through space by the wheel, I suddenly had to think of my clan—generation after generation, the Winters founded the works, built them, expanded them, with driving energy but also driven, created this work of art of the steel and machinery industry, a monumental, flexible sculpture that now reaches into the clouds and darkens the sun over the local landscape. At its heart: progress—the Great Flywheel, whose turning has long since been governed by the law of profit. God knows they all profited from it, Theophil Winter, Elsazar, Ulrich, except that for a long time they failed to perceive that this machine they were steering and constantly expanding was actually driving and steering them, lifting them up and down and up again, as time went on. Perhaps my father was the first to feel dizzy on becoming aware that he, as steersman, was himself being steered—chained, with no possibility of ever freeing himself, to the wheel that swung and turned him and all those who depended on him, up and down and into destruction. Look at him; look at them all: Uncle Ludwig, Aunt Esther, look at my mother, power-obsessed and irreproachably noble, inhumanly saintly. Or Uncle Paul, and somewhere the specter of that murder is still haunting our history.

Or Gret? By noon she has already drunk her three doubles. And then there is myself—for the time being paralyzed. Sometimes I think that the fact that we were all, directly or indirectly, bound to the wheel of those plants has put its stamp on everything in our lives: our upbringing, our goals, our way of loving, seeing, thinking, not to mention our actions.

How quiet it is now, one A.M. I can hear the rain outside the open window, gently pattering on the leaves—after a violent lightning and hail storm. Will the thunderstorm return toward morning? At last it's cooled off. From time to time a moth swerves in and flutters around my desk lamp. I watch it crawl away, exhausted, into the pattern of the curtain. I expect you are fast asleep in your oversize bed. Or are you also sitting there writing, writing to me and telling me about your day? At dinner tonight on the covered terrace of your hotel you were doubtless unable to avoid the invitation of that nice couple from Denmark, probably on their honeymoon, who spoke to you from the next table; you joined them on a walk through the little town and then, sitting in a wicker chair at Silvio's Bar, discovered how pleasant it is to chat with those bronzed Swedes and Norwegians. Or at the swimming pool today—or on a bus trip to Lacoste and Gordes—you arranged to have a candlelit dinner with the intelligent wife of an architect from Le Havre, at one of the elegant restaurants above Saint-Rémy, and the pale lawyer from Lyon and his sporty, amiable friend, sure to be called Henri or Lucien, invited you both onto the dance floor to the music of the Spanish cha-cha-cha trio with Hammond organ, so at the moment you are a moth-woman of the night . . . ?

How much do I know about you, dearest Lis? For me you are still a creature coming from far away. From a history that, in this century alone, has been dramatically ruptured three or four times; from a Germany that has been plowed up three times, bombed to bits, split in two and occupied, vanquished, leaving the grim memory of the time of delusions: the delusion of national honor, the Führer principle, of blood, race, and world salvation. Yes, you and I: despite our languages being so closely related, we are the products of two totally dissimilar histories. Think only of childhood—that of your parents, my parents, my childhood and yours. If I imagine myself having been born, like you, in 1943 in Chemnitz, into a Lutheran background, at a time of almost nightly air-raid alarms, of the incipient collapse of the Third Reich; if I imagine that my father, a teacher, had been killed in Poland or Norway or Africa as a captain in the artillery; that in the days of coal pilfering and black markets my mother and I had traveled through the ruins of cities to Munich and that later, aged seven, I had ended up with relatives in Andernach am Rhein, surrounded and brought up by adults who, as both victims and perpetrators, had to forget what their former life had been—how and what would I dream, how and what would I think, feel, do? How would I see myself?

Contrast with those imaginary early experiences my actual child-hood, here in Jammers, in a small state made up of small states, for almost two hundred years without war; no empire, no First World War, no Thousand Year Reich, no national collapse. A childhood in this house here in its own grounds, with the stables, the orchard beyond, the wash-house, in the general history of this country of Switzerland with its leisurely developments, its unbroken traditions, even those that may be crazy or lethal. Although that is far from being everything that put its imprint on us, we, Lis, are the products of two worlds. The similarity of the language—and even that is merely superficial—is deceptive. We belong to two profoundly dissimilar cultures.

I believe that our only chance of staying close to one another for a long time will be if we bear this in mind, don't you agree? So, once again—how much do I know about you?

During the night just past there were more intermittent thunder-storms. At one point I was suddenly roused by the windows banging and bluish sheet lightning flickering through the room, so I had to get up and close the window. Immediately I lapsed back into dreams of which I remember only that I was crawling, climbing through shafts, through an endless system of shafts, chimneys, sewers under the town. I woke up, exhausted by fear. Even now, as I sit at the desk, a cup of coffee in front of me—it is not quite ten A.M.—this vague but ghastly fear has not quite left me, even though the leaves outside are now gleaming as if cleansed in all that sunshine.

The reason I am telling you all these details is not merely to describe how I spend my days. I think I am also trying to put off what I still have to tell you—I don't know whether I should laugh about it or yield to the temptation to let it drive me mad. What do you say to the following:

Just before nine I went down to the kitchen to make myself some coffee. You know my niece Barbara. Today she was not in school, as she normally is at that hour, but sitting at the table in the pantry, as if waiting for me. Without preamble, in a despondent voice, she began to speak. We were alone, by the way; Sepp and Herminia could be heard from the washhouse, engaged in some little argument.

Barbara told me that because of what happened she had hardly slept. And went on to say that she had been with Aunt Esther late yesterday afternoon: "You know her stories, Uncle—yesterday she was in especially good form. Or should I say, especially wicked? First she carried on at great length about one of those strikes at the plant, and how your father, standing outside on the steps, spoke to the thousand men who had entered the grounds. You've heard all that. But then suddenly she started talking about your mother. I know Aunt Esther didn't like her, but now I believe she hated her. What do you think?"

That was my impression too, I told her, or perhaps one should say she loved her brother, my father, more than anything in the world.

Barbara hesitated. "Then she went on to tell the bathroom story again. I told her I didn't wish to hear about those terrible things any more, but she just laughed."

"I know," I said. "She's relentless that way. The first time she told me—I was about fourteen—'You should know, Thom, that your mother Lilly is the person who has my brother Ulrich on her conscience,' I began to cry, and I yelled at her, 'Take that back this instant!' Frieda stopped me from going at her with my fists. But that time too, Aunt Esther just laughed when I ran out of the room and upstairs to my mother. After a dramatic confrontation between the two women, Mother wanted to forbid Aunt Esther the house. Aunt Esther threatened to publicize the whole story. There were few things Mother shrank from as much as being talked about in public. Besides—there was, after all, Aunt Esther's vested domiciliary right. So Aunt Esther came out the winner. However, from that day on until after Mother's death she never again appeared at table in the Paneled Room. She did not give up making her terrible accusations; at best she formulated them somewhat more indirectly, by hints such as 'You know how my poor brother met his death,' or 'Let us for a moment forget what happened in those fifteen minutes behind the locked bathroom door: let God be the judge.' And somehow she succeeded. Although I have always refused to believe the bathroom story, such phrases as 'You know what a woman's eyes are capable of' have pursued me to this day.

Oh yes, she dripped her venom aimed at my mother so carefully and persistently into me that there were at least times when I began to believe that Mother had systematically driven my father to drink and eventually to his death."

Barbara looked at me. "Uncle, is there any chance that you too hated your mother?"

An odd question, wasn't it? Can one in this case make a neat distinction between no and yes? We are supposed to love our parents. Any other emotions that might exist are kept locked, in me too I suppose, behind armor-plated doors.

And Barbara again, with her solemn brown eyes: "But might it be that Aunt Esther had tried to incite me with her stories, to make me her ally in her war against her sister-in-law? Perhaps even her tool, her weapon?"

What should I have said? Aunt Esther has always been a woman full of contradictions, eccentric, a bit sinister too. In any case, she succeeded in binding me to her with her ever-new outlandish inventions.

"Yesterday," Barbara continued, "she told me about your mother's death—she laughed—something about a pillow—and 'Thomas,' she said, 'ask him, child, if you want to know how her unnatural death came about before she had properly begun to die.' She laughed. 'Thomas, *he* knows about it.' It wasn't until I had left the room," Barbara said, "that it dawned on me: That's monstrous, that sounds as if you—" Barbara fell silent.

Can you imagine, Lis dearest, how I felt? Like yelling? Laughing? Yielding to madness? Rushing across to the old woman and grabbing her by the throat? Dear Barbara. I could understand her bewilderment. "Now listen," I said, and I told her everything—about our arrival here, about the entry in Aunt Esther's diary, what it set off in me, and about my search ever since. And now this: myself as the one I'm looking for? A ghastly joke—no, not a lie, the insane cannot lie—let us call it rather the macabre notion of a woman whose mind has been corroded by age and hatred and evil fantasy. Then Barbara saw the whole thing in that light too. Poor old woman, damage to her faculties now increasingly affecting her—what else can we do, as long as she's still with us, but let her be, and in her confusion and malice, go on spreading her dangerous, scandalous stories? What do you think, Lis? Of course I'll have another try at catching Aunt Esther at a lucid moment, so as to have a very serious talk with her. Is there a hope? What can be going on in that brain, that heart? Is her hatred of my mother now also being aimed at me, the son? I am at a complete loss.

Dearest Lis, what do you say now?

By the way, I was up at six this morning, took broom and shovel from the closet downstairs by the kitchen door, and swept up the broken pieces of the Madonna with Child, then tipped all the debris into the garbage can. The only thing I brought upstairs with me is the metal crescent moon. It is lying here on the desk—it will be useful for opening what I hope will be your numerous letters.

I must hurry to catch the mail. More tomorrow.

I hold you close and kiss you.

Your Thom

In Those Days

WHO IN THIS HOUSE CAN REMEMBER HERMINIA'S PREDECESSOR IN THE kitchen? Thom had never known her. In 1934 Käthe Zandl, from the Tirol, had given notice without stating a reason, and, at the age of forty-two, returned to her native Austria. Nothing had been heard of her since.

Mother, of course, as well as Father and Grandmother Helen and Aunt Esther, Uncle Ludwig, or Sepp, would each have had little stories to tell about her. For instance, how at Christmas she used to weep in front of the Christmas tree; how she was scared almost to death when—in 1931 or '32—an infantry unit headed by six drummers marched smartly up from the town and past the box hedge below. That whenever Father, for whatever reason, lost his temper in the Paneled Room or the hall, she would immediately drop everything and silently disappear into her attic room. She couldn't stand men who shouted, just couldn't stand them.

In Switzerland toward the end of the 1920s there were still, unlike in Austria, well-paying positions for cooks in private houses. About one hundred eighty francs a month plus board and lodging. Käthe had an illegitimate son, Aloys, so her salary was only one hundred fifty francs, but she had managed to obtain permission for Aloys to study theology at Innsbruck, the expense of which was borne by the bishopric of Innsbruck. Furthermore, Mrs. Winter, since they were about the same size, once gave her a silk blouse she no longer wore, and later a navy-blue winter coat that showed no signs of wear. At Christmas she was given an extra fifty francs.

Still, she was described as having been tall, gaunt, somewhat re-served, but with a kind heart. Every beggar who came to the door received something from the small change in the kitchen. And she could sing, she really could: especially when she sang "Tirol, Tirol, Tirol, you are my native land, o'er every hill and dale," everyone in the house was touched.

Tall, gaunt, a kind heart, a good cook. Quince jelly was one of her specialties. Anything else? What else would there be to tell about her? And that she could sing—but only when she was alone in the kitchen; then in her strong contralto voice she would sing "Tirol," or "Captive in the Moorish desert," and at the part about the swallows flying home again her voice would suddenly break off.

Did Käthe listen at the pantry door to the Paneled Room when there were guests? When there was talk in 1929 about inflation, unemploy-ment, and between 1930 and '35 about the crisis in the Swiss machine-building industry? Or when Father's first wife, Hortense Winter, died? When Father told his sister Esther about his forthcoming engagement to Lilly Schaub, daughter of the comb baron?

Wash the quinces; slice thinly, unpeeled, cover with water, and cook slowly until fruit is soft. Strain juice through a cloth and boil with sugar, using 850 grams of sugar to one liter of juice. When juice begins to jell and a drop barely slides from side of spoon, skim off any froth, pour hot jelly into jars, and seal. When it came to sealing the jars, Grandma Helen is said to have insisted on using pig's bladder skin, while Käthe preferred the modern method of melted paraffin wax, metal clamps, and rubber ring. We no longer know how the argument was resolved, but the fact remains that Herminia later used the good Swiss method of sulfur and pig's bladder.

Cooking time: 5 to 10 minutes. Use remaining fruit pulp to make quince jam (see Quince Jam).

Was that Käthe Zandl's life in Switzerland? A few fragments in the memory of those who have now died with them? Is she still alive? Does she still remember the big, dark house, the comings and goings there, and how, when there was a change in the weather, the faucet over the kitchen sink would suddenly start to drip? Remember the happy hours that once every three weeks she was allowed to spend on Sunday afternoons at the domestic servants' club down in the town? Or the festive atmosphere in the house after Adolf Hitler won the election in that neighboring country to the north—Hitler who was, after all, a Catholic and an instrument of Providence? Did Käthe still harbor a secret love for the man who had fathered her illegitimate son? Who or what—apart from the land of Tirol—might have been the object of her hopes, her secret longings?

After allowing the jelly to cool in the jars, cover with a thin layer of melted paraffin wax and seal.

Mark jars with crayon and store in a dry, cool, dark place.

Tall, gaunt. Somewhat reserved. A kind heart, a good cook, a good contralto voice. She gave notice without stating a reason. In 1934, after being employed for eight years, she left Switzerland.

As Thomas Winter was sipping his morning coffee, Herminia came into the pantry and placed the newspaper beside him. What did he think would happen? She sat down across from him with her cup. He saw the bold headline: "Negotiations! End of strike?" and picked up the paper.

"At 3 P.M. today, delegations from the Winter Corporation management and the trade union are meeting for a first round of negotiations. The object, as announced, is to find a way out of the situation created by the workers' strike. The corporation's spokesman, Mr. Felix Aufdermauer, emphasized that, although the management of Winter Holdings foresees no possibility of departing from the plans for reconstruction as already announced, the details of a social plan for those affected are to be discussed."

What will happen? Thom looked up. "What do you think, Herminia? Who will have the greater staying power? Who will have the stronger—economic—arguments? Will it come to an occupation of the plants?"

Her sister Margot, said Herminia, was inclined to be pessimistic. It was, of course, wonderful that after forty-five years of "labor peace" the workers had rediscovered the old, the only effective weapon—the strike; she hadn't expected that at all. "But Margot also says, 'If necessary they will call in the police, or even the army. And we know what will happen then, remembering the strikes of the dyers, of the mechanics, and the general strike of 1918.' "

She is probably right. Thom read the report through a second time.
Presumably the union would try at least to extend the period of adjustment
to the new technology to ten or twelve years, while at the same time
demanding concomitant measures—early retirement, retraining programs, possibly work programs undertaken by the town, the canton, and
the federation. In addition, a phased reduction of work hours—it was
unlikely, in André's opinion too, that more could be achieved. The bad
part: in other industries, watchmaking for instance, similar reductions in
the work forces were under way.

They sat there silently. Thom skimmed through the rest of the paper
as he sipped his coffee.

Beirut. The leaders of the P.L.O. (Palestine Liberation Organization) are said to be prepared to withdraw their 8,000 fighters from the
Lebanese capital, regardless of their declared intention of fighting to the
death. The question was, as stated by . . . , where to

Visas required for Turks. Federal Councillor Furgler justified the
measure by citing the increase in illegal labor and the abuse of the right
to asylum . . . eventually to benefit genuine refugees

Terrorist extradited to Germany. Gabriele Köcher, the terrorist being
held in a prison in Canton Bern, is to be extradited to the Federal Republic
of Germany at that country's request. This decision was taken by the
Federal Court in Lausanne.

Start of race in Basel. With 170 cyclists, the Tour de France boasts
a record number of participants. Top favorite is, of course, Bernard
Hinault. For the first time

Warsaw. Jaruzelski in the crossfire of forces . . . curfew to be lifted
. . . demonstrations . . . in support of the banned "Solidarity" union as
well as the release of

Reinforcements for cantonal police. Following the swearing-in ceremony, one woman police officer and eighteen police candidates were
inducted into the Solothurn cantonal police. After a year of intensive
training . . . the great, the long-awaited moment . . . musical offerings
highlighted the ceremony in the Old Arsenal

On the page headed "Jammers City News," he studied the photograph showing a wide expanse of meadows dotted with shrubs and clumps
of reeds between grassy patches with wild flowers. The caption read: *Once
a rich biotope, today a desert.*

As he ate his bread, Thom drew the page closer. Surely that looked
familiar? Those were the meadows close by the River Aare, on the border

between Luterbach and Jammers. What did it mean, "today a desert"?

The article didn't take long to read. The background: The meadows were owned by Pharmacom, a subsidiary of Winter Holdings Incorporated. In the spring of 1981 Pharmacom (which also produces artificial fertilizer) had applied for a permit to build a factory and warehouse complex. In opposition to this plan, the community of Luterbach, in conjunction with the Solothurn Nature Preserve Association, had filed a protest with the cantonal government. Their argument was that the (unzoned) area, covering roughly half a square kilometer, represented an important recreational site and, in particular, a natural biotope unusually rich in small game and species of birds and butterflies; it should be declared a nature preserve. Application and objection were currently pending.

Subcaption: Pharmacom not squeamish.

Yesterday members of the Nature Preserve Association discovered that every shrub, clump of reeds, and grassy patch is now completely withered. Those plants that are still standing have been hit by a kind of blight. The ground is littered with dead birds, rabbits, and butterflies. There are no signs of live insects or worms. The biotope has turned into a desert. There can be no doubt that the area has recently been sprayed with poison. On being questioned by this newspaper, a company spokesperson responded with the single sentence: "The spraying of an area by its owner is not a criminal offense."

Thom put down the newspaper. Had Herminia seen this, he asked, pointing to what he had just read?

He couldn't take it. This day-after-day misery. Day after day? He couldn't even summon up indignation. Whatever was compelling him to stay on in this house seemed to have taken possession of him so completely that any new information that reached him was instantaneously rejected by his skin.

He finished his coffee. As he got up and walked to the door he heard Herminia mutter, "Shocking!" She was still reading. Then she looked up. "Can you believe it! That would never have happened while Mr. Winter was still alive!"

Thom was already in the doorway when he said over his shoulder, "Are you so sure?"

•

*   *   *

Perhaps it was because, for the first time during these last few days, he had once again noticed the old crucifix with the gilt body of the crucified Savior in the Paneled Room. Here from time to time, for as long as it took to recite seven or twelve Hail Marys, he had had to kneel and do penance for some sin or other—a penance that, at the age of eight or even fourteen, he had sometimes imposed upon himself.

Or was it merely because of the feeling, as he was about to go up the stairs, that momentarily, here on the landing in the curve of the staircase, there had been a smell of candles—who in this house, where the temperature was again approaching thirty degrees Centigrade, would have wanted to light candles?

Or had it been nothing more than Barbara's voice, that call sounding through the open front door, the words indistinct, just the high voice of the seventeen-year-old calling up from the driveway to one of the windows, directed at someone or other, and the way it reminded him of his sister Charlott: Charlott's furious expression, the fearful and accusing look, as she stood on the parapet of the Old Bridge, balancing high above the water, already nineteen, in her light, perhaps flowered, full-skirted summer dress, perhaps with puff sleeves, calling down to him, "I'll jump! I'll jump from the bridge, and when I'm dead it'll be your fault!" She called down, "Either you promise me not to go there this evening, not to go to that woman, or I'll jump! Now: will you promise?"

But whether it was the crucified Christ or the smell of candles or Barbara's voice or perhaps only the notch or little dent in the worn banister that he now, leaning lightly on it, felt under his middle finger: one or the other and everything together carried him back to that summer day, a Friday, carried him back into the dim light of Saint Sebastian's Church, into the confessional, found him in the swimming pool, everything almost simultaneously during the ten seconds or so it took to get from here on the landing in the curve of the staircase over the nine remaining stairs all the way up to the gallery—here, and there, and under the branches of the wild cherry tree beside the Aare in the dark with that woman and at almost the same time on the Old Bridge with Charlott and here on the stairs, on his way up, with the smell, no doubt imaginary, of candles.

How could he have known at that time what was going on between Charlott and the woman? Was her name Andrea? In any case, her name had sparkled like gold threads in black silk. In the weeks before that, she had appeared from time to time at the swimming pool, always quite suddenly, as if surfacing from the waters of the Aare as they flowed beneath the pillars of the bathing establishment. In her leisurely crawl she would swim one length, then climb dripping up the little ladder, and when she stood under the shower Thom couldn't resist walking over, as if casually, to within six or seven steps of her and watching her abandon herself to the jet of cold water, twisting this way and that with her long brown hair. How shamelessly she turned her body, offering her long thighs, her hips, to the water, pulling her black swimsuit above her breasts far enough away from her skin for the jet of water to plunge down perhaps as far as her stomach. Once while doing this she turned her face toward him, toward Thom. He couldn't look away, he felt caught, then she smiled at him. He quickly walked off. But when later she lay in the sun on her red swim towel in the grass behind the pool, he would circle around her, at a distance. Or up on the sun deck with Charlott, he would sit so that he could keep her in sight over there on the grass without Charlott noticing. Then when he stood up Charlott would promptly ask, "Now where are you off to?"

To look for his cousin Rolf, he would reply, or for André. He took care to walk casually as close as possible behind the perhaps twenty-year-old woman so that at least for a few seconds he could see her, out of the corners of his eyes, stretched out and yawning at the sky as uninhibited as a cat, or sitting up, running her fingers through her hair until with a toss of her head she would make the brown waves ripple down her bare back to below her waist. She seemed not to care in the least that she had that lovely face with those green eyes; not even her breasts under the close-fitting swimsuit seemed to bother her, in fact not even the little dark hairs between her thighs either side of the triangle of her swimsuit. And from time to time she would nonchalantly touch up her lips with a pale red.

Yes, Thom began to hate her. He knew that he now went to the swimming pool solely in the hope of seeing her swim toward him. And he knew that at night, when he went to bed, he would again be putting on that harness with the two shoulder straps and the two bands for his wrists. His mother had told Frieda to make this contraption out of strong, tear-proof cotton, with two narrow tapes for his hands. He had had to try it on in front of Mother and Frieda, and it turned out that the two tapes to be fastened around his wrists were too long; Frieda had to shorten them. Now, after he had slipped into the harness, closed it in front with the little hooks, and fastened the tapes around his wrists, they were still long enough for him to move his hands at chest level, but they were also

short enough—so short that, even when Satan in the guise of a shameless
woman attempted to lead him into sin, he was protected from the temptation of touching his sex organ with his hand.

Late that August afternoon, a Friday, he had still known nothing
about Charlott meeting the motorcyclist on the previous evenings and
going with him twice to the clay pit for Moto-Cross training. And only
later was he to hear from Charlott about the quarrel, without any details,
between Andrea or Ariana and herself, and how Ariana had said to
Charlott, "Listen, pigeon—you'd better stop bothering my friend now,
or else—" and Charlott said the woman looked at her and smiled, "how
old is your dear brother anyway, fifteen?—or else I'll make a man of
him!"

Even if Thom had ever heard that phrase before, the words "make
a man of him" couldn't have conveyed much to him. Neither at home
nor within the confines of the convent school in the mountains, where
he had now been living for almost three years exclusively among pupils
and monks, had there been anybody, male or female, who might have
taught him the meaning of that forbidden, darkly lustrous word "sex."
He had remained alone with his feverishly trembling curiosity. When
he joined in the laughter at the other boys' jokes, it was merely so as not
to betray himself as uninitiated. From his mother he knew that one day,
the day he and his bride entered the holy state of matrimony, it would
be soon enough to find out all he needed to know about such things.

Still the dimly lit staircase; still five or six more stairs up to the
gallery; and once again Charlott balancing with outstretched arms on the
parapet of the Old Bridge, and kicking out at the man with the toes of
her high-heeled shoes. Ariana—or was she called Andrea—was coming
up from the grass (he had seen her in the swimming pool over Charlott's
shoulders) toward the steps to the sun deck. As she climbed the steps,
she looked up through the beams.

She proceeded to put down her bag and stretch out on her red swim
towel on one of the wooden lounges, diagonally across from Charlott
and Thom. Charlott turned away onto her stomach, saying—although
at the time Thom didn't know what she meant—"That snake!"

When Thom stole a sideways look at the woman, she was rubbing
one leg with suntan oil. Her leg, with the knee slightly drawn up, glistened
in the sun. The woman tossed back her hair; she looked across. Still he
couldn't turn his eyes away. He felt his heart pounding in his throat.
Now—quite unmistakably—she winked her right eye—yes, she was wink-

ing at him, at him, Thom. When he tried to wink back with one eye, he found he could only blink, not wink. She laughed—the woman laughed.

Charlott, lying beside Thom, was absorbed in her book, so couldn't see how hot and flushed his face had become. She didn't see the woman beckoning Thom, and she knew nothing of the trembling in Thom's limbs as he got up and in wonderment, suspicious wonderment, began to walk over until he finally stood in front of her. Still laughing, she held out the little bottle of suntan oil to him. And, suddenly serious, she asked if he would please rub some on her back, where she couldn't reach.

Thom walked around her and, while she bent her head so that her hair fell forward, knelt down behind her on the wooden deck. "Go on," she said. "Don't be scared. And a bit harder, if you don't mind. Your name's Thom, isn't it?"

The hum of voices, the shrieks coming up from the water, the heat of the sun, and the smell of oil and soap and of the woman's cool skin. "You're Thom, aren't you?" He heard Charlott calling him but didn't look across to her. He rubbed the skin between the shoulder blades. The woman laughed, bending forward. "You're tickling me!" Thom was still incapable of uttering even a yes. He heard her say that he was to call her Andrea. Andrea, or was her name Ariana, anyway it was a name with a halo, and as he dribbled three or four more drops of oil onto her right shoulder, he heard her say she had to talk to him. "Are you even listening?"

Again Charlott's voice: "Thom! Come here at once!" If he had time, Andrea said, this evening, at dusk, up at the little Pontonier's hut—all right?

Thom stood beside her. Now, with her sunglasses covering her green eyes, she looked up at him. He heard himself say yes. He walked back the twelve meters around the corner as if in a daze, the sound of the rushing waters of the Aare thundering in his ears. This evening, at dusk. It had sounded like a promise. Like a vow.

Yes. He said yes even before Charlott began to cross-examine him. Charlott was now sitting up. "What else did she want? To see you tonight? That rattlesnake! Do you know what kind of person she is?" "Yes," he said. "You mean *tonight*?" "Yes." Before his eyes, the sun exploded in sheaves of flame. "A hussy!" said Charlott.

At dusk.

A hussy.

Yes.

"Oh, you numskull!" Charlott hissed. "A snake! Now tell me where! And don't keep saying yes, you idiot, and wipe that silly grin off your face! She'll seduce you, you hear? She'll fleece you!" But whatever disaster Charlott predicted for him, it glistened like black silk. Like Andrea's oiled skin when the sunlight played on it.

Charlott's "Never! D'you hear? Never!" already sounded as if she understood. Was she crying?

He saw Andrea get up and gather her things. As she approached the steps she laughed, raising her hand to Thom, raising three fingers as if making a vow. Yes. He responded with the same gesture. Even if Charlott did betray him at home! Even if she did walk on the waters of the Aare— there was nothing in the world that could prevent him from keeping his vow.

Charlott was weeping softly as she looked for a handkerchief in her swim bag. "For crying out loud!" she said. Her tears glistened. "My brother! My little brother! He'll catch syphilis! And when I think of Mother! My brother. He'll become the prey of that she-devil—but Christ will point to his black soul and hold me accountable: me!" Charlott looked up at the sky as if hounded by the voices of the damned. Thom knew that when she gave vent to her feverish outbursts it was useless to argue with her. She was carried away by those words to some place where he could not follow her. "I'm going for a swim," he told her. And again Charlott: "She's going to make a man of this child! She's already be-witched the child!"

Thom felt almost like a man as he walked down the steps. The Aare glittered

while, still here in the dim light, he walked up the last five or six stairs to the gallery, through the lost times of then and now. He was not walking particularly slowly; by now, after that rendezvous with Andrea, it was Saturday afternoon, and he was kneeling in the Capuchin mon-astery church in one of the front pews on the right. In the pews ahead of him there were people too—women, only a few men. In the dim reddish light of the church there was a smell of cold incense, and now also of those candles burning in front of the altar to the Virgin Mary. From the confessional against the right-hand wall of the nave came intermittently the murmuring voice of the father confessor.

With him, with Father Hieronimus, it was safe to assume that, provided no mortal sin was involved, he would rarely impose a penance of more than a dozen Hail Marys. But how about now, when it was a matter of the satanic lust of a mortal sin? And anyway, when his turn came in about ten minutes, what words was Thom to use to confess his sins of last night to Father Hieronimus?

He saw himself pushing aside the red curtain of the confessional and kneeling in the darkness before the wooden grille, with the priest sitting behind it and, being slightly deaf, moving his ear close up to it. To Thom's "Praised be Jesus Christ" he would reply, "For ever and ever amen," and now he was waiting, waiting for Thom to begin his confession.

Eight more minutes perhaps. As he knelt, Thom covered his face with his hands in order to concentrate. How was he to begin? Last night just after nine I met Andrea down by the river. Or go back even farther? Perhaps like this: Charlott and I were walking across the Old Bridge at six o'clock last evening. I had been hoping that Charlott wouldn't refer to it again. But halfway across the bridge she suddenly pulled herself up onto the parapet and, keeping her balance, walked forward a few steps, stopped, and then, Father, she demanded that I promise not to go there that evening. "Or else—I'll jump; see? When I'm dead"—yes, that's how it had been. A man wanted to lift her down, and she kicked out at him with her high-heeled shoes. "Stop right there! Or I'll jump. And as for you: do you promise?"

Charlott in her full-skirted dress. Balancing with outstretched arms. I have sinned against the commandment of Love thy neighbor. I called out, "How can I not go, since I've been bewitched? I made a vow! Come down—come on, or, if you prefer, jump!"

Charlott said, "I'll count to three: One—two—three!"

Father, I have—yes, perhaps this would be the best way: I have sinned—I called up to Charlott, "I'm leaving!"

Charlott jumped. Her loosened hair fluttered up as she fell, and she disappeared beyond the dark parapet. When I rushed over and looked down—people were already gathering around me, all staring over the parapet into the river—there was nothing to be seen but the water rushing and foaming past the bridge piers ten or twelve meters below us. Was Charlott dead? Knocked unconscious by the impact, dragged down into the depths by the eddies?

Someone shouted, "There! Down there!" pointing a hand down river. Yes, at last Charlott's flowered dress came in sight, and Charlott trying to swim free of the pull of the tide over to the right toward the railway station. Thom knew he would have to confess everything to Father Hieronimus. How else could the priest render him absolution? And it was true: Thom was choking with fear, trembling from his knees up to his hips when he tried to call for help. His first mortal sin was that he had not loved Charlott, his neighbor, as himself. On the contrary: he had hated Charlott when she jumped, and he had acquiesced in her risking her life for him—for him! No, he hadn't loved her even when he finally ran off along the river bank toward the station, now shouting for help and waving and pointing to Charlott as she swam toward the bank; he was merely glad when, her hair straggling over her face, she finally touched bottom, and pulling herself up by some branches, her flowered dress plastered to her body, waded up out of the river. And when, panting and sobbing, she stood in front of him, in the little crowd, he could think of nothing better to say than, "But you always said you could walk on water!"

But now that other, that second mortal sin? Suppose Father Hieronimus were not satisfied with the all-encompassing confession that he, Thom, had sinned in thought, word, and deed against the Sixth Commandment? Suppose the priest wanted more precise details and asked, "And then, Thom? Yes, what happened then? And when Andrea embraced you and pressed herself against you, what did you feel?"

"Bliss and terror at the same time, Father."

"And when she suddenly kissed you on the mouth? What happened when you lay side by side under the wild cherry tree by the river, and the moonlight filtered through the branches onto you, Thom: Did you touch her then? Did you feel true love or sinful lust? And your heart— was it beating fast? What did you whisper?"

"How do you expect me to tell you all that, Father? I felt many things, all at the same time, and on the Aare in front of us wisps of mist were dancing, like the souls of those spewed out from the mouth of God, curving down from the railway bridge like suicides, and when Andrea touched me I was rigid with love. I felt icy, I was on fire, my soul was on fire. We lay side by side, we embraced, we kissed again and again, I felt Andrea's hands and her body and its mounds, felt her tongue, the Aare thundering by as if from far away; and when, utterly exhausted by love, we looked up to the sky, green and red and white stars passed over us, blazing their trail through the drifts of the Milky Way.

"No, I couldn't think of Mary, our pure Mother of God, not then. It's possible she might have protected me, but I am not sure whether I really wanted her protection—perhaps I didn't. I was flooded with the scent of Andrea's hot skin. The moon sparkled darkly overhead; then it emptied and trickled down onto us through the wild cherry branches."

From the organ loft came the first heavenly chords. No promise of mercy from them either; they sounded more like revenge and judgment.

Now there were only three people, now only two, kneeling outside the confessional. Four more minutes perhaps, then Father Hieronimus would turn in the darkness toward Thom, with his whisper that sometimes gave a whistle, and ask the question: "Are you prepared to forswear sin and repent everything? To repent everything with a sincere heart?" Thom covered his face with his hands again. The heat in the chill of the church made the sweat pour off him; he shivered. "And do you promise never to see that poor fallen creature again?"

The echo of Father Hieronimus's voice resounded through the nave, reverberating from the walls, bouncing back from all sides. "Never again? Do you promise? Do you swear?"

Suddenly Andrea's voice was there again too. "Here, can you feel? Can you feel me?" Fallen creatures with brown-gold hair were tumbling through the air onto the Aare. At the sound of the Divine Judge's call they crawled away under the wild cherry tree. The organ in the loft grew louder and louder. It was the call, the call of judgment. "True love, Thom, or sinful lust? Are you prepared? Do you promise? Te Deum, Domine!" What was Mary, our heavenly Mother, doing?

The angels of wrath and frenzy finally overwhelmed the organist; now bereft of his senses, he intoned the war cries and trumpets of the heavenly hosts. Thom knew the man: he had the corroded face of the secret absinthe distiller.

Suppose Charlott were to decide to tell Mother everything?

The organ collapsed. When Thom uncovered his face, he saw Father Hieronimus emerging from the confessional. He smiled, looked apologetically toward the red flame of the Eternal Light, then nodded at Thom and the elderly woman beside Thom. He lifted his stole from his neck and over his head, kissed it, and placing it over his arm went off toward the high altar.

One more, one last step, and Thom had reached the top of the staircase, and as he walked on through the gallery, the woman kneeling beside him stared at him. "Now what?" she whispered, an angry flush spreading over her face. She stood up. "I came over specially from Läufelfingen!" And suddenly raising her voice, as if Thom were to blame: "Who's going to forgive me my sins now?"

And she repeated, as if Thom were the one to know the answer, "Who?"

Leafing through the Festschrift III

. . . YET THESE ADVANCES IN TECHNOLOGY AND THE CULTURE OF THE nineteenth century are also matched by and reflected in the history of the Winter enterprises. Here too the path led from handicraft, but also from the exploitation of water rights, to a large-scale modern industrial complex.

As early as 1908 Theophil Winter, the founder, noted: "Switzerland is a country lacking in raw materials. Hence we will not long confine ourselves to iron-smelting. Our trump cards are (1) refining, (2) quality, and (3) diligence, diligence, diligence."

In 1842 the first steam hammer—bringing from Poland the technique of obtaining fluid pig iron—and with that the important step toward

was Wilkinson's invention of the cupola furnace—that meant it was now also possible—as well as the beginnings of temper-casting. Elsazar Winter's incorporation of the annealing process in the treatment of castings around 1850 represents a significant act in the history of our works.

not until the sixties of the last century. In this way steel-shaping by the casting process was introduced into our foundries. The first rolling mill was set up in Winterthur about 1867, in Choindez in 1869, in Mühlenthal and Schaffhausen in 1870.

were the first steel-mold foundries in Switzerland, supplying steel castings to mechanical-engineering companies at home and abroad, for the construction of locomotives, dynamos, and electric motors.

simultaneously with the conversion in 1907 of the simple trading company to a family corporation—but only now the third decisive step: the company starting its own machinery production. With a wide range of boilers from the Lucerne plant as well as

In 1912 the first diesel locomotive in the world was built in our

Winterthur plant. At the same time, the addition of new buildings to the foundry in Jammers as well as building extensions in

In the Dovecote

The fact was, you had to know how to handle a marten trap, especially when it came to tying the decoy pigeon to it. But Mr. Ludwig never listened to him, to Sepp; he always knew better. Sure, martens could also be caught alive, with a simple box trap, but not with the box-board trap devised by Sepp himself. This was constructed so that if the marten wanted to get into the box, wanted to get at the pigeon, it had to step onto the board behind the hole in the box. Now, if a marten weighing even as little as three hundred grams stepped on the board, the iron ring would whip around and kill the marten. That was a box-board trap, intended to kill. With that spring above the pulley you could have killed a young fox. You had to tie up the pigeon, the decoy pigeon, good and tight beyond the hole in the box, then push the board up to the hole, engage the iron ring, set the spring, carefully push in the board, and put on the cover: now the trap was set.

Martens are more cunning than foxes. They can pick up the smell of a human a hundred meters away, so Sepp would end up by taking a piece of pigeon meat and rubbing everything with pigeon fat.

And yet Mr. Ludwig had been lucky. A squashed thumb, that was all. That ring could have cut off his hand.

But now he too had been dead and gone for a long time. As an inventor, a big shot among other inventors, but when it came to practical matters, when it came to the marten trap or the horses, a person must have the right instinct, like Sepp, a good nose. Now there were no more pigeons, no horses, and it must have been ten years since Sepp had seen the last marten. For all Sepp cared, that was fine too. After all, he would soon be turning seventy-six. What more did anyone want—he'd never needed much space. The attic up at the house for the night, and here these four by two-and-a-half meters, a mattress, some pillows, a blanket for chilly days, on the wall the shotgun and the photograph with Mr. Ulrich on it; and when Sepp lay there and raised himself on his elbow he could look through one of the old pigeonholes and see the stable yard and the whole length of the avenue. What more did he want.

And he had the right to live here in the Winter mansion. Even if Gret or Gret's husband, that Mr. Glur, should ever get a notion to sell the estate, no one could deprive him of that right, for free too; that was in the land-title register, forever. In addition, free board plus the seven hundred francs a month from the Old Age & Survivors' insurance—that was plenty for him, and he had made himself nice and snug up here.

The only thing a person might wonder about was whether he shouldn't take down that postcard from Benni Kunz. For ten or fifteen years Benni had been all right; they had gone off on jaunts together, to Frohburg, Chasseral, or to the Bölchenfluh, and every Tuesday and Friday evening to the Waadtländer Hall to play cards with Jakob and Oettu, but now, all of a sudden, since the strike at Winter's, Benni had turned spiteful again. In the middle of a game he would start on that ancient business again. He would even bring up Sepp's father: "Hadn't he been a foundry worker and one of them? But you? All you've ever done is wait hand and foot on Ulrich Winter."

How had it been then, in November '18? Sepp's father, during that general strike, always out front; and when Colonel Sonderegger mounted those machine guns at the railway station, one of the first to be crippled. Shot in the hip. "At least he was one of us. But you," asked Benni, "where were you, in '32? And when the dyers went on strike, and even children and mothers were wounded just because they were looking down on the street from upstairs windows? Or on the 'night of blood?' Whose side, Sepp?"

They had been through all that a hundred times, and for years and years not one of them had spoken to Sepp. Until one day Benni turned up and said, "Now we're both on the scrap heap." And did Sepp feel like a little game at the Waadtländer Hall?

Bernhard, of all people. As a foreman at Winter's it was his job, after all, to pass down orders from the top; what else was a foreman but an overseer? They said he could be pretty rough. And anyway, the mechanics' strike at that time was illegal. They had been on strike for six weeks, and at Winter's the first sympathy strikes had already started. All illegal. The union secretaries had said so themselves, and even written: Anyone on strike is acting illegally. "Those high-and-mighty secretaries," Benni said, "that Konrad Ilg and Uhlmann and Vollmer, they've stabbed us in the back. We are the basis, after all, not them, and we happen to be on strike. A vote on the strike by a strike, that's what it was. Those fellows had been hand in glove with the Red police chief, and it was precisely this socialist and comrade who distributed live ammunition to his men—why do I say distributed, he deployed them with the order: At the slightest resistance—shoot!

"Don't talk to me about those secretaries, Sepp, about those union bosses. They actually organized the strikebreaking, right here in Jammers—did you ever hear of such a thing? But not one of us went back to work. Sure, when they turned up in the foundry with the strikebreakers, we beat them up." Benni did admit that much. "Always the same old trouble," he said, "with the bosses of the Socialist Party and the union—they're voted in at the bottom by the left and come out on top at the right."

Benni could really work himself up into a rage, and so could Jakob. "Listen, Sepp," Jakob had said. "People like you are just the kind they like up there. They sent you out with your knuckle-dusters and your blackjacks—you fellows, against your old coworkers!"

"What do you expect?" I asked them. "You must have known that wherever there was any rough stuff I was always available, and it was common knowledge that you were acting illegally. After all, it was your own union bosses who arranged the pay reduction with them, not me. We were young fellows in those days, feeling our oats, and that evening, since Mr. Ulrich didn't need me to drive him anywhere, I stuffed the blackjack into my pocket and off I went, to the Old Town. What do you expect? Even the Red town council had banned your demonstration. Even your strike committee had called it off.

"I know exactly how it was. At the time we had this Trakehner gelding in our stable. It was a day in June, a sultry June day. I had led out the gelding and taken him over into the shade. I had bought four new horseshoes; I still had enough hoof nails. I was just removing the gelding's old horseshoes and was about to trim back one hoof when Mr. Ulrich came down from the house.

"His voice was lower than usual. 'It's about time something was done,' he said. 'The wildcat strike,' he said, and it was gradually spreading. Although the police were alerted, waiting to be dispatched in order to maintain law and order, they couldn't go ahead just like that, not just like that. 'Let's suppose,' and Mr. Ulrich laughed. 'Let's suppose a few hefty young fellows like you, Sepp, go down to Helvetia-Platz this evening and start a bit of a ruckus, what do you say? Then the police can wade in with a couple of squads and put paid to all that, what do you say? But watch it, Sepp, we don't want a free-for-all—you'll be outnumbered. A bit of provocation here and there, then beat it—is that clear?' "

Of course Sepp hadn't told them about all this. "What do you expect?" he had said. "There you are, ten or twelve happy fellows, out on the town, having a drink here and another one there, and you suddenly find yourselves in Helvetia-Platz and in front of us all those people, hundreds of them standing there and more and more arriving, all silent. From the far end someone shouting out over the heads about capitalists and pay cuts—and of course it's not unlikely that someone will call out, 'You're illegal!' or some such thing, 'Go home!' Well, and then? It doesn't take long for a fist to fly!"

So it did come to a regular free-for-all—at first down at the end, where the street comes in from the Union Building and Bastian-Platz and Lang-Strasse. Sepp and his friends couldn't possibly see that there were some four thousand people standing in Helvetia-Platz. And Sepp had knocked down only two of them, one was a plasterer and the other that floorlayer, by the name of Flückiger, whom he later occasionally saw from a distance. "Anything else? You can't nail us for the fellow who got killed! Not us!"

A marten trap was not a toy. You had to know how to handle it. Sepp had built this box-board trap himself. Now it hung outside in the shed above the steps. Every May and June, and again in November, he had used it to catch up to five ordinary stone martens, the kind with a white bib. Once he had even caught a pine marten in the trap, a good eighty centimeters long. That one had been especially cunning. And tough! It had killed seven pigeons, and pigeon eggs were lying around all over the place. But then the trap had finally done it in—or rather, Sepp and Herminia and Charlott had been having supper in the pantry when suddenly there was a loud wailing outside in the passage and Gret came through the kitchen, sobbing, standing red-faced in the door, her straw-colored hair hanging over her face, repeating as she sobbed, "This is animal torture! It's still alive! It's still twitching, it's trying with its hind legs to pull its head out from under the iron ring! And blood all over, such lovely fur, spotted like robins' eggs. It's still whistling!" She was wailing, but Sepp asked, "How about the pigeons—it's been killing them, hasn't it?"

Coming up past the stables, she must have heard the marten in the dovecote. Frankly, Sepp had also been surprised that it was still twitching, but then it was a pine marten; they were bigger, they were as tough as rats. Sepp had stood up. "It's all right, my dear," and, taking the rabbit-killer, he had shot the marten in the back of the neck. Next day he had skinned it and stretched the pelt on a frame to dry, behind the washhouse.

Zoller the fur dealer had said, "Well, well, Sepp, yet another of those?" and as usual, had taken five francs from the till and placed them on the counter, but Sepp had merely shaken his head. "I don't think I need tell you," he said, "you don't get one like this in a month of Sundays," and he had started to pack up the pelt again. "Thirty," Sepp had said, or he would take it to Zurich on Saturday. So Mr. Zoller had to go back to his till again.

True, the following Saturday he had treated himself to a few extra doubles. At the Traube he had even paid for a round. On his way home, on Gold-Gasse, the police had even taken away his bike. "You can pick it up tomorrow after your porridge," they had said. But Sepp had just laughed. "Shooting, that's what you're good at! Shooting at people. But has any of you ever caught a pine marten?"

In the middle of the game Benni had said that Sepp must have known they would start shooting, since he had provoked the free-for-all.

How could Sepp have known? Sure, at the time of the general strike, that Colonel Sonderegger with his machine guns, but that had been the military, after all. But he'd been surprised, he must admit, when suddenly a police squad came driving up and started shooting into the crowd. After all, policemen weren't normally supposed to shoot. Four thousand people, the whole of Helvetia-Platz filled, but just when they were slowly getting ready to march off down Lang-Strasse, those fellows arrived: first some warning shots in the air; then, when the crowd started picking up paving stones, shots aimed at the legs. One man was killed. Others seriously wounded, fifty of them, all on the orders of that socialist, Police Inspector Wiesendanger. Yes, how could Sepp have known? He had never been interested in politics. "Or are you suggesting something else?" he had asked Benni. "Are you trying to say that Mr. Ulrich knew?"

Sepp had laid his cards on the table. "If that's what you meant, I'm leaving," he had said. And stood up. "Mr. Winter has put bread on your tables all your lives." And Sepp had left.

Why did Benni have to stir all that up again now? Just because of this strike. They should be working, like other people, and later everyone would have their Old Age & Survivors' insurance, and Mr. Ulrich had always treated Sepp fairly, no one could say more. Maybe Sepp would take down Benni's postcard after all.

Here at least Sepp wanted to be left in peace. So there were some people who died earlier. So they were dead longer. And then there were some, like Sepp, who didn't die until they'd lived long enough.

And as for that pine marten that hadn't been killed right away and had gone on twitching for an hour—after all, Sepp hadn't intended that either.

Munich, March 24, 1937

Dear Ulrich, beloved brother,

Yes, I arrived here safely. But even the comforts of the sleeping car did not prevent me from lying awake on my journey through the night.

I am not happy about the turn taken by our conversation at the station. How could you construe my remark about your wife's demeanor as disapproval? There is no doubt Lilly and I are totally dissimilar by nature. Consequently, even during the many weeks I have just spent at home, it was not possible for our relationship to become cordial. But that I disapproved of Lilly? No! I have the highest respect for your wife: her great qualities, her artistic talents, her intelligence, the charm of her attractive, unquestionably strong personality—and her fine educational background, which surely no one would deny. No, my remark that she was apparently still refusing to adapt to our family is a criticism of you— if I may say so—rather than of her.

Lilly seems to me to resemble a young mare that has not yet been broken in. A risky comparison, I know, yet—and this applies to many women of her generation—her training, if I may call it that, was neglected. The parents and educators of these women concentrate their efforts on raising sons to true manhood. While the daughters are brought up to devote themselves to essentially female accomplishments, of late they have been permitted—quite rightly, too!—to study intellectual matters, if that is what they actually desire. However, as regards the necessity of practising the proper attitude of a true life-companion to the husband, their education is being grossly neglected. When I consider, for example, how our mother spent her entire life in absolute devotion on the one hand to us children and on the other to the loving support of her husband,

I find myself wondering where such selflessness is to be found among younger women today. Enamored of themselves, they revolve, it seems to me, around their own person; the noble social task that, particularly in our social sphere, has been allotted them by marriage is no longer sufficiently taken for granted. Lilly—and that is all I wanted to emphasize—is no exception in that respect. Yes, I admit to being confused by the violence with which she acts out her emotions: the way she can dance, play the piano with such passion, but then in a trice abandon herself utterly to her tears—she, a mother of two daughters, after all! What she needs, dear brother, is the gentle guidance of your strong hand. Wasn't it Nietzsche who spoke of the golden whip for which woman positively yearns?

But now to turn to something else: Your approval of my chapter regarding automation has really given me profound pleasure, besides encouraging me. And with your reference to the eighteenth century and, in particular, to the mechanical flute player of Vaucanson, you found a wonderful illustration of what I have in mind but which I had not yet succeeded in formulating clearly. Meanwhile I have looked it up: as early as 1738, according to Diderot, the flute player was presented by its ingenious designer to the Académie in Paris. Did you know that the flute player has movable lips, a movable tongue—to act as an adjustable valve!—and its leather fingertips open or close the holes in the wooden shaft of the flute? What a minor marvel! It actually embodies in a nutshell the concept of automation!

The practical application of this can mean only: on the one hand, of course, the continued *mechanization of production*. Now that—thanks mainly to the conveyor belt—we have already achieved mechanization in the field of transportation with the railway and the automobile; now that cotton mills and even abattoirs are equipped with our machines, we must turn our attention to the mechanization and electrification of kitchen, household, and bathroom. You know my old refrain: diversify, brother dear! And let us not underestimate the importance of small appliances! Irons, fans, toasters, wringers, vacuum cleaners, electric ranges, refrigerators, and cans—these are the ideal containers for concentrated soups, baby food, cat food, etc. Vast markets are opening up here. Are we to leave them to the dealers? No. We shall soon see ourselves compelled to attach trading companies to our flagship of mechanical engineering, so that we may not only produce our goods but also sell them directly to the consumer!

However, much as all this must be our objective, one area of concern remains: too much importance is still being accorded the intervening human hand. In other words, we must approach actual automation, the full robotizing of production, in concrete terms. This means the elimination of the human being as an interference and cost factor. Wireless telecommunication! It closes the technological gap! Given the tremendous expenditure of will power, of the truly fascinating awakening of national energy such as is now taking place here in the German Reich in the name of the New Order, the robotizing of armaments is no longer idle speculation.

I can see you shaking your head with a smile. Ludwig and his visions, his castles in the air! I do not think so. Here—and I am telling you this both as an intuitive artist *and* as a technically competent natural scientist—the old, the great idea of totally automated warfare is finally within reach! A matter no longer of decades but of years!

More about this before long. Two more things: On my tour of inspection to the plants at Schweizerhalle, Winterthur, and Lausanne, I was struck by the poor posture of many of our employees—in the offices too, incidentally. What has become of him, that proud worker in the Winter plants with his firm, upright gait? I suggest that, with a view to improving the physical condition of the employees, a program of brief daily exercises be introduced; these could be performed in shifts in the factory yards, in small or large groups, under professional supervision. As a flanking measure it would, in my opinion, be necessary for our regional directors to insist—if necessary with some gentle political pressure—that closing time in bars and taverns be advanced from midnight to eleven P.M.

And now finally: Director Berger has shown me the mounting number of files dealing with complaints from local inhabitants about soot emissions from our factory smokestacks. Berger seemed at a loss. You ought to take a hand in this matter. That constant grumbling! There should be no shilly-shallying here! Make the situation perfectly clear! In such cases the truth *has* to be brief and unvarnished.

I congratulate you, as captain, on the fact that our Winter fleet is now once again moving full steam ahead on a successful course. May the blessing of our Lord be upon you and on all those entrusted to you!

Yours ever,
Ludwig

The General's Politics IV

1. DESCRIBE THE SITUATION IN SWITZERLAND AFTER THE FRENCH CAPITulation of June 25, 1940. The wave of sympathy for the French people; the consternation in our country.

So from now on Switzerland is an island encircled by the two Fascist dictatorships.

There is a growing touchiness on the part of the rulers of Nazi Germany and Italy in regard to the Swiss press. Illustrate the relevant attempts at pressure, both internal and external. Against this background, emphasize the attitude of the editors in chief (Bretscher, *Neue Zürcher Zeitung*; Oeri, *Basler Nachrichten*; Schürch, *Bund*), who steadfastly and admirably cling to their right to freedom of expression, and how with their critical views, especially of the Third Reich, they are a thorn in the flesh of our Foreign Minister Marcel Pilet-Golaz as well as General Guisan. The General demands press censorship and urges the removal of the above-mentioned journalists from their posts (!).

The diplomatic double game vis-à-vis Germany; rumors about substantial concessions, about the pro-German sympathies of leading industrialists (also in U. Wille's circle), about terrorist acts of the national-socialist fifth column within Switzerland; but above all: as a result of the government's silence and the increasing food-supply problems, a mood of hopelessness rapidly spreading throughout the population.

2. On the first day of the truce in France: Federal President Marcel Pilet-Golaz (Foreign Minister) finally addresses the Swiss people (over the radio): "Swiss citizens!" Would the speech clarify the overriding question: accommodation, or resistance to the end? Military resistance even now that the country is militarily encircled? Would not such resistance be suicide?

Quote the famous speech verbatim. First point out: It contains not a word about the life-and-death dilemma. An analysis undertaken by numerous commentators is faced by a disconcerting verbal mélange:

(a) there is mention of a "partial and graduated demobilization";

(b) Europe would have to find a "new balance" to be achieved "without regard to obsolete forms";

(c) "obstacles" would have to be "removed" in order to achieve "the necessary accommodation to the new conditions";

(d) the Federal Council (government) must be equipped with new "powers of authority";

(e) "The time for inner rebirth has arrived. Each one of us must divest himself of his former self";

(f) "Swiss citizens, it is now up to you to follow the government in its capacity of confident and devoted leader (. . .)."

Satisfaction in fascist circles inside and outside of Switzerland. Outrage among the parliamentary groupings that are still determined on resistance and form a majority; outrage also in the officer ranks of the militia. Pro-Nazi professional officers, however, made use of the speech as an excuse to remove General Guisan's portrait from barracks (and, incidentally, to throw knives at it). Outrage or profound dismay also among the population as a whole.

Quote W. Rings: "How could a government demand blind confidence when it failed to reveal how it intended to act?"

The speech, given in French, was read over the radio by Pilet-Golaz's Federal Council colleagues Etter in German and Celio in Italian. Nevertheless: all seven members of the government were jointly responsible.

The question remained. So what would happen in the case of a (constantly threatening) German attack? Would the government, would the General, issue battle orders? Or would one of them, or both of them, capitulate?

Would the General if necessary order unconditional resistance against the will of the democratically elected government to which he was, after all, subordinate? So: Putsch? Patriotic rebellion?

3. (a) Describe: How the old Frontists with their dedication to the idea of a Führer state came creeping out of their hiding places again. How they formed two new parties, and how their delegation was granted audiences by the government (!).

(b) Reaction to the accommodative speech in the Federal Parliament was spontaneous and swift. It was simultaneously a reply and a protest: coming from below, from the people, and the gist of it was: Whatever tactics those fellows up there dream up, we will fight. If it comes to that, *we* will issue the necessary orders for that ourselves. Like mushrooms after rain, *secret armed commandos* shot up out of the ground in countless villages and towns; within a few weeks, some 120,000 armed volunteers were operating in the 2,800 (newly formed) local militias, in some cases also independently. Remarkable that these volunteers were recruited from among men not militarily organized.

The General was silent.

"What *was*, once upon a time? No, don't ask me, because what *was* became the substance from which you too have come; because in that which has gone down the reaches of time, farther and farther down, into the Aare to be swept away into the Reuss and the Thur, swept down and away into the Rhône and the Rhine, because in all that is also the beginning of those who are still alive or have since been born. Quite possibly that's all forgotten now, carried out to sea, and from there it returns in rainy nights over the land of the two rivers. Remember that. Write it down. Make it into your story-machine before you, too, go down the Aare. Bring it to the surface.

"But that wasn't the right word," she often said. "Not that one— not adultery, oh no! Your Lilly lost only her heart then. Do you understand?"

Aunt Esther had closed her eyes; her head resting against the cushion in her armchair, she sat with her hands holding the ball of wool in her lap, and for many minutes left him, Thom, aged fourteen, to himself with those strange words. Adultery. What was he supposed to understand by that? And what did it mean when someone like his mother lost her heart? Not until, after that long interval, Aunt Esther started to speak again, her voice hoarse, dark, and this time low, as if from coming from the distant past, did he suddenly grasp that today she wasn't telling her story to him, even though it was he who was listening to her, here on the stool with his back to the wall. She looked across to the little round bridge table, across to the Voltaire chair upholstered in dark red damask, and when she said, "Ulrich," and "I will never forget that face, never ever, even beyond my grave," she was merely talking into the time into which she had returned while telling her story, to an afternoon or an evening or a night several years ago, probably soon after the war. And it wasn't Thom she was telling, but Thom's father Ulrich, describing what had happened or what she chose to believe she had experienced a few years earlier still, when there was war all around and peace reigned only in this land of Switzerland, protected by God and our brave officers and soldiers.

Although Thom had only a dim memory of that time, he did remember this much: that in 1942 and '43, when he was four and five, those gloomy blackout curtains would be drawn or hung across the windows at nightfall; there was not much butter but a lot of mashed vegetables, and Charlott and Herminia used to admonish Thom to think of the starving children in wartime Finland and of the Polish children, and how much worse things would be if the Russians were to come. On the grounds where now there were lawns again and a fine show of flowers, long rows of potato plants and string beans had been growing; in the attic had stood two barrels of sand, with a shovel beside them in case incendiary bombs fell from the sky, or just in case; in the cellar, cartons of canned food for survival; in the stables, the billeted soldiers, sleeping on straw like the Christ Child, and the horses and ammunition carts, and occasionally the rattle of distant rifles when the "enemy"—identified by the white bands around their helmets—was trying to capture Jammers.

And sometimes Mother had stood with Thom at the open window, where, listening together, they could hear the distant roar of engines in the sky: night bombers flying into Germany.

Aunt Esther blew the smoke of her cigarillo past Thom. Where the February sun slanted into the room, the smoke billowed up, revolving, catching the light. In an undertone she said only, "You must know that yourself."

For an instant Thom saw the American bomber again, in the midday sun, the bomber hanging aslant in the air as it dragged a black plume of smoke in its wake. It made a slow loop, then a wing broke away. The plane disappeared behind the roof of the barn.

"That's something a man must know for himself, whether he is a good husband to his wife. For me, anyway"—she hesitated, gave a little laugh—"in this respect I must admit I could understand Lilly—if you are either on leave and spend all day and half the night at the plant and come home practically asleep, or most of the time you're with that artillery detachment somewhere back there in the Waadtland Jura, and it's permissible to knit you a few socks and write you a short letter every two weeks—for me, anyway, that wouldn't have been enough. I say that as a woman. You must try and imagine what it was like here—the officers in the house, every room occupied, every bed, plus extra mattresses, then the constant coming and going of messengers at all hours of the night, the staff kitchen over in the washhouse, the stables full of horses and soldiers, and a dozen or so young lieutenants around the pantry table; a few captains and the major in the Paneled Room, and when they'd finished their evening meal, the card games and the drinking." She laughed.

"Quite often they would bring along a hand organ, a saxophone, or a bass fiddle, and sometimes they would introduce some women from Jammers to your pious Lilly as their fiancées. Fiancées indeed! Even Lilly behaved as if she saw and heard nothing when the fiancées slipped out of the bedrooms in the morning and crept downstairs and out of the house. After all, it was, in a way, war, and when one group was discharged or transferred to the Alps, it was immediately replaced by another. What could one do? Again the house would smell of pipe smoke and leather, of sweat, it smelled of men, of wood fires in the garden, and of longing— c'est la vie, my dear! We had to be glad that we managed to defend the innocence of your daughters. No, no, no adultery, but I think you have a right to know what occurred then, in November '43, with your wife.

"The Paneled Room looked like a casino. Lilly was playing Skat with three officers over in the corner; I was playing bridge with the major and his staff officers; at the round table by the tiled stove a game of chess was going on. The man with the hand organ had fallen asleep on the bench beside the stove. One last game, and we would have been in bed just before midnight."

For a few seconds again Thom saw the bomber on fire, the bright sky with the tilted bomber against it. It seemed to be sawing off the tops of the hickory oaks with its drooping wing, but it only looked that way. Three, then four and five parachutes opened and floated high up over the roofs of the town while Aunt Esther was telling about how the door suddenly opened. "You know what Sepp's like. When he's excited he can hardly get a word out. At first he just stood there, stood in the doorway."

In the bright sky, dangling like hanged men, the Americans with their parachutes slowly floating down. "You could have cut the smoke in the Paneled Room with a knife." Aunt Esther described how she had walked toward Sepp and on reaching the door had switched on the chandelier. It was then that she saw the prisoner; Sepp was pulling him toward the table by a rope, and: "No, I shall never forget that chalk-white face. Behind them stood one of the sentries, his helmet pushed back, his rifle at his hip.

"They had tied his hands behind his back, and Sepp was holding the rope as if he were leading a dancing bear into the room. But that man wasn't dancing. He was staggering. Sepp had to hold him by the arm, and if you ask me that fellow was hardly more than skin and bones—a lanky bag of bones, his clothes flapping about him, and as I said, that face: white—with those dark, hollow eye sockets, the scanty, stubbly hair—as white as a harlequin. They untied his hands. He sank into the easy chair pushed toward him, yes, sank right into it. Then, his head sunk on his chest, he fell asleep, almost before we had recovered from our surprise.

"Or he wasn't asleep yet, he opened his eyes again, raised his face, looked at all of us, standing there at a loss as to what to say or do—looked at each of us in turn out of those dark hollows until he managed to say, 'Où vivez-vous! Où vivez-vous!' It sounded as if he meant: Where do you live, on what distant star! His head fell forward again.

"Then the staff doctor came up and took his pulse. Your Lilly brought a glass of water. No, we didn't find out that evening where he had come from or how. Thom—long since in bed—was moved to Herminia's room, so the stranger could now sleep for fifteen straight hours in Thom's room; then, nursed and looked after by the staff doctor and your Lilly, he began to eat, first cautiously, then more and more voraciously. Three days later, in the afternoon, he sat with a blanket over his knees in your armchair, which she had pushed up to the open veranda door for him.

"Now, bit by bit, his story emerged. Of course we had occasionally heard the letters KZ, and we knew what kind of stories were being circulated about concentration camps, *Konzentrationslager*, but until now they had been mere reports from far-off lands somewhere up there in the north and east, where there was a war going on and a New Order that we only partially understood—KZ, for us half chamber of horrors, half atrocity story: what really lay behind those letters in terms of death or life was beyond our grasp, until those November days. The stranger, Gaston Nougier by name, had been picked up a year earlier in Avignon and transported to Germany, to the concentration camp in Sachsenhausen.

"Two of them had escaped from there. The other prisoner was

caught. What that meant could be imagined when Gaston, by way of illustration, grabbed his throat with his right hand and pointed upward, as if he too were dangling from a rope in the camp."

She talked on. Not to him, not to Thom. Her voice, as if coming from the distant past in the warm February room, the sun slanting in almost as far as the glass-fronted cabinet, and Thom pictured that tall Gaston, that prisoner, traveling by night through southern Hesse down into Baden, appropriating frozen pants and a shirt and jacket from the washing line behind a farmhouse; somehow managing to hide for two days, among wine barrels from the Palatinate, in a freight car en route from Karlsruhe to Singen; making his way, always at night, from Singen across the Swiss border at Thayngen to Schaffhausen.

However, if he had imagined that this meant freedom, he was mistaken. Although a pensioner's widow hid him for two days in her basement laundry room, where at last he could get his teeth into some hot food, and sleep, sleep, Gaston also discovered that anyone entering Switzerland without a visa, without a passport and a work permit, would be handed over forthwith to the authorities in the German Reich, deported and handed over. He heard about fines and imprisonment for Swiss citizens who harbored illegal immigrants without reporting them. Nevertheless, the widow Maria Stock took Gaston Nougier in a potato sack on a farm cart across the Rhine bridge, then on foot as far as Benken, to her brother's. From there he got a ride on a motorcycle from a salesman for women's underwear who charged him a fare of twenty francs plus danger money of sixty francs. They left at eight in the evening, heading via Glattfelden and Dielsdorf for Jammers, where it had been arranged that the Frenchman would be taken in by a factory foreman and his wife.

The two men didn't get very far. Engine trouble forced them to stop on a stretch of open road; and when the headlights of two motorcycles appeared in the distance, Gaston disappeared from the road across the fields into the night.

Aunt Esther drew on her cigarillo. "Now you can work it out for yourself," she said. "You don't need to wonder what someone would do on those bare, frozen, snow-swept rapeseed and potato fields, after having watched the military police drive off with his rescuer, probably because there was something wrong with his papers—drive off with him and that address in Jammers where Gaston was to have been dropped off. All the Frenchman knew was that he was supposed to have been taken to some people in a town called Jammers.

"So he begins by stumbling southward until he reaches a little copse; here, to avoid freezing to death in the night, he seeks protection from the north wind under some bushes.

"At first light he continues across the open countryside, following a stream, shelters out of the wind beside a dilapidated farm shed on the exposed plain, then at some point approaches a farm, comes to a halt, hears his own breath rasping, hears a dog barking and the clinking of empty milk containers.

"He watches for a long time, then takes a chance, and to the constant barking of the farm dog, approaches the barn door in a wide detour. Light falls from it. He comes face to face with the farmer's wife as she stands in the doorway, the strap of the milking stool around her hips, broad-faced, and himself asking, always in French, for 'Shammers.' Until at last she understands him. Until she understands, hesitant, suspicious, and calls her sixteen-year-old son. In the warm barn, with its smell of cow dung, she gives the Frenchman two glasses of milk still warm from the cow while he sits on the bench beside the milk containers. The boy brings a piece of bread and two apples, and with gestures and her few words of French she indicates that he can't stay here—forbidden, keep going, Jammers still a long long way off, yes, toward the town of Baden, yes, vers là-bas, oui, très loin, direction Baden et après la ville de Brugg, and the boy has to go to the cheese factory before school so the stranger can ride on the back of his bike as far as the bridge. Toujours direction ouest et sud, and the names of a few villages that Gaston Nougier forgets, Siggenthal and Stilli and again Brugg.

"The day spent in the storage shed of a shut-down sawmill. Or at best in a hay barn beside the railway, but the passing trains are guarded by soldiers.

"Or a dog sniffs you out in a garden hut that you, frozen stiff, have broken into; the dog chases you out into the fields again.

"The old man driving the approaching beer wagon in the forest briefly reins in his horses, looks you up and down, then urges the animals on as if he had seen a Communist.

"Or the doors or lighted kitchen windows on the outskirts of the village, the peering faces, the eyes that measure you from head to toe, and hardly have you opened your mouth when the windows, doors, and faces close.

"Or then the schoolchildren, walking along in little groups; from them, from the older ones, you hear: Brugg? Yes, that way and the wooden bridge there and the cement plant in the distance, straight ahead; then they suddenly gape and run off without looking back.

"Then again a piece of bread through a window, even a piece of cheese—mais: allez, non non, allez, go away, and then, again from an old woman, a glass of hot tea hastily passed down through the window after cautious looks all around to make sure no one is standing behind the windows next door—allez-y, monsieur!

"He walked on, walked through snow, always toward the west-south-west, keeping to the edges of the forests on the southern flank of the Jura Mountains.

"God knows how he did it. Sepp, at home on leave for three weeks, had found Gaston at 11:30 that night, down in the avenue in a light snow flurry; lying on the ground, propped against one of the chestnut trees."

Thom could picture his father sitting in the Voltaire chair, raising the sherry glass to his lips and drinking. Saying nothing and listening. Saying, "Yes, go on." Or directing his eyes with their dark pouches, his tired, alert eyes, at Aunt Esther, and saying—this was 1946 or '47—"Yes, of course, Lilly told me about that Frenchman, and that he stayed in the house for seven weeks, until the major billeted in the house helped them obtain an internee pass for him. Hadn't he been an editor or something?"

"You know—I needn't tell you—what it was like in those internment camps. Gaston Nougier was sent to a camp near Frauenfeld. From there he worked in a cannery, for one franc an hour and up to fifteen hours a day.

"Then, here in the house, she nursed him back to health, bringing to his bedside whatever could be obtained on the black market from the farms in the valley; and when he finally stood out there at the top of the steps in the morning sunshine, newly arrayed in a made-over brown suit from your wardrobe and ready to leave for the camp, he looked almost in good health, tall, a fine figure of a man in his mid-forties. We had all come out to say goodbye, only Lilly was missing. Finally she appeared in the doorway, in her smart shirt blouse, her hair up; she saw us, hesitated. But then she walked down the steps and over to him and, as if it were the normal thing to do, embraced him. Downright shameless, the time she took over it. She didn't even wipe away her tears as she walked back up the steps to the front door, and now we could all see how she felt about marriage and faithfulness—do you understand?"

For a few seconds the burning bomber again roars before Thom's eyes over the hickory oaks, a gigantic fish, a shark hanging athwart the bright sky with the plume of smoke and the five hanged men against the sky behind it. It swoops above the chestnut trees in the avenue, thundering as it suddenly disappears behind the roof of the stables, no no, not adultery, Thom's mother with her hair up goes toward the stranger, she embraces him, her idea of faithfulness, you could easily have counted to three before the roar dies in the boom of the explosion coming from the forest beyond the town.

Aunt Esther leaned forward to stub out her cigarillo in the ashtray. "Now you know. And now you no longer have to wonder why the lamp on your wife's desk, upstairs in the Blue Room, is often burning until two in the morning. And why your Lilly goes to the post office every third day. Now you know what's going on; after all, you have a right to know, and now perhaps you can also figure out why, ever since then, the door to her Blue Room has been locked from the inside when you want to go to your wife, as a man, and no amount of knocking and pleading is going to help you, idiot. But it is also a sin the way you've let yourself go to the dogs since then—that's something you have to be told too."

Aunt Esther fell silent. Thom sensed that behind her closed eyes she was far away. Until she went on, and now, as before, she couldn't have meant him, Thom: "You can, if you must, do something about adultery. But the sad thing is: What can you do about a lost heart?"

Time
of the
Hedgehog

O r she would suddenly whisper, as if it were the Great Secret—a
secret between Thom and her alone, whisper in the torpid afternoon,
"What above all must you learn, Thom, if you want to become a man?"
Even though he would promptly respond bravery-courage-honor-wisdom,
she wanted to hear more from him, and Thom had to learn the meaning
of gritting-your-teeth, and that if you wanted to become a man you had
the right to use the virtue of cunning when faced by a superior opponent.
He tried this out in his mind, tried to circumvent the superior opponent
so he could grab him suddenly from behind. "Courage alone," said Aunt
Esther, "is stupidity," so sometimes Thom would stand stockstill as he
let his opponent approach and would wait to overpower him until the
opponent believed that Thom's resistance was broken. "Like a toreador.
Like our General Guisan, understand?"

In matters of honor, however, Thom had to learn that ahead of all
else came a woman's honor. It was up to him, as a man, to defend it,
whenever and wherever. The same applied to family honor—whenever
and wherever, "and you can lose your good name only once, Thom,
that's why, secondly, male honor is a man's most precious possession.
So fight in such a way that you can appear at any time before God and
country with a shining shield.

"But how can you expect to be brave, to be courageous, able to
defend honor at any time, if all this is but sounding brass to you?" Beyond
the window the heavy fresh snow that had fallen during the night was
glistening in the trees. Or the scent of blossoms drifted through the room.

Or fall had painted the leaves brown and red, and sometimes a blackbird flew out of the espalier with a loud twittering, and one of the ripe pears could be heard falling heavily through the leaves and striking the ground. Then Thom had to stand by the open window and twirl the ratchet until all the birds flew away into the Gütsch copse.

"It follows, then," she would say, "that wisdom is the foundation on which a man builds his life." Thom knew he was now going to hear about knowledge again, and that wisdom consisted on the one hand in recognizing all men, objects, and events for what they were as well as in their relationships to each other, and on the other in seeing them as they related to God, death, and Eternal Life. And once again she would tell him that knowledge was therefore the prerequisite for wisdom. Though all this made sense to him, sitting there on his stool, aged ten or eleven, by the open or closed window, his problem was that his brain simply wasn't big enough yet. Of course there were many things he already knew without having to think hard. So if Aunt Esther were then to light her cigarillo and ask him, "All right, Thom, what are we Swiss?" the response would come easily: "A nation of brothers." If she asked, "Since when?" he would know: "Since 1291." But no matter how he tried to keep in his head all those columns in the book she always gave him to study, he found it hard, for instance, not to confuse the name of the town encircled in 1941 by the German Afrikakorps, under General Rommel, with Toledo. And how in the world was he to relate to God and Eternal Life that parachute jump of Rudolf Hess's over Great Britain the same year? How was he supposed to remember how the Russians managed to halt the German panzer army before Moscow, since he couldn't find Stalingrad on the globe and it even took him a long time to find the Volga? To be sure, he had no trouble remembering that in 1941 the United States had established bases on the Galapagos Islands, which belong to Ecuador; and he would certainly never forget the staggering surprise attack by Japanese dive bombers on the American fleet in Pearl Harbor. But who was the commander in chief whom Adolf Hitler dismissed in order that he might personally take over the supreme command of the Eastern Army? Why did Thom have to learn that Virginia Woolf's novel *Between the Acts* was published in the year of her death? When did German troops start attacking the Soviet Union? Why was Heydrich, the Reich Protector of Bohemia and Moravia, assassinated; and who, in an act of reprisal, razed the village of Lidice to the ground? And was Thom to be haunted even in his dreams by the image of all the men in that village being shot? What was the purpose of American and British troops landing that same year in Morocco and Algeria? And what was Thom supposed to make of the words "final solution," and how was he ever to grasp what was happening from 1941 on in Auschwitz, Maidanek, and Dachau? That the scientist Enrico Fermi was the first to produce atomic energy by a chain reaction in the splitting of uranium on December 2, 1942, at 2:30 P.M. Chicago time, was not hard to remember; but what was he to answer if Aunt Esther proceeded to ask, "Very good, Thom, now tell me the five consequences of that successful experiment?" Or the novel *The Turning Point*, by Klaus Mann. Or when did Mauckly and Eckert develop the first large-scale electronic calculator? Who directed the German color film *The Golden City*, with Kristina Söderbaum? Who personally gave the order to execute hundreds of members of the Leftist underground organization, the Red Chapel? In what way was the first naval defeat of the Japanese in the Solomon Islands of significance for the war in the Far East? What is the name of the artist who is now world-famous for his animated cartoon *Bambi*? When did the popular fighter pilot Ernst Udet commit suicide, and why? And which Soviet general was in command when the German Fifth Army under General Paulus was trapped at Stalingrad? When did the painting *Marlene* cause a scandal in New York, and what is the name of the actress portrayed? Did the German painter of that portrait, Max Ernst, owe the prevention of his deportation from the United States to Ernest Hemingway or Peggy Guggenheim? What is the name of the private detective played by Humphrey Bogart in *The Maltese Falcon?* Who was the producer of the première of Bertolt Brecht's *Mother Courage* on April 19, 1941, at the Schauspielhaus in Zurich? Is the German reply to the nylon stocking challenge called "Persil" or "Perlon"? When was the Communist Party banned in Switzerland? To how many rounds per minute was a machine gun's rate of fire increased, on the basis of a development by Ludwig Winter: 700, 1,000, or 1,200? What happened in 1942 at the Mardi Gras ball in the concert hall in Jammers when the orchestra struck up "Alexander's Ragtime Band"?

Many a time Thom could only sit there and repeat, "I've forgotten." Then Aunt Esther would shake her head and once again threaten to tell him no more stories—"None, do you hear, you birdbrain?"—and supply the answers herself. At night, when he fell asleep over her history book, she was suddenly there, a great bird with folded, gray-speckled wings, her eyes glowing red from within, her beak coming closer and closer.

Behind her stood Mother and Grandfather Elsazar and Grandmother
Lilian and Great-Grandfather Theophil and Uncle Ludwig. They did
not speak. They looked at him as if he had besmirched the shining shield
of honor.

How does it come about? At five o'clock on the afternoon of a certain
June 30, 1982, a man like Thomas Winter takes down some gardening
boots from the shelf and a spade from Sepp's array of tools on the wall;
then, whistling softly to himself, he walks past the stables into the
avenue, and from there into the overgrown garden, the kitchen garden, enclosed by a thick box hedge, and here he begins, spadeful by
spadeful, to turn over the nearest bed, which is barely discernible under
its blanket of weeds. He works at the excessive speed that betrays the
amateur.

Amateur by inspiration, because while sitting at the shady stone
table on the terrace, leafing through rather than reading the newspapers,
he had felt a sudden urge to shake off his ruminations and do something
useful. Something physical, something visible and tangible that might
even have productive results—not right away but, who knows, in the fall
or next spring—potato plants might sprout there, tomatoes or peas might
ripen. But was now, midsummer, the right time for that? At the moment
he didn't want to know.

He worked. Soon he took off his shirt; perhaps he had underestimated
the temperature a bit. He tossed his shirt onto the box hedge. Naked to
the waist yet sweating, he dug the spade into the ground—which, though
moist below the surface, was hard—jerked the haft back, and turned over
the clods, causing plantains, dandelions, and strawberry roots to become
buried under their own fertile soil.

How does it come about? How does memory function? In which
zones of the body, of the human brain, is the past stored? The past, or
which parts of it, and how were they selected? Which reflexes, often
triggered by minute factors, come together in such a way that a person
like this Thom, who, his back already aching, is digging over the bed,
suddenly sees himself again in scenes from his childhood that he has
been trying for years to forget? Placing his boot once more on the edge
of the spade and thrusting the sharp blade into the earth, his foot and
hands guiding the spade felt it strike something hard when only halfway

down into the soil. He shoveled the object up into the light and bent down to toss the stone aside onto the path. His hand, his fingers, told him that the object he was holding was not a stone; it turned out to be a piece of stamped tin. He stood the spade upright in the earth beside him and with the fingers of both hands pressed and scraped away the dark lumps of earth from the object until he found himself holding an oval piece of metal, now suddenly much lighter—unmistakably the hollow form of the toy fish with which he used to bake those amusing dolphins in the wet sand, in the sandbox among the fir trees on the Gütsch hill—or, at this moment, as he examined the metal object, its curving shape, wavy and ribbed—some specks of pale blue in the fish's scales still adhering—or, at this moment, in the sand by the little Aeschi lake, close to the water's edge but not so close that the shining incoming waves could lick away his sand fishes. How does it come about that this man of forty-four is standing in the overgrown kitchen garden holding the rusty toy, and at the same time on this very afternoon, aged about five, is squatting at the water's edge baking his fish, dazzled by both suns—one on the water and the other already low in the sky, in that scene by the lake as if it were now?

Thom laid the fish on his shirt on the hedge and continued turning over one dark clod after another. As he went on digging, the scene did not go away. It became painful, too distinct, frayed; separate images kept flashing up in it, to give way simultaneously, at brief intervals, to others—strangely enough, to images of that evening when his mother had told him to accompany his father as he went off, drunk, in his pajamas and dressing gown, his bare feet in felt slippers, out the front door and into the night—an evening when Thom was already ten, twice as old as he had been beside the Aeschi lake—when his mother had ordered him to accompany his father as he staggered down the steps into the snow flurries of that night.

Thom had walked up the few steps from the little sandy beach to where his parents were lying in the meadow. He sat down on the grass between the two deck chairs, under the sun umbrella. On one side of him was his mother's yellow summer dress with its pattern of dark yellow moons; on the other side Father, in his white trousers and blue shirt, and from where Thom sat his fingers could touch his mother's foot as it swayed gently up and down in its leather sandal, and at the same time his father's white tennis shoe. The top half of his parents was hidden by the little two-wheeled tea trolley that the woman in the white apron had

pushed out. Between the legs of the trolley he could see Gret far out on
the raft, where she was sitting, her feet in the water, with three other
children. She waved, she called out something. Father waved back. An
ant was climbing up Thom's leg; when it reached his knee, Thom would
squash it. It felt good to sit here by the tea trolley and between the two
deck chairs, in the shade on the grass. Mother handed him down his
bottle of pop. Strawberry pop sucked through a straw was Thom's favorite.

He heard Father say, "It can't go on much longer—now, after
Stalingrad. Then we'll all go to Scheveningen. Or what would you suggest—Spain?"

Mother laughed. "Surely you don't believe that your Germans have
already been beaten? Granada," she added. "Granada, Almería. Remember? And on the way back Our Lady of Lourdes—"

The previous evening Father had come home on leave from the
army bringing Thom twelve lead soldiers and a wooden cannon drawn
by six little horses. It looked almost exactly like Father's cannons in his
regiment: each detachment had sixteen cannons, only much bigger, of
course. Father had explained to Thom the difference between a cannon
and a howitzer. Five days' leave. "And in the fall I'll be home for three
months. Then we'll take a trip. A vacation!" He laughed. Leaning forward
in his deck chair, he refilled his glass from the bottle of wine that he
took from the ice bucket on the tea trolley.

"You're right, all the frontiers will still be closed in the fall. So let's
just go to Lake Lucerne: Weggis, Vitznau! What do you say? *Prost!*"

In order to stay in the shade Thom shifted slightly away from the
trolley. Now he saw that there was a smile on Mother's face. "You know
what would be lovely?" She hesitated. "Just for once, we two alone—
just you and I. Like in the old days. Oh, how lovely that would be!" She
squinted into the sun.

Father twisted the umbrella pole toward the sun so that Mother's
face was once again in the shade. "Thank you," she said, and Thom
heard Father laugh. "Like in the old days? Better! Much better! What
do you think! During the day a boat trip, why not? And in the evening
we'll have a bang-up dinner somewhere—how about the Waldstätter Hof
in Gersau?" Mother smiled again. "Oh, Ulrich! And at last we'll have
some time again? Time for walks beside the lake—time for each other?
I was afraid it would never be like that again."

Gret called out something from the lake. Father waved, his arm
raised high. "Never again?" he said. "How can you say that! Why, now

it's really going to begin—life, I mean! Production has increased enormously! And the children are doing well—what more do you want? Never again? You must be joking!" He drank up his wine. "Better! Much better! Of course we'll have time for everything. We'll—": he hesitated, broke off.

Thom heard his father pouring himself some more wine. "Miss! Oh, Miss! Another bottle, please!"

Thom hid his face in his hands. He could feel something inside him going rigid: his muscles tensed even before the words RIDING CROP came to his mind. Sitting motionless between the two deck chairs, he didn't want to see anything more, not the sun sparkling on the water, didn't want to hear anything more, neither the shrieks from the water nor Gret's happy cries. At five years old, this much he knew when he was with Mother and Father, like now, and everything was good and warm around him: he must not trust his feeling of happiness, not for long. That sparkling feeling. No. Don't move. Make yourself small. Be there as if not there. How quickly the riding-crop feeling could be in the air and around you! A slash through the world, a blow from a riding crop—suddenly, yes, without warning, and Thom already knew what would come next, he felt it, knew it, could already hear Father perhaps saying again, "Much better—where did you get *that* idea—you must be joking—of course there'll be time, loads of time, and in the early morning you'll be kneeling in the nearest church or chapel, beseeching your Heavenly Mother for strength! And mercy for him, the sinner, your husband—oh, you can really drive a person up the wall with your stiff-necked martyrish expression! That's what you want, isn't it? Strength to drive me up the wall? Admit it!" Father would drink up his wine and refill his glass and drink up, a new bottle would come, more refilling, more drinking up. The sun must have dropped behind the mountain. The second sun, the one in the water, had drowned. Thom shivered. "Much better, dammit! I've had enough! The bill, please!" Mother was standing at the water's edge, calling Gret to come in. Thom stood up. "Come along," Father said. "We men will go ahead." Thom ran along beside him.

And stood there or turned over the soil—how did it come about that in broad daylight he was trotting along beside Father at the lake in front of the Seehotel, and simultaneously he was here in the kitchen garden busy driving the spade into the soil, but while he lifted out the clods of earth and tipped them to the right—they glistened with dark moisture in the late afternoon, the two ends of a severed worm coiling around themselves—everything smelled cool, and at the same time and as if doubled and tripled he was trotting beside Father across the field, brightness, brightness of snow in the night, brightness and dread of the riding crop in his memory, simultaneously—how was it possible, how did that come about? How did it come about that Thom felt that the worst part was not Father's presence, not even those—to Thom totally incomprehensible—abrupt switches from joy to fury—no, not even Father's rage-suffused face, nor his eyes above their dark pouches, nor his curses, greatly though he feared them—no, the worst part was Mother's silence. Hardly ever did she cry. No matter how much Father raged, she was silent. Didn't she know that by her silence she provoked him to ever wilder outbursts? For days following such scenes she would talk to no one, not even Charlott or Gret; and only when she eventually, often in the middle of the day, called for Thom did he know what to expect.

He trotted along beside Father. Behind the Seehotel, Father paced up and down. Thom retreated to the far side of their parked black car, facing the forest, and sat down on the running board. He could hear Father muttering to himself. Or Father suddenly shouting, "Aren't you ever coming? Those damned females!" Thom made himself small. Don't move. Be there as if not there. When they were finally sitting in the car, Father drove off with a roar of the engine. In the curve leading to the gravel road, a jolt shook the car: Father had ripped the bumper off a car parked on the right. Gret and Thom, who were sitting in the back, looked straight ahead. They knew that Father could observe them in the mirror.

"Much better! That damned Blessed Virgin of yours! You've got it all nicely figured out again!" Driving across country, through villages. Hardly any traffic, except for farm carts or people on bicycles. Even Thom knew that now, in wartime, gasoline was precious; only important people like Father were allowed to drive cars.

At some point Father fell silent. Thom looked straight ahead between his parents' shoulders. Beyond the long hood he could see the car constantly swerving to the left of the road. When Father narrowly avoided a horse-drawn hay wagon, Mother and Gret screamed.

On reaching home Gret and Thom ran up the steps and straight into the kitchen. Gret reported, "He's at it again!" and she and Thom fled upstairs with Charlott into Charlott's room.

Charlott's eyes, wide open and round as cherries. And then? Where had Mother sat? But why—two bottles? Three? So suddenly? Why? Why?

There they sat, Gret and Thom on Charlott's bed, Charlott on the floor in the corner beside the closet. Her cheeks were pale. They were all listening.

And suddenly Charlott said, "Can you keep a secret? Do you swear? And you too?" Her voice dropped. "It's all because of me. I know it. Four weeks ago I decided to renounce the faith." Her voice barely trembled as she said: "I've left the Catholic Church. See that?"

She pointed to the wall over her bed. "There's nothing there," Thom said.

"You're wrong," Charlott whispered. "There's no Jesus Christ on the Cross anymore. Don't you see? And there, beside the door, the little pitcher of holy water? And over there: the Blessed Virgin of Einsiedeln— all gone. I put the crucifix and everything into a box, with a stone, and tied it up. And buried it all in the fir copse."

"But why because of you? Do you mean God's punishment?" And Gret added, "Maybe you've just gone crazy. And anyway, how did you renounce the faith!" Thom couldn't quite imagine that either.

But again Charlott, saying, "If you can't understand, why should I tell you about it? Let Thom find out for himself when that riding crop gets going again! And you," turning to Gret, "you should really be old enough by now to understand." It was, after all, a sacrifice. She had been to Saint Sebastian's Church. One afternoon, the church almost empty, and she had gone right up to the communion bench and uttered that most wicked of all curses—"you know the one"—then walked back down the center aisle to the door. There, without touching the threshold, she had left the church.

Father's voice could be heard from downstairs. They listened. Charlott stood up and opened the door a crack, then turned her face toward Thom. "Today you're not going! That's right, Gret, isn't it? Today we simply won't allow it." Thom crept under the quilt. He could feel himself trembling. There was no sound from Father. Was the silence to be trusted? Since at any moment that voice might be raised again and echo through the house: "Where's Thom? Thom, go at once and bring me my riding crop from upstairs! I won't let myself be bamboozled by anybody, least of all by my own brood! Come on, come on, down with your pants—lie down here!" Yes, since the voice of the big heavy man who was Thom's father might once again bark hoarsely through the Paneled Room while the crop came down on Thom's bare buttocks, his thighs, and his back, again and again.

Charlott reported that Father was on his way up the stairs. She switched off the light. "He's stopped. He's listening. Can you hear?"

After a while Father came padding along the gallery and past them. The door of his room shut behind him. Gret lay back on the quilt. Through the quilt Thom could feel with his feet that she was sobbing. Charlott had sat down again in the dark in her corner. The voice did not return.

Perhaps this time Father hadn't thought of the riding crop. That was a possibility, after all. But even if Father's voice were to call him now, even if blows from the crop were to descend on him again: that was not the worst. Worse than that were the words his mother used when she became worked up, the words and the way she whispered them to him, in an even but searing, threatening tone: "You've taken leave of your senses! You with your black heart! Do you know that the Devil will get you?"

Gret, still lying on her back, spoke to the ceiling. "But why because of you? And if you renounce the faith—that's not a sacrifice! A mortal sin, that's what it is! And if you've left the Church, that makes two. And 'God damn me' makes three. You're crazy—three!"

When Charlott used that voice, nothing could bring her around. One mortal sin, and you go to Purgatory. Two, and you'll end up in Hell. Three, and Satan will come for you on the spot.

"Charlott, I'm scared," said Gret. "Perhaps Jesus will forgive you? I'll pray three rosaries for you—please go and confess, please!"

And Charlott: "Why can't they understand?"

There was now a tear on Gret's cheek. "Do you really want to go straight to Hell?"

"Yes," said Charlott. Gret sat up. She began to laugh, she was laughing, almost soundlessly. "There's no way you can do that. You're just crazy, that's all."

"Why not?"

"Because Satan doesn't take crazy people." But Charlott was already talking again. So, in order to free Father from Satan's clutches, she had promised herself, body and soul, to Satan. Three mortal sins. So she had uttered the dreadful curse, she had left the Church, and the only thing she hadn't quite managed yet was to renounce the faith. "Not yet," she said. She looked at Thom and Gret. "Suppose our Heavenly Mother really did conceive without sin, and suppose Jesus Christ really did redeem us, what then? Do you see what I mean?" Tears on her face now too.

She still had these doubts, she said, still, and so she hadn't fully kept her bargain with Satan, and that was why Satan hadn't let go of Father yet. "Do you understand? Because of me!"

As she got up and switched on the light, "But I'm sure I'll be able to." She smiled.

Yes, how on earth did it come about? How could that all be right there again? Now snow was there, snow flurries; great sails of snow were drifting over the plain below; in the sky they hid the white disk of the moon. Now Thom and Father were walking across the fields, the snow stinging their cheeks and eyes. From time to time Father had to wait for Thom to catch up. He took Thom by the hand. Thom kept thinking, but in his pajamas, with only his bathrobe over them, and wearing a hat, that wasn't right, and only his felt slippers on his bare feet? After all, Mother had told Thom to put on his blue windbreaker over his sweater and knee pants before sending him off after Father. This much Thom knew, that Father was heading for one of the taverns over in Kappel. Father wouldn't stand for having his wine locked away from him in his own house, no indeed. "Would you, Thom?" "You had better run after him," his mother had said, "and at least see that he doesn't fall down somewhere and not get up." Yes, Thom was proud. Now instead of Father holding him by the hand, *he* was leading Father. Beyond the snow sails they could see the distant lights of Kappel. Father laughed. "We're both going to catch our death out here, what do you think! Come on, Thom, let's go!"

Yes, how does it come about, how does it work? Will those ancient, those blurred, flickering images, their sounds, smells, and horrors, never disappear?

Leafing through the Festschrift IV

THE GREAT WAR OF 1914/18 BROUGHT INTENSE ACTIVITY TO OUR plants—but slacked off again—could not avoid the consequences. The crisis spreading from the United States of America

The primary cause of the worldwide crisis was—army of unemployed—more than one-third of the Winter work force. Plummeting prices were followed by currency breakdowns as well as protectionist—

together with a serious agricultural crisis—toward the end of the decade this cumulative deterioration led—and contributed to a political polarization

Seen as a whole, however, thanks to the adaptability and entrepreneurial spirit of our management under the dynamic leadership of Mr. Ulrich Winter, the low point of the Depression was passed in 1933/34—once more a steady upward trend

in particular, the widening scope of our products—among them, marine engines with direct fuel injection and a thermal efficiency of 47.3 percent, at that time a record achievement, as well as

In 1936 the construction of the compression-molding works (plastics of all kinds) for radios, telephones, etc., in Solothurn was

the first single-tube steam generator for hypo- and hypercritical pressures and temperatures up to 650 degrees Centigrade could be erected in Brussels, and one year later two additional, improved installations in Lyon and Zurich.

the armaments sections now also underwent a rapid capacity-expansion. Specifically, in the area of machine-gun and hand-grenade production, the types developed by the Winter plants in Lucerne and Liestal achieved impressive increases, with both domestic and foreign sales

In 1938 the hands and heads of more than 6,000 persons were employed in the manufacture and sale of our products. By way of comparison: When the corporation was founded in 1907, there were 800—a twelvefold increase in production as well as

Saint-Rémy, July 1, 1982

My dear Thom,

Your express letter arrived barely an hour ago. It is five P.M., and I am lying on a large many-colored knit blanket given me by Madame Hussin—lying here in the garden behind the hotel. Above me the rustling in the plane tree, around me the sparkle of light as if the sun were scattering handfuls of silver dollars through the branches.

Your story about smashing your mother's plaster Madonna—your search is obviously putting you in touch with some explosive material within yourself. Just as well that its force, now that you are approaching it, is directed outward rather than against you. As I reread your letter, the question just occurred to me of how many such images from childhood I ought also to bring to the surface and destroy.

Or what you write about the wheel and its momentum, about the Great Machine, and how, no longer controlled but controlling, it has dominated and defined you all, you and your clan. I can't get the picture out of my mind. Mustn't we all by this time have the feeling that we are caught up in the Great Machine? It rotates, rotates us in its unleashed autodynamics; those who still believe they are controlling it are themselves controlled? An added danger: the machine is becoming more and more abstract, more and more inconspicuous, it seems to me. Its tone is becoming more and more friendly. Only a gentle hum proclaims its encompassing presence. In accordance with its own electronic impulses and reflexes, its rays penetrate walls, bodies, and psyches with its programs. Malfunctions are not ruled out, but the remedy for them is discreetly programmed in. What will happen when their enormous energy potentials explode one day?

Recently a colleague of mine at Radio Free Berlin invited us to visit her at the station's switching center, where she works as a controller. All those images and sounds which that digital technology enable them to pick up and broadcast across countries and, by satellite, across continents! Afterward, four of us sat in our office discussing the question of where, perhaps even tomorrow, installations of this type will autonomously control traffic and production, service sectors and agriculture, planning, and the leisure time of carefree individuals. The Great Machine—yes, a nightmare vision of the last few decades: it is now reality. You know Renate—she said something like, "Men's mania for omnipotence is devouring their own children—including us."

On the way here, between Jammers and Bern, I read the *Weltblatt* you bought for me at the station. A full-page ad extolled the precision instruments of the Winter Corporation. Even before we reached Bern, I saw through the train window a factory complex with the eye-catching block letters of the Winter Corporation with the big W—Winter Air-Conditioning Systems, Winter Electronics.

There was a man sitting across from me, a heavyset fellow wearing suspenders, and I asked him who owned this Winter Corporation, curious to hear whether he knew.

He lowered his newspaper, *La Suisse.* "Oh, some holding company or other, I suppose. And that in turn is owned by three or four other concerns, some West German, some American. Or the other way around:

the Winter Corporation owns seven other concerns, and the major banks are involved, and United Technologies, Minnesota, U.S.A., registered in the Bahamas—these conglomerates are all connected and their holdings so interlocked that everything dissolves into anonymity. Perhaps," he went on, "you now want to know who's liable for all of this? Capital. And that, as we know, has only limited liability." The man smiled. And switched to French: "Qu'est-ce-que vous voulez?" he said. It sounded as if he meant: That's life.

But you were asking, my dear: What do I know about you? I've already told you quite a lot. Father's death when I was barely two years old. A captain in the Wehrmacht, killed in January 1945 east of Glogau on the Oder. So all I had was my mother, to whom I clung until I was nineteen, and my brother Klaus, who was two years younger than I. I told you about Mother's suicide, also that Klaus drowned a year later while swimming in the Rhine. Her death, his death: for a long time after that I was convinced that the people I loved must die. So I am still grateful to Wolfgang, even though our marriage didn't work out; he made it possible for me to discover that that terrible equation was not inevitable. Yes, my mother was the center for me, especially when, after the long journey from Chemnitz via Munich, we landed at her Catholic relatives in Andernach. I could not warm to them.

She was spontaneous, warm-hearted, generous; a bit sloppy, not averse to stretching a point, left Heaven to the devout, and Hell too. What bound me to her so strongly was her way of always being unstintingly there for me even during my fits of rebellion. Yet as a clerk in an architect's office she didn't have an easy time of it. So it was all the more terrible for me that while I was away on a three-day school outing, and my brother was at boarding school, she should slip away from life, with pills. To this day I am searching for the reason. And I am only gradually beginning to forgive her the betrayal. As for her having instilled in me her ideas of conventional female behavior—what else could she have done? At least through her I found out that self-confidence and financial independence are essential to my autonomy as a woman.

When I picture my mother, with her rather chubby cheeks and her cheerful laugh, and then that sudden end, and when at the same time I visualize your mother's photograph on the black sideboard in your house, her dark-blond hair done up in a braid that, judging by the half-profile, seems to continue down her back; the starched white collar above the pale blouse; the eyes severe, the mouth too, in spite of the smile on her face—two female portraits, two lives of women who are linked in that they did not accept their fate as being a mere sacrifice. (By the way, as I contemplate them I find myself wondering where, somewhere between them, I might fit in. . . .)

But apart from this common factor: How far apart the two are, if only in each one's personal history and in each one's death! What a social gulf, what differences—you are right—in the general history that they, each in her German-speaking country, lived through. Now I understand what you mean when you write that we belong to two different cultures. And I still haven't spoken of our fathers, neither of mine—I could speak only about his absence and of my longing to have spent, at least once, a day of my life with him—nor of yours. The fact that he seems close to me when you talk about him, close in spite of his compulsion to seek oblivion and in spite of his terrible riding crop, close in the almost monumental contradictions in his nature, is because of you: your animation when you speak of him. I can see you sitting at night at my kitchen table on Schlüter-Strasse in Berlin as you said, "God, yes, I was devoted to him."

Two worlds of background and experience. Do we have a chance, we two? For after all, we are here now, each with our baggage, separated by less than seven hundred kilometers. I wish that at this very moment you would sit down on this blanket, on the grass that is already sunscorched even here under the plane tree. You would lie back, as I just did, and overhead we would have this leafy, many-ribbed dome.

Do you know what I would show you? Of course you couldn't know that, about five meters above me, a red squirrel has retreated into the first fork. I would show you how you can see only its delicate nose and the little triangular ears above it, if you look carefully.

And would tell you, while the squirrel keeps its eyes and ears on us, about my experience with the little animal, yesterday and a hundred years ago.

I was sitting here yesterday at this time too, leaning against the trunk of the plane tree and reading the Meinrad Inglin novel you recommended so highly when you gave it to me.

I had the book in front of me on my drawn-up knees. Suddenly I was startled by a small stone falling just past my forehead onto one of the two pages; it rolled across the print and the margin, leaving behind a trail of purplish spots. Then I realized it was a cherry stone newly released from the fruit. Under a plane tree? I looked up. Overhead, in the fork, just like now, the squirrel was sitting in plain view. It was laughing, believe me, Thom: it was laughing.

But that's not the end of the story. To start with, I read the passage in the book that had been marked, so to speak, by the rolling cherry stone. Ammann Senior is talking to his son Severin, the journalist, who is complaining about his brother Paul, as follows: "He is possessed by that typical arrogance of the literati who consider themselves above criticism even if they have no idea what they are talking about. I am sorry, but he is a hopeless case." Although you're not one of the literati, but still something of the kind, do you suppose the squirrel was trying to warn me with that passage?

Seriously, though: a little later—I hadn't yet read as far as the outbreak of World War I—a scratching noise, also a sound as if someone were discreetly blowing his nose, startled me and made me look up again. This time I jumped up. Barely an arm's length above me, clinging to the piebald tree trunk as if stuck to it, was the squirrel, upside down, its little head thrust forward, and again it seemed to be laughing at me. Only its pointed ears were moving, listening. Or was the cute creature trying to tell me something? For almost a minute we regarded each other across the two meters between us; then in a flash the squirrel turned around, its head now uppermost against the trunk and its tail pointing down, and I noticed that a tuft of fur was missing from the tip of its bushy tail. Yes, the tail looked as if about five centimeters had been cut off the end of it, or, for all I know, bitten or shot off.

And now it was winter; the little orchard behind my uncle's house in Andernach, on the edge of town, lay deep in snow. Through the dormer window in my attic room I could see the squirrel, sharply outlined against the gray sky, sitting in the bare branches of the big pear tree, when from down below a shot rang out. I knew the squirrel; we had already made friends the previous spring. At the time—I was about fourteen—I had often placed a chair beneath the sloping ceiling and climbed out through the window onto the roof; there, before Mother came back from work, I was more or less safe from the acrimonious voices of our relatives in the house. The red squirrel, as it scampered up and down the tree, had often kept me company for half the afternoon, all through that summer and fall. I used to talk to it. I called it "Lilliput." I knew where it retreated into its hole in the tree at midday.

Now another shot from Uncle's BB gun. Hit a second time, the animal twitched and tried to hide high up in the bare treetop. Another shot, this one missed. I began screaming into the gray afternoon: "Stop! Mur-der!" Another shot from below the roof gutter. The squirrel fell off its branch: some two meters lower it managed to cling to some branches. I screamed up into the sky. I saw Lilliput, badly wounded, fall from the tree; the light body disappeared below the roof gutter. When I ran downstairs, Uncle Josef was standing in the kitchen doorway, saying to Aunt, "Just like '41 in Croatia! The partisans also used to hide in the trees!"

Uncle's hands and the knife were bloody when he came out of the laundry room. And outside in the snow, dark blood too, and Uncle Josef's footprints. Close to the tree trunk I found a tuft of reddish fur. It had been the tip of the squirrel's tail. I took it and put it away with my hair ribbon, Grandmother's silver brooch, my brother's milk tooth, the uniform button, and the two letters, all of which I kept in my silver box hidden beneath my underwear at the back of the closet. Filled with all that stuff, including the tuft of fur, the box is still in my closet on Schlüter-Strasse.

Can you understand, Thom: For quite a while, and as I was still standing in the garden behind the hotel in Saint-Rémy, watching the squirrel as it showed me its bushy tail and what was missing from it, I knew at the same moment that in my room, in my silver box, in Andernach and Berlin, I had the missing tuft. Or should I say that here, suddenly and after twenty years, I once again had the squirrel that had been missing from the tuft all those years? However that may be, I said— softly so as not to scare the squirrel—"Hello Lilliput! How are you?" With its little head turned toward me, its ears pricked, Lilliput laughed back. Then the squirrel took its time climbing back up the tree trunk and resumed its post above me in the fork, as if wanting to keep an eye on me. And there it is again today, jauntily sitting just above me.

By now it is 10:30, and I am sitting at a small table in the lobby, while across the room the TV set is entertaining the other guests, and I must admit to feeling somewhat useless and romantic when I read once again how your search is leading you into ever more confusing labyrinths. (After dinner I went for a walk in the town, the air still very warm, and then, almost a regular customer by now, drank my rosé sitting outside Silvio's Bar.) So now, to go by Aunt Esther's wicked old wives' fantasies, you are supposed to be the person you're looking for? I can only marvel at how calmly you report on this somersault of the whole thing into the absurd!

I intend to arm myself with a veritable panoply of patience. But what should I wish for you? I keep wondering. Also patience? Persistence? Vulnerability, or perhaps rather the fleece of invulnerability? In any case: Be alive! And I hold you close.

Your Lis

P.S. My good feelings for you: Yes! But half an hour ago, while rereading this letter, written late last night, I suddenly felt that they are not the whole story! I brought the letter with me when I came for breakfast on the terrace, intending to drop it in the mailbox at the corner. So while I was sitting at my little table waiting for my breakfast and squinting into the bright sunny weather out there in the park, I was overcome by rage. It was—no, it *is* rage at you. Why on earth should I be spending my vacation in this little town of Provence, pleasant though it is, left all alone?

How intensely I had been looking forward to sharing these days with you! Looking forward to being at last without a clock, with no need to solve any job problems, meet any deadlines, to having—geographically separated from all pressures of work—three whole weeks here to ourselves—time to discover each other by discovering a landscape together. Why should I, all alone, absorb the people here and all this beauty, the cloud formations, the churches, antiquities, trees, as well as the horrors of destructive industry? By becoming aware of these things together, we could at the same time become aware of each other. We could embrace, even argue occasionally, about me, about you, without my having to be in the office by eight o'clock and you at your work. Why should I allow myself to be deprived of all these possibilities, allow them to be destroyed at the very outset—for the sake of a cause which, I know, is very important to *you*? How did I suddenly get pitched once again into the role of the self-denying sympathizer? You abandon yourself to your memories, your traumas, your stories of your history—I feel cheated, Thom! Yes, you're cheating me—in a manner of speaking and, of course, involuntarily— with this search for your own and your family's past, this search for your own self. I am outraged! And what's more, filled with jealousy of your mother, who apparently still manages, twenty years after her death, to claim your attention to the extent that I am left with the role of the faraway sister who is so full of understanding. I hate her!

I know—if I were in your place I could probably act no differently from you. And I also know that if, contrary to that compulsion of yours to solve this terrible riddle, you were to arrive here by the first possible train, you might be physically here, but: could you detach yourself from that riddle? You see that once again my understanding nature is forcing me to exonerate you and to transfer my rage—but to what? To the great Absent One, the author of our life story? To what is called Fate? Let *it* at least be cursed! Whoever may be the novelist who has concocted our story, I'd like to kick him in the shin, I'd like to see him in Hell.

Five minutes have passed since the Hell wish. I went for a walk—highly incensed, I must admit—in the park and finally took my first sip of coffee—rather watery, by the way. My small fist that was defying the gods is now unclenched; sunshine and birdsong are warming my soul again. Don't rejoice too soon—I won't take back a thing. But at least one consoling thought has struck me. Whether or not you find the answer you are looking for in that decaying house, this journey through the catacombs of your childhood will change you, no matter what happens. Will enable you—I feel convinced of this—to open yourself toward us, toward our shared present. You will be liberated from a piece of the past.

So, my dearest, accept this rage as a part of me. Together with my hope. Together with the wish for a long, close embrace!

Your Lis

The General's Politics V

WHAT ABOUT THE ECONOMIC BACKGROUND—E.G., THE RAW MATERIAL basis—to Switzerland's political actions?

What was the economic scene behind the myth that the people of Switzerland, united in solidarity, were determined to resist at all costs?

Describe:

1. Switzerland's close-meshed ties with Nazi Germany even before mid-1940; their subsequent intensive reinforcement.

2. German demands and pressures.

3. The total economic exposure of the little island of Switzerland (4.5 million inhabitants in 1941) completely surrounded by the Axis powers.

4. Export: of high-quality, militarily essential goods and services from Switzerland to the Third Reich (machinery, weapons, watches, etc.).

5. Imports from the Third Reich: of raw materials, especially iron,

coal, fuel, chemicals. Thus in 1943 Switzerland imported as much as 14 million tonnes of coal (60 percent of its requirements) plus 1.3 million tonnes of iron (50 percent of its requirements).

In other words: From mid-1940 on, an export blockade by Germany and Italy would have sufficed to ruin the Swiss economy within a few months (not to say weeks). And what would be the use of any army, however determined, to an encircled country deprived of its economic basis?

6. The "battle for agricultural production": According to Professor Friedrich T. Wahlen's plan, "every piece of land was listed in a production registry and, wherever the plan called for it, opened up and planted. Even recreation areas and parks were turned into grain and potato fields" (Rings, *Switzerland in Wartime*). However, the Wahlen Plan raised agricultural production by no more than 10 percent. Point out here the differentiated rationing system for food, etc.

7. In terms of raw materials Switzerland was, as shown, susceptible to blackmail. The resistance strategy required "trump cards" that could be used to compensate, at least partially, for the disastrous effects of this dependence.

Possible "trump cards" for this were:

(a) from a military point of view: the mountainous terrain that favored the defender over the attacker;

a strong, well-trained, and by now well-equipped army imbued with a determined fighting spirit;

shrewdly staged defense preparations, aimed always at exacting the maximum price for a potential conquest.

(b) from a politico-economic point of view:

Possession of the Alpine crossings, especially the Alpine tunnels, which could be blown up within hours. They were placed at the disposal of the Axis powers: 1,800 carloads of German goods moved daily through Switzerland to Italy.

Credit system: Switzerland was more than an efficient supplier of the Third Reich; it was also capable of granting generous credits (clearing credits). By the end of the war, the German Reichsbank owed Switzerland as much as 1.2 billion francs.

What other factors would ensure that the rulers of the Third Reich would remain interested in the continued existence of a neutral, more or less autonomous Switzerland? Possible answer: the bank vaults. Were there any (relatively) safer places in which to store hoarded stocks of gold and looted valuables than the secret numbered safe deposit boxes in the armored vaults of Swiss banks—also for the personal requirements of the rulers?

8. The General's politics—also vacillating! (cf. following paragraphs)—aimed at resistance.

The government's foreign policy wavered between resistance, concessions, and accommodation.

Beyond this—deliberate—double game, Switzerland's policy vis-à-vis the Third Reich is shown to be completely contradictory, even schizophrenic, in light of the economic cooperation, especially in the sphere of arms exports.

Incidentally, the violations of the neutrality principle by *these* activities would appear to be considerably more flagrant than Guisan's violations deriving from his relatively one-sided alliance policy.

Example: On June 21, 1940, immediately after the armistice between the Reich government and France, Mr. Fierz, head of the ordnance department (in the Swiss military section), went to Berlin to offer the Reich government additional services on the part of the Swiss armaments industries (cf. Edgar Koeppel, *The Problematic Nature of Swiss War Matériel Exports 1939–45*; also Peter Hug, Bern, on the same theme; also Daniel Dürst, *Swiss Neutrality and War Matériel Exports*, dissertation, Zurich).

Fierz's mission was obviously a success. After his return, Fierz called upon his former employer, the firm of Bührle AG, in Oerlikon, specializing in armaments, to "deliver as speedily as possible to Germany." The head of the Swiss Department of Commerce reported that "no stone was left unturned to promote exports to Germany across the board." Such appeals by Swiss authorities to private enterprise are to be "deemed clear violations of Article 6 of Hague Convention XIII" (Koeppel). "Even the minimal stipulations of the Hague Convention were violated in at least five different ways" (Hug). Unfortunately it is not possible to cover all of this far-reaching area within the limitations of this study.

At least point out: The economic policy of the Bern government, together with the major Swiss banks and certain industries, gained very considerable profits from this dependence on the Third Reich. While that can be seen as a shrewd, cunning "David vs. Goliath" policy, the fact that all over the country, starting in the summer of 1940, Swiss machines (including those of small subcontractors) were producing for the German final victory is remarkable for more than its neutrality aspect.

(Question: What information could "our" director, Mr. Berger, give about such exports by the Winter Corporation?)

Obviously: This export policy of Switzerland toward a regime whose policy was typified by everything Auschwitz stood for contains unmistakable elements of Switzerland's historical shared guilt in the Nazi crimes.

In conclusion make clear: Neither the arms exports nor the other "trump cards" mentioned offset the paradox: Any military resistance to, any defense preparations against, Hitler's Germany on the part of the General remained economically dependent on that same Germany.

(Also quote Jakob Tanner here: *Federal Budget, Currency, and War Economy*.)

Passages IV

MARTEN HUNT, AT NIGHT—THAT WASN'T LIKE SOME MERRY CHASE through stables, fields, or forest. It was sitting on a half-empty sack of flour in the storeroom under the stairs to the gallery, it was a target rifle in the hand under the arm of a thirteen-year-old and the flashlight to be switched on by Cousin Rolf, two years younger, when those soft scratching noises made by claws on the wooden beam above the old vinegar barrel announced the arrival of the marten. Marten hunt, at night—that had little to do with hunting and a lot to do with smells and listening open-mouthed, and with waiting waiting in the dark. Or hearing Rolf, close beside him, breathing hard in his excitement, then briefly the smell of vinegar would waft across from one barrel, and from the other barrel, covered with a piece of old muslin, would come the smell of elderflowers steeped in sugar water and a little kirsch, silently foaming and fermenting to produce Herminia's special bittersweet brew, laced with woodruff.

Or there was also a smell of horse sweat and leather from the two saddles hanging over the banister on the right when, after Aunt Esther's and Uncle Ludwig's ride, Sepp had slung them onto the wooden railing where the cellar stairs went down into the vaults, haunt of the cellar witch, or the mass murderer Dillinger, or the vampires, or the souls of the damned.

It was waiting and staying awake, staying awake, don't nod off and start up at the slightest wingbeat of a moth fluttering against the wire grille of the store cupboard where, wrapped in a damp linen cloth, the hunk of Emmentaler cheese was sweating and slowly turning saltier; waiting and starting up in the dark and feeling your heart pounding in your throat because this barely audible sound was not the moth against the grille and not the beams—those beams that, working in the stress between the warmth of the evening and the chill of the night, seemed every so often to groan—no, it had to be the soft scratching of claws, the sound so long awaited, by now past midnight, of the marten's paws, and for a second, or as long as it takes to raise and aim a target rifle, its safety catch already off, and simultaneously to nudge Cousin Rolf as a sign to point the flashlight at the black beam and the rough plaster wall behind it, now, right now

for this one second, or two, the marten, although the light had not yet picked it up, appeared in a shining cone of light, was there, erect, startled, rigid, its foxy head raised, its ears pricked, in its eyes a wild, bloodthirsty flicker, standing there, a king of the night, otherwise betrayed only by tracks of blood in the poultry yard or the dovecote—was there, brought to bay, caught red-handed, an open target in this silence that roared in your ears

but now and only now did the cone from Rolf's flashlight fall upon beam and wall. Only now, beyond the notch and the dancing bead along the barrel, was there nothing to be seen, no marten, only the rough oak beam, dried out over a hundred years into iron and blackened by time in front of the plaster wall, no marten on it, only now a shot and already pointless, marten hunt, that was still the fluttering of the moth against the cupboard grille, was waiting waiting and scratching sounds and vinegar smell, it was the flaring up in the darkness for two seconds of the dreamed and longed-for image, was sitting there and a shot and that little bullet hole in the plaster and that bit of dust in the air and a sweetish smell of powder and a marten that, at least this night, refused to come.

Then suddenly again the feeling that he would go on poking around in the past until the end of his days. Suppose even death were not final, not deadly enough, and he were to search the house and the smells and images and voices through all eternity for that one clue?

Hatred was what killed people by people. So all right, or all wrong.

Did he now, on July 1, 1982, on the seventh day after discovering that entry in Aunt Esther's handwriting, did he know any more than this truism? Hatred, and its covert origin, fear?

On this Thursday morning he was again standing at the open window of the Blue Room, again as if paralyzed, before him between the two hickory oaks the distant view of the roofs of the town. Even they, the oak trees, his allies from the old days, were there, raising their crowns aloft, yet he felt as if with their lush foliage they were no longer shining at him in friendship. They stood there absorbed in themselves. Yes, in the increasing folly of his search, even they left him to himself.

Yesterday evening, after working in the garden, he had walked from the washhouse across the rear terrace and into the house. From the hall he had seen Frieda, carrying a tray, step out of the kitchen into the dim light of the passage. He had approached her. Would she please tell Aunt Esther that he would like to look in on her in five minutes.

Frieda had stopped, nodded as usual, but, already turning toward the door of the suite, said this was not possible, it wasn't "a good time for her—you understand."

"Please, Frieda, it's important."

With her free left hand she opened the door. As soon as his aunt felt better, she would let him know. It was only when she was inside and carefully closing the door that she looked up at him. Her wrinkled face showed fear—or rather, showed the scared determination of an accessory. As if the old lady were at death's door, she whispered, "Nothing must excite her—nothing, Thom!" And without waiting for his reaction, she shut the door as if forever.

Feeling his rage mounting in him again, he had gone across to the kitchen, taken the bottle of wine and a glass from the cupboard behind the door, and sat down at the table. After the first gulp, forcing himself to be calm, he asked Herminia what was the matter with Aunt Esther.

Herminia was standing at the sink, stripping leaves from a head of lettuce. "In this heat," she said. The water from the faucet splashed into the colander. "Digging over flowerbeds, in this heat! Early morning's the time for that!" She shook her head. And now he must surely be tired. Thom took another gulp. After turning off the water, she brought the colander to the long table. And just then, before he had asked his other, his big question, she said, "Surely a person must be able to forget! That's what I tell Gret, and I'm telling you too!" And after a while: "Why don't you say something?"

What could he have replied? When Herminia started preparing the salad dressing, he got up and went into the Paneled Room. Then, after a taciturn supper, Samuel had entertained him with the problems arising from the development of the electronically controlled hydropump system for mountainous and desert regions. Moreover, he was able to report that the employees at the Seveso branch had gone back to work.

"What concessions did you have to make?"

"None," said Samuel.

So the hickory oaks out there could no longer be trusted either. Who could have so greatly feared, so greatly hated, Lilly Winter, née Schaub? Might it have been a settling of accounts from her earlier life as the unmarried daughter of Thom's grandfather Jeremias? What he knew about her from those days didn't amount to much. At thirteen she had been the owner of the first bicycle for miles around. She had attended high school, the only girl in her class, had graduated in economics from a boarding school in Fribourg, and—surely daring for her time—had gone on to study chemistry, including two years in Berlin. He saw her for a moment: her face very close, very animated; she used to laugh when she described her two years in Berlin, seeming for a few seconds to be illuminated within before resuming her usual consciously impassive expression, her voice again slightly breathless but calm, and then she would say she had come back, her father had needed her in the head office of the comb factory, and that was where she stayed—"then we got married."

Had university, had Berlin, been her first attempt to break out? Thom sat down at the desk. He had been surprised at Susann's amazement when he had casually mentioned his mother's two years in Berlin. Susann was anyway forever trying to persuade him to talk about his mother, although he found the subject rather embarrassing.

But now he didn't want to think about Susann. Please, Susann, not now. I know that with your—as you doubtless thought, subtle—questioning you wanted to persuade me to examine my relationship with my mother more closely. "Men always remain Mamma's little boys"—one of your phrases. I admit it was your amazement and your comment, "She must have been an unusually emancipated woman for her time," that made me realize that Mother's at least sporadic insistence on independence, her rebellions, were for a woman of her generation indeed amazing. Fair enough. For the moment that wasn't the point. Or was it? If he continued his thoughts from there—Aunt Esther's hatred of "power-crazed Lilly"; the rare but relentless dueling scenes between his parents, in which Father must usually have come off second best; or again Aunt Esther, who, as convincing proof of Mother's moral turpitude, had repeatedly told him how Lilly Winter, a scant seven days after the general mobilization—"and your father had hurried off to his artillery unit on the field of honor, and anyway all or almost all the men, all the real men, were already on guard at the frontier—that's when Lilly in her raw-silk two-piece had our chauffeur drive her to the works, and up she went to the board room floor, imagine that! Mr. Berger, the treasurer, and two other men unfit for service were the only executives in the building. She summoned them. And then gave them her instructions, as if she had never heard anything about responsibilities, signing powers, and authority in a properly conducted enterprise such as the Winter Corporation, or had never heard that machinery construction in particular is men's business, and that the woman's place has always been in the home looking after the welfare of husband and children. She is said to have spoken in the slightly bored voice of a teacher, you know how she can be—as if she found it tiresome, tiresome for the listener, if she had to repeat a sentence. Even when she said, Would they *kindly* supply daily work reports by nine each morning, or would they kindly submit all decisions involving expenditures of over twenty thousand francs for her approval, she was arrogant enough to say it all as if she were giving orders.

"Berger—you must know him, that giant with the bushy eyebrows—that sly dog of a Berger is supposed to have cleared his throat and said something about a board resolution that entrusted him, Berger, in the case of a general mobilization, with the sole responsibility for all financially relevant decisions pending the return of Mr. Winter from his military duties."

Thom had listened. He had sat on the stool beneath the window and listened to this story, which he already knew. He knew he mustn't take anything for granted. Even if Aunt Esther had told a story three or five times, each time in almost identical words, at some point she might pause, as now or in those days, might lean her head against the back of the chair so that her white, still abundant hair would puff out beside her temples; and if then, with that smile, she would slowly, as if tentatively, and softly resume speaking, you could—Thom could—be almost certain that she would from that point on tell the story differently, expanded by a new twist, and sometimes sharks would suddenly turn up on the streets of Jammers, or the goats from that other story, the one about the billygoat and the gypsy, would be browsing among the branches of the ash tree, browsing high up in the treetop.

Or she did not smile. Her voice would tremble with rage, carrying through the open window into the afternoon, and she would suddenly cry out, "That woman, a mere relative by marriage! And do you know what she even had the impertinence to say? She was half-sitting on your father's massive desk, as if the big executive office were her boudoir, and she said, 'So much the better, Mr. Berger. So much the better for you if the responsibility for each decision is shared by the majority shareholder, the Winter family, which I represent here. Exceptional situations demand exceptional solutions, don't you agree? Rest assured, my dear Berger, your experienced advice will be indispensable to me'—more or less in that tone, you understand, and it is just as well that my dear departed brother came home on his first leave only four weeks later. At that time, you see, we didn't even know the addresses of our officers in the field. Anyway, he was here for thirty-six hours, drove to the factory, and on his return immediately summoned your mother Lilly to the Paneled Room. What happened then was one of those scenes you're familiar with. No, he didn't beat her, my brother never did that where women were involved. But at least then, in that one instance, he made it clear to her where the line was drawn. True, years ago, with his consent, she had bought a block of Winter Corporation shares with her own money— barely a hundred thousand!—but on condition that she give her lifetime proxy to her husband. It is *that* Winter, the member of the family carrying the highest responsibility in the company, who is the sole and personal representative of all the family shareholders' votes. That's how it has always been done in our family, since the days of your grandfather Elsazar, and that was how it was to continue, mobilization or no mobilization, and that much my late brother made clear. And that there are women's affairs and men's affairs. Where would we all be, Thom, if we were to start erasing the borderlines between the two? Just look at the Bolsheviks— how far have they got since they entrusted the management of their heavy industries to their riflewomen!"

Thom could hear her voice as he leaned back, still upstairs at the desk. Was that perhaps the clue?

He wrote: Apparently Lilly Winter was constantly trying to go beyond the limits of her allotted sphere of influence in the house and grounds, to reach out for the levers of power where she assumed them to be—

does her rebellion represent her sin and now at least a hint of a clue to the motive? Could her apparently, or allegedly, violent death have been something like a delayed revenge? Crazy idea—maybe. But at least make an effort to see the whole story from *this* aspect?

He went back to the window. No, even the hickory oaks were no longer to be trusted. There they stood, their branches now suddenly combed cityward by a gust of wind, and for the first time he noticed that, although the leaves glistened in the sun as if oiled, the two trees with their many dry branches at the top were clearly not in good shape. He reached for the two window panels right and left, pushed them shut, and turned the cast-iron handles.

Then he went downstairs.

Assuming Thom had stopped in the gallery outside the library: he would have hesitated. That smell again. He would have gone in. Outside two of the three windows, the left shutter was closed. Here on the east side the gale from the recent thunderstorm must have blown shut the heavy wood-slatted shutters, darkening the room.

Thom walked across. He pushed open first one shutter, then the other; the blue paint, rough on the surface, flaked off at his touch. He turned up the iron brackets. Closing the second window he looked down and saw Sepp coming out of the washhouse. The late-morning sun reflected from Sepp's bald head.

And assuming that Thom were standing once again in front of that pile of company and family rubbish. He would bend down, pick up a file, "Balance Sheet 1942," turn the pages, but feel not the slightest inclination to penetrate those columns of debit and credit, investment and yield, profit-and-loss calculation, as they marched across page after page. The only thing he read was: "Proposal by the Board: 20 percent of the profit of 7.4 million francs, which is 21 percent higher than last year, to be applied to depreciation; the dividend to be increased from Fr.30.00 to Fr.45.00 per share."

So there it was, that famous Swiss war profit. It really didn't look all that high. Oh well. Apparently even at that time his father, so often impaired by his addiction, had no longer been the towering captain of the Winter Corporation ship extolled by Aunt Esther. Thom put back the file. No, let the stuff rot here!

And assuming that Thom had walked by the dark-red cabinets, he would have peered through the glass doors and seen, obscurely behind the reflection, those books, those old, now brittle volumes, leather or cloth bound, with their gold lettering; here the Romantics, all in silent, vertical order, there the classics, the writers of the Enlightenment, Montaigne, Rousseau, Diderot. He stopped. Now, close up, reflected in the glass in front of the dark bindings, he saw himself, saw his head, dimly, saw at least the outline, the dark curly hair, the upper rim of his spectacles. The head and shoulders formed something like a gray silhouette; where it fell on the glass, the volumes in the background stood out more clearly yet, as if they—silhouette and books—had been printed one on top of the other in an underexposed photograph.

He read: *Tristram Shandy*, read: *The Demons*, read: *Myths of Classical Antiquity*. Or this one—how did Faulkner's *Go Down, Moses* get here? It didn't belong among Father's books, let alone Great-Grandfather's. Thom had bought the book while at university in Fribourg. So there they all were again, his heroes from the time when, home on vacation from boarding school, he had spent the days and half the nights up here. Over there had stood the round table on its curved pedestal, over there the second of the two armchairs, on the wall above it the reading lamp —it was still there. Table and chair had disappeared, probably taken away by Charlott after Mother's death? Gret had allowed him and Charlott each to choose a few pieces of furniture for themselves.

As he continued to move past the glass-fronted cabinets he saw, beyond the reflection, those shelves with the big gray cloth-bound annual reports of the Winter Corporation. He was familiar with those too. When he was commissioned in the mid-sixties to write a jubilee volume about the company, he had spent six months studying these documents and making notes, although with very little sense of personal involvement; the Winter Corporation had been the world on which he had turned his back. His father's world. The fellows over there: Dostoevski, Laurence Sterne, Chekhov, Turgenev, they had been his allies; they had accompanied him into those other worlds, those of the imagination and quiet insanity—into spheres, anyway, in which Father's, as well as Mother's, visions of his career at the Winter Corporation, and whatever other of their wishes and ideas for his existence, could no longer reach him.

From outside came the sound of the distant surf. Thom sat down. He could suddenly see himself, sitting in that armchair under the reading lamp at the round table, aged twelve or fifteen, a book on his knees or on the edge of the table in front of him. He kept his eyes closed. He was sitting here in the library on that fortress of the rocky island, high above the sea. Or—while he heard Charlott reading aloud—he was imagining himself standing at the tower window gazing out into the winter storms. The waves, foam-capped and tumbling, came rolling ceaselessly in from the northwest, smashing onto the reefs at the foot of the cliffs on Thom's island.

If he leaned out the window, he could see his guards far below. In their breastplates, with their lances over their shoulders, they paced slowly up and down the outworks and ramparts. Who was holding him captive here? And why? Because he was the only person who knew the magic word? What power had banished him to this place? He felt as though the guards, the battlements, the towers, the whole fortress complex existed only on his account.

Yes, the Winter mansion, the grounds, the stables: they had all turned into a place of exile for him, turreted, accessible only from the sea. All communications between him and the guards was forbidden. Like a banished hero of legend, he lived here far from Mycenae, far from sunny Attica, so he called his island "Aulis." He seldom saw the monks in the Temple of Apollo on the south side of the fortress: only when he was led to the temple, at the change of the moon. On clear nights and days he could hear their singing.

It was only his sister's message that kept him alive. A fisherman had sailed past the island and, his powerful voice drowning out the gale, had called up to Thom, "The wild beasts will rescue you in the eighth year! That is what your sister bids me tell you!"

The guards laughed at the fisherman. Even though Thom had no idea how wild beasts could rescue him here above the rocky cliffs, he had faith in the message. Charlott's voice had sunk to a whisper the first time Thom heard the story from her. He had wept too. And had listened as Charlott went on telling him and Gret about the sister, how she wove a robe for her banished brother and artfully embroidered it with wild beasts. In the eighth year, when she had finished her work, she sent the fisherman to Thom; after landing on the island secretly at night, the fisherman scaled rocks and walls and tossed the robe, tied in a bundle, through the narrow window of Thom's cell. Now Thom understood. The following day he donned the robe. The wild beasts shone in terrifying red. When the warder brought his food, he became petrified with fear. In his disguise, he rushed outside. The guards screamed and fled. Thom scrambled over the battlements and climbed down to the sea and the waiting fisherman. They sailed in the direction of Tauris, where his sister was expecting him.

How often in those days, and over how many years, had Thom lived and relived that story here in the library? Here, or at the monastery boarding school where his mother had taken—or banished—him, when he was barely twelve years old? He had a fleeting vision of her: In the visitors' room in the outer building of the monastery, where women were permitted, he saw her rise from the armchair and draw herself up. "It's time." The tall monk promised to keep an eye on Thom. Thom flinched under the long, white hand of the man in the black habit, the hand on his shoulder. He looked at the black sandals showing under the habit. It's time. So. Yes, Thom longed for her to leave right then, without kissing him goodbye. He was sure he didn't have the strength to hold back his tears any longer. But then she put her arms around him and gave him a quick hug and a kiss. "Time to go."

In the anteroom the monk knocked three times on one of the three doors, the one with the word CLAUSTRUM on the lintel in gold lettering. The door opened. "Go ahead, Thom," said the monk. "Keep straight on and report where you see the door marked PRAEFECTURA."

He stepped across the threshold and walked a little way down the long colonnade with its vaulted ceiling, then stopped. He didn't know yet that within ten minutes he would be sitting in the chair of the barber, the brother who would casually cut his hair down to a short stubble. He didn't even know, or couldn't imagine, that from now on and for many months he would not be allowed to leave the monastery behind its high encircling walls; and that within half an hour he would be standing, shorn, with other monastery pupils, new boys like himself, in the tailor's room, dressed in the close-fitting black garment that buttoned down to the ankles and up to the stiff collar under his chin, around his waist the cingulum, the broad black sash, and look down at himself in amazement.

He turned around. The door was still open. Beyond it, in the anteroom, in full light, his mother in hat and coat; beside her the monk. His mother came forward as far as the door. Without putting her foot across the threshold forbidden to her as a woman, she looked at him. The tears were running down his cheeks; when he tried to wipe them away his lips tasted salt. Dimly, with smarting eyes, he saw his mother nod. He responded with a tiny wave, then turned around again and walked straight ahead, into exile. And wished his sister would weave the robe, weave it with lightning speed, embroider it with the terrifying wild red beasts, and send it to him by way of the man with the sailboat.

Yes, there too, in seclusion, in the pure realm of men, he had so many times taken refuge in that one passage of the old myth, had heard Charlott's voice and the roar of the sea; daydreaming, he had spirited himself, and now the monastery too, away onto his isle of Aulis. There he had lived for hours until Gret, sounding the gong in the hall, summoned him for supper; or before his eyes closed in the dark as he lay in his narrow bed in the wooden cubicle at the monastery school. Again and again he saw himself, saw himself for a few seconds in an old photograph standing in the walled schoolyard; the yard around him was empty. He stood there in his black garment like a convict, disguised; waving, so it seemed, with his right hand, and smiling. He had never liked this picture of himself—yes, a thirteen-year-old convict made to wear the black stuff that was already getting shiny with use; trying to cover up his terribly obvious subjugation with that fatuous smile. Even his smile betrayed his sense of shame. But this child had already learned to be manly. To smile when humiliated, when exiled. One who accepts harsh rules as having been given by God and Mother. Clench your teeth. Smile. But don't you be deceived! I am not merely a victim! You will all be amazed! Yes, I have deserved the exile, the punishment. But one day I shall have served my time. Then I will return! That awkward smile, perhaps even more the child's defiant, erect posture, also contains a shadow of sorrow—or perhaps of the question: Is this what life is about?

She was the one. She had brought him here. Father had let it happen: but he had other worries, didn't he? Actually, this was what was done "in our circles." A few years at boarding school, that will make a man of Thom. The monastery school enjoys an excellent reputation. Haven't leading politicians and quite a few Catholic captains of industry been among its graduates?

But Thom was convinced that, if his mother really loved him, she would never have brought him to this terrible monks' prison. She had wanted to get rid of him. "You'll be the death of me yet!" Hadn't his mother cried out those very words simply because Thom, missing the squirrel with his slingshot, had bloodied the shoulder of one of Gret's schoolmates? Hadn't she shouted, "You devil!" or "Keep out of my sight!"?

And for four days after every such vituperative outburst, she had consistently ignored him. Not she but Frieda or Herminia filled his plate at table; not she but Frieda came, after he'd slipped into bed, to cover him up properly, to say his evening prayers with him, and, after dipping her finger in the little holy water pitcher, make the sign of the goodnight-cross on his forehead. When they were all kneeling in front of the statuette of the Virgin, his mother would say, "Now we will say three more Ave Marias so that our heavenly Mother will crush the head of the serpent Satan in Thom's sinful heart."

To be sure, at some point after such days she would come into his bedroom and turn on the light again, then sit down on the edge of the bed and stroke his forehead and cheek. At last there was a smile on her face. "Well then," she would say, "let us two make peace again." He would quickly sit up, put his arms around her neck, and press his cheek against hers.

Of course, yes, *hers* had been the power, *she* had banished him, betrayed him: she had punished his love for her. Such were the no doubt sinful thoughts he had suddenly dared to think, at night in his wooden cubicle in the monastery. He had even, while lying there in the dark, whispered to himself, "I hate her, I hate her!" And sometimes in his rage he had punched the pillow with his small fist. Yes, during such nights he knew he wanted to be bad, really bad—she had a surprise coming to her! The rage had been like a release.

But then one of Charlott's letters had arrived. She wrote: "Now I know the truth. Herminia told me. And then I asked Mother herself. She actually wept over your defiant letter. Do you know what she said? 'How am I supposed to protect my little boy from Father's riding crop? Here in the house? Only behind those walls is Thom safe.' You see? None of what you write is true. She loves you, Thom! Now that you know that, you'll postpone your suicide, won't you? Please, brother dear, be patient. I'm so very much looking forward to your coming home at Christmas."

Such a letter from Charlott had taken all the momentum out of the hatred he had finally admitted. If what Charlott wrote was true, he had hated Mother for no reason—which rendered his guilt all the greater. And now even suicide would have been pointless. So all that remained to him, torn as he was this way and that, were his daydreams, when he could spirit himself and the monastery and the Winter house away onto his isle of Aulis. It was now his place of exile and refuge, in one.

Outside the windows the bright noonday light of the hot July day.
Thom stood up. He shivered. On his forehead he felt cool sweat.

Did he have a fever?

In Those Days

HOW DID THE DAYS PASS? ON A VERY ORDINARY WEDNESDAY AFTERNOON,
say, in 1942 or '43, when Herminia sat at the kitchen table stringing
beans with a knife, and Frieda was about to make some of that sinfully
expensive Indian tea for Aunt Esther; while Charlott tipped meat and
bone scraps (brought twice a week to the back door by the butcher boy
with Herminia's order) into the remains of yesterday's oatmeal and began
to boil it all up for her Alsatian—at that time she still had an Alsatian:
what might have preoccupied them, those three in the kitchen? Even
though war and politics were men's business, the three women knew,
each in her own way, the magnitude of the threat posed by the history
passing over their heads. They were sure to know that since the fall of
France in June 1940, the little country they inhabited in the center of
Europe was, for the first time in its history, completely encircled, in fact
trapped, by one of the parties to the war, the German-Italian Axis—an
island spared by the war; determined on military resistance, but a midget
in the face of the German Reich and its troops accustomed to victory,
with the German press constantly threatening that now, the war on the
European mainland having come to an end, the special case of Switzerland would be "taken care of" by Hitler's Western army "on its way
home."

But could this threat, long since a commonplace, be a topic of
conversation among the three women in the kitchen? Or did they discuss
the battles between the British and German troops in the desert, the
second or third conquest and reconquest of the Tunisian town of Tobruk?
At most, Lilly Winter might tell them about such events in the fighting
that was moving farther and farther away to the south and east; she might
come from the Paneled Room through the pantry to the door and try
and explain what she happened to have heard on an English radio station
in the middle of the afternoon while sitting by the window.

She wanted to understand all that was going on. Every Friday evening at ten minutes past seven, when the Swiss national radio station Beromünster broadcast Jean-Rodolph von Salis's World Report, she would sit beside her radio. She often made notes, often brought out the world atlas to show her two daughters—Thom was too young—where General de Gaulle's units had landed in North Africa, where General Guderian's armored spearheads were on the move again, and where the retreating Soviet Russian troops were carrying out their scorched-earth tactics. When Ulrich Winter came home around nine o'clock from one of his numerous meetings at the plant or in Zurich, the blackout blinds had been lowered, and she would sit down with him and tell him about what was not yet in the papers.

No, probably neither Herminia nor Frieda nor Charlott was thinking about those military operations. At most a sigh might be heard: Is this going to last forever? And what will it be like if the whole world belongs to them? Herminia was telling herself more than the other two that the next job was to dry the beans, all eight kilos, so first string them, then thread them, and where was that Sepp again, he was supposed to heat up the stove in good time. Or had Frieda heard from Mrs. Esther, as she called her, about the breakthrough of the battle cruiser *Scharnhorst* from the Atlantic by way of the heavily guarded English Channel toward Norway, why Norway? Or why was Mrs. Winter so happy about the news on the radio that the French fleet, in order not to fall into German hands, had been scuttled in the naval port of Toulon; or that six months later, in May 1943, the German Afrika army group had capitulated, and 252,000 German and Italian soldiers had been taken prisoner by the British? Possibly the three women argued about whether these soldiers were now unhappy because they couldn't fight anymore, or were more likely to be happy to be prisoners? "For them," Herminia said, "the war is over—yes, they're lucky," and Frieda took the cookie tin from the cupboard, put it on the table, brought a newspaper from the pantry, spread out the ration cards, and proceeded to jot down the number of coupons on the margin of the newspaper. The basic daily ration per head was: bread 250 grams, potatoes 550 grams, noodles 33, flour 17, legumes 10, sugar 37, butter a scant 7 grams, and how were 550 grams of vegetables supposed to be enough; on the other hand, wasn't half a liter of milk a day a little too much? Herminia was allowed to cook meat only three days a week, but how, how, since the ration amounted to only 50 grams? Sure, Mrs. Winter had been able to convince the head of the rationing office that Sepp, obviously, but also her husband Ulrich Winter must be classified as "heavy workers," so each of them received an additional 50 grams of bread and 20 grams of meat per day. But even clothing, even shoes, had been rationed for almost two years now! Well, Charlott and Frieda knew that when the secret supplies of lard or smoked ham in the cooler beside the cellar stairs began to run low, Herminia would take Charlott's bike and ride off toward Kestenholz, where her grandmother lived with her sister on the farm, and from there she always came back, under cover of darkness, around eight in the evening, with two bulging leather holdalls on the carrier. At times she was more than cheerful, not to say tipsy. That was her grandmother's coffee; she would laugh when she said that.

Then one day Mrs. Winter was standing in the doorway, on May 31, 1942. At first she merely stood there, wordlessly watching them at their work. Terrible! She looked at them out of her dark eyes. "Last night more than eight hundred long-range British and American bombers attacked Cologne—everything, including the residential areas. Cologne is a burning city of rubble filled with dead. Come up to the Blue Room, please—we must say three rosaries for the dead."

How was it? How did the days pass in those years?

It was her voice; it was the way she strung the words together. Or the way she would look across before uttering the words she particularly loved. The way she could stretch words or intone them in long, rolling sentences. She would often repeat a word until it began to sparkle. And when she described how it suddenly began to snow, Thom, it just snowed and snowed, you can't even imagine, it snowed and snowed outside the window, or it snowed in Rome, and Thom was in a taxi with her and Mayor Hunziker and the rector of Jammers University, driving along the streets of Rome through the snow to the Palazzo Veneto, where the Duce was impatiently waiting for them, the delegation from the north. Yes, she could turn words into webs, into stories, or even spaces; the very word "snow" became a word that spun itself spiderlike around him even in his sleep. Or the way she cried out, "Impossible!" A word like a room behind bars. Uttered by her, words like "Palazzo" and "Duce" were transformed into cathedral naves in which Thom could wander around filled with awe. And "hand grenade"—"you remember I still had my hand grenade in my purse": at that point, when that word came, Thom was always reminded of Jericho and how Lot's wife was turned into a pillar of salt.

But first she would tell him about her cousin Francesco Obreggio. Originally called Franz Obrecht, he had been a watch manufacturer from Grenchen, a capable man whose native land became too cramped for him, so he went to Italy, to Genoa. His white villa stood high above the city and the sea. Despite his great wealth, he was inventive. His misfortune: that he was a thorn in the flesh of the Lord Mayor of Genoa, do you understand, she asked? And even if Thom didn't understand, and even if he told her so, Aunt Esther had already gone beyond that to where her cousin Francesco Obreggio employed some sixty people in his watch factory, an excellent little factory in Genoa, but could he be blamed for that? Simply because he was more capable than those Italians who preferred to lie around in the sun? "A man who wants to get ahead in life, Thom, must have an idea. Hard work and efficiency are important, but there are three principles you should remember: don't work alone— work in such a way that you have other people working for you. And here's the second principle for your future life: don't work with your own money—work with other people's money. Then, because you have debts, the government can't collect taxes from you, and when the great inflation comes your debts will become smaller and smaller and your revenue bigger and bigger."

She said "revenue," but even if Thom had now wanted to know what inflation and revenue meant, she was already busy explaining the third principle: that you also need an idea. Otherwise you'd be a loser all your life.

Aunt Esther's cousin's idea was simple enough. "Swiss watches are the best in the world. Francesco Obreggio manufactured Swiss watches in Genoa just as he had previously manufactured Swiss watches in Grenchen. Why did he do it in Italy, Thom? Right. Because it was cheaper there. Are we to blame him for that? You see? And because Swiss watches are the best, they are entitled to be the most expensive, my cousin said to himself, so he produced cheaply and sold expensively. The only question was whether he would find enough buyers for his Swiss watches. He did. Sales rose like a thermometer in hot water; he found buyers, and as time went on he produced and sold more and more of his top-quality Swiss watches, sold them in Italy and from there all over the world. Now you will say, Well, that was a good idea, your cousin became a rich man, but what does that have to do with Mussolini?"

She gazed out into the snow flurries. It had been snowing, she said, and again Thom saw her and himself and the rector of Jammers University in the taxi in the snowy streets of Rome, and how all the taxis and horse-drawn cabs were getting stuck in the snow while the Duce and leader of all Italians was waiting for them. Aunt Esther said, "We're getting there, but first you have to know what a crook this Genoese *sindaco* was, and how we tried out Uncle Ludwig's new invention, an oval hand grenade, in the clay pit. But first comes the honorary doctorate for Benito Mussolini, and after that you'll hear about the plan that took us to Rome in the summer of 1936." She smiled. "Not exactly a run-of-the-mill plan, but everything in its own good time."

Thom said, "But Aunt, snow in summer? In Rome?" But by now she had moved on again to that crook of a lord mayor of Genoa who wanted to get his hands on a smart Swiss watchmaker's money. So she had the *sindaco* summon her cousin Francesco to his palazzo, made him appear before Thom as soon as the servant had left the room, and had him say, "Signor Obreggio, here are the documents. By circumventing the laws of the *Repubblica Italia* you have made a fortune. Either the watches you are manufacturing and selling as Swiss watches are in fact Swiss watches, in which case you have cheated our government out of 200 billion lire in customs duties and I have to arrest you; or your watches are Italian watches, in which case you have grossly violated all the rules of good faith, and I must arrest you as a swindler. You must be prepared for a sentence of up to twelve years' imprisonment." According to Aunt Esther, this *sindaco* and cutthroat smiled, went back to his big desk, and sat down. "Well?" he asked her cousin. "Signore, the choice is yours. Or do you see a third possibility?"

Aunt Esther told Thom he must be proud of this Swiss citizen in Italy who declared that he insisted on his rights. He had been born a Swiss, as a Swiss he had designed his watches, and as a Swiss he would answer for his company. His watches were Swiss watches.

The *sindaco* persisted, maintaining that these were watches financed by a company registered and located in Genoa and manufactured by Italians in Italy on Italian machines, in other words: Italian watches.

Thom saw his cousin or second cousin once removed draw himself up, proclaiming that he would fight for his rights, and again Thom was proud of him, when that fox of a super-*sindaco* actually said, with lowered voice, "Perhaps, signore, there is a third possibility. Won't you sit down?"

"And what might that be?"

"It would mean that I would *not* arrest you. And that I would not hand over the documents to the court today and not tomorrow. It would mean my declaring the documents to be incomplete and demanding additional proofs. More and more proofs. That I would continue to pursue the case, but slowly, do you understand? For seven years? Ten years? And you would go on producing and selling your watches, on and on. Until one day I send you the word *Addio*, whereupon you will depart without delay to some other country of your choice. The third possibility, you see, would consist in my being a humanitarian: or rather, in becoming one."

"Good enough," said Francesco.

"Very good," said the *sindaco*. "Now all we have to do is answer the question of how we two intend to induce me to be a humanitarian." The *sindaco* smiled. "Have you any ideas, Signor Obreggio?"

Aunt Esther looked across. Thom knew what foxes look like. And when she exclaimed indignantly, "That fox!" the word and Aunt Esther were one and the same. Snow was falling outside, and the fox retreated into its den beneath the roots of the felled oak, up there on the west rim of the clay pit. But its tracks in the snow betrayed it.

Aunt Esther's cousin Francesco rose to his feet. "Even if you put me behind bars for many long years, I will never agree to your dirty deal! I demand a trial!"

Obreggio, the manufacturer of Swiss watches, was led away by two guards. Shortly after that, one of those lousy Italian courts sentenced him to twelve years' imprisonment plus a fine of 200 billion lire. Interventions on the part of the family, even at the highest diplomatic level, were fruitless.

When Aunt Esther cried out the word "impossible," Thom had a vision of Cousin Francesco behind bars. And now when she came to the hand grenades, the Italian air force was flying to Abyssinia to take part in the Italian blitzkrieg—that was in 1935/36—and Emperor Negus, that bloodsucker, retreated with his resplendent court into the mountains of Abyssinia. At the same time, the air force of victorious Benito Mussolini began to fly to Spain too, where General Franco's brave soldiers were in need of hand grenades against the Red flood. Thom knew that, when it came to events and trends of world-historical significance, Uncle Ludwig had nothing short of clairvoyant gifts—Aunt Esther had no hesitation in calling them "prophetic" in this instance, so that Thom knew what was bound to come next.

Today it pleased her to keep this part of the story short. She passed over the fact that Uncle Ludwig not only had foreseen the Wall Street panic of 1929 but had prophesied Hitler's election victory of 1933, and as early as 1938 had predicted the flood of refugees that would pour into our little country. Without a doubt Aunt Esther, in contrast to Uncle Ludwig, simply liked Benito Mussolini better than Adolf Hitler—he was greater somehow, greater as a statesman and as a human being, you understand, Thom, but even this she mentioned only in passing, and even Uncle Ludwig's studies, his years of research, and the way, after working all night, he would turn up for breakfast gray-faced, discouraged, and exhausted because he hadn't been able to bring his designs for the rocket car or the Big Bomb, the boomerang principle or the unmanned factory, to ultimate completion, yet he never gave up, never, do you hear?—today even those achievements were barely touched upon. Regarding the hand grenade, she merely said, "As long ago as 1933 he was already telling me, and writing to me from Munich: 'Dear Sister, once again there is a smell of war in Europe. More than ever will it be a war of machines. This ominous trend demands that we, the executives and shareholders of the Winter Corporation, invest a great deal of inventive imagination, much advanced technology and capital, and I mean today! Our Swiss principle of neutrality will compel us to offer *all* parties to a war the possibility of benefiting, share and share alike, from our industrial capacity.' "

At that time Uncle Ludwig had not yet been overtaken by insanity. He was not yet wandering about the house day and night, talking incessantly, as Thom was soon to see for himself. He had been working for two years, not without success, on his invention of the hand grenade, a new type of grenade, upstairs in his laboratory, as well as with a technician in the workshop behind the welding shop, which had been placed at his disposal for his experiments. No, while the snow fell silently past the window and Thom was already looking forward to the scene with the Duce of the new Roman Imperium, she proceeded to describe how Uncle Ludwig surprised them all by standing up, one evening after dinner in the Paneled Room, tapping his glass, and announcing, "My dear family, the hand grenade according to the Winter system is now reality. I refer to the oval gas attack hand grenade designed on a three-chamber principle. It guarantees, first, an explosive force on the traditional pattern of a radius of twenty-five meters; and second, a lethal effect by gas on any living creature within a radius of forty meters. The practical tests undertaken this afternoon on our testing ground in the clay pit yielded positive results. I cordially invite you all to a demonstration in the presence of our top executives next Friday. This will be followed by a little ceremony in which the grenade is to be given the name"—Uncle Ludwig is said to have smiled as he alluded to the mythical Greek goddesses of revenge— "the name of Erinye."

Words like cathedral naves, like hot-air balloons above the cliffs of Aulis. She would soon come to the suffering and disgrace of Francesco Obreggio in the Genoa prison, Aunt Esther said, before telling him about the hand-grenade demonstration in the clay pit. Words like rooms behind bars; like the dying of rabbits, like the screeching of magpies accompanying the matricide as he fled, or like glossy black rabbit fur. The drive to the Hupper clay pit in the three shiny black limousines. The arrival of the guests. The whole group advancing to the edge of the cordoned-off area, a point beyond which the lethal droplets of liquid gas were guaranteed not to reach. And Thom's father, representing the board of directors, briefly congratulating the inventor and expressing his own conviction by asking, "How else can future wars be avoided than by a balance of strength? Toward this end we of the Winter Corporation wish to make a contribution throughout the world from the base of our neutral country. History teaches us that common sense is not enough to banish the scourge of war. Only those heavily armed opponents who are *forced* to recognize that the price of victory is the death of the victor himself will sit down at the negotiating table and outlaw war for all time."

The way the words echoed in the wide circle of the clay pit. And only now did Aunt Esther mention the test animals: the rabbits, tightly tethered to pegs placed five meters apart across the testing area. Between them, little towers of varying height, steel towers with observation slits, simulating armored vehicles, the tanks and machines of future wars. They too contained, so one heard, trussed-up test animals—chickens, rabbits, and rats.

Oh yes, Thom could well understand that Aunt Esther wanted to move on as quickly as possible to the scene with Benito Mussolini, whom she found so congenial, and lambaste that crook again, the Duce's adjutant with the rank of general. But there was no escape: first she had to describe the throwing of the test hand grenades; how, at a safe distance at the edge of the clay pit, they all watched Uncle Ludwig and the technician, a certain Mr. Droll, while the two men stood at the chest-level safety wall, each holding a grenade, and Uncle Ludwig shouted to them both the command: "Prepare to throw!" The two men ducked. Each placed the hand holding the grenade on his right knee. "Eyes on the target!" Simultaneously they raised their heads so they could glance over the wall at their target and immediately resume their crouching position. Aunt Esther hesitated. She seemed to be debating whether this time she should again tell Thom that after the third dual throw Uncle Ludwig looked back and called out to ask whether any of the gentlemen would care to volunteer for a throw. Since none of the gentlemen spoke up, Aunt Esther stepped forward. She hesitated, she deliberated, but then, with the astonished murmurings of the top executives in her ears, she walked across the ground—in those days she didn't yet have an artificial leg—and presented herself to her brother.

Uncle Ludwig told her exactly what to do: "Pick up the grenade, take cover, get ready to throw, grenade on knee, glance at target, take cover again, and don't drop the grenade whatever you do!—at the command 'Throw,' release the catch—like this, you see: When you press the two halves of the grenade together in your fist, the time fuse inside will be released. After that you will have six seconds before the detonation— enough time for you to swing back your arm, throw, and take cover again. This is how you count: a hundred and one means press together and ignite; a hundred and two means swing back your arm; a hundred and three means throw."

But at this point Aunt Esther decided to skip this whole episode of the demonstration in the clay pit, and how she herself had put on the helmet and with her own hands ignited one of the oval gas hand grenades as she murmured a hundred and one, after having handed her purse and binoculars to Mr. Droll and taken off her white crocheted gloves; how, murmuring a hundred and two, she had straightened up and swung back her arm, and upon reaching a hundred and three had thrown and promptly taken cover again—decided to skip all this as well as a description of the truly terrifying blast. She merely mentioned Uncle Ludwig's invention of the grenade and that he had tapped his glass and made his brief announcement of the success of the test; then, without further digression, she began to speak about the awarding of the honorary doctorate. Probably she wanted for once to spare Thom the vision of the rabbits torn to bits by the grenade.

Even Uncle Ludwig's positively inspired fourfold idea had to pass without mention, although it was behind or above his invention: 1. A future war will be a war between machines remotely controlled by humans. 2. An easy-to-handle grenade of triple-chamber design must be developed, one whose initial effect, the explosive effect, can kill humans and put machines—meaning tanks, armored vehicles, and even planes—out of action; and whose second effect, that of liquid gas, will kill soldiers even *inside* the machines. This second effect must be founded on the ability of the lethal gas substance to penetrate every nook and cranny of the machines, to corrode all organic material, to eat its way through all clothing and all flesh down to the bone, at the same time spreading lethal vapors. 3. The effect of the grenade must be absolute and, in the truest sense of the word, terrible. 4. All potential parties to a future war must be supplied with this weapon in such quantities and so even-handedly that no potential aggressor will ever again find the courage to start a war.

Today, Thom sensed, Aunt Esther wished to concentrate on her audience with the Duce. In 1936, she began, Jammers University, on the occasion of its Five-Hundredth Jubilee, decided to bestow an honorary doctorate on Benito Mussolini. To quote: "Does not our university have a duty to honor the man who has achieved such truly great things in the field of the social sciences? The man who will leave behind him a trail that will never"—Thom, do you hear?—"never be obliterated from history?" The news hit the town like a grenade.

"True, some malicious voices were also raised. Thus, for instance, *The People*: 'An honorary doctorate for whom? For the dictator who is destroying democracy? For the extremist who is smashing Italy's glorious Left and incarcerating its leaders?' Remember this, Thom: Great men are great by the fact that they do not please everybody but unswervingly follow their own path of greatness." In any event, Aunt Esther volunteered once again, this time with her local knowledge and her considerable if inaccurate command of Italian, as interpreter and guide for the three days that Benito Mussolini was to spend as a guest in Jammers. The organizers, under the chairmanship of the rector of the university, gratefully accepted Aunt Esther's offer. Indeed, they did an excellent job. Starting from the Duce's arrival at the main station, with speeches, maids of honor, large numbers of students sporting corps colors, with the government in a body, with choirs in native dress, cadets forming a guard of honor, and five bands for the procession through town, to the climax of the festivities in the Great Hall of the university, with Federal Councillor Motta as the official speaker: everything was prepared down to the last detail.

So the announcement by the Italian Embassy in Switzerland that during the days in question the Duce would be prevented by affairs of state from participating in the celebrations was received with profound disappointment, although Aunt Esther emphasized that she could fully understand. The Duce's spiritual and even physical dedication to his mission of leading the masses of the people on their path through history demanded sacrifice and renunciation, especially in the matter of accepting personal honors. After Thom had promised to look upon Benito Mussolini as a model in this respect, Aunt Esther, "to make it short," switched to her journey, the memorable journey undertaken in August of that year with Professor Kunz, rector of the university, and Mr. Hunziker, mayor of Jammers. "Who, Thom, in this land of ours so lacking in appreciation of greatness can boast of having had what amounted to a private conversation with a man who, though certainly not without his faults, has set his lasting imprint on this century?"

Thom had no answer. "You see?" she said, then passed over the splendors of the St. Gotthard Pass, Lake Como, the theft in the wagon-lit compartment between Milan and Rome, passed over the suite at the Hotel Esplanade in Rome; even the inability of Roman drivers to keep their vehicles under proper control in a violent snowstorm in August, a subject on which she normally liked to dwell, was now of no importance to her. The trip by taxi, however, and how "we started to sweat blood because the car stalled, and no windshield wiper with the snowstorm reducing visibility to less than ten meters," or how "the taxi started to skid and span right around in the curve beside the Colosseum while the Duce was expecting us at five o'clock for an audience at the Palazzo Veneto, and how we all—Professor Kunz, Mayor Hunziker, and I—had to get out and push the taxi at a run all along the Via del Popolo with the taxi driver continually shouting 'porco miserio' the whole way and the clock already pointing to five fifteen"—all of that she did mention.

"Yes, but your plan, Aunt, your plan with the hand grenade?"

Now Aunt Esther laughed, her face foxy again, and Thom could wander through the word "audience" as through a palace. We were the delegation from the university and town of Jammers. We were there to present the diploma for the honorary degree. But apart from that—I see you've been listening carefully, Thom—I had two objectives in mind. First, as a gift for the Duce, I had secretly instructed the welding shop to provide a silver casing for an oval gas hand grenade engraved with the words: Per il Duce—la granata del pace. I thought how wonderful it would be if on my return I could surprise my brothers Ulrich and Ludwig with a substantial order from the Italian head of state, an order for the production of, say, two million grenades. At the same time I was determined to ask the Duce for the release of my cousin Franz Obrecht languishing in his Genoa prison. The storm was still flinging snow in our faces as we hurried up the steps to the entrance of the Palazzo Veneto. General Felloni (about whom I shall have more to say later) received us with his crafty face beneath the plumed helmet. Two minutes later we stood in the great audience chamber on the second floor; after a few moments the two palace guards opened wide the doors, and Benito Mussolini in person appeared.

"Il Duce! What a man, Thom! The sash across his chest, decorations glittering, he raised his hand, stuck out his chin in the well-known manner, and shouted in a thunderous voice, *"Mi Svizzeri bravi—salute!"*

Thom didn't have much time to linger over her words. He loved it when she spoke of the "historic mission," of "Providence" having chosen this man, and of the "secret of his personality"—words in whose dark mystery one could wrap oneself as in brocade vestments. Then Aunt Esther, after curtseying deeply, had introduced the gentlemen of the delegation and herself, and the rector of the university had read out the document bestowing the honorary degree on the Duce. Aunt Esther had then approached the Duce and presented him with the document, even though it had suffered some slight damage from the snow. In her purse she still had the hand grenade, silver edition.

And just imagine, she said—no, exclaimed: "The Duce clasped me to his breast and kissed me! In his eyes were tears of emotion, tears of gratitude! It was a while before I too regained my composure. Gallantly taking me by the arm, the Duce led me into the more intimate adjoining room, where a magnificent buffet and a wonderful vino spumante had been set out for us. The gentlemen followed, accompanied by that perfidious adjutant general." Thom listened. She described how it snowed. Snow was falling so thickly outside that the roofs of Rome disappeared from sight. Under the sparkle of the magnificent chandeliers—"chandeliers," what a spiderlike word, a word like the glitter of rising stars!—the Duce sat down beside Aunt Esther on the brocade-covered sofa. Thom could hear the Duce whispering, always in Italian of course, "What a pity, my dear, that we are not alone!" While the Duce shyly stroked Aunt Esther's left hand, Thom found that he also preferred Benito Mussolini to Adolf Hitler: he seemed somehow more human—yes, one of the great men of this world, but always a human being too, who radiated warmth, one might almost say benevolence, and Thom listened as Aunt Esther proceeded to talk to the Duce about the Abyssinian war, which was still going on.

This was intended as a bridge to enable Aunt Esther to open her purse and take out the hand grenade in its silver covering. Surprised, the Duce read the inscription. And was even more surprised when Aunt Esther began to unscrew the silver top. This, she said, was her gift to him, the weapon that would prevent any future war. Still twisting the top, she mentioned the inventor and explained the epoch-making concept of balance of power, then lifted off the silver lid. For a few seconds even Benito Mussolini was struck dumb before exclaiming, *"meraviglioso!"* and asking, *"un prototipo?"* He took out the grenade, which was painted gray, examined it, and, scarcely hesitating, extracted the safety pin by its little leather tab, at which point Aunt Esther and Thom turned pale, knowing as they did that even slight pressure on the oval grenade by the encircling fist would be enough to ignite the fuse that six seconds later, would cause the grenade to explode.

Aunt Esther hadn't been able to say, to this day couldn't say, whether the Duce was so experienced in matters of weapons technology that he could calculate the risk accurately at a single glance and acted accordingly; whether he was just extremely courageous as well as full of confidence in the power of the Almighty; or whether he assumed—although in this case mistakenly—that any prototype was bound to be a dummy.

The Duce having reassured her, she could now hand him the envelope containing directions for use and a price list, at the same time emphasizing that delivery of the grenades could, of course, only be made simultaneously with deliveries to all other European states, and furthermore she would now like—an entirely personal request—to ask for clemency, for the clemency of the Duce dei Popoli Italiani, for her cousin Francesco Obreggio and his release from the Genoa prison—here, this letter contained all the information on this scandalous miscarriage of justice—when the Duce stood up. Affairs of state, cara mia, and he added that he would take a personal interest in this relative of Aunt Esther's.

And already he was at the door. They had all risen; the Duce was still holding the grenade with its safety catch released. He turned once more toward them, *"mi cari e bravissimi Svizzeri."* While he expressed the hope that Switzerland and Italy would continue to enjoy the same friendly contacts that had existed ever since the battle of Marignano, his left hand, as if playing with the imperial orb of the Roman empire, threw

the grenade thirty to fifty centimeters into the air and caught it gracefully.
He kept tossing it casually into the air; then he finally threw it across to
his adjutant general, that crafty-faced scoundrel with the plumed helmet,
at which Aunt Esther fainted. Thom tried to interpret the words "imperial
orb," words with the dimensions of a Palazzo Veneto, words that evoked
a celestial sphere, but just then Aunt Esther came to again. Her first
thought: It was all a dream. Her second thought: What a good man this
Benito Mussolini must be for the Almighty to allow him to survive the
greatest mortal perils unscathed!

"But that general!" she exclaimed. "I was suspicious of him from
the very beginning." So she had not been surprised when, a year later,
the news made the rounds of the press that an Italian armaments manufacturer had developed an oval gas hand grenade that in its terrible
effectiveness outclassed all that had gone before; the Italian Army was
now the strongest in the world, and finally invincible. Aunt Esther had
reason to believe that that adjutant general was the principal shareholder
of the successful armaments factory. Nor was she at all surprised that
Uncle Ludwig's *registered* letters of protest to the Duce remained unanswered. Thom remembered asking the question that had always puzzled
him: Why, in that case, hadn't the Italian Army remained invincible?
Aunt Esther hadn't heard him. She kept her eyes closed. At least: she
said, and now Thom rejoiced with her and they ran together up the stairs
to Uncle Ludwig's laboratory in the annex behind the house—at least:
only a few weeks after the conversation with Benito Mussolini, there was
a phone call from Genoa, imagine! No mistaking that dear, familiar
voice, "I'm free!" her cousin Franz cried, "I'm free!" A word like a balloon
soaring above the Alps, a word like Manhattan or a sailing ship crossing
the ocean. In contrast to earlier occasions, when Aunt Esther had had
her cousin merely write a sad farewell letter from his barred cell before
hanging himself from the bars—may his desperate soul rest in peace—
this time she released him into freedom, into the wide open spaces of
the hills of Mexico.

Thom's question as to the invincibility of the Italian armed forces—
"armed forces"!—had for the time being to remain unanswered. Aunt
Esther opened her eyes. She looked across at him. "The Duce," she
whispered. "My Duce."

Saga of Origin IV

BRAN AND EUROPA PLANTED A NEW RACE. EUROPA SHOWED BRAN HOW to drain the swamps with dikes. She also bestowed on him the skill of riding in boats on the water. Their children flourished. They sailed southward on the River Rhône as far as the island they named Crete. They sailed northward on the River Rhine and founded the mark they named Danamark after Dana, the primeval mother, and the vessel of abundance granted them intoxication and all that they needed.

Thereupon Dana summoned her son Bran into the mountains. Bran set out on the journey with his men. In the gorge, at the place where Bran had struck down Gwion, an ash tree was growing up into the clouds. In its crown the goat was browsing. They lay down under the tree for the night.

Toward morning Bran was wakened by the roar of the lion, the screech of the eagle, and the hiss of the snake. Bran remembered Dana's messenger having told him, Fear not on your way the cave beast, even though it has seven heads. Once again Bran espied the Great Cave, its entrance now guarded by the creature that was lion, eagle, and snake in one. Seven heads grew out of it.

All day long Bran fought with the beast. When the sun dropped into the western sea, he had struck off six of the seven heads with his sword, and the beast rose into the air.

The men carried Bran on branches through the mountains. Bran, exhausted by the battle, slept.

Hadn't they always treated him at home as "the littlest one"? To this day he resented it when people changed the subject the moment he joined them. Even as a three- and four-year-old, he had lived with the feeling that all grown-ups and even his two sisters were permanently involved in excitingly beautiful or sinister experiences. *He* was told to play with a toy train that couldn't even fly.

But he had been wide awake. He had made it a habit to note the subtlest sounds, even the pitch of whispered voices behind closed doors; fleetingly he would listen at the half-open kitchen door and through the noise of water splashing into the sink or the clatter of dishes, greedily drink in at least snatches of the voices of Herminia or Charlott and Gret, or a word or two of their conversation: always tracking down secrets, words that were often unknown to him and as dark as the stables where the horses—or was it moose, buffalos, elks, and unicorns?—shifted gently against their clinking chains. If he were then to enter, he would look at once into their faces as they fell silent, trying to make out what the eyes, the half-open mouths, and the expressions of feigned attentiveness to him were striving to conceal.

What did the phrase "Jewish capers" mean? If he asked Gret, she would snap at him, "Shut up, Thom! That's none of your business!" Or Herminia, scraping turnips at the kitchen table, would shake her head in disapproval. "When you're older."

Or Mother: "Where did you pick *that* up?" A little later, hidden by the curved uprights of the gallery banister, he heard Mother berating the cook downstairs as if Herminia had betrayed the grown-ups' secret.

It took him many a long day to find out that the phrase "Jewish capers" had to do with the great family row of a few weeks earlier.

Shortly after supper, before Father came home from the office, Thom had been sent off to bed. He had already slipped under the quilt and was waiting for Mother and her goodnight kiss. Light from the gallery shone through the half-open door. He heard Father's car, heard it drive up to the front steps. At almost the same time, from outside his door, from the gallery, suddenly Sepp's voice: "That's not my job!" And right after that Mother; her voice had that dry sound it acquired when she raised it: "You'll help Herminia carry that laundry basket down right now, or else—" Thom ran barefoot to the half-open door. In the dim light from below, at the point where the gallery ended in the short passage to the salon, he could just make out Sepp's bulky figure, with Mother facing him, and Herminia was there, and Gret—her hand over her mouth as if she were laughing or about to cry. Sepp was still hesitating: "Or else?"

Thom's mother stepped forward. "Or else you'll be fired!" What Sepp mumbled was unintelligible. Herminia and Sepp bent down almost simultaneously. Thom just had time to see them lift the big hamper and carry it forward before Mother reached him, pushed him back, gently but without a word, into his room, switched on the light, and closed the door.

So there he was, shoved aside. What was happening outside the door? Suddenly, for the merest blink of an eyelid, he saw again those black eyes, that thin face, that little black moustache, those eyes looking at him as if saying, Please, son—please. In a language that sounded strange to Thom, the man said, "Not a word, okay?" and laid his finger on his lips under the black mustache. That afternoon Thom had been sitting on the top stair outside his room. When he heard the motor start behind the house and the chain saw begin to wail, he had stood up to go downstairs, intending to watch Sepp and the two other men sawing wood.

As he rose, half turning, he saw the black figure, or rather, saw the bathroom door behind him open silently and the man staring at him, hesitating, then opening the door wide and nodding at Thom with that pale face. And the man beckoning Thom. Thom closed his eyes, then looked again. The man was still beckoning. The man said softly, but not with a Swiss accent, "Come here." When Thom stood before him, looking up, the man said, "A secret, do you understand?" And with his finger to his lips: "Not a word, okay?" Thom nodded, then watched the man hurry away on tiptoe and disappear in the little passage to the salon.

A secret, he thought. What was that? Not a word, okay? he thought. Suddenly he ran down the stairs as fast as he could. He had to find Gret. She was four years older than he, she was eight, almost grown-up.

Gret was sitting at the pantry table making herself a teatime sandwich with some black jam. Would he like a sandwich too? Then she looked at him. "What's the matter? Why are you so upset?"

When he told her his story, she suddenly put a hand in front of her face and closed her eyes. Dear God! Then she started biting her fingernails. This much he understood: the man came from far away, from Poland. "A Pole, understand? The police are looking for him. We met him up at the reservoir, Charlott and I. Now we're hiding him in the salon. Only Herminia knows about it, and Frieda. And now you, Thom."

What was that, a secret? Why were the police looking for the man? Why wasn't he allowed to tell anyone, d'you hear, not a soul? "Above all, not Father. Promise? All right, kneel down, Thom. Place this hand on your breast. Raise the other hand. Now—like this, see?" stretching up three fingers. "Come on. Can't you even stretch three fingers for an oath? Never mind, then: say after me: I, Thomas Winter, swear by God and the Holy Virgin Mary not to betray the secret to anyone."

That was what he swore, word for word.

Again, or still, he was standing in his pajamas, shoved aside, behind the closed door of his room. Outside Sepp and Herminia could be heard carrying the laundry hamper downstairs; he could hear them groaning, hear the wooden slats bumping on the stairs, hear "Careful!" and Mother saying in a loud voice down in the hall, "Oh, there you are!"

Thom opened his door again and walked to the balustrade. Sepp and Herminia had just reached the bottom stair. Herminia was panting, trying to catch her breath. Father, not yet in sight, must have entered the passage from the porch. Through the uprights of the banister, Thom could see the part in Mother's hair. Then, loudly, Father's voice: "Now I want to know exactly what's going on here!"

Mother: "I don't even know what you're—"

Father broke in. For heaven's sake, the police had been searching the works for the past two days, from top to bottom, the warehouses, the entire plant area. For days they had been questioning, not to say interrogating, the foremen and office staff—everyone, in fact, including even himself. Father was breathing hard, seething with rage. "Now the aliens department of the police has been on the phone to me: a local tip-off— do you know what they want to do? Search my house! They'll be here any minute. So listen to me, Lilly: if it should turn out that this damned, this goddamned Pole is German and Jewish and has been hidden by one of you, here in the house—and behind my back at that!—I'm telling you, there'll be hell to pay!"

Mother said that was too much for her all at once. "Come, Ulrich, let's talk it over calmly, one thing at a time—come, let's go in."

Father burst out again. No, he wanted it clarified here and now, on the spot. "Charlott, Gret! And you, Esther, all of you, Herminia! And you too, come on, come over here, the whole lot of you!"

Thom hesitated—he too?—then slowly walked down the stairs. Secret! Swear! Not a word, okay? A Pole, and German. He didn't understand. He couldn't combine these words and the man with the black eyes into a story that made sense. Downstairs he stood behind his mother. Gret was in tears, hiding her face behind Herminia's back. Charlott said, "We have sworn an oath. But I am ready, you can torture me, and I shall pray to the Early Christians."

And Father: "She must be out of her mind again! Are you all out of your minds? Esther, what's going on?"

Aunt Esther was standing with Frieda in the open door to her suite. She had to cough. "Don't make such a racket, Ulrich. I know nothing."

And Thom's mother: "And if the police want to come—of course they're welcome to search the house—search *your* house. You have nothing to hide—so why worry?"

Father turned his face this way and that. Looking past Mother, Thom saw Father's left eye twitching. "Frieda, come here! Now tell me straight out: is there a strange man in the house?"

Frieda stepped forward. By this time she was in tears too. "I didn't see anything, I was just sewing upstairs in the sewing room—the girls," she said, "they told me I had to swear—"

Sobbing, she ran off into the kitchen. "Come on, Herminia," Mother said, "Take that stuff outside."

Sepp and Herminia lifted up the hamper again and carried it past Father along the passage toward the front door.

The doorbell rang. Charlott ran to the entrance, overtaking Sepp and Herminia in the porch, where there was some congestion. First the laundry hamper out the door, then two men in uniform in the passage, and Father inviting them, "Do come in—by all means, good evening, Mr. Born, Mr. Zaug! Have a look around!" Thom heard his mother saying, "Perhaps you would like to start from the top? This way, gentlemen." From the stairs she told Gret to take Thom into the pantry. Frieda sat down on the bench in the corner, pulled Thom down beside her and, as if to protect him, placed her arm around his shoulders. And Charlott? Gret was scarlet with fear and eagerness. Rushing into the Paneled Room she called out, "Where's Charlott gone? If only nothing goes wrong!" Thom still didn't understand. Those words—"a secret," "the Pole," and "not a word, okay?" and a German and a Pole: they still didn't add up to a story. Were they still looking for the dark man? Frieda shook him by the shoulder. "Just you be quiet!" Suddenly she burst into tears again. "They're searching everywhere—the whole house!"

When Gret called Frieda, Thom followed her into the Paneled Room. It was dark in there, but with enough light coming in from the big lamp outside over the front door for Thom to make out Gret's head at one of the three windows. "Just look—all those people!" Unable to see out over the windowsill, Thom pushed up a chair and knelt on it. People everywhere, standing on the steps and below on the driveway, in the lamplight. Or were they on the point of leaving? "Policemen, see?" Gret was breathing hard. "Three," said Frieda, "three of them! And there's Charlott!"

And Gret again: "Is he safe? Look, Charlott's coming up!"

Yes, people were beginning to walk away down the drive in groups. Some of those still on the steps were laughing. A man's voice, muffled by the windowpane, calling up to the house, "Are you sure you've searched the laundry room thoroughly?" Again everybody laughed.

Gret, Frieda, and Thom filed back into the light of the pantry. Charlott came through the kitchen, beaming. "I can't believe it!"

And Gret: "Is he safe?"

Charlott sat down across from them with her back to the kitchen door. "Slowly now," she said, "one thing at a time." Thom felt Charlott was being a bit self-important because she had so much news to tell them. Gret kept saying, "But tell us, is he safe?" and "Hurry up!" Or Frieda, laughing, or now and then exclaiming, "For heaven's sake!"

Charlott was enjoying herself as she slowly told the whole story; even Thom could now more or less keep up when Gret and Frieda were told first what had happened three days earlier at the Winter plant, as they laughed, as they listened, watched, and were there when the three policemen arrived at the foundry to arrest the Pole. The men in their mechanics' overalls, their welding goggles on their foreheads, stopped working. The Pole? They exchanged glances, and one of them said to the policemen, "I wonder where he's gone off to this time?"

And another: "Didn't he just go through that door into the casting shop?"

And yet another: "He must have gone down into the rolling mill," and another one said, "The Polish fellow—isn't this about the time he's supposed to pick up the control tags from the planning office? Right now"—the man laughed—"he's probably having a quiet smoke behind the garage on his way back here!"

Frieda and Gret were flushed with excitement as they followed the policemen into the casting shop, accompanied by Mr. Lutz, the foreman. Here too, the men claimed either not to have seen the Pole at all, or to have talked to him just a few minutes earlier. "Yes, right, he was here a moment ago. He went over there to the assembly room. He must be in the casting shop. He must have gone across to the rolling mill. Wasn't he supposed to take the reports to the office by ten o'clock?" And on through the afternoon, at three, at five: "He was here only a minute ago." And "What do you want him for anyway? He's an internee, they're legal, a Pole, Siblevsky, we just call him 'the jolly Pole' because he has such a stock of funny stories!"

Charlott laughed. "It went on like that for two days. Although of course everyone at the plant—almost everyone except for Father and his assistant managers—knows he's a German, *and* a Jew—an illegal. One evening after work they brought him out of his hiding place in an air duct in the casting shop and hid him for two nights and a day in a cellar in the Old Town while the aliens department of the police arrived from Bern to question people all over town."

Why upstairs in the Small Salon, and why all those people outside? And if he was a "Pole," why a Jew, and if he was a "Jew," what did that mean? Words! How, with so many strange words, could he ever have understood why all that happened and why Father was so angry?

"But is he safe?" Gret asked.

And Charlott again: "You remember how we suddenly came face to face with him among the hazel bushes up there by the reservoir? And how startled we were? And how he told us about the men from the plant trying to get him out of town in a delivery van? But the exits were all blocked by the police, who searched everything. I heard they even fired at him from behind when he had a chance to escape."

Mother came in through the kitchen and paused in the doorway. "Thanks be to Mary," she said. "They've left." And to Charlott: "But what was all that suddenly going on outside?"

In the Paneled Room the light went on. And a moment later Father appeared from there in the door. "Now listen to me," he began, broke off, looked at them all. "What's going on?" Thom sensed that the anger was gone. He saw Father lean against the doorpost and take a cigarette out of a package. Almost calmly he said, "For a whole year we've been employing this Jew at the works! They palmed him off on us as a Pole, as a Polish internee. What a dirty trick! They say he was smuggled across the border from Italy, some big shot in the Jewish Resistance. At the plant he was known only as 'the jolly Pole.' " Mother broke the silence with, "Tell us, Charlott, what was happening out there?"

To Thom, Charlott already seemed almost grown-up. She turned her face toward Father. "But do you promise not to be angry any more?"

"What are you talking about, 'angry'? So: what happened?"

"Gret and I hid him upstairs in the salon. Now you know." Father drew on his cigarette. He said nothing. "Everyone had to swear an oath," Charlott continued. "An hour ago Herminia heard from her sister in town that the police were going to search this place." Then: "Is Sepp back yet? There's a rumor that the police were tipped off by someone here in the house!"

Father was still shaking his head. "I can't believe it! Don't tell me he's still around?"

Mother said quietly, No, she had arranged for him to leave the house.

When was that?

Charlott, and then Gret, began to giggle. Gret managed to say, "In the laundry hamper!" and now Thom noticed that Mother had to bite her lip in order not to laugh too. Father still hadn't caught on.

"Sepp and Herminia," said Charlott. "Didn't you see them walk past you with the laundry hamper? And all those people outside? I went out with them and they carried the hamper right through the crowd down the steps. At the bottom the police corporal stopped them and made them set down the hamper. Everyone wanted to see what was inside. The corporal looked in and picked up the laundry, but of course the Pole was lying there, and as he sat up, his eyes full of fear, a movement went through the people like wildfire and they crowded even more closely around the hamper with the Pole inside, and around the corporal with his two policemen. Then," Charlott went on with a laugh, "the corporal asked Sepp and Herminia, 'Since when'—he hesitated, looking slowly into the faces all around—'since when has mutton been transported in a laundry hamper?' All he added was, 'Take the stuff away! And anyhow, folks, what are you all standing around here for? Get along, go home, all of you!' "

At this point Gret and Frieda laughed out loud; Charlott did too, with tears in her eyes. Mother was laughing into her handkerchief, and when Thom dared to look across he saw that, although Father was still slowly shaking his head, laughter was beginning to spread across even his face as he stood there seeing and hearing his household burst out laughing after surviving the common danger—so much laughter that it was beginning to shake him, and all his anger had vanished: Father was laughing, joining in with the rest, so that Thom suddenly wished the shared laughter would never end.

Now at last Thom could combine the strange words into a story, into a jolly story about a jolly Pole, or at least into a story with a happy ending; for Ephraim Siblevsky the Jew observed the end of the Third Reich from his category of "Polish internee"—not as a Polish Jew—

happily ensconced on a farm in Rickenbach, district of Jammers. But it was a long time before Thom understood the words "Jewish capers." It was only many years later that he realized the difference between "capers" and "papers," and what a "J" stamped on such papers could mean. Only then did he begin to understand how a single letter could turn a jolly story into an entirely different one; a life-and-death story.

Time
of the
Victors

He had wanted to say, But it wasn't like that. Yet on she went, speaking from her armchair in the slowly waning light as she wound her ball of wool. And from the music room next door came the sound of Gret tinkling on the piano, over and over again the same seven or eight notes.

Not like that.

Had Aunt Esther forgotten that he had been present? That he had been the first to enter the porch through the glass door with its pattern of red, green, and yellow flowers and open the cellar door to the steep steps? He had wanted to say, But I heard him myself. That groaning coming up from the cellar. And Father's voice at times getting loud, angrily loud as he cursed away down there, but then it would once again sound like the growling of a wounded bear. "I did see him myself, it's less than a year ago, Aunt Esther"—but she carried on as if it were a legend from ancient times.

To be sure, yes, Father had gone to Bonn where, as the head of a trade delegation of Swiss industrialists and parliamentarians, he had met with the heads of the Federal German Ministry of Economics for some difficult negotiations. A year earlier, then again six months earlier, in the spring of '52, there had already been lengthy negotiations, first in Bonn, then in Basel. There had been frequent talk between his parents and at table about those discussions with the Germans regarding tariffs and a European economic order: that much even Thom, aged fourteen, had understood.

Now Father had telephoned ahead, calling from Basel: "We've won!" And Thom was to tell Mother that he, Father, would come home after dinner with some of his friends from the delegation—"a little celebration, we've earned that, haven't we? Tell her about nine o'clock, and don't forget to go down into the cellar right now and bring up some wine, fifteen bottles of the Nuits-Saint-Georges, and put them in the Paneled Room next to the sideboard." Aunt Esther told Thom not to ask her about details—"at any rate, it was a great victory. Also a personal victory, my brother Ulrich could be proud. Your father's decisive move was that in the preceding months, on two trips to Strasbourg, he had succeeded in coming to an agreement with the French and British, without the Germans knowing about it. The victorious powers still have some say in Germany in economic affairs too, you see. The entire export industry of our country should be deeply grateful to your father!"

While she carried on with her story and Gret continued to practice that difficult passage at the piano, Thom saw himself and Gret helping the men off with their dark coats in the passage, then the two of them sitting with Mother in the Paneled Room at the very end of the table, which together they had pulled out to its entire length; or Thom walking around the table carrying the claret basket and refilling empty glasses. It had been Mr. Sarasin, Thom remembered this well, who tapped his glass, stood up, looked around, and said, "Friends, a battle has been fought. How does the poem go? 'See, the conquering hero comes!' I'm a banker. Liberal principles. Breaking a lance for private industry against state intervention as supported by the German delegation. Simply magnificent, the way you, my dear Ulrich Winter, conducted the negotiations, luring the German side into the trap, forcing them to lay their cards on the table. A historic moment. The way you introduced the victorious powers as a Trojan horse, so to speak, into the opponent's fortress, then, in a bold stroke, doubled the stakes with the trump card of our country's wartime neutrality. Psychologically too, a masterpiece! May I ask you to rise, my friends? Let us raise our glasses to the victor, the head of the delegation: Ulrich Winter!"

Thom and Gret looked on, astonished, embarrassed, as even Mother rose to her feet and there was the clinking of many crystal glasses across the table. Father beamed from ear to ear. Yes, Thom was proud of him too.

Was it really only a year since that celebration in the Paneled Room? Only a year—and how could Thom have known, when he and Gret kissed Father goodnight at ten o'clock, that it would be the last time?

Ulrich came to her suite, she told Thom. After the guests had left, there was a knock at her door: he was laughing, and when he sat down he said, "You should have been there, sister darling!" "And I'm telling you, Thom, he was sober! Not for years had I seen him in such good shape! I'm not saying he hadn't had anything to drink at all. Two or three glasses perhaps—but you know he could still tolerate a good deal. In three days, he told me, he was expected at the Federal Parliament in Bern to report on the results of the negotiations. No, on that memorable evening he wasn't in the least drunk. Remember that!"

Was she lying? Or did she want to provoke him? Thom was no longer a child. At fourteen he had long since developed the wild animal's nose for impending danger. From the lower end of the table he had observed the minute changes in Father's face—not merely the faint reddening of that highly porous facial skin, not only the sagging around the mouth, the increasingly feverish glint in those brown eyes. He had noticed—watchful, ever watchful!—the movements of those hands becoming vaguer, more erratic, as he spoke, and his voice, too, growing louder and louder, clear though it remained at first. But the very way Father laughed or slightly slurred his words was indication enough for Thom.

While Aunt Esther was telling him how, after the departure of the guests, Father had continued to sit in his study over his papers until far into the night, how at about two A.M. he had gone down into the cellar, slipped on one of the bottom steps, and lying there with a broken arm had called for help, Thom could once again hear the muffled wailing from below—Thom was lying under the quilt in the dark—a distant wailing interrupted by the whispering nighttime silence in the house, and suddenly he knew it was Father, that he had once again reached that point. Thom sat up. Again that fear. Again he saw himself, and his father ordering him to fetch the riding crop from the back of the big closet in the attic, and himself, Thom, coming back into the passage carrying the riding crop, walking slower and slower toward the Paneled Room, like a person sentenced by some incomprehensible authority to be tortured simply because he was the sole male descendant, sentenced to be tortured simply because of his gender and because a man must learn in his earliest years to endure injustice and the terrible pain of the whip, of the whip coming down ten, twenty times on buttocks and back and arms and backs of knees and shoulders and even on the head, to endure it like a man, without complaining or crying out.

Father was prowling around the table in the Paneled Room. If Thom were to enter now, he knew he would have to place the whip on the table, let down his knickerbockers, and lie head down over the arm of Mother's leather armchair in front of one of the east windows.

His hope: that Father had already reached the stage where he no longer drank wine but only gulped down schnapps out of the bottle and would very quickly be so drunk that, as he swayed, he wouldn't have the strength to hit properly; or that Thom this time, this one time, would finally manage—he was thirteen, after all—to be a man, a man who, although feeling the lashes as they flailed down blow by blow upon him, feeling the whip like a red-hot branding iron leaving its marks on his bare skin, had by now learned to clench his teeth so fiercely that no sound would pass his lips. So that at some point Father would stop panting and yelling at him, "Not a sound! D'you hear me, you young puppy?" and stop thrashing too, amazed to see his son now straighten up, pull his suspenders back over his shoulders, and say merely, "I'm leaving now." Father could, if he wanted to, read triumph in his eyes: "Sure, you're still the stronger, and the welts on my back and my ass are bloody, but I'll never whimper, never beg again—never! And it's dawning on you now, today, for the first time: it won't be long before you will have to confront me, man to man, and it won't be long before you realize that you are an old man; and I will train every day, I'll grow stronger and stronger." Hadn't it been Mother herself who had told him, Thom, not too long ago, "Don't forget—one day you will be stronger than he"?

All that passed through his mind as he sat there listening to Aunt Esther and at the same time sitting up in bed straining to hear. Aunt Esther said, "He must have slipped on the damp stone flags down there and fallen, breaking his arm above the elbow. I am sure you can imagine, Thom, how hellishly painful that can be. So there lay my poor brother— no wonder he called for help! But who was to hear him at two o'clock in the morning? The door leading to the cellar was closed. The door to the porch was closed; Charlott wasn't home, she had gone back to her boarding school in Fribourg, and we were all asleep. Only your Mother —who, if not she, should have stayed awake or awakened? *She* should have heard him right away, since she—"

As always, when she was upset, Aunt Esther lit a cigarillo. The flame flickered twice in the dusk, and Thom saw the reflection in Aunt Esther's eyes: they had been turned on him the entire time.

"No," he said, "it wasn't like that at all. I *had* heard him. I sat up in bed for a while, then went out, listened, ran across to Gret, and together they"

Aunt Esther wasn't listening. She sat there, leaning back, smoking, and went on with her story. "If you ask me, she didn't want to. She heard him, heard him call for help, but for the longest time her hatred would not allow her to do her duty by him! At least her duty as a Christian!"

"No, Aunt, no"—while Thom was trying to tell her how it had really been: Gret in her nightgown had first listened at the door to the Blue Room, opened it a crack, listened again, closed it and said to Thom, Mother's asleep—come along, and together they had

but Aunt Esther had already resumed her story in the gradually darkening room. Now she was talking about Sepp and Herminia, how the two of them had eventually managed to drag the heavy, injured man, half-unconscious from pain, up the steep steps, "while your mother merely issued a few directions instead of going straight to the telephone to call Dr. Muralt! Can you believe that a woman, especially that one— can you? What did you say? No no, we're not concerned with you here, you really mustn't keep interrupting your aunt with some trifling details— no, do you hear?"

Thom fell silent. Yet all he had wanted to tell her was what had happened, that he was the first to go through the porch beyond the colored-glass door, that he had opened the heavy door to the cellar and noticed that the dim light in the vault was on. Then he heard and saw his father lying down there on the stone steps. Apparently he had tried to get onto his knees and heave himself from one step to the next. Gret and he had gone down. Father was whimpering as he lay exhausted some three meters above the little landing from which three further steps went off to the left to the first cellar vault.

When they reached Father he started wailing again, those long-drawn-out lamentations of his. Raising his head from the edge of the stone steps he looked up: "It's you!" The words came out thickly. "Yes, Aunt," Thom said, "he *was* drunk. He couldn't even get onto his knees. And it was only his right elbow on the step that kept him from slipping. I climbed over him to the bottom and tried with both hands to support one of his shoes so as to give him some resistance. Gret pushed her arm under his to help him up, but that made him scream and curse. This was when we realized that his left arm must be injured. In his right hand Father was still holding the neck of a broken bottle, grasping it as if it were his last weapon against the specters of despair. We did our best to encourage him, and together we tried to lift his heavy body. But again and again he slipped from our hands, and we were afraid all the time that he might start sliding down the steep steps."

At that point Thom had suddenly seen Mother in the open door at the top of the steps, as if she had been watching them for quite a while, standing there in her long blue housecoat with the gold belt. The porch light was shining just behind and above her, obscured by her head, so that her hair seemed surrounded by an aureole; she was beautiful, an angel, Thom thought, the angel of salvation. "Wait!" she called out. "That's more than the three of us can handle!" She disappeared, to return very shortly with Herminia and Sepp. And now, trembling with exhaustion, trembling in the chill air of the cellar, they watched Sepp and Herminia drag Father, one step at a time, up the stairs. Thom could feel Gret groping for his hand; when he looked at her he saw the tears on her face. She whispered a word, repeated it. Now he understood: "The victor," she was whispering.

"But never mind what you say, Thom"—Aunt Esther was still speaking—"your mother Lilly must have known how dangerous such a fracture is. She should have phoned Dr. Muralt immediately! Can *you* tell me why she didn't do that while Sepp and Herminia were still carrying my poor brother upstairs to the gallery and into the bathroom next to his room?"

"But none of us knew yet what was wrong with his left arm!"

Aunt Esther laughed; she laughed. "Even before they had hauled him upstairs, Lilly must have thought up her plan! She was giving a few directions, and now will someone please explain to me why, when he was finally seated up there in the big bathroom in the wicker armchair, groaning with pain—why she sent them all away, Herminia and Frieda and Sepp, and then actually locked the bathroom door from the inside? I'm only saying, It all fits! Not even then, so your mother claimed, did it occur to her to call the doctor. First my beloved brother had to be dead before she decided to do so!"

Thom had risen from his stool. He could feel himself trembling again. "Stop! You're lying! You're lying, Aunt! She simply wanted first to wash his face and hands, wipe off the blood, put on a temporary bandage"—but Aunt Esther carried on with her own concocted version, speaking into the room that was now quite dark: the whole ghastly story, on and on she went, and how after fifteen minutes, according to her,

Lilly Winter had turned the key again from the inside. She stood in the doorway, looking exhausted, her disheveled hair falling over her face.

"Why are you staring at me like that? And why are you talking like that? Listen, just calm down and listen to me. You are his son. Who, if not you, has a right to know the truth? All of it, understand? No, I insist, keep quiet now and let me tell you what happened!"

Thom was still standing. No, he didn't want to hear that to the end, not that! But even when he closed his eyes and pressed both hands against his ears; when, stiff with rage and fear, he moved past the bridge table, past Frieda sitting over her embroidery frame; when he opened the door to the passage and suddenly dashed up the stairs in the dark—Aunt Esther's voice pursued him, those words piercing him like daggers. "So Lilly Winter stood, panting, in the bathroom door, and after pushing back her hair from her face she merely said, "Now he is dead!" Aunt Esther went on: "You know our dear old Doctor Muralt! In all innocence he filled out the death certificate: Embolism resulting from a fracture of the upper left arm. In other words, he suffocated. But suffocated actually from a blood clot or from a wet bath towel over his face? You know what I think. And she knows too."

Thom went to Gret's room; she was not there. In the dark he flung himself face down on the bed. He and Gret had followed Herminia, Sepp, and Father up into the gallery. Then Thom had joined Gret under her quilt. Here, in Gret's bed, he had pressed his sister's head to his shoulder, felt her warmth, and her sobs as she fell asleep. Here, where he was now burrowing his face into the cool pillow, he had also been asleep when suddenly his mother had been there. He had awoken with a start to see her sitting on the edge of the bed. "Are you both awake? Thom? And you, Gret? I have something to tell you. Your father is dead. We must all be strong now. He died five minutes ago," she said. With her hand she had stroked the damp hair from their foreheads, first his, then Gret's.

In Those Days

THEY SAY THAT AT ONE TIME HERMINIA HAD HARDLY MISSED A SINGLE dance put on in town, although only those on weekdays and—Mrs.

Winter insisted for reasons of propriety—only until 11:30 P.M. Entertainment on Saturday evenings was—as Pastor Zemp of the parish church repeatedly made clear to his flock with his bone-chilling, hell-fire sermons—forbidden for Catholics, especially Catholic young women. They also say that she, Herminia, had fallen in love so seriously at the New Year's Eve dance at the Hammer in 1943 that the Winter household was already afraid she would hand in her notice because she planned to get married. The fear proved unnecessary. Herminia said no.

In any event, every Thursday, when the *Stadt-Anzeiger* arrived, Herminia would sit down with a cup of coffee at the pantry table so that the light from the east window fell over her left shoulder onto the newspaper. Beside her were pencil and paper and a pair of scissors.

Entertainment evening in the concert hall. DANCING. To the Swiss Melodies Band. Admission Fr. 1.80.

Cinema Palace: *Dancing with the Emperor*. Starring Marika Rökk.

Entertainment and DANCING. Everybody welcome! Doors open 8 P.M. Many surprises! Door prizes! Music by the ever-popular Echo vom Weissenstein Band. Sponsored by the Jammers Catholic Athletic Club.

Herminia merely glanced at the housing and vehicle offerings, but she was always on the lookout for bargains.

Lowest prices for remnants of all kinds! Spielmann-Bucher Fabrics. Ladies' tailoring on premises.

Specials: Overstuffed armchairs only Fr. 160.00 and up. Complete bedroom furniture sets Fr. 380.00 and up.

China, the timeless gift! Unique offer from our wide selection: Coffee service, blue floral pattern on white, for six; 16 pieces only Fr. 27.50! Bastian-Platz Shopping Center.

Would Herminia have read this offer two or three times, would she have marked it, perhaps cut it out? And for two minutes allowed herself to dream of receiving her own guests in her own little house for coffee and cakes, sitting at the table with them, and on the table would there be little silver knives and spoons gleaming in the candlelight, the new coffee service with the blue flowers, and would her husband, her future husband, carry a bottle from the walnut sideboard and fill the little silver beakers with kirsch made in Zug; and she, Herminia, would she cut the first slice of the homemade nut or carrot cake with the silver cake knife? Hadn't she, in the closet in her attic room, kept her silverware in the two leather cases with their velvet-lined trays? For what purpose? And for what purpose did she go to the trouble of polishing the silver every

six months? No. After all, she had twice in her life said no to men—
one of whom had even been divorced—who had asked for her hand in
marriage. She had made up her mind. She wasn't prepared to give up
her status as an unmarried Catholic young woman for the sake of some
good-for-nothing man. Here, as cook in the Winter household, she had
her place. And anyway it was time to start preparing the potato and cheese
soufflé for the evening meal. She went into the kitchen, put on her
apron, and began peeling potatoes at the table.

Thom took the bottle of apple cider from the refrigerator, filled two
glasses, placed them on the kitchen table, and sat down on the stool
across from Herminia. From the table drawer he took out a paring knife;
Herminia and he peeled the potatoes together.

Was it really almost forty years ago? As a boy of four or five he had
knelt here on the stool, and Herminia had taught him how to use the
little metal shapes to cut cinnamon stars and Milan hearts out of the
dough. Of course Herminia's hair had turned white long ago, and though
her face was wrinkled her eyes still looked shrewdly through the glasses
she now wore. But she was plump, still lively, the way Thom had always
known her. Close-mouthed too. Yet now, even before he had asked a
question, she said, "She came in here. She sat down on the stool you're
sitting on. Suddenly she said, 'I believe I knew this young fellow by sight.
Executed! Shot as a traitor to his country. A man from here, from town!
You know the family, the Kullys? He was a student, a lieutenant. They
say he was a spy in the pay of the Germans, that he betrayed military
secrets.' "

Lilly Winter, Herminia said, had been very much alone during
those war years, especially in 1942 and '43 when Thom's father was
constantly away with the army or on business. So she often used to come
and sit with her, with Herminia, in the pantry or here at the table. Before
that, all they had ever discussed was the day's menu, shopping, the
laundry, and household supplies. Or the maids, who, as Thom knew,
changed almost with the seasons in this house. But then. To be sure, in
Zurich Mrs. Winter had her old schoolfriend, Verena Vontobel, Thom
would remember her. About once a month she went to visit Mrs. Vontobel; she corresponded with her, sometimes stood in the passage and
talked to her on the phone. Who else was there?

Mrs. Winter needed someone; she wanted to discuss what was going
on at the time. She listened to her London broadcasts, and she and
Herminia would sit together in the Paneled Room listening to Radio

Beromünster, to Professor von Salis's World Report—though they sat together only when Thom's father wasn't there.

For a moment there was the sound of Herminia's breathing. She had begun to slice the peeled potatoes. Yes, she said, at that time she too had started reading not only the *Stadt-Anzeiger* and the Catholic *Der Morgen*, but also the newspaper clippings her sister gave her. Every Thursday from eight to ten thirty she spent the evening with Margot on Säli-Strasse—which, incidentally, she still did. Her brother-in-law—did Thom remember him, Isidor Strub, foreman at the Winter plant? He had died years ago—anyway, the Strubs belonged to the Red Assistance, and both were members of the Social Democratic Party. Margot was on the union's education committee; Herminia had even had to go along with her to lectures three or four times. Did Thom understand? Quite often there had been comrades from Basel and Zurich at their place, visiting Communists in hiding, and even anarchists. There had been lively debates, and Margot was constantly giving her articles from the socialist newspaper *Das Volk*. "You must read this, and this, and this too!"

"You know, Thom," said Herminia, "right here in town we had a real big Frontists' nest. In 1940, when Germany was winning on all fronts, they started holding public meetings again."

Oh yes, Thom knew about that, knew what he had read in books about the Frontist movement. But he had never concerned himself with the recent history of his home town except as it related to the Winter company's history for the Festschrift he had composed. He had probably even avoided it instinctively, he said—largely because he didn't want to know too much about his father's political stance in those years.

"No, no," Herminia said, "your father was never a Frontist, no more than, say, his Skat partner, Otthmar Walter the publisher. All those two had was a certain affinity with the Front and with Hitler and Franco. Margot used to say, They'll side with anything that's against the Left. Many of the upper-class people here in town felt like Ulrich Winter, and like Otthmar Walter, who was widely respected as a publisher and a leading Catholic-conservative politician. Margot and her husband called it a slight touch of Fascism. Until well into the war years, they approved of Hitler, yet at the same time they were in favor of defending a free Switzerland. They were against Leftist godlessness, against Bolshevism, against the Jews, who owned the department stores: to that extent they agreed with the local National Socialists. On the other hand, certainly from 1939 on, they were defenders of Switzerland—a Switzerland, however, that was to undergo a radical renewal in line with the New Order.

"I know," said Thom: "reactionary patriots, but certainly not anti-Fascists."

Herminia nodded. So did he realize what a conflict she found herself in? "Once, when I used the word 'anti-Fascist,' your mother immediately asked, 'Where did you pick that up?' And what did I imagine it meant? So I began, tentatively, to tell her about the discussions at Margot's and Isidor's. I passed on to her some of the articles Margot had given me. Your mother had recently read an enthusiastic book about General Franco published by Otthmar Walter. She also lent me a book called *Atrocities in Spain* from the same publisher. 'That will open your eyes and your sister's to what would happen here if the spirit of godless Bolshevism were to triumph here too!' I took this book, after I'd read it, to the Strubs, and the result was another evening of arguments about Red and Brown, about Franco, Stalin, and Hitler. Who was I to believe?" Herminia laughed. "I really didn't understand much about all that political stuff. Margot was strict: 'When are you going to start using your head, my girl?' So there were times when I would come home at ten thirty on a Thursday evening from those discussions with the Strubs and their friends, and from the passage I would hear through the open study door the Skat players—often including Father Zemp and Dr. Muralt as well as Dr. Bircher from Aarau—arguing about whether this country could still afford the Jewish and Leftist refugees, or whether the boat was full. Or they were indignant over the case of that police captain from St. Gallen, Paul Grüninger: in defiance of orders from the department of aliens, he had permitted some two thousand Jews to enter Switzerland from Austria, thus saving them from the concentration camps. He was taken to court, lost his job, and had to pay a fine. The argument in the study was about whether the sentence hadn't been much too mild. When I went into the pantry, the light was on. Your mother was sitting there, white-faced, distraught. I can see her looking at me! 'That man was found guilty of saving human lives! What has happened to Christianity? The virtue of charity? Why don't the bishops—'

"The rift," said Herminia, "went right down the middle during those years. It went right through this house, through the town, through the country."

Herminia stood up. The potatoes were peeled and sliced. "Preheat the oven," she said. And had Thom seen the latest *Stadt-Anzeiger?*

Passages V

TO WRITE IT DOWN OR NOT. TO COMMIT THIS STORY WORD FOR WORD TO paper or not: even while sitting in the Blue Room again at her desk, he felt he must bring *his* face up close, once more right up close in his mind, just this once; then maybe he could consign him too to the past, once and for all, and the rain and Hurricane and all the fear and loneliness and rage that had been pent up inside him; consign them to the past, together with that sudden onslaught of an autumn thunderstorm.

A frost had descended on the grounds; the leaves gave up their last resistance. One morning, fog coming up from the Aare and the town suddenly surrounded the house as if arsonists had been at work during the night. It was noon before the hickory oaks and the lilac bushes emerged from it, dripping wet; the fog sank or drifted away, and even the sun came out and shone as if nothing had happened. But Thom couldn't help thinking: that again today

but the mental block, while Aunt Esther droned on with her story about that gypsy who had been killed down in the Old Town beside the Aare, on and on, but that one sentence, that half sentence of hers, had been enough to make him lose the thread she was spinning again. He had simply not been able to get past the words, spoken as if they were of no importance: "You know, his face at times," she had said, as if this didn't touch upon the innermost core of all the fear that he so often tried in vain to forget before falling asleep or even during the day—"his face at times"—and perhaps only because she had also said, "you know," hence that mental block, and he had tried, while she carried on with her gypsy story, to endure his father's face as it suddenly loomed close to him: the downward-slanting corners of the eyes, that nose, slightly reddened, slightly porous, from alcohol, the graying mustache; the full lower lip and again those watery brown eyes, rapidly changing from angry to crinkly, soft when smiling, and wide open again, wide with rage; and Thom had suddenly stood up and walked past her while she went on talking to herself that afternoon, walked through Frieda's room into the passage, the hall, out through the porch and across the back verandah and the sunlit gravel down into the stable yard, with no clear idea of what he intended to do in the semidarkness there with Hurricane, that idiotically named mare bring his face up close again or at least make it possible for it to loom close to him again, now, this morning, as he sat here at the desk leaning back in the armchair: Father's big face, now wearing that lopsided smile, and with it summon up or bring close that hour or so he had spent beside the mare's long head as he sat in the manger in the semidarkness, his legs dangling, lost in thought in the miasma of horse manure straw barley and swarming flies. Suddenly he had known two things: that after the last few days of Father's subdued agitation and exaggerated calm, his alcoholic phase was due again today; and second, that should it again occur to Father to send him for the riding crop in the attic closet, he, Thom, at fourteen, was from now on not prepared under any circumstances to let himself be whipped, come what might.

Hurricane snuffled persistently at Thom's neck and shoulders, her soft chin hairs and moist, velvety nostrils tickling Thom's ear; when the long-legged Hanoverian mare snorted, her breath was hot. They knew each other. Not that Thom was a horseman; he had twice been thrown in the paddock; and after Sepp had teased him about his swaybacked seat, Thom had only occasionally gone riding, for barely an hour, just to exercise the mare, and whenever possible at dusk so people wouldn't recognize him. No, Hurricane was Aunt Esther's horse; now and again the mare would also be ridden by Uncle Ludwig after his stallion had to be put down because of a broken hind leg. They knew each other

back to Father's face: from the stable door Thom could see the black limousine, see Mr. Wenger opening the car door at the foot of the steps, and, since Father was very slow getting out of the car and walked unsteadily toward the steps, he could already see, right then, that the time had come again, so he dashed off to the back verandah and into the house up the stairs three steps at a time in his sneakers and into the gallery and up again until he flung open the closet door in the attic, but this time not the riding crop, no, the revolver, the heavy, saddle-colored case, and again with no real idea of what he was about to do but now quickly down the stairs in the dark. He stopped in his room just long enough to pick up his brown woolen jacket, the one with the zipper, then went into the hall and heard Father's cheerful singing in the passage and in the Paneled Room. Passing Herminia in the kitchen with her "What's going on?" and astonished look, Thom took half a loaf of bread from the cupboard, stuffed two apples in his pockets, and was already in the storeroom under the stairs when he heard Father calling him; leaving the saddle lying across the banister he took along only the thick yellow saddlecloth and dashed outside. He received a shock: in those three or four minutes a greenish-black wall of clouds had risen up behind and above his ash tree, and dusk had already extinguished all the colors of the autumn evening. Thom ran toward the stableyard, through the gateway, and into the stable from the rear. He put the bridle on Hurricane, pushed the bit between her teeth, tightened everything, and led the mare out into the open. Then he slung the saddlecloth over her back. From the cornerstone he managed, at the second attempt, to get astride the saddlecloth, and thus, still in his sneakers and with no saddle, he rode off. As he trotted down to the end of the avenue and turned right, away from town, the first heavy drops were already falling. An October thunderstorm, a storm erupting onto the almost bare trees. Now he realized how much he needed the stirrups. Although in the second lesson Sepp had tried to teach him how to ride without stirrups, Thom still had great difficulty posting in time with the mare's trotting rhythm. As he rode through the residential area, the rain drenched them both with cascading water, and all around was darkness. Although gallant Hurricane flinched at every thunderclap, she heeded the reins

or summon up the abandoned clay pit with the burned-out brickworks and think how Thom had left the pavement and turned onto the gravel path to ride along under the trees in the dark, how he eventually found the half-overgrown approach to the clay pit and rode on until he was under the sloping, ruined roof of the brickworks. Summon the night sounds, the cry of the Little Owl, and how Thom, even in his jacket, was shivering with wet and cold and yet, sitting now in the northern part of the brickworks where they faced the pit, sitting on some boards and charred beams in that open shed, didn't want to remove the saddlecloth from the mare because horses so easily catch cold in the wet. The storm tramped with hobnailed boots across the corrugated-iron roof and across what, twenty years ago, may have been the entrance for the tipcarts coming from the clay pit and that had survived the fire; it certainly was no place for the long-legged mare and the fourteen-year-old boy to linger. He was determined he would rather catch pneumonia or even die than ever again submit to another whipping. Let Father rage! Let him smash vases and glasses and whatever else! But if it should occur to him to organize a search, maybe even summon Charlott and Mother and Gret and extort a confession from Charlott as to where Thom might be hiding, and then turn up here, perhaps with Mr. Wenger and Sepp, then Thom would, and he swallowed hard at the thought could now be heard only in the distance, and the rain stopped almost as abruptly as the thunderstorm had begun, although water was still dripping all around. The wan light of the half moon showed up rivulets and glistening puddles on the ground. Hurricane neighed with annoyance, or perhaps she had already caught cold. Charred tree stumps on the way up to the pit; spindly bushes thrusting up between the twisted rails. Suddenly hungry, Thom began to munch on his hunk of bread, from time to time groping for Hurricane and offering her bits of bread and pieces of apple on his open palm. Then he would sit down again on his pile, watching and listening, listening or turning around with a start at the unaccountable sounds of the night in front of or beside or behind him. And all the time fighting off sleep

yet at some point he would suddenly wake up, then, his back against a wet wall, drop off again; or he would suddenly feel his shoulder being nudged and for a moment not be sure whether it had been a ghostly hand or the mare's nose hovering dimly over his face against the night sky. "Hurricane," he would say, "stop that! I'd rather be home too." He took out the revolver and placed it, the safety catch still on, beside him on the pile. And nodded off and woke up again, wide awake, jumping to his feet because what he was now hearing was a motor, and because on the beams above him headlights shone, so he was coming—Charlott, no doubt in tears, must have confessed—that must be the Mercedes limousine approaching, the sound of that motor, it had to be Father stopping on the south side of the ruin. Then the voices: first Mr. Wenger, then Sepp, and now Father calling out, "Thom!" He didn't budge. If it weren't for this damn mare—but where could he have hidden her? Then he did stand up, quietly, the revolver in his right hand, and take cover by crouching behind his pile of charred lumber

and once again summon up those downward-slanting eyes above their pouches that face reddened by alcohol and sadness that face of the man who was his father. Thom could feel his own resistance as he sat at his mother's desk; yes, resistance to reliving it all, right to the very end, yet at the same time knowing that only once more, just this once more, and he would be rid of that face. And how, crouching in the cold, drafty, ruined brickworks, he had followed the wandering spotlights and seen and heard Mr. Wenger and Sepp moving around in the chaos of still-standing or half-collapsed walls and rubble and nettles, and heard Father coming around toward the rear along the overgrown path on the west side and calling for him

Thom stood up. Should he clear out, following the rails up into the old pit area with its mounds of rubble craters bushes puddles of water, right now, or stay where he was—stay and defend himself to the last with the revolver? Then Hurricane neighed, and in an access of renewed rage and no doubt ludicrous heroism he called out, though in a shaky voice, "Here I am! I'll shoot!"

For a few seconds, silence. Outside, the stumps of the charred trees were now gray in the early morning light. The mare neighed again. From the west, along the ruined building, light approached: Father's flashlight. It shone toward him, away from him, and when Thom, although his whole body was trembling and his teeth were chattering with cold, took two steps forward and called out "Halt!" the beam of light struck him full in the face.

Father came closer. "Thom! There you are!" and stopped. Thom could tell that his father was not drunk. "Thom. What's this nonsense! Come on, be sensible!" From the left, from inside the building, the two beams of light wavered toward them. Father switched off his flashlight. It was probably Sepp directing his beam for Father to see where he was stepping, and Thom saw, just within the spotlight, the shoes in the muddy ground less than four meters away. He held the old service revolver at chest level. "I'm going to kill you now."

The words were out. Just don't weaken now—just don't

Father came closer. Sepp's flashlight revealed him up to his hips, and from the left a light fell on Thom too; his revolver gleamed, trembled. Three more meters. Now. But Thom could not press the trigger.

"Come on, don't do anything stupid—Thomi, do you hear?"

Now. In the faint morning light Father's face was there before him, came closer, came closer closer—but the trouble was, there was no anger in those eyes, no hint of punishment, only something like gentleness or even compassion; maybe that was even worse than the true fatherly calm with which Father took the revolver from his hand and dropped it on the ground. And drew Thom gently to his breast for a few seconds, and said, "My boy"

so much so that he had had to summon that face again and again through all those dreams and years until this, perhaps last, time; and perhaps now Thom would be able to consign that face, and that night after the thunderstorm with Hurricane, to the past and, written down or not, let it sink away into the vaults, into the rubble of those irretrievable years.

*   *   *

Jammers, July 2, 1982 (Friday)

My faraway darling,

Now you have told me something else about yourself—I mean, also about the child you are (once were). I am touched when I read and reread how you used to sit in the attic window in Andernach, alone, talking to your squirrel Lilliput. Then that horror brought about by your gun-crazy uncle. It is when you tell me something like this from your past, and what hurts you, that I feel I am beginning to know you. The feeling is still there when I put down your letter again on the desk here; it will stay with me, briefly perhaps, while I get up and begin to walk up and down in the Blue Room, which I am making more and more my own; yes, I still feel I know you—and am already aware that in a few moments you will have slipped away from me again, a different person, with all your very own vulnerabilities, and the fear, the longing, and the images inside you to which I am once again a stranger. And I fall back into myself, into my exile, into my solitary cell. The awareness that to be left alone is one of our fundamental agreements apparently loses little of its misery even when I live it at first hand: that is, as the counterpart to closeness. No matter how much I rebel against it, as I do now, it remains. Even calling it both terrible and banal is of no help to me.

What will happen when we are back in Berlin again? But you'll first come here, won't you, and then two or three days later we'll return together?

To Berlin—but where? You to your Schlüter-Strasse, I to my apartment? Do you remember the combination we wanted to find? Buying autonomy by staying alone—I've been practicing this for two years now, and I must say I've had enough. Just as that symbiotic marriage with Susann became too much for me. You've told me similar things about yourself, including your living with Kurt. We wanted to find the right combination. But how, Lis dearest, how? We two, belonging to the generation between "no longer" and "not yet"? Probably I am worrying—theoretically at that, about something that we can discover only by experience. One thing I'm sure of: that often, very often and on many nights, I have wished I could wake up toward morning, emerging from some dream or other, able to feel you beside me, hear your quiet breathing, and in the first light of dawn from the open window see your hair on the pillow beside me and your profile. And, in a very male sense, feel myself to be the one who watches over your sleep.

Last night, while this day was just dawning beyond the window, I was wakened by a noise from the gallery outside my door. It was a kind of giggle; at first I thought I must still be dreaming. When I heard it again, I got out of bed and in the dark opened the door. Outside, in the dim light of the three wall lamps, I saw my sister Gret. Now that I'm writing about it, I wonder whether it wasn't only a dream after all. I received a double shock. First, because my sister was wearing that turquoise-blue housecoat—the same color, the same soft sheen as on our mother's housecoat. The same gold belt—which certainly emphasized the difference between Mother's slim figure and Gret's heavy body. Then the eerie part was that she was dancing and at the same time giggling, and again she would hum, hum the little tune that Father sometimes used to sing, and when he did we knew he was drunk: "Once again the roses bloom," only that Gret was humming it in three-quarter time and dancing slowly, very slowly. She was unquestionably drunk. As she swayed about she kept losing the rhythm and would reach out for the balustrade or one of the columns, trying to regain her balance; then she would start revolving again, charming and ungainly, her eyes closed. Suddenly she said, "How are you, brother dear?" Then, revolving: "Will you join me in a little dance?"

You can imagine that, standing there in the door, I didn't feel like dancing. Gret giggled. Again she reached out for the balustrade and leaned against it, then fumbled in her pockets until she found her cigarettes and lighter. "Do you believe in eternal life?"

How should I have answered? I decided to say I did: "Of course, Gret." She tried to light her cigarette. "You're crazy. Eternal life—" she hesitated, and waved the thought away. I told her I was sure that after death we dissolved into our basic substances, into millions of atoms, thus becoming part of Mother Earth's eternal cycle of death and new life. Even our spiritual energies—"Do you follow me? Are you listening?"

Gret shook her head. "You're stupid, Thom. I want it to be the way they've promised us. I want to rise from the dead." She was laughing again. "Really, you know. I want to see Father, I want to walk toward him and put my arms around him. And then? Then I'll ask him. And he will tell me what happened here that night in the locked bathroom." Suddenly she looked at me as if she were the schoolgirl of long ago, almost impishly, with strands of hair falling across her face. "Haven't you realized? How I have wanted only one thing: to be different from her?"

Gret actually had not heard my question, or she had ignored it. She repeated a few times, "Quite different. And now—do you see me? Haven't you noticed?" She was smoking avidly. "She insinuated herself into me. First only a little, then I became more and more and more like her. But now? She, the irreproachable one! Look at me! There's a chance that I'm a culprit too. An accomplice, if you like. But otherwise—I have now"—Gret laughed and dropped the ash on the floor—"I have now become like Father. He weighed ninety-six kilos. Today, Thom, I have managed to get there too—ninety-six! And as for drinking, I'm almost as good at that too." She crushed out her cigarette on the dark-red balustrade and tossed the stub over her shoulder into the hall. "Don't worry, brother. I'm not going to order you to fetch the riding crop from the attic. I'm not going to beat you. Not you. You, my ally! I love you, Thom. Do you remember the oath we swore? Let's stick to it." She came toward me, swaying slightly. "Why don't you go back to sleep?" She put her arms around me and kissed me on both cheeks. "My poor ally." She shuffled off toward the stairs, then turned around once more and, her hand on the balustrade, said, "Do you see any—any!—reason why I shouldn't drink myself to death? There you are, then!" She giggled and walked down the stairs. All I could do was go back to bed, where I fell immediately into a dreamless sleep.

What, Lis dearest, am I to do with all this? With this undisguised announcement of deliberate self-destruction? You will understand how sorry I am for my sister. What she said about being an accomplice—she said it while she was drunk—am I to take it literally? And come to the conclusion that I have solved—almost solved—the riddle that I have been finding more and more sinister? "Accomplice": wouldn't that have to imply more than one perpetrator? I am suppressing the temptation to write at this point: Come! Please come soon! But I want you to know that without you—well, I would probably have come to grief here long ago. The fact that you exist, exist for me, even though you are a day's journey away from me—this bond with you is for me, if I may use a metaphor, the rope that holds me in the present, in the everyday world, while I find myself descending into ever new, ever deeper cellar vaults.

There's a lot more I could tell you. About a long walk I took with André up to the old castle ruin, and about the strange discussion we got into during which I now feel we were talking more and more at cross purposes. This depressed me. What a man! How independent, clear, and generous in his thinking! Yet he is still, at fifty, living in that little house in the Old Town, tied to his mother's apron strings, if I'm not mistaken. Although I don't wish to encroach on the preserves of psychology, I do have the impression that it is this mother who is blocking him, so it is no coincidence that although he falls in love with a woman every six months he is incapable of relationships that would be more than, or go deeper than, mere affairs; in fact he admits as much himself. This fear we men have of a love that gives itself, that surrenders itself! Where does it come from? As you see, I say "we." You know why; you know the bitter secret of my impotence, you know how I long to break through this barrier in me. But it is there—always at the very moment of the most blissful embrace: a kind of prohibition. Or a punishment? For what? And imposed on me by whom? Perhaps after all by myself? I can remember this not being always the case. From the age of eighteen to twenty-five, although I was no doubt an awkward lover and probably more nervous than I would have admitted, I had no trouble achieving an orgasm. Then, about six months after Mother's death, the barrier appeared, went away, came back again. And remained. I remember how for years Susann and I assumed that the root of my inadequacy lay with her. A friend of mine in Zurich, a doctor, advised me, half jokingly, to have a try with a prostitute. I did, several times, and that finally forced me to acknowledge my own incapability. However, I will follow your advice and make a last attempt: as soon as we are back in Berlin I will seek psychotherapy treatment.

But back to my walk with André—just one more thing, and I must admit it disturbed me deeply. As I said, we had this long discussion about the destruction of the world by us, its inhabitants. André calls this process the daily matricide by men exerting their power, an aggressiveness arising, he says, from the fear we men have of nature, which ultimately cannot be disciplined as men would like. A pretty bold thesis. Well, after a beer at the Berghof we were on our way home. When I asked André where, in that case, he saw any hope, he answered, in his dry manner, "Hope? No, no hope." It sounded like a judgment. I must admit that, no matter how hard I look for an argument to refute his gloomy assessment of our chances, nothing useful occurs to me. When Gret asked me her question, should I have given her a similar answer? No hope? No reason?

I have just realized how many blank sheets I have filled again in this letter to you. But what a relief to be able to tell you about my experiences and the things that preoccupy me here! Don't let these rather dismal accounts interfere with your well-earned right to enjoy summer in Provence to the full.

My loving caresses,
Thom

P.S. One hour later. Lis, I'm not feeling well. A despondency that seems to pervade my whole body, like a fever. I keep feeling so lost. Really, Lis, it's as if my dream machine were now running in the daytime too. Whether sitting in my room, or lying down, or strolling in the grounds, I feel split down the middle like a person who, while awake, observes himself wandering about the house or outdoors through a fairy-tale landscape. Even the hall downstairs opens up, and in horror I watch myself moving out into a crater landscape of gigantic trees draped with hanging moss, of giant ferns, of plane trees as tall as television towers and festooned with lianas. Here and there lions, snakes in glowing colors. You know those paintings by the douanier Rousseau, don't you? Something like that. But terrifying. Am I losing my mind? Crazy. So I do say it after all: Please come.

In the Dovecote

HE HAD RECEIVED THE PISTOL AS A GIFT FROM MR. ELSAZAR. A HEAVY semiautomatic, seven point eight. As Elsazar Winter had told Sepp, a pistol must be taken care of like a woman. Sepp had been twenty-one at the time. For his birthday.

But while he lay here in the afternoon heat, in the semidarkness of the dovecote, his head resting on the pillow filled with cherrystones; while he half sat up and with his left hand raised the lid of the box and groped inside for the leather case, the light wavered before his eyes and suddenly he saw again the little pigeon feathers, hundreds of them, white and speckled in many colors, or speckled brown and blue like the eggs of the swamp owl; they swirled up from the floor as if blown by a storm or as if someone had fired a shot into the fluttering pigeons right here in the dovecote when it was full of pigeons; they flickered right before Sepp's eyes, whirling like snowflakes, causing him to withdraw his left hand from the box to shield his eyes for a few moments, and slowly the feathers turned into a hovering cloud, a thousand swaying floating pigeon feathers, before beginning to sink, sink like snowflakes, soundlessly; then they and the wavering light were suddenly gone, the little room was once again swept clean, no pigeons, no more downy feathers, and only Sepp muttering something like "I'm getting old," or "Maybe this is what dying is like"

but probably he had only dozed off: was it any wonder, in this heat? So when he stretched out his arm again and groped around in the box, touched the leather case, lifted it out, put his hand in again, and felt the little canvas bag of cleaning materials at the bottom and lifted it out, one of those big horseflies flew in through a pigeonhole he had left open. It buzzed around overhead in the room, bumped against one of the roof beams, and fell to the floor. Sepp took out the pistol. Then the horsefly was there again, flying angrily back and forth past Sepp's left ear. Now it was hanging upside down by its suction feet from the beam above him.

Sepp raised the pistol. Just to try. Target practice. He half sat up. With his carpenter's pencil he had drawn a breast on the opposite wall. A female breast. Only one, shaded at the bottom. He held the pistol with both hands, slowly lifting it from his stomach; as he raised it, he closed his left eye and began to sight through the notch at the bead. Now he had it in the notch. Precisely in the middle of the notch. Barely dancing in it. Higher, slowly higher. When, by looking across the notch and the bead, his one eye had sighted the lower edge of the breast on the wall, bull's-eye, he pressed the trigger, but only mentally, not really. He emptied the whole magazine, six bullets. Not really, of course. He knew that in this confined dovecote a single shot would mean no more eardrums. He wasn't crazy, after all. Aiming practice. A fellow had to keep in shape. Especially when his strength was failing. The pigeon feathers whirled up, fluttered, subsided. Shooting at pigeon feathers! For a moment he had to laugh himself. He lowered the pistol and put it down beside him on his right, under the pigeonhole. Pigeon feathers—that was like dying. Now for the canvas bag; after lifting it onto his stomach, he undid the leather thong.

The slender barrel brush. The little can of gun grease. The spare firing-pin spring. The awl. The spare firing pin. The glass wool and the cleaning threads. At the sound of Barbara's voice outside, he raised himself: he could see her through the upper pigeonhole. She had brought out a lawn chair from the washhouse and was lying on it in the slanting sun under the fir trees, beside the avenue. Once again she called up to the house. Barbara had something of Mrs. Winter in her. She smelled like her, like her grandmother. Sepp didn't like her. Barbara, wearing sunglasses, was reading a book. Sepp put on his glasses, better for distance. He watched her. She was wearing blue shorts. Her arms and shoulders were bare. As for breasts, breasts like a real woman's, nothing much to speak of yet. Granted, she was only seventeen. He didn't know why, but sometimes he hated Barbara. Her voice too. Like Lilly Winter's.

He laid his head back on the pillow and proceeded to take the pistol apart. First: unload it. Second: remove the magazine. Third: unloading movement. With this semiautomatic Mauser model, the pivot screw had to be removed with a screwdriver. Four: take out the loading mechanism. Five: the barrel, and then finally the pin: one always had to take care that the spring didn't flip the pin out as one twisted it free of the two tiny restraining cams; Kuhn had shown him how. But he had learned how to shoot before that; Elsazar Winter and Mr. Ludwig and Sepp used to drive out to the clay pit in the evening to shoot at tin cans. But the proper care of a gun, that he had learned from Kuhn. They used to call him Doctor: a code name. Kuhn would say, "Now we're Fascists." They had practiced on targets shaped like men, also in the clay pit. That had gone on for quite a while, then one day Kuhn had asked all five of them whether they were prepared to shoot and kill a man if necessary?

"I'm in charge here," the Doctor had said, and Sepp, when it came to his turn, had had the right instinct. "Why kill?" he had said.

That Kuhn! A real highbrow, and for a while he had been over in Germany illegally, in Stuttgart, to be trained as the future Gauleiter for German-speaking Switzerland. "What do you mean, 'why?' " Kuhn had asked, and yesterday Sepp had recognized Kuhn right away on Markt-Gasse, though he hadn't seen him for forty years. Even at a distance, just by his walk, his body always turned a bit to the left. And when Kuhn came closer and stopped, and they looked at one another, Sepp had said, "You're still wearing those same round glasses."

Kuhn had not laughed. "I see you're still in good shape," he had said. "D'you know whether the beanpole is still alive? And the fellow with the repair shop?" And finally, "Now, Sepp, just tell me one more thing: Was it you who squealed on us, or Lina?"

"Are you nuts?" Sepp had said. He had addressed Kuhn as "Doctor" as in the old days, in 1942. "Do I look like a squealer? And it wasn't Lina either. But she's back in the country again too, living with her daughter in Lucerne—you can ask her yourself." At that time the Doctor had gone across the border at night, back to Stuttgart, so one heard. On orders from the German Consulate, it was said. Sepp had kept the newspapers of April and May 1942 right here beside him in the box; they contained the whole story, including a photo of Kuhn, with the caption: "Did 'the Doctor' order the murder? Those arrested aren't talking." No, he, Sepp, had had the right instinct. And when he had asked, But why kill? Kuhn had replied, Because it was an order. And because the fellow was a filthy Jew. "And because we will first have sentenced him to death, we the secret Special Brigade of the National Front. And because we'll go even farther: all the Jews, is that clear?" Kuhn had banged his fists on the table. After that, Sepp stopped going to the meetings, and when he went to the Stern for a beer Lina had come up to him and said in a low voice, "Listen, I'm not going there any more." The following Sunday Sepp and Lina had gone to a movie together, *Immensee*, and that was how things started between Sepp and Lina. But that was another story, and he didn't want to think about it now. A sad one.

First of all, give the casing and loading mechanism a good polish. Then the magazine: press out the bottom panel, pull out the spring, polish everything. Several times. He jumped when the horsefly started noisily flying around again. Wherever could it have come from? He tried to slap it down with his hand, but that was just as futile as when the horses used to try to drive away the flies with their tails. He wished he had a horsefly smoke pot. Long ago, in sultry weather like this, when they still had horses here, Sepp used to hang horsefly pots in front of them—break up pieces of coal with a hammer, throw them in the pot, cover them with a bit of tarpaper and a few drops of gasoline, set a match to it, add a lump of resin, another of tar, and hang the whole thing in front of the horses. Although it had smoked and stunk like sulfur, at least it had kept the horseflies away.

That fellow Kuhn. Actually he was from Basel. "After the final victory we will bring Switzerland back into the Reich!" Sepp first learned about the murder from the newspaper. Anyway, he had an alibi for the night of the murder; he had spent that evening and all night with Lina. They happened to have had the right instinct. All right, slap a Jew around a bit, that wouldn't have bothered Sepp much, so someone went a bit too far. But kill? The members of the Special Brigade of the National Front of Switzerland hadn't known that cattle dealer personally. Arthur Bloch, from Bern. After the cattle market they had told him they had another pregnant cow, a bargain. The beanpole was driving when they took him to Lager-Strasse, into a garage. The Doctor and the other two were already waiting. When the garage door was shut and that big fellow Bloch got out, they smashed him up with iron bars. Maybe he was already dead. Then they shot him, for good measure. A real execution. After that they sawed him up, put all the separate pieces into three milk cans with some rocks, loaded up the cans, and sank them in the Aare under the railway bridge. The missing Arthur Bloch was found a week later, caught in the grate spanning the Aare, in the three milk cans, each of which also contained a note: "Sentenced to death. Because he was a Jew." And "The executioners of Jammers have done on a small scale what we ought to have done long ago on a large one. Swiss citizens! Open your eyes and judge!"

A gun barrel had to be well cared for, a gun barrel most of all. If only because of the condensation. The groove inside the barrel could easily become plugged with solidified grease, which on firing could lead to an excessive buildup of gas in the barrel. The groove gave the bullet the necessary spin around its own axis as it flew on its course. First the little cleaning rod—without the brush but with the cleaning threads attached—had to be pushed down the barrel, pulled out, in again, out, in, several times. Then attach the little brush, and now a bit—just a bit—of grease on it. The bullet would reach its target only if the groove gave it enough of a twist and the twist kept it on course. There was a smell of gun grease. In the army Sepp had been in the supply corps, where they had been issued only bayonets, no firearms. It had been the Doctor who had first shown him, Sepp, and the others. Now carefully push the grease brush in again, pull it out, in again. Several times.

Later an agent had been arrested, a man from Stuttgart who had brought the Doctor money, explosives, and detonators, as well as instructions. At the code words "Rustle of Spring," bridges and railways were to be blown up. The Doctor and the organizers behind him had planned to set up an armed terrorist group. The horsefly was now clinging by its feet to the wall on the left. From time to time, without flying away, it would buzz. Without his glasses Sepp could not have seen its gray-and-black-spotted wings vibrating as it buzzed. Sepp looked through the barrel toward the rear pigeonhole. Several times. The inside shone, freshly greased, silvery. Then he began reassembling the parts, in proper order. Raising himself just enough to check through the pigeonhole whether anyone was coming up the avenue, he saw Barbara again. She was still on the lawn chair, reading. The shadow from the west had now crept up above her hips. Her hair made her a bright patch in the sun, in spite of her sunglasses. Sepp sank back again.

Just lie there for a while. Eyes closed. Over in the washhouse he had been standing at the work bench; he had removed the trigger cam from his semiautomatic and clamped it into the vise. Using the finest of his nine files, he had started to file down the trigger cam, just the tiniest bit, at most half a millimeter. The Doctor, that fellow Kuhn, had told him up at the clay pit, "When you fire you tend to veer to the right. Your Mauser has too much first pressure." He filed away, carefully. Suddenly he was aware, aware that she was coming. The light on the vise in front of him darkened. Sepp turned around. She was standing in the doorway. Mrs. Winter came closer. He saw her eyes moving rapidly between himself and the parts of the dismantled semiautomatic beside the vise.

Lie there. With closed eyes: breathe in, breathe out. He groped for the semiautomatic beside him, opened one eye, aimed the weapon at the horsefly on the wall to his left. Squinting through the notch and holding the Mauser with both hands now, he tried to bring notch, bead, and horsefly into line. But everything was dancing. The pigeon feathers began to flutter about again, whirling and swirling, then, more slowly, they drifted down upon him, around him, like flurries of big snowflakes: strange, once again those little speckled feathers, must be something to do with his right eye. His forefinger found the pressure point on the trigger. The horsefly vibrated, its whole body quivering. Now Mrs. Winter was looking only at him, and Sepp saw that she was suddenly afraid: Lilly Winter was afraid! She wanted to say something, hesitated. "There are rats in the cellar again." He saw her breasts rising and falling under her blouse.

Sepp resumed his filing. In the door she turned to say, but in a voice that was too quiet, "I don't want to see any weapons in this house, any guns," before going out into the bright daylight. Sepp could feel that old tightness in his chest. The pigeon feathers were gone now. The horsefly gave a loud buzz, took off at great speed, and circled noisily over his head, several times, before flying angrily out through a pigeonhole into the open. He could still hear it circling outside and then flying off.

Sepp took down the semiautomatic. Raising himself again on his right elbow, he looked out. The shadow from the west, from the terrace, had reached Barbara's breasts. Her head and hair in the sun looked bright,

round, and when Sepp closed his left eye again Barbara's head looked
like a bright target, and for a second the sunglasses were the round black
center. Bull's-eye. But Sepp was now too tired to practice aiming; somehow the heat and the swirling pigeon feathers had tired him out today.
He sank back again. Lie there. Just lie there.

Something like despair seized him. He wrote and wrote. What he should
do was conjure everything up, pry into the remotest corners of the house,
the town, the country; whatever life had been lived there should be noted
down, committed to paper. How had Aunt Esther put it? Thousands
upon thousands of sentences ought to follow. But even if he were to fill
five hundred, or even a thousand, pages with sentences, the sum of all
that would never be the whole, would never be more than the selection
of a selection of a selection, chosen and evaluated by Thom's own
consciousness.

Sometimes the feeling that the other time was stronger in him than
the time on the clock—that time of cosmos, stars, and planets. As in
dreams, that time would sometimes race, then slow down, stand still, or
skip. It seemed to be chaotic and permanently in conflict with mechanized
time. Two times, two scales: simultaneously? But inside himself weren't
there also two languages in a similar relationship: this persistent, only
seemingly chaotic, associative confusion of words in constant conflict
with a mechanized, disciplined, normal language?

Contradictions. Contradictions.

He was startled by a knock at the door. He turned around and, when
the door opened, saw Barbara standing there, leaning against the door
jamb. "Do you know what's happened?" In her blouse and jeans she
looked as if she had run all the way here from the bus stop and up the
drive. "The plant!" she said. "They've occupied the plant! And the bridge
too!" She was fighting for breath.

He gradually learned that because of the out-of-town delegations, a
union meeting had been delayed until ten o'clock that morning. The
union leaders reported on Thursday's failed negotiations: management
had rejected the demands; the only thing it had wanted to negotiate was
a social plan, but this in turn was rejected by the union. The outcome
was then discussed. The union's proposal to go on strike for two hours

each day was voted down. The union secretary's appeal for moderation led first to loud protests and soon to tumult. So the discussion had been broken off and adjourned until next Wednesday.

However, about a thousand workers had begun to occupy the main building and the foundry. And shortly after eleven o'clock, strikers had driven their cars and company vehicles from both sides onto the bridge and parked them there all over the place, including the sidewalks, altogether over a hundred vehicles.

Some three hundred workers, said Barbara, were now standing at each approach to the bridge. She had just come from there. She had seen banners that said, "First occupy, then negotiate!"

"Why don't you say something, Uncle? It's—it's fabulous, don't you agree?" Her eyes, her dark Gret's eyes.

"Fabulous? I don't know," said Thom. "But I can understand their fury. The question is only—" He broke off. For a moment he could hear Barbara's breath again.

"From now on they intend to block the bridge every midday, from eleven thirty to two," she said. She laughed. "Super, isn't it?"

Thom mumbled something like, "Hard to believe!" And went on, "Here, in strike-free Switzerland? The trouble is, you know, that such things usually end badly in this country. First they'll use tear gas, then water cannon and rubber bullets. And if that doesn't do the trick, they can still call in the army. And the army will arrive with tanks. Don't you see?"

"You mean, they might even shoot?" The laugh on Barbara's face had vanished.

Thom nodded. "They'll shoot."

Here, right here, on the lowest of the three stone steps leading up to the front door, was where he wanted to sit. He loved these massive old steps, this smooth Jura limestone. The doorposts too, and the sill, and all the window casings were of the same pale stone, here in this house as well as most of the big buildings from the preconcrete age throughout this area, they and the pale cliffs towering about the wooded slopes of the Jura Mountains north of Jammers.

Yes, this is where he had been sitting, just as he was now. The afternoons with their scent of fuchsias and their yellow light had seeped away in an infinitely broad river basin, or the sea of Aulis, in the days when clocks were still no more than boring toys for hobby types like Thom's cousin Rolf; for Thom, the position of the sun had told him enough about the time of day. That, and the cool air rising from the grounds over the steps toward evening. As early as the first week in March, the pale blocks of stone had been warm from the sun. When the fiery circle of the sun began to hide behind the hickory oak, then sank lower and lower in the fir trees of the Gütsch copse, the shadow spread downward over the house wall, at the same time creeping across the terrace until everything was covered. Sitting on the step you could feel through your pants the stored warmth still being given off by the stone, even in the shade, until it was almost time for supper.

Over there the grown-ups had been sitting around the stone table, some family celebration or other—or had it been V.E. Day? That day, May 8, 1945, when Mother had shaken him awake, her face radiant. "A great day, Thom! Just imagine: the war is over—thanks be to the Mother of God!" In her excitement she had paced back and forth in the room. "Peace, golden peace!"

What could that have conveyed to Thom, aged seven? War? At least this much he knew or had picked up from hearsay or pictures in the newspaper: that war meant burning houses, starving children; meant the roar of bombers during the night over the town, and somewhere in the world soldiers marching or lying in trenches and killing each other. War meant that Rommel, the Desert Fox, was advancing with thousands of tanks toward Egypt, and people were being killed, and constant air-raid warnings and bombs dropped on towns and bodies and march music, all far away, and that dreadful voice of Hitler's on the radio, blackout curtains and only a scraping of butter on bread: actually, nothing that would have made much difference to Thom in his comfortable existence here at home and as a pupil at the Frohheim school. On the other hand, things did happen: soldiers in the house, in the stables, drilling in the yard outside the barn, soldiers planting potatoes down below the steps where now the neglected roses were choked by weeds; or at night the rattle of machine guns from maneuvers outside town, and always those sirens. War, real war: that was still beyond comprehension, a specter in some far-off place. Thom knew he was living in a country that was being preserved from such horror by its brave soldiers and by Mary the Mother of God. So now there was peace? What could that mean for Switzerland, the island of peace? What else for Thom than the continuation of his dreamlike life?

It was Herminia who was able, that afternoon, to explain to him what peace meant: The threat of German tanks invading Jammers was finally banished. All the bells in town had started ringing at nine that morning; at ten Mr. Schwartz, their teacher, had made a little speech in which he impressed on Thom and the entire class that they must be eternally grateful to the victorious powers, France and England, and especially to the United States of America, for liberating Europe from the terror of Hitler's Germany, but also for stoutly resisting the Red tide of Stalin's Bolshevist armies at the very gates of Western Europe with their "Thus far and no farther!" And, oh yes, there would be no more school that day.

So now, an hour ago, the cars had driven up for the little family celebration. Thom, for the first time that year wearing shorts, knee socks, and sandals, had had to start off wearing his cotton-knit top with the blue-and-white sailor collar, but after lunch, when the temperature rose to twenty degrees Centigrade, he was allowed to take it off. Like his sisters, he had been told to shake hands with the relatives as they arrived around four.

His mother and Frieda were still busy decorating the stone table already set for the tea party; Sepp was bringing the garden chairs, which, recently repainted, sparkled white in the sun.

Then they started to arrive. First Aunt Elsa and Uncle Theodor, getting out of their shiny new beige car. Charlott, Gret, and Thom were sitting on the steps and stood up as their mother walked across the terrace to welcome first her sister-in-law, then her brother, with a kiss. The children approached them, but when Uncle Theodor laughed—which sounded like neighing—Gret pulled away her hand and ran off up the steps, where she remained planted beside the door, her back to the wall. "Come here!" But Gret shook her head. Thom submitted to all the kissing and returned with Charlott to his place on the steps up to the front door. Uncle Theodor laughed.

Gret! What was the matter with her? The familiar furrow appeared between Mother's eyes. Everyone looked up at Gret. In her face were laughter and tears. She swallowed, bit her lip. Then she came out with it: "Because he neighs! He neighs like—" Gret burst into tears. Uncle Theodor laughed; fortunately at that moment Father's black limousine

swung around the bend in the drive, followed immediately by Dr. Muralt's car. More greetings and handshakes; more how you've grown and
kisses on cheeks. Aunt Esther emerged from the house with Grandmother
Helen, and up the steps came Aunt Fanny and Uncle Hans, and Aunt
Margrit from Como with Thom's favorite cousin Tildi in a wonderful
white ruffled dress. Tildi hugged Thom and kissed him; he smelled her,
felt her press her body against his, which made him blush, and she kissed
him twice on each cheek. Then she joined Charlott and Gret to sit down
behind him on the steps, and the three girls began whispering about
Uncle Theodor, about Aunt Fanny and her wide-brimmed red straw hat,
about Uncle Ludwig's goatee, and about Mrs. Muralt's large bosom.
Thom heard the girls giggling behind him. Just then Frieda came through
the door with the tea trolley. Charlott, aged thirteen, had to help her
carry the cake-laden trolley down the steps; then Charlott wheeled it over
to the table. Frieda arrived shortly after with the tea.

Truly peaceful, that day when peace had arrived. Thom, sitting here
on the step, his elbows on his knees, a cigarette between the fingers of
his right hand, had a brief vision of Uncle Ludwig circling the happy
group around the stone table as he took pictures with his new camera.
It occurred to Thom that he should have come across those photos up
in the house in some drawer or other, photos that Thom had once looked
at again with Charlott, Gret, and Samuel, ten or fifteen years ago. They
had had a good laugh over them; suddenly Gret had pushed them away
and stood up, in her eyes that old angry flash. All that ancient stuff!
What did it have to do with her? She wanted to live now—now! She
had hurried out of the room. After that Thom had also lost interest in
Uncle Ludwig's snapshots.

Strange: now he wanted to recall them. As if turning over the pages
of an old album, he saw the photos and at the same time his own fragments
of memory pass rapidly before his mind's eye, over and over again: that
cheerful tea party; the ladies' summer hats; his father suddenly jumping
up; the argument between Mother and Uncle Ludwig; the bewildered
faces of the relatives as they ate their cakes, drank tea and later champagne—Aunt Margrit's round astonished eyes, and Charlott whispering
behind Thom, "Like a pear—doesn't she look like a pear? And Uncle
Hans, do look: a real polar bear face!" The three girls giggled again, and
now Thom couldn't help laughing with them. Or else: the whole garden
group enveloped by the shadow of the hickory oak, but in that shadow
the many hundreds of sun dots scintillating on faces, or flashing off a

fork or knife. Everything was sprinkled as if by snowflakes; or: the cake on the plate on Thom's knees smelling of burnt sugar and vanilla, of caramel candies, and from under him, from the stone Thom was sitting on, the stored warmth rising. What did sun-warmed limestone smell like? Sepp, in black vest and white shirtsleeves, bringing out the champagne. And the popping corks flying into the lilac bush.

No celebration without Uncle Ludwig getting to his feet, tapping his glass, and, usually starting with a joke, launching into a speech. "Today, on this truly historic occasion of the capitulation of the German Reich, let us raise our glasses to peace! Long live peace! From this hour onward may it endure forever!" No joke, then; Uncle Ludwig continues in a serious vein. Even the girls behind Thom fall silent as Uncle Ludwig now begins to speak about the future. About this new magnificent step forward in progress. "The war, terrible though it was, has produced a vast abundance of technical inventions, the peaceful use of which will open up entirely new perspectives for our Winter enterprises. What we are looking at is new technical materials, new alloys, aluminum and plastics, at chemo-metallurgy and other exotic developments, at the tripling of steel refining, but at the same time at—diversification! Now that our chief competitor, Germany, is down and out"—Uncle Ludwig's voice cracks—"now that the Russians will not hesitate to scrap the German industrial plants or to dismantle them in order to re-erect them in gigantic production centers beyond the Urals, we are ready to accept the challenge. Ulrich! Let us take up credits! Let us press forward with research! Let us invest in the new products! The Americans need Europe as a trading partner; they will not be stingy when it is a matter of encouraging reconstruction. In two years or three, or even tomorrow, we will enter the wide-open markets of reconstruction not only in Germany but also in Italy and France, and even in England, with our good Swiss precision machine tools, our synthetic fibers, our refrigerators, our electrical appliances for the home and industrial production!"

Thom saw his father trying to curb his rhapsodizing brother, but his "Easy now" had no effect on Uncle Ludwig's enthusiasm. Ludwig's voice grew even louder. Now he was talking about the construction of huge electro-turbines, about dams, huge reservoirs and pumping stations, about freeways that were to open up our country and all of Europe from sea to sea and as far as the remotest Alpine valley so that people would at last become better acquainted! "Castles in the air?" Uncle Ludwig looked challengingly around the group. "Pipe dreams? I am telling you,

I am prophesying, that in ten to fifteen years there will be hardly a Swiss citizen left who does not own a car, and that vehicle will be equipped with the engine I have developed to the point of assembly-line production—the maintenance-free Winter gasoline engine!"

Both Aunt Fanny and Uncle Theodor applauded vigorously. Uncle Ludwig smiled—behind Thom, Charlott murmured, "You see? A wolf face!"—and lowered his voice. "And that is by no means all. You are the first to be told: I have invented something that scientists all over the world have been feverishly looking for: the practical extraction of the energy that is released by splitting the atom. An inexhaustible, a titanic potential, let me tell you! Ulrich!" Uncle Ludwig raised his voice again. "My dear brother, you are the chief executive and the spokesman of our board of directors! I know how you are torn between risk on the one hand and responsibility for the whole on the other. Throw them overboard, your perpetual misgivings! While our competition throughout Europe has been destroyed or is on the brink of ruin, we, the industrialists of an intact economy that has been spared by war, now have a truly unique opportunity. Barely ten years after the Depression we have at our disposal modern plants, financial reserves, and trained personnel of the highest caliber."

Like a prophet from the Bible, Uncle Ludwig stretched out his hand and gazed into the distance. "I see the sweeping, open country between the Jura and the Alps, between Lake Constance and Lake Geneva. Where today there are only pastures for cattle and fields of wheat, we will build highways, build transmission lines, build for ever-improving production—factory after factory. Let Egypt and the Ukraine produce the wheat, Argentina the cattle, and Canada the milk: we in the heart of Europe opt for the third industrial revolution!"

The group applauded. "Ludwig, what a brain you are!" Uncle Hans raised his glass of champagne. "He's right! Your health, Ludwig!" Even Father nodded several times and also raised his glass. In principle, he said, he must agree. But, as they all knew, being a practical man he favored a policy of "one step at a time."

"And you know what the first step will have to be—apart from taking up credits, of course?" Although Uncle Ludwig had sat down, his voice still drowned out the others. "Opening up our family company to investors from Switzerland *and* from the United States. Five or six well-funded partners as minority shareholders! And right away the second step—we will expand production! We will build a factory for plastics processing, in practical terms a molding plant where we will produce everything from telephone casings to electrical plugs, from radio casings to refrigerator housings, products for tomorrow's Pan-European market! For what purpose did our parents leave us those two farms in the Rychenwyl? About a hundred hectares of land? We can count on state subsidies for an access road and railway sidings. For a start, I am reckoning with three hundred new jobs; soon there will be a thousand! The whole wide valley is ours for production plants, warehouses, apartment blocks—in fact, a satellite city!" Again the aunts and uncles exchanged nods. Father asked whether Uncle Ludwig could provide him with a written résumé of these ideas on paper; he would have an estimate drawn up for the whole project. "You're right, Ludwig, it's certainly worth discussing."

Suddenly, into the silence, Grandmama's voice, sounding angry: "Discussing—*that?* Not with me!"

The girls behind Thom stopped their whispering.

"Mama!" Father spoke with deliberate calm. "You love that valley. Your Rychenwyl—I know, I know! We also enjoy driving over there in the evening or early morning, my brother and I, hearing the mating call of the pheasant, catching sight of a herd of deer. After all," he laughed, "we're avid hunters too, because of our love of nature. But what do you expect? To make an omelet without breaking eggs? Surely you're not serious. What used our father to say? Good feelings make for bad business. Is progress to be—"

Grandmama interrupted him. She rarely spoke, and usually she smiled only when she disagreed with the other person: "Never mind, then. If that makes you happy." But on this occasion she interrupted Father. "I grant that you are the heirs. But the usage rights to it are still mine. Without my written consent there can be no change to the Rychenwyl, let alone any construction on it. And that holds good until my death." Now she smiled. Her slight figure sank back in the wicker chair. "You won't have to wait long for that now—a consolation, my dear sons! In September I will be eighty-five—"

Uncle Ludwig had risen. He took a few hasty steps along the terrace, stopped, drew on his cigar. The smoke shot upward, twisting in a great cloud above his head, rose higher; in the sunbeams above, it caught the light as it formed an expanding mushroom. "Either we, we ourselves," he said, "take charge of the future, or it will be determined by the competition that tries to impose its will on us. I repeat: we are standing on the threshold of a new age. We, the majority shareholders of the

Winter Corporation, bear the responsibility for the rails of progress being laid in the proper direction—today! In the eyes of history you, Mother, share in this entrepreneurial responsibility toward the people of our country!"

Grandmama's face was drooping to one side. "Please," Mother said softly, "can't you see she's fallen asleep?" She straightened the lap robe over her mother-in-law's knees.

Thom, still sitting there, flicked his cigarette stub over the edge of the terrace. When he placed his hands beside him on the stone he could feel the warmth through his palms. As Gret had said: "Why bother with this stuff from the past?" And he? Here he sat, now, in the early summer of '82, letting himself be drawn down almost addictively into this maelstrom of images of that "old stuff." Yes, at least resembling an addict— or was it something else? He knew that feeling; it overcame him quite often: he wanted to ask someone about a mutual acquaintance from the past, but the name was gone. What *was* his name, that tall, thin fellow, you remember him! His name—we used to see quite a lot of each other in the old days in Zurich—a name, two syllables, Thom had it on the tip of his tongue, he was getting quite distracted, couldn't get away from this idiotic lapse of memory, tried to visualize that person, to describe him over and over again, but his companion obviously couldn't help him. Thom would almost panic. Ridiculous, these tricks played on him by his memory!

He had devised a method of handling this kind of annoying situation: what he had to do was recall the circumstances of the last time they had been together with the nameless one—you remember, the three of us were sitting in the Pfau Restaurant, he was telling us that wild story— how he had become a minor character in a comic novel—yes! that fellow with the horn-rimmed glasses, light brown hair, about my age—and usually the name would pop up. Why didn't something like that happen now? Had his mother's murderer been sitting at the stone table? Why was he able, day after day, to immerse himself in the memories of bygone days; why was it that, although each time he recalled that afternoon it was with more and more of the minutest details, he still could not come up with the name that must be there somewhere, barely below the threshold of his consciousness? He could feel it, feel it almost on the tip of his tongue. Why didn't his method work this time?

Suddenly a boom, followed by a roar that immediately swelled to an ear-splitting thunder. Thom looked up, his hands pressed to his ears.

As if shot out of the pale-blue sky, a formation of four pursuit planes plunged across the town spread below him, streaked up—two or three seconds—into the sky again as if piloted by a spectral hand, then quickly shrank to a speck and disappeared. The noise died away.

Thom shivered. He stood up and stretched his limbs. A blackbird, its feathers fluffed out, was squatting on the stone table that was by now in the shadow of the old lilac bush. When he turned toward the front door, the bird took off protestingly in the direction of the fir copse. He passed through the porch and into the dim corridor, where he switched on the light. On reaching the dark sideboard he stopped and looked at the picture above it. Hadn't he already seen it a thousand times? That Holy Family enclosed in its heavy gilt frame, painted by an unknown master of the Italian baroque? Dominating the foreground, in gold-embroidered brocade, the Madonna with her little gold crown, bending smilingly over the well-behaved doll on her lap. Behind her, above her, already darkened by patina, the bearded face of Saint Joseph; to the right and left in the background, the ox and the ass. No, at the moment he had no further desire to go on delving deeper and deeper into that afternoon of the day of peace, into those ancient family pictures. He didn't want to know—not now—what had led up to the quarrel, that same evening, long after the guests had left: the quarrel between his mother and Uncle Ludwig and the way they had shouted at each other in the hall and on the stairs. Hadn't Mother tried earlier to restore the peaceful atmosphere around the table by bringing out her guitar? No matter how much he resisted, he saw, Thom saw her, heard her, his mother in her mid-calf dress—something light-colored, flowered—standing behind Uncle Hans's chair, obviously a bit tense as she plucked a few soft chords on the guitar and announced that she was going to sing a song—to celebrate this special day. Thom, sitting on the step still warm from the sun, was embarrassed when the company fell silent, and in the silence his mother began to sing in her strong, dark voice to the sounds of the guitar—to sing of past summer days, of a poppy blooming in a wheatfield; how it withers, how the snow comes, but one day it will be summer again and it will bloom again—the poppy so red. But he clearly remembered how his eyes had smarted, and how at the end even the girls behind him had clapped enthusiastically. "And to think," cried Uncle Ludwig, "that she wrote the words and music herself!" The whole group had applauded his mother again, and Thom too had been proud of her.

Although something in him suddenly began to resist the surfacing of those long-forgotten photos, those images, scenes, smells, and sounds of long ago, he now knew, as he continued along the corridor and into the hall, that he had to pursue them—but no longer in a logical search for motives for the deed. He must become purposeless, that was all, yet he must not stop meandering through the past, prepared for the unexpected. What, he wondered, should he do to achieve the purpose of becoming purposeless? To switch off thinking by a mental effort, hoping that, if he succeeded, he would gain the revelation he was looking for?

However, as he crossed the hall the memory assaulted him again: with a sharpness he had never heard from her, Mother had said to Uncle Ludwig, "All your progress—that's sheer madness!"

Thom and Charlott had been standing in the door to the kitchen. Charlott had pressed him against herself from behind as if to protect him, but at the same time also herself. She was the one who later explained to him what it had been about. Here, on one of the bottom stairs, Uncle Ludwig: from the sideboard he had picked up Mother's guitar with its colored ribbons and, obviously tipsy, had started strumming on it and bawling something out into the hall. Father had not been there; had he driven Aunt Margrit and Tildi to the station? Uncle Ludwig had been rhapsodizing again, something about progress, humanity, technology, and a historic day. Had the quarrel started over the guitar? For a few moments, words flew sharply back and forth, and suddenly Thom could sense thunder in the air, Uncle Ludwig's explosive rage. Mother, it seemed to Thom, had calmed down when she told him that we should not subject everything to industry and its laws—more and more factories, more and more exploitation of God's creation. It sent cold shivers down her spine, she said, to visualize what Uncle Ludwig had been talking about out there on the terrace. "Are we not ourselves part of creation? If you and your kind destroy the foundations of life—the countryside, the lakes and rivers—aren't you also destroying us? What in the name of Heaven is the matter with you men!"

Mother was now in tears. And the Rychenwyl—of all places! Pressing her handkerchief to her mouth, as if dumbfounded at the sight of a ghost. Suddenly she ran past Uncle and up the stairs.

Uncle Ludwig stayed where he was, dangling the guitar by the neck like a dead goose. Slowly he raised it in front of him and, his hand clasping the neck, held it for a moment horizontally. Was he about to start strumming again? He lifted one knee: in a single movement he smashed the guitar across it; the strings emitted a brief discordant sound.

He flung the broken pieces into the hall. "Women!" he muttered. Passing Charlott and Thom as if they were not there, he stomped through the passage to the front door.

The next day, it remains to be said, Mother didn't appear for lunch; she claimed to be having one of her migraine attacks. Thom went upstairs and knocked at her door, gently so as not to startle her, then stood in the darkened room beside the bed. She turned her face toward him. "Ah, Thom," she said.

"Does it hurt?" he asked, meaning the headache. "What times these are," she said softly. And: That she was just sad. Just sad, sad. "Can you understand that?"

Leafing through the Festschrift V

AND IN PARTICULAR, STARTING IN 1939 A BRISK RECOVERY. WITH THE Western Allies as well as with the German Reich, we developed
    principally in the production of machines and war matériel.
    During this period the share capital was increased in stages to eight million
    made immense sacrifices for the defense of our country due especially to personnel absences resulting from general mobilization
    thanks to the cooperation of the government and the military command!
    the difficulty of importing sufficient basic raw materials (iron, coal, etc.) leading to painful cutbacks in the output of our plants, especially in the years 1942–45. Nevertheless, our management succeeded
    Continued expansion. Installations for heavy nickel-plating and construction of hydro aggregates as well as for earth-moving equipment and transportation systems were added or enlarged; also new production centers in Winterthur, Lucerne, and Liestal for our specialties of semifinished steel, steel rods, and steel profiles.
    1946 saw the beginning of a new chapter in the annals of the Winter Corporation. The opening up of the company to outside investors led to a substantial broadening of the company's own capital base, at first to 12 million. Moreover, the policy of diversification under the leadership of Mr. Ulrich Winter was resolutely pursued

the newly erected plants in Langenthal and Zurich for refrigeration, communications, and transportation technology. In addition, the incorporation of eventually three planning and engineering departments for the following assignments

in 1952 as a result of the sudden accidental death of our president, chief executive, and spokesman for the board, Mr. Ulrich Winter. His will always be our heritage *and* our obligation!

This picture, seen through the open door of Gret's bedroom: Gret, kneeling on the old, damask-covered prie-dieu; in front of her, kneeling, Urs; beside her stood Barbara. Before them, in the corner and at eye level, the Cross with the crucified Jesus.

Walking upstairs into the gallery, Thom had already heard the murmured prayers. Our Father who art in heaven.

Thom suddenly became aware that he was pacing agitatedly up and down between bed and desk, also murmuring words, sentences. Am I being unfair? Is this supposed to go on and on, one generation after another, and yet another? No, it wasn't that Gret and her children were praying to Christ. It was all that lay behind this in the way of Church, of God the Father, of power over the souls of children. The whole apparatus of Thou shalt not. Of suppression and dominance, dominance!

He could feel himself becoming more and more worked up. No, his anger wasn't directed at that carpenter's son, that man from Galilee. Him and his "Love thy neighbor as thyself" I can respect. But Lis, do you understand? This Church—I can speak only of the Catholic one—creates a climate, one that it has continued to generate for the last fifteen hundred years. It generates a thinking, a feeling, a perception, in billions of human beings. God knows it is a product of its society; but at the same time, with its terrible doctrine of sin, guilt, and the suppression of instincts and sublimation of suffering, it shapes society, shapes structures, shapes human beings—to this day, Lis—try to understand this madness, this outrage: to this day!

To be sure of missing nothing, it stands at the cradles of the newest born, imparting its blessing. In the schools at every level, almost imperceptibly, it pervades the Christian image of man with which we have been inoculated. Mothers and fathers are its zealous agents when it is a matter of instilling the true Catholic, authoritarian consciousness in us.

And of implanting the male and female virtues, humility, the sense of impotence, of guilt—yes, over and over again, of guilt! Thus it helps prepare the ground for ever-new forms of fascism.

So who is this Church? With endless patience it has developed through the centuries its highly differentiated moral codes, a net in which we inevitably become entangled. As we flounder in it, now guilty, it is the Church that forgives us the sins it has invented. Is not the Church, the holy and only true Catholic Church, alone empowered to dispense the grace of God? Who is it? An absolutist state that, anticipating Orwell by centuries, has insinuated itself into our heads, our psyches, into the actions and laws of the states we call Christian.

Didn't you too believe that was a thing of the past? The distant past? No, the feudal state lives on, supported by an army of millions of worthy, often even kind-hearted officeholders in the lowest and humblest ranks of this hierarchy. But: above these are the prebendaries and the provosts, those cultivated bishops, abbots, and archbishops in their seigneurial residences; those cardinals living in palaces who do not fail to pay the occasional visit—and on foot!—to the slums of the world—blessing, judging, forgiving. What entitles them to bless? Who allows them to forgive? Where are the people who have resorted to their democratic right to legitimize the Church's power? Nothing of the kind. He who is elected with the total exclusion of the public: the Generalissimo under Saint Peter's dome has consecrated them. That is supposed to satisfy us: the Pope, who lists (not even ironically) the word "Patriarch" among his official titles, and to this day, Lis, to this day presides in the style of the Byzantine emperors over a resplendent court in Rome to the glory of himself and God. He actually permits the laws of his Church to refer to him as "God's vicar on earth," and more outrageous still, as infallible—modestly, of course: infallible solely in matters of faith and when speaking ex cathedra. What arrogance! What an appalling fantasy of power.

No, Lis, I am not going to write this in a letter to you. But do please understand: I know what I cannot keep silent about. I must get rid of it, here, like this, so that you will perhaps at least hear my murmurings. The Church has been secretly wreaking havoc in this house for more than a hundred and thirty years. When I think of all the children it so gently turned into cripples! Here, and for centuries on every continent, millions of adolescents, of young human beings, were driven to spiritual torment and fear of Hell by those princes by divine right in their gloomy soutanes, branded as heretics when they raised their heads and, if they were women, dragged as witches onto the pyre and blessed while the sound of their screams was smothered by the flames. They were humiliated until they learned to regard impotence and exploitation as a blessing, since consolation awaits us in the next world.

Granted, my faraway Lis, if the spirit of the times should be so disposed, this disciplining whose goal is dependence can sometimes loosen up a bit, and church dignitaries are now wearing sweaters and jeans. After all, by this time they can rely on droves of therapists attending to all the souls they have damaged. When in doubt—and I am far from overlooking those magnificent exceptions in the footsteps of Saint Francis of Assisi, in fact I applaud them!—when in doubt they end up aligning themselves, as they have always done, with the powerful of this world, Lis: to this day.

Oh, Lis! Where are they, the Christians who, in the name of human dignity, rise up against their masters? Who refuse to go on being duped by the guilt-instilling image of their sexless Heavenly Father? Refuse for themselves and their children? Yes, they do exist, in little groups here and there. Church from the grass roots! Christian men and women who rise to claim liberation for themselves and all others! Where is this divine spark if not in ourselves? Oh, Lis!

The General's Politics VI

THE RÜTLI ADDRESS:

FOLLOWING THE CAPITULATION OF FRANCE, AND AFTER THE SPEECH OF Federal President Pilet-Golaz that served to compound the confusion:

(a) existing military defense preparations: all the divisions of the Swiss Army, 450,000 men plus auxiliary troops, were deployed, deeply staggered, along the borders, especially to the north and east. A considerable mobile reserve remained in the interior at the General's disposal. During the preceding year or so, pillboxes, road barriers, tank traps, defense positions, and dugouts had been built; troops were trained and drilled in, among other things, the complex coordination of branches of the services. Equipment that in August 1939 had still been inadequate was improved piece by piece. (Insert here a chart showing armaments expenditures 1938–45.)

(b) as of June 25, 1940, troops of the Axis powers completely encircle Switzerland. What does this mean to an army command? What options does it have?

Set out: what would now be the advantages and disadvantages of a strategy aimed at defending Switzerland's 1,800-kilometer-long border? Advantages and disadvantages of splitting up army units into small partisan or pursuit groups operating in specific areas? Other options?

The General still maintained his silence. Uneasiness and apprehension in the population rose to new heights when it became known that individual troop units were moving at night out of their prepared defense positions and toward the interior of the country. Lower-ranking commanding officers were given no reason for the order. Was it because of the increasing pressure of the Axis powers? Was the front line to be thinned out? Was it to be shortened?

(c) the Rütli statement of July 25, 1940: describe how General Guisan finally makes an appearance in a dramatically staged action.

How on his orders commanding officers of all ranks, from army corps down to battalion, 650 senior officers, arriving from all parts of the country, assembled in Lucerne and boarded a steamer (!) to cross Lake Lucerne to hear the General's statement up on the Rütli, that meadow high above the lake on which in 1291, according to legend, the first Swiss communities formed their Confederation and sealed it with an oath. Point to the massive security measures. Even so: Why did the General accept that extraordinary and obvious risk—of an attack from the air, for instance? Comment of one ordinary soldier: "All the eggs in one basket."

(d) standing in a wide semicircle, the officers listened to the speech. No copy of it exists. The taking of notes was not permitted. The General relied on its contents being passed on by the commanding officers to the troops and by the latter to the population throughout the country. Duration of speech: slightly over half an hour. The General spoke without a written text, in German, relying on cue words on a slip of paper held in his hand. At the end, the officers were handed an army field order pointing out, among other things, the necessity, in view of the new situation, of moving into new defense positions. (The regrouping had already begun.)

(e) contents of speech: only one brief passage has been passed down as authentic. The speech began with the words: "I have deemed it important to gather you together at this historic place, on this soil so symbolic of our independence, to explain the situation and speak to you as a soldier to soldiers. We find ourselves at a turning point in our history. What is at stake is the existence of Switzerland. Here, as soldiers of 1940, we will draw strength from the lessons and the spirit of the past so that we may resolutely confront the present and the future of our country and hearken to the mysterious call that emanates from this meadow. . . ."

(f) in the solemn tone of these sentences there seems at first sight to be nothing in the words themselves of concrete instruction or response to the "malice of the time," as the government put it. Quote statements made by participants. They agree that the object of Guisan's address was to clarify the situation and challenge the country to offer determined, united resistance and to continue defending Switzerland's independence, if necessary by military action. Apparently it was the combination of three factors that finally provided this clarification: the address was given on the tradition-hallowed Rütli meadow; the General personally addressed the assembled commanding officers at this venue; the army field order in question removed all doubts as to the military-strategic consequences resulting from the situation described in the speech.

(g) the wording of the army field order: "What was unimaginable a few weeks ago is now within the realm of possibility: We can be attacked from all sides simultaneously. The Army must adapt itself to this new situation and occupy positions that allow an effective defense on all fronts, thus fulfilling its historic task. . . . It must suffice to know this. . . . You must believe not only in our birthright but also in our strength, the strength with which, if each one of us is possessed of an iron determination, we will offer successful resistance. Soldiers! On August 1 you will bear in mind that the new positions to which I have assigned you are those where, under the new circumstances, your weapons and your courage will make the most effective contribution toward the welfare of our native land. . . ."

Note: (1) the firm resolve to resist is emphasized; (2) the new strategic concept of the "Alpine redoubt" (first known by the French term *le réduit*) is briefly outlined. Deal with this in the next chapter. For reasons of secrecy a detailed description of the new strategic concept was not feasible.

(h) elaborate on the General's sense of dramatic gesture, of the richly symbolic staging of the Rütli address calculated to foster a feeling of common purpose.

(i) describe the extraordinary and unifying effect on the Army and the population at large. The highly approving comments in the media and among the people. Quote a young officer, R. H. Wüst: "Now we know what we have to do and why we do it." Describe the protests coming from pro-Nazi circles within Switzerland.

(k) above all: which of the General's politics were exemplified in his action? Abroad: the applause in the anti-Fascist and liberal press of the Western powers demonstrates that the words of the commander in chief of the Swiss Army, while fully respecting neutrality, were interpreted as an unequivocal vote in favor of the democratic cause and against the Fascist dictatorship.

The protests of the Axis powers in their press as well as expressed in formal diplomatic representations to the government in Bern, combined with their threats, are proof of the same interpretation, but this time from the opposite point of view.

At home: the General's action as "the right word at the right time." Furthermore, it was clearly at odds with the vacillating, confused attitude of the government and its spokesman Pilet-Golaz. For his chosen course, however, the General could invoke his mandate.

Yet what is also apparent here is (again) an element of insubordination, rebelliousness, of coup d'état, in the General's attitude toward the political, elected authorities in the overriding issue of the time. His appeal (as documented in his Rütli address) for unity in a determined, even military resistance, constitutes without any doubt the brilliant "staging, no less, of the will to decide" (J. Tanner). His course was clearly intended to be one that ran counter to the government.

P.S. The idea of a "staging" does not acquire its full significance until the General's action is seen in conjunction with the country's dire raw-material situation. The supplying of Switzerland by the Third Reich was what secured the economic basis that could have made military resistance to that same Reich possible. . . . Unthinkable that the General on the one hand, and the leaders in Berlin on the other, would not have known this. . . . A staging!

P.P.S. Have just read the article by Felix Müller in the Weltwoche that André gave me yesterday. Amazing! Until now only the above-quoted passage of the Rütli speech was known. Müller reports: The director of the federal archives, Oscar Gauye, recently came across a draft of the speech consisting of more than twenty pages. The draft was composed by Major Bernard Barbey, Guisan's closest collaborator, after discussions with the General and at his request. According to the draft, the General also included the following points (hitherto unknown to me) in his speech:

He sharply condemned defeatist attitudes in Switzerland, and at the same time demanded a "national propaganda" to encourage the "resolve to resist to the utmost."

The "spiritual national defense" must be directed not only against National Socialism but also against Communism.

Unlike Germany, Italy was very favorably disposed toward Switzerland; all the more deplorable, therefore, that certain newspapers and personalities were sharply critical of Italian Fascism. Robert Grimm (federal counselor and one of the best brains among the Social Democrats) was rebuked with particular asperity for this.

Whether this passage about Grimm was actually included in the speech as delivered seems to be as unclear as the possible omission of the next passage. Evidently Guisan had to shorten his speech for practical reasons (delayed arrival of the lake steamer). However, by comparing it with numerous other Guisan texts, interviews, etc., Gauye successfully demonstrates that the General's political thinking is authentically expressed in this passage.

It begins with an appeal for the "renewal of political institutions" and goes on: "What is presently occurring in Europe will affect our country and our political system and may even lead to a modification of our federal constitution. We must continue to develop and adapt ourselves to the new political conditions in Europe, but by our own efforts and without copying foreign models. I am convinced that the old party attitudes have become obsolete. . . . We must remain true to ourselves, and that is why a national renewal is necessary. . . ." Then, to top it all, comes the ominous phrase about having to strive for a "corporate order" (authoritarian form of government in which parties are eliminated, à la Mussolini).

I had not known that the General held such extremely reactionary political views.

Was it really the smell of marjoram? Mightn't it rather be lavender—the smell of lavender from the linen closet and the smell of violent history that hung there in the room? He had only to summon up this mixture to see her before him as she sat there in the lengthening shadows and smiled, telling him to imagine the four letters—the *T* and the *R* and the two *E*'s. Now he was to close his eyes and visualize the four letters together in one word.

"What do you see?"

"There you are!" she exclaimed. "We have the words; I need only say 'tree,' and you see a tree"—she laughed—"not just any tree but your tree," and for an instant Thom gazed in wonder at the tree that had sprung up in his mind, not just any tree but the ash, the giant ash behind the house, in whose branches hung the four quarters of the globe, and when Thom looked up the goat was browsing in the crown and the kestrel sat there trilling.

Then, when Thom said "tree" to Charlott, upstairs in the sewing room—Charlott loved to shut herself away in the sewing room with her nose in a book—and she finally grasped that it was a game, she would reflect. "Come on, come on," Thom would say, "what do you see?"

Charlott would shake her head. "What am I supposed to say? I see the fir copse and the apple trees and the hickory oaks. I see the silver poplar and the two copper beeches, I even see my jasmine bush. A tree? Oh yes, there's the pear tree, there it is," and Thom knew that Charlott often went down to the huge pear tree beside the drive at the end of the grounds. She would stand under it in the midst of hundreds of small, sugary-sweet pears spread around the tree like a carpet, slit or burst open from falling onto the asphalt or the meadow; Charlott standing there, looking up, more and more little pears falling from the branches, late summer; bees crawling and buzzing around on the carpet, barely able to take off with their bulging nectar bags, then flying away low over the ground.

Or Aunt Esther would say "lake": Thom saw the Aeschi lake. Or "town": Thom could see his town and Jerusalem, Rome, and the Eiffel Tower all in one, and the crumbling walls of Jericho. Or cloud and wolf and eagle, steamer and Zeppelin; it was a game between Aunt Esther and himself, the word-movie game, and he never failed to be astonished.

"But what do you see when I say 'sharpened file'? When I say 'Geneva,' and 'Empress Elisabeth of Austria' whom the Austrians called 'Sissy'—what do you see, Thom?"

Thom laughed. He saw the town of Geneva with the walls of Jericho on Mont Blanc, he saw Mont-Blanc Bridge in Geneva and the carriage with Empress Elisabeth of Austria, he saw all those thousands of people and heard the cheering as the Empress drove across the bridge in her carriage through a rain of flowers. This was one of those dreadful Aunt Esther stories that Thom loved.

She tossed him the words like balls. Assassin's head and sharpened file and rain of flowers, the hanged man in his cell and the doctor cutting off his head. Of course, now that so many different things came together in one story, the word-movie worked only when he remembered everything Aunt Esther had already told him about it. How could he have forgotten what the year 1898 looked like, and that glorious September day when the town, bathed in noonday light, was positively vibrating with the festive activities of all those crowds that had gathered in Geneva? Forgotten the carriage drawn by six white horses, the coachman in tailcoat and top hat? When Aunt Esther said "that anarchist," it sounded like a foreshadowing of the evil deed. Thom saw him, saw that anarchist Luigi Luccheni standing silently among the rejoicing crowd on Quai Mont-Blanc; and when she said "revenge," the very word was a black cloth in which the anarchist Luccheni kept his sharpened file concealed while the carriage approached.

Aunt Esther had been there. Just as it had always been in her nature to be present without fail at the scene of the great, the crucial events in the history of Switzerland and of the whole world—whether in Paris or Sarajevo, in Saint Petersburg, Berlin, Paris again, or in 1830 in Warsaw at the outbreak of the uprising against Nicholas I, always on the spot— so on this occasion too, her infallible instinct for what was to happen, for significance as such, caused her to stroll, as if by chance, through Geneva, and at the sound of the cheering crowds she had hurried, carrying her pale English umbrella, to Quai Mont-Blanc. When she said, "And if I live to be five hundred years old, I shall never forget that murderer's face," Thom saw her having to thrust her way through the serried ranks of people on Quai Mont-Blanc until she stood where Providence—"No, Thom, we have no other word for it"—had led her: to the side of the assassin.

"Beware of anarchists," she often said. "Anarchists plant bombs, stab with knives, and rape. They stop at nothing. Their vengeful feelings render them blind. Anarchists are capable of anything at any time." Thom knew this. Thom could see the muscles working in the murderous face of the anarchist Luigi Luccheni. As the imperial carriage with its six white horses, the crowd cheering and the Empress waving through the rain of flowers, came nearer and nearer, this man must have been under enormous emotional pressure. Aunt Esther was prepared to admit that he was a handsome fellow. But an Italian. He was employed in the construction of the Lausanne railway station. And an anarchist.

Her words like balls. Word-movie. Rain of flowers. Nearer and nearer. Preceded by two mounted cavalry colonels. The jubilation. The clip-clop of the horses' hooves. The cheering, and the flowers raining down, the jubilation. The Empress of Austria, loved and revered by her subjects. Being cheered. Nearer and nearer. "Sissi! Sissi!" Thom was there. "And at that very moment, Thom!"

At this point his eleven-year-old heart always missed a beat. He couldn't prevent her words from making him see—in fact share in the experience, in the suffering—the Empress's crown sparkling as she caught sight of Aunt Esther in the almost uncontrollable, applauding, cheering crowd and called out, "My friend! I am expecting you for tea!"—couldn't prevent the blackhearted anarchist from making a dash, at that joyous moment, toward the open, flower-strewn carriage, leaping onto it and snatching the sharpened file out of his black cloth of revenge. The file flashed in the sun in the assassin's raised fist, then plunged into the heart of the imperial-royal mother of Austro-Hungary.

Thom sobbed. His eyes smarted. The mother of the defenseless and the powerless. An appalling, ghastly deed. Europe wept.

For once Aunt Esther left open any discussion of what would have happened if the deed had not been committed. Would the meeting between King Victor Emmanuel and Czar Nicholas II near Turin, with all its consequences, have taken place or not? Would Spain have sold the sugar island of Cuba to the United States for twelve million gold dollars if the Empress of Austro-Hungary had lived to be eighty instead of only sixty-one? And how about the antitrust laws in England? Is it even possible that the war—I am referring to the First World War, Thom—need never have taken place? And then what: what would have happened, what would not have happened?

Even though all that for once remained open, Aunt Esther loved to let Thom discover, by means of the word-movie game, what a wealth of different times showed up if a person used not only nouns but verbs, verbs in their multiple tenses. So instead of saying, "Europe wept. But in 1936 I made another trip to Geneva," she said, "So Europe had wept. And thirty-eight years later I made another trip to Geneva." Thus spaces, spaces in time were created, and thus Thom could see and live through the story and its unfolding in three staggered time-spaces: once in the present, with the assassin's head in the tall glass jar filled with formaldehyde upstairs in Uncle Ludwig's lab, while he sat here playing the game with Aunt Esther; then, behind that, and shimmering through the space of the present, in the immediate past in which Aunt Esther and Uncle Ludwig made another trip to Geneva in 1936; and then, of course, the time of the dreadful deed itself, in 1898, which had now been shifted from the immediate past to the remote pre-past by Aunt Esther's verb inflections.

Thus he heard, and in his mind's eye clearly saw, Uncle Ludwig, tireless in the pursuit of his research, corresponding with the state attorney's department in Geneva. "You see?" laughed Aunt Esther: "Tireless. Insatiable. My brother Ludwig." And again Thom traveled with her and Uncle Ludwig to Geneva, in the big Mercedes, the one with the pane of glass between Mr. Wenger at the wheel and the two passengers—or should Thom be included?—behind.

The very day after the crime, the anarchist Luigi Luccheni was arrested at the construction site of the Lausanne railway station. After a brief trial he was sentenced to life imprisonment. Twelve years later, "the black avenger of the evil deeds of the rulers," as he called himself, hanged himself in his cell. It was thanks to Ludwig Winter, a young researcher in Jammers, still scarcely known in 1910, and his connections with prominent personalities of the Republic of Geneva, that, although the assassin's headless body was buried, the severed head was preserved in formaldehyde in the Geneva mortuary as a valuable specimen for future research. How Ludwig Winter finally succeeded, twenty-eight years later, in acquiring Luigi Luccheni's head for the paltry sum of a thousand francs is another story. "Mr. Wenger drove us home from Geneva via Neuchâtel in the big Mercedes we owned in those days. I held the glass jar containing the assassin's head and covered with a black cloth on my knees."

Geneva. Neuchâtel. Biel. Olten, and finally Jammers. Aunt Esther knew that Thom was familiar with the great question at that time preoccupying them—herself and her brother, and Thom's father, even Herminia. "Where in the human brain, Thom, is the seat of evil? The seat of that force that continually entices a human being, against his nature—that, after all, is God-given and therefore good—to create evil?" There in the Mercedes, on the way home and while talking to Uncle Ludwig, Aunt Esther was touched by the breath of greatness emanating from the bold vision of a brilliant researcher. She was holding the glass jar on her knees. In the brain of the assassin's head floating in that jar, Uncle

Ludwig, using the most modern, the most sophisticated equipment and microscopes, would unlock the secret of human criminal energies. She recalled—they happened to be passing through Biel—that he had exclaimed, "And then, my dear sister, we will start performing a brain operation on the entire human race, in groups, until evil has finally disappeared from the world!"

The brain. The assassin's head. Glass jar. Words like balls: they caused you to roam as if weightlessly from the present to the remote past, to the past, and back to the present. And caused everything to blend into one, into the multiform and time-fraught space of a single story. Thom had a momentary picture of himself upstairs in the lab standing beside Uncle Ludwig, and of his uncle saying, "Very well. I'll let you see it." And he walked over to the big closet on which stood the glass jar covered by the black cloth of revenge. Uncle Ludwig pulled the cloth away. Luigi Luccheni, anarchist and murderer of the Empress, unshaven, lower lip drooping to one side, one eye staring straight ahead, the other upturned. Thom had gazed at the head in the glass jar, his hand over his mouth. Only when he had left the lab and was on the stairs did he begin to cry. He had run all through the house looking for his mother.

"You see?" Aunt Esther lit a cigarillo. "That's life." And now he mustn't ask her again how long Uncle Ludwig would have to go on with his research before finding the seat of evil in the human brain. "What," she laughed, "are thirteen years of research when measured against the ten thousand years since our expulsion from Paradise? He'll never give up, not my brother!"

Again there was that smell of marjoram or lavender and the smoke of history. The giant ash behind the house was standing in the room, casting its long shadow across Quai Mont-Blanc, across the Empress's carriage and the crowds in Geneva. Sharpened file. Jericho. Assassin's head and rain of flowers. How weightless words could make you! How far they carried you through space and time, first to one place, then another. Were there then no boundaries for them? Now suddenly something in him was thinking, and Thom laughed again: No. No boundaries. No boundaries anywhere throughout the four quarters of the globe.

Conversations with André IV

". . . BUT LET ME EMPHASIZE RIGHT NOW! I'M WARNING YOU! PLEASE THINK very carefully, Thom, whether you want to be persuaded by me to start even wondering about what stamps you as a man. The dictatorship of the patriarchy within us, within us also as a society, will not permit even a few critical questions as to the nature of your masculinity. Sanctions are ready and waiting to pounce. If you don't keep such questions to yourself, you will be regarded at best as an eccentric, an outsider, a weirdo. Men feel threatened—especially young men: at the cost of much repressed pain they have learned in their first seventeen or twenty years what it is to be truly a man, they have used this to construct their protective armor as a second nature, and finally gained what we glibly call an 'identity.' And then along come those who cast doubt on all this— including the inculcated success formulas and the prospect of easy money?

"Or take men of forty or sixty. In their case, added to this memory of years of early training is all they have meanwhile experienced, accomplished, and achieved, achieved as men. Or still hope to achieve, something they can have a chance (at least theoretically) of achieving only as men: privilege. The all-too-often puny privileges of the little man who sees himself as a great male. Power, even the mere illusion of it, being the goal of lonely male dreams. Those dreams, that power, those achievements—who will be brash enough to call into question that entire system of models and values? No, Thom, you won't be able to count on many allies. When in the history of patriarchy have those in power ever voluntarily surrendered their power?"

"So it's hopeless?"

"Hopeless. Unless—unless the evolution of enlightening thought were to advance in our day to the point where we become capable of the hardest thing of all: of thinking against our own interests. Of literally calling into question the roots of our social and private existence. Of renouncing power."

André leaned back. But that wasn't nearly all. Hadn't women been trained, in our phallocentric history, to direct all their thoughts and emotions toward "the man"—the right one, of course? André smiled; he was warning Thom, yet again! Thom should try an experiment, try challenging the notion of this "right" man as a norm. The reaction he would have to expect from many women would be one of incensed rejection. "Adapted" women, he said, were not prepared to sacrifice their self-image (likewise acquired by dint of many sacrifices), and along with that, what their fathers had been and what the man of their dreams was. Although even today at least 70 percent of women would still assert their pride in not being feminists, they would with equal pride despise a man as a nonman if he were to admit his resentment at the stamp of patriarchy. But even among feminists, André went on, a man who questioned masculinity would have to look far for sympathetic ears, let alone allies. He might expect to hear a (readily understandable) sigh, and comments such as: And now, to add insult to injury, we're supposed to feel sorry for men as they suffer in their role? Or rejection, such as: Is someone capable of such resentment a real man? Seriously, Thom should consider twenty times over whether he wanted to embark on this thorny subject. The worst plight in which he might find himself hadn't even been mentioned yet: the permanent state of being at war with himself, at war not only with his own sense of self-worth but with the whole value system entrenched within him. Once Thom acknowledged this resentment, one doubt would lead to the next, one feeling of insecurity to the next. Diffuse guilt feelings would surface; his relationship to himself, to his social position, his profession, his friends (women and men), might be fundamentally impaired. He would see the world, his environment and everyone in it, more and more clearly in a dazzling, alien light, and grow increasingly fearful of the latent aggressiveness aroused in himself by his doubts. The pretensions of the great of this world would gradually come to seem absurd, like the clowning of a lot of Zampanos. And as for being sheltered in the hierarchies and in his own unchallenged role, he could say goodbye to all that forever.

Now Thom was laughing too. Sounded absolutely irresistible! But where was the argument that might persuade him to expose himself to these prophecies?

André hesitated. He would say it again: autonomy. "Yours. And that of us all. Are we then, we men and women of the white man's culture, to go on for centuries reacting like insects? At the mercy, like insects—even though we consider ourselves long since enlightened—of reflexes imposed upon us by our role? Can we, imprisoned as we are, discover and put to the test alternatives in feeling, thinking, acting that are, after all, part of freedom? Isn't it," André wondered, "isn't it the precondition of freedom, and the essence of human dignity, that we perceive the falseness of the predestination imposed upon us by the role of gender? Isn't it here that enlightenment and painful self-enlightenment must begin—isn't this the beginning, in defiance of all sanctions, of the first chapter of solidarity in political resistance?"

While it was true, André went on, that a society dominated by patriarchal values harmed *everyone*, victimizing women by humiliating them, women were not his subject; the question preoccupying him was the way this society was turning us men into severely handicapped, insensitive idiots who were incapable of love—in spite of all the privileges we enjoyed. The nature of this process—yes, the longer he thought about it, the more crucial this question seemed to him, if only to the survival of nature and the human race. And, of course, to our communal life.

Time
of the
Hunt

Sometimes when Thom visited Aunt Esther, he found her reading the newspaper. When she read her beloved *Vaterland*, she wore her glasses. Whenever the printers in Paris or the French railways were on strike, which meant that the mail did not deliver her *Figaro*, she would confide her many thoughts to Thom concerning the worldwide collapse of all moral standards. Yet it was a sin to believe that man was bad by nature! "The grace of Almighty God, Thom!" It was this that made some of us human beings capable of the most wonderful achievements in painting, music, and literature, and those of scientific inspiration to which we owe our progress. No, not all of us were accorded this grace. Many of us, all too many, were lazybones. In despair over the fact that in their youth they had wasted the chance of developing their minds through ceaseless endeavor, many, all too many, turned to crime, and this despair accounted partially for Satan's constant success in establishing the realm of the wicked in this world. But to those who in their early years developed their mental capacities in unremitting diligence and increased the capital of their knowledge—to them would be accorded the grace of an exceptional place in humanity. They walked in the light.

Then she would go back to reading *Figaro* or *Vaterland*. "Take those American physicists! What inspired minds! They have developed a rocket that explores the highest layers of the atmosphere at an altitude of 88,000 meters. Here, see?" She paused to reflect. "My poor brother Ludwig! I hope he doesn't read this report. If only he had emigrated to America, that brain so richly endowed by the Almighty with the inventive spirit!

I am sure he would have long ago invented a rocket capable of flying twice—no, four times as high! But what can you expect? The fact that he went out of his mind is simply the tragic consequence of his fate: that of having too great a spirit in too small a country, one that is lacking sufficient funds for research.

"Ah, Thom, what times are these?" While Thom was still wondering about an answer, she had already gone on to her other topic. She loved to expatiate on the stupidity of politicians. "What do you say now about this Harry Truman? When he wiped out two cities of those perfidious Japanese with his atom bomb, one could assume: a man of character. But today? Today he permits the Russian bear to set up a blockade around Berlin! Permits the expropriation of land in Czechoslovakia! Permits, without a murmur of protest, the awarding of the Nobel Prize to that abnormally inclined Frenchman—what was his name?—Anatole Gide! Fails to protest when a Communist in Paris by the name of Sartre is allowed to drag the holy Catholic faith through the mud with his rubbishy play aptly titled *Dirty Feet!* Why doesn't the president of the victorious United States of America simply drop an atom bomb on Moscow, the headquarters of world Bolshevism? And, while he's at it, on Paris? Beautiful Paris! I would be sorry, of course. How many happy days have I spent there! But when a city wallows so deeply in a sink of iniquity, it is necessary to make an example of it. What if Harry Truman were simply to haul the spiritual ringleaders, those Sartres and Camuses, those Moravias and Kasacks, before a tribunal? Didn't he have the top Nazis and war criminals condemned to death by a tribunal in Nuremberg, have those ambitious boors, those thoroughly unprepossessing characters Göring, Keitel, Streicher, Kaltenbrunner, and the rest of them, sentenced to be hanged? Yes, why not a tribunal for the protection of true Christianity from the criminals of atheism?" She laughed.

And right away, as she turned the pages of *Figaro*, her eye was caught by a picture of a statue showing a number of blocks of stone, rough stone slightly polished. "See? And how has this so-called artist, Henry Moore, entitled his misbegotten object? *The Family!* I suppose it's true," she went on, one eye remaining closed and the other wide open looking past Thom over to the fir trees, "that your old aunt has suffered all her life from the violent death of her dear departed George for the very reason that he made it impossible for us to found a family. Isn't the family the most important as well as most sacred cell of our people? And it is the family, thus one of our greatest treasures, that is being not only mocked but deeply insulted in Paris by this English anarchist!"

Thom knew no one with such strong feelings as Aunt Esther— except perhaps Charlott, who was always finding new words for weeping, or rage, or contempt and hatred, and never hesitated to use them. Sometimes when Aunt Esther raised her voice and downed her sherry in a rage, he was afraid that at that very instant she might have gone mad. But even when breathing noisily, she almost always found her way back after such outbursts to the events that had claimed her particular attention. Nor were they chiefly those of this little country that had been left in peace by the thunderous advance of world history. Her object was to keep Thom's eye focused on the interaction of events on a world scale, and simultaneously to let him know her honest opinion of the deeds of the Great Men of this world. The way she jumped from Harry Truman back to Benito Mussolini, from him, the Duce, to such crafty figures as Stalin, to the founding of the United Nations or to that incredibly brave Swedish Count Folke Bernadotte who, as a go-between, was murdered in the Holy Land right after the founding of the state of Israel: all this was part of her spiral thinking, about which she loved to tell Thom. The main thing was that Thom should learn to recognize how world events interacted.

Because Thom knew that she had been personally acquainted with Benito Mussolini, he was not surprised that she often referred to his death. A horrible, violent death! It reminded Aunt Esther of how our Lord and Savior Jesus Christ was first acclaimed by his own people, the Jews, then nailed to the Cross.

Was Thom prepared to admit that it was a shameful deed on the part of those Italians? Thom was. To have not only shot their own Duce— when, Thom, and where?—in the village of Giulino di Mezzegra on Lake Como, April 28, 1945—correct!—but also hanged him—together with his mistress!—in public, naked and by his feet: wasn't that loathsome? Thom admitted that it was.

Even when lying in bed at night, he sometimes heard Aunt Esther's voice, smelled the smoke of her cigarillo, and tried to find the answer to her question as to what times these were. In the dark he saw Ho Chi Minh above the rice fields of French Indochina, saw the Marshall Plan come across Europe, saw the civil war in China with Mao Tse-tung as leader, and saw that fool Harry Truman. He visualized the murderers of Wolfgang Staudt's movie *The Murderers Are Among Us*; denazification went, an old woman, from door to door in Germany, and Josip Tito returned victorious from the mountains of Yugoslavia and seized power. The mutual assistance pact between the Soviet Union and Poland knocked on the window, making Thom start up from his first sleep. The black market in Berlin was at the door demanding 1,100 Reichsmarks from Thom for a miserable kilo of coffee, holding a sharpened file in its hand. The class struggle swept over Italy on horseback, the strike of the generals brought traffic to a standstill, Palmiro Togliatti, the Communist leader, was recovering from an attempt on his life: now, in the dead of night, he planted himself with his red flag on the roof of the barn across the way and proclaimed the dictatorship of the proletariat in every country of the world.

Thom drew the quilt up to his eyes. For a long time he lay like that in the dark.

Saint-Rémy, July 3, 1982

Dear Thom:

Your letter still troubles me, and even our talk last evening on the phone hasn't helped much. True, the way you modified your "Come," the way you described your outing with Samuel and your niece up "the mountain," the lovely weather and your longing for a swim—all that sounded cheerful enough. And that you feel it is time to tear yourself away from the "monsters of the past" and make straight for here—how could I have been anything but glad! Besides, you have freed me from the dilemma I was thrown into by your plea for me to come to you. You know, I'm afraid I would have had to remind myself of my wish, cherished during all those months of hard work at the radio station, to spend these three weeks of vacation here in the sun, the way I imagined them. I know that in doing so I would have hurt you. And myself. But how am I supposed to continue my efforts to break loose from my indoctrination as a woman if, when the beloved calls me, I instantly forget my own life and rush off to him because he misses me? We two have talked a lot about independence and how essential it is to a true commitment. This insight, so hard to translate into reality, does not for either of us, I know, exclude solidarity when one of us is in genuine need. So my question on the phone as to whether you really couldn't manage without me amounted also to an offer to come if necessary. No, it wasn't like that,

you replied with a laugh. Another two or three days, you said, and you
would be on your way to Saint-Rémy. But later, and probably in a dream,
your laugh sounded almost artificial to my ear. It was as if you were
trying to hide, even from yourself, what is weighing on you.

Wouldn't it be possible for you, without actually breaking off your
search, to suspend it for a few months? I am sure you would find here
the relaxation you need as much as I do. Yesterday the Danish couple
from the next table took me in their car to a swimming pool, and today
I walked there. In the garden of an old farmhouse, three young people
have built a pool, shaded by old plane trees, and beside it and in front
of the house a bar with a little restaurant, rather like a club but open to
the public. There, in the surprisingly cool water that flows directly from
the Alpilles, I realized again how the problems that in my four walls in
Berlin often seem to tower sky-high above me, actually, when seen from
there, scarcely reach my shoulder. I am sure the same thing would happen
to you. And so now I am the one who writes: Come! Your riddle, which
is after all twenty years old, won't run away from you! If, as I gather from
your letter, all that scrambling around in the cellar vaults, and the monsters down there, are a serious psychic threat to you—so much so that
you have to feel "confused" and "as if split in two," and the riddle seems
an "ever-growing threat" to you—then, Thom, my dear, the point has
been reached when you need to gain some perspective. Incidentally: on
our way to Switzerland, didn't you solemnly promise me that, although
you would do some reading during this vacation, even look through your
old files—sniff around a bit in the mornings, as you described it—you
wouldn't do any work? Now you are haunting your old family home,
and in spite of your feeling of paralysis doing some highly demanding
work. And writing the words that scare me: "Am I losing track of myself?"

End of sermon! Needless to say, I too am constantly thinking about
where we will be heading when we return to Berlin, what form our joint
lives will take. Sometimes—and especially now, when you are so far
away—I want to live with you as closely as possible. I picture us looking
together for an apartment with three or four rooms and settling in there,
with lots of space. When I think of Renate, the way she and Michael
seem to have vanished from sight since living together this past year, I
am consumed with envy. And the very next moment am suspicious again.
Could that, at least for us two, work in the long run? I have been
observing—here in the hotel too, by the way—the state to which men
and women are reduced by the much-touted symbiosis. Oh yes, at first

the couple are full of love, full of courage and the desire to be together; to their own surprise, they tell each other all about their lives, are tender and caring, phone each other three times a day, desire each other, have each other, sleep in a double bed, think up dream journeys, even make one of them come true; financially they are at last secure, the first child arrives, perhaps a second one—so what are they lacking for lasting happiness?

Inescapably, the daily round is always there, as it was today and will be tomorrow—a workaday world inside the home and out; the minute insults in the hierarchies at the machine, the cash register, in seminars or at the office, humiliate her, him or her, and both. Why was *he* the one to be passed over for promotion? Why wasn't *she* rather than her co-worker given a raise and the vacant office on the fourth floor? A special night-school training course failed to live up to its promise; it certainly didn't help to paper over the wear-and-tear of their life together: the television is now on every evening, and for hours. Has the supply of things to talk about been used up? The daughter's speech defects have become worse again. The rituals of going to bed, taking turns at brushing teeth, one last cigarette in the kitchen while he, more tired than usual tonight, is already falling asleep in the double bed—I don't want to go on describing what we both know. And how the question, Was that all? feeds the silent resentment against the partner: Why hasn't she, why hasn't he, halted this gray, creeping failure? What happened to love, to longing and desire? The dull feeling, constantly pushed aside, that actually it is the partner who is to blame sometimes leads to violent arguments; but they too become more and more infrequent, as infrequent as the loving embrace.

Am I being cynical about the commonest form of a life together? Kurt accused me of this. Of course there are exceptions, the happy couples, even when they share a home. And to counter the insidious crumbling of love through habit, there are energies that can prevent that crumbling; one of them, I suppose, is the utmost consideration for each other. Will we be among the exceptions? I personally feel as you do: we are prepared to see the dangers, we don't intend to give up the knowledge that in our destroyed world, conditioned by alien influences, autonomy and the commitment between two autonomous individuals are an objective worth fighting for, don't you agree? The outward form in which we live this commitment will, I believe, either simplify or complicate the task. Our two small apartments—an expensive privilege. I'm all for keeping them—aware, also, that separation and self-denial are necessary for the success of our lives as a couple. Move in together? Live together? I am afraid that, if we shared a home, I would have to make an even greater effort than I already do not to slip into the ever-ready, (also) comfortable wifely role. As you know, that already happened to me once. Never again! And you? The latent patriarch in you: wouldn't he be all too easily inclined to assume the husband's classic role? I can already see us: you reading the newspaper, me cooking and sewing on buttons.

Again you write about your inability to enjoy sex with me. I repeat, Thom: we have plenty of time! I feel sure we will find the source of the fear that is blocking you. It will melt away once you have regained the basic confidence that you used to possess but which through some experience or other has been impaired. The thought of what you are doing at this time makes me believe that those journeys into your and your family's past, together with your mulling over everything to do with your mother's death, will enable you to explore the hidden "cellar vaults" in yourself, where, I am sure, you will also find yourself. Strange: in this connection I suddenly thought of the phrase "self-experimentation"— Thom's self-experimentation?

And another thing: I don't believe it's necessary for you to understand, now or even tomorrow, everything that comes across your path. At some point the solution to the riddle will present itself to you; I really believe that.

Here at the local post office, where I hand in an express letter almost every day, the young man at the counter already greets me as an old friend. He said he'd like that too: a love letter every day! I must hurry— he closes up at five.

But I still have time to ask you to give my regards to André and tell him that the future of our patriarchally damaged world is really not as hopeless as he sees it. We, the man and woman in the street, and our resistance do make a slight difference, don't we? And our refusal to give up uncovering the causes and kinds of damage in ourselves too!

It's quite strange: today on my half-hour walk beside the cypress hedge to reach the swimming pool—the hedges were already exhaling the first noonday heat, and on the green strip between the tire tracks red poppies are still obstinately blooming—while I was dozing or reading in the shade, writing to you or watching the Ping-Pong players—as I walked back to town at three, had a shower, and sat down in my usual place on the shady terrace in front of Silvio's bar—I constantly caught myself telling you the thoughts going through my mind. As if you were walking or sitting here, as if I could put my hand on the back of the wicker chair beside me or on your hand, and we didn't speak, or we talked, I listening to you, you listening to me. A continual exchange between us of words, gestures, looks; I bring them so vividly to mind that I can feel you, here, beside me, close. But you remain a figment, a mythical creature as it were, especially since the nice old retired gentleman from Alsace has sat down in the chair next to me. From time to time he tells me of his annoyance with the people of the Midi, who for money will permit any kind of devastation of their beautiful country. He also loves to tip me off as to what I should look at and where I should go for a particularly good meal.

Your merely imaginary presence has so far (although not always!) helped me to enjoy my solitary state here.

But now, after your last letter, your illusory presence reinforces the certainty that you are far away, and now also reinforces my fear—a vague fear for you. I have a feeling this fear is growing. It is beginning to darken my days and nights here. Could it be that, over and above the depression you have written about, something untoward has happened to you? Will you please write to me immediately and tell me I am merely in danger of succumbing to a stupid, indefinable female fear?

A love letter, yes! I hold you in my arms.

Your Lis

The General's Politics VII

THE STRATEGY OF THE "ALPINE REDOUBT"

IN MID-1940, IN AGREEMENT WITH HIS ADVISERS GONARD AND GERMANN, the General decided to concentrate the army forces on the strategically most important areas of the country: on the Alps with their passes and tunnels for north-south-north traffic.

Quote Guisan's memorandum of July 12, 1940: "Switzerland can only escape this threat of a German attack if the German supreme command becomes convinced that a war against us would be lengthy and costly. . . . If we should become involved in the struggle, it will be a matter of extracting the highest possible price from the enemy."

The decision meant, first:

Shortening possible fronts.

Concentrating forces in the central massif of the Alps.

Using and expanding the old fortresses at the invasion gateways in the Alps: Sargans (east); St. Gotthard (center); St. Maurice (west).

Blocking and preparing the destruction of all crossings over or through the Alps.

Developing the Alpine wall into one colossal fortress.

Also, in the event of an attack: destroying bridges, roads, railway lines, factories, throughout the country.

At the same time, it meant that the protection of the frontiers was left to the relatively poorly equipped forces of the regional border-defense units. The heavily populated lowlands, with the agglomerations of Basel, Zurich, Bern, Neuchâtel, Lausanne, and thus almost the entire industrial production base of the country, remained under the protection of merely a few light brigades.

Describe the rationale, still from a purely military aspect, of this new concept: With the concentration of forces on the redoubt, it was necessary to neglect the frontiers as well as large parts of the habitable and industrialized areas. A defense of these areas against the large German panzer units now threatening from all sides was doomed at the outset; yet it was precisely those mobile, motorized German divisions that would be unable to make full use of their speed and firepower in that steep, trackless Alpine terrain. They would be forced into a protracted infantry battle from one natural pocket into another, in a terrain offering obvious operational advantages to the entrenched defenders.

1. What were the political consequences? For the population, the regrouping now under way came as a shock. Four-fifths of them saw themselves, together with the country's industrial installations, forsaken by their army; saw themselves in their towns and villages as helpless victims in the path of the threatening German panzer juggernaut.

The government in Bern scarcely reacted to the decision that proved once again that the General, by word and action, was continuing the high-handed pursuit of his own course running counter to the government's trend toward accommodation. Gritting its teeth, the government appears to have swallowed it as an "acknowledgment of military logic."

2. Insert here: reflections on the nature of a coup. In this case, what

was still "legal," what "legitimate"? If a putsch is carried out by a general against a government elected by an elected parliament, is such action legitimized by the mandate accorded the general by parliament? Must one grant that for him, and in the evaluation of his political actions, unlawful conduct may be in the rightful interests of the democratic state? According to constitutional law: No.

3. Describe the new diplomatic representations made by the Axis powers to the government in Bern. Protests by Von Ribbentrop and Ernst von Weiszäcker on behalf of the Reich government against this "renewed saber-rattling" by General Guisan: the Führer was outraged, etc. (Originals dated August 10, 1940, in the federal archives in Bern.)

4. Economic consequences: In 1938 federal expenditures for defense stood at 200 million Swiss francs but rose, especially after mid-1940, to over 2.5 billion annually (1944). This exerted a positively Keynesian stimulus on the Swiss economy, which in turn may explain why the bankers and industrialists did not violently object to the Alpine redoubt project, although it deprived them to a large extent of the Army's protection. They calculated, and once again they concluded: We shall profit. (Perhaps my fellow historian Jakob Tanner could direct me to the original documents for this?)

5. Reaction of the population

(a) Strange phenomenon: After the first shock, as all reports and testimonies agree, a widespread though somewhat mixed approval of the Alpine redoubt and its consequences became apparent, although economic and military circles in favor of Nazi Germany dubbed the General's decision a "suicidal idea." Critical voices of the lower ranks as well as of the population as a whole cursed the "top brass": Was such a display of force in any sense worthwhile? In the last analysis, what or whom was the Army protecting? A "native land" that belongs to the landowners and the banks? In the name of which Switzerland, which social order, was a potential bloodbath being preprogrammed?

(b) A revolt of the critics did not take place. On the contrary: More even than the strategic logic, it was the sheer heroic aspect of the new concept that exerted a galvanizing fascination. In the dire situation of 1940, the fact that the General ordered the most uncompromising, the harshest variation of "resistance at all costs" seems to have swept the exposed population along into an attitude of heroic defiance: "We'll show them!"

6. Was the General obeying his mandate with his strategy of the

Alpine redoubt? The mandate demanded that, "deploying all appropriate military means," the General preserve both "the independence of the country" and "the inviolability of the territory."

(a) The German attack did not take place. The Alpine redoubt was never tested militarily by any opponent as to whether it was actually capable of maintaining Switzerland's independence and the inviolability of its territory.

Clearly, in order to be able to concentrate the military resources in one-third of the territory, at least two-thirds of the territory had to be largely deprived of protection by the Army. This was intrinsic to the redoubt concept, which simply accepted the "violability" of these large parts of Swiss territory. Accordingly, the second part of the mandate was not carried out; it was neglected.

(b) Was it neglected in favor of the first part of the mandate? Was the concept of the Alpine redoubt appropriate for the maintaining of Switzerland's independence?

In the hope of at least approaching an answer, we should visualize the scenario: An army moves out from its positions that had been consolidated during the past year. It marches off, regiment by regiment, company by company, bag and baggage, through the lowlands into the Lower Alps, for nights and days on end. Towns, villages, and industrial plants, including the women and children, the old, the blind, and the lame, are left behind by the Army. Slowly their heavily loaded, heavily armed columns, most of them on foot, advance along the roads over the passes into the rocky heights of the Alps with their three- and four-thousand-meter peaks, leaving their supply base, precarious enough at best, farther and farther behind and below them. Some 250,000 men are on the move, with their tens of thousands of vehicles; cannons, howitzers, munition carts, supply wagons, are horse-drawn. The entrances to the thinly populated high valleys are blocked by fortifications, infantry forces, and artillery. Beyond and above these blockades, airfields are laid out. High above rugged cliff walls, tunnels, shafts, and cavities are blasted and drilled into the Alpine massif; massive armored doors are welded into the cliffs; behind them, supplies are piled up in the caverns.

In graphic terms: the supreme commander withdraws with the bulk of his Army from the lowlands into the natural fortress of the Alps. Two-thirds of the country, four-fifths of the population, remain outside, at the mercy of an attack on their open settled areas. The drawbridges to the fortress are raised. Behind and above them, the Army has entrenched itself. The supplies brought into and stored in the fortress are sufficient for about a year.

Who or what, which or whose independence and inviolability, is being defended, protected, maintained, guarded?

History did not require that the concept of the Alpine redoubt be put to the test. The question of whether or not it was correct from a military and strategic point of view must remain open here. We do know the result: that from mid-1940 to 1944 the Swiss Army was protecting only itself, itself and a highly abstract idea of national autonomy.

7. But how can this action of the Alpine redoubt be reconciled with that other action: the demobilization of approximately half the Army ordered by the General as early as July 7, 1940, some three weeks before the Rütli address? Was that demobilization to be seen as a gesture, an obeisance in fact, to the new "force of circumstances" in Europe, in other words: to Fascism?

In my assessment of this—clearly contradictory—policy of a deliberate double game, I find myself for the moment at an impasse. . . .

The story of Charlott's pheasant included, as Thom knew, three hunters, four beaters, and six hunting dogs, as well as guns, horns, flocks of birds, partridges, a pheasant, and Charlott. Charlott with her red windbreaker. And also an early morning in mid-October.

Anyone wanting to tell this story would need to use long sentences; anyone wanting to read it would have to sit down, or preferably lie down, with plenty of time, and be able to picture a pheasant running through the underbrush or the reeds out into the open where it begins to flap its wings and flies off, shimmering, into the sun—in the old days when there were still pheasants in these parts.

But even to describe a pheasant and its flight, long sentences are not enough. And where to find the adjectives for the sheen of its dark green cap? For the scarlet of the wattle around its eye, for its white neck ring, for the iridescent colors of its plumage between gray and dark red on the breast and in the long, pointed tail feathers? And how is someone who has neither seen nor heard a pheasant for twenty years or more to describe the double squawk, the throaty kork-kok, when the pheasant flies off into the marshland?

The preamble is quickly told, of course. A pheasant hit by a single bird shot in the wing joint can no longer fly. Chased by the hunting dog but being a fast runner, it escapes in the underbrush, loses a lot of blood, looks for water, and, exhausted, settles down in the bushes beside the Aare to die. One afternoon in August 1945, Charlott and her friend Ruth are paddling their boat upriver in the shade of the bushes on the banks. From the water the two girls, both fourteen, are looking for a place to land where they can spread out with their baskets on Charlott's big towel. Sometime that evening Charlott finds the wounded bird on the riverbank; together the two girls manage to catch it. An hour later Thom is allowed to look at the wounded pheasant in the washhouse: in a large, round willow basket, a nest of hay containing the pheasant, its lustrous green, brown, and red plumage, its tail feathers projecting beyond the basket. Its head raised, the pheasant looks at him fixedly with one round eye. The injured wing has been firmly bandaged to the plump body. All encouragement fails to persuade the pheasant to drink from the water or peck at the scattered wheat kernels. Two days pass before it begins to feed.

Ten days later: Charlott is lying on the lawn chair in the sun behind the house, near the summerhouse. This time she is not being guarded by her Great Dane, Whirlwind. Instead, the gold-gleaming pheasant struts around her like a peacock, apparently still unable to fly. But when Charlott sticks out her tongue and places a wheat kernel on the tip, the pheasant jumps from the ground onto the chair arm and pecks the kernel off her tongue. And if Thom dares to come closer than seven meters, the pheasant comes running, rears up before him, and angrily spreads its wings; it hisses: a hissing guard.

Just a few days later it flies, flies whirring around the house, circles the fir copse, calling and shining in all its glorious colors, before disappearing to the south, toward its old marshland.

Charlott—this also is part of the preamble—laughs. That was what she wanted, for her pheasant to fly again. To fly away one day to the place where it belonged. That was what she wanted, wasn't it? "It's flying again, my Whir-whir can fly!" Charlott wears a Sunday-morning face. But Thom already knows: that evening she will be sitting at the kitchen table with moistly glistening eyes, and at some point Herminia will say, "Now listen: it's time to stop choking back your words." She will say something about love and suffering, my girl, you should know by this time that they belong together like a pair of shoes, and Charlott will jump up and, scarcely out the door to the hall, be heard sobbing her heart out all the way up the stairs into the dark.

But within another few days everything is all right again because Charlott is wakened at 6:30 in the morning by a tapping at her window. She rubs her eyes, looks at the window again, gives a shriek, and dashes to the window to fling it open and put her arms around her long-tailed friend in all its shining plumage. The kork-kok and Charlott's whispers mingle. Although Whir-whir no longer pecks the kernels off Charlott's tongue, she swears that the bird gently rubbed its beak against her tongue.

What else? That all through September, every three or four days, Charlott received a visit on the windowsill from her admirer in the crimson plumage? That October came, and the time of the hunt, the sun was beginning to set earlier in its sheaves of fire, and a business friend from Italy, a gentleman with a valet and carrying over his arm a dark overcoat with a black fox collar, came to spend three days in Jammers where he was put up at the Schweizerhof? And that it is with him that the story of Charlott's pheasant really begins? For in his honor and for his entertainment, Father had arranged a hunting party for the following morning. Nothing big, a little outing to the marshland, a little shooting party, just Father with this gentleman from Parma, and Father's friend Dr. Von Sury and his hunting dogs; then, as beaters, the faithful Boschung from the factory as well as Tscharland the gamekeeper, and of course Sepp. Not forgetting the valet.

Doubtless it was due to no more than forgetfulness that Father omitted to mention the hunting party the previous evening at dinner. So how would Charlott have found out about it? Instinct? Or had she watched Sepp taking the two shotguns down from the wall in the hall that afternoon and carrying them across to the washhouse? Or had she been wakened at five in the morning by a creak on the stairs, had she started up from sleep, run to the door in the dark, opened it a crack, and, seconds later, seen down in the lighted hall her father in his dark green jacket and gray knickerbockers slipping the flat metal flask into his outer pocket? In any case, five minutes after the black limousine had left the garage and disappeared down the avenue, Charlott, buttoning up her red windbreaker, ran across the back terrace to her bike, lifted it down the steps, and rode off.

Skilled hunters like Father approach the marshland downwind, noiselessly, and at first light. Between bog patches and open channels, wide swaths of reeds, lakes of reeds, there is always some firm open ground with clumps of trees, copses with dense undergrowth and, reaching high above them, scattered birch, alder, and old willow trees interspersed with candlelike poplars. What hunter would not love to shoot a grazing buck! Or a fox, frightened by the noise of the beaters, that is forced to cross a clearing! But for whom is it not a high point of the hunt when with a single shot he brings down a bird flying high overhead?

The three hunters had the wan morning light behind them as they walked along the river path toward their stands. They advanced cautiously, in single file, ducking under autumn foliage, trying to tread quietly in their rubber boots. Ulrich Winter led the way. At some point he stopped to allow the others to catch up. Here in the dark under the canopy of trees, the meager beam from his dimmed flashlight revealed the narrow path turning off to the left, away from the Aare. Then, with his double-barreled gun under his arm, he proceeded warily along the little path. After two minutes he and his two companions had reached the wide clearing, its flat expanse bathed in the glow of the rosy dawn light; like a sweeping U, a dense belt of trees surrounded the meadows that spread for some two hundred meters before them.

They were lucky. Although the fog down there was often almost impenetrable, that day there was only a trace, drifting eastward in thin veils. Father pointed toward three clumps of tall bushes—stands one, two, and three. The guest from Parma was allotted the stand in the middle of the clearing. The three hunters each pushed two cartridges into the breech; then came a final synchronizing of watches.

The whole thing was done expertly and tactfully. In a half murmur, half whisper, Father, speaking in French, explained the procedure. At 6:20 sharp, over to the left, in the east, Tscharland—who had the valet with him—would start beating from the far side of the belt of trees. That would give each hunter a first and possibly a second shot from his stand as soon as the birds flying over the clearing showed up beyond the barrels. Six thirty-five: this time, far to the right, over to the west, old Boschung would start beating. There would be a second, indignant wave of partridges and pheasants, snipe, quail, owls, ducks, jays, perhaps even a blackcock flying over the clearing: again, shooting was in order. Fifteen minutes later it would be Sepp's turn to beat: the noise he made coming from beyond the belt of trees would ensure that the game birds fleeing from the middle section would be forced to fly over the clearing again. Pheasants—the gentleman from Parma obviously knew his stuff—often take off close to the ground for only thirty meters or so; fast runners, they try to evade their pursuers by escaping through the undergrowth toward their nesting sites.

Dr. Von Sury smiled. "Three classic chess moves, so to speak!"

The three men fortified themselves with a swig of Armagnac from Ulrich Winter's hip flask; then slowly, unobtrusively, each walked to his well-camouflaged stand. There were still five long minutes to go before 6:20.

But here Charlott must be mentioned again, how and where she came upon the two cars parked at the fork, dropped her bicycle at the side of the road, and flushed by the wind, exertion, and fear for her Whir-whir, began to run, following the boot tracks in the dewy grass, although they were hard to make out in the brightening morning light. Again it must be told at length how Charlott imagined as she ran that she would creep up on Father and the two other hunters from behind and snatch their guns from them, or that she would be in time to warn the game birds of the entire marshland and summon them all to a distant place beyond the Aare, or that she would strangle the dogs, or that she would simply entice her pheasant friend from the undergrowth and, carrying him in her arms, run away, or would place herself in front of the gun barrels and calmly declare, "Whoever kills the pheasant will kill me too!"

But wasn't she much too late for all these possibilities? She stopped for a moment. She listened, straining her ears. All she could hear was her own heavy breathing. Around her, large bushes crouched like old crones with gathered skirts, whispering their predictions of the disaster. Charlott looked back. Behind her, on the path she had been running along, another big, fat bush crone with disheveled hair and red-hot, dripping eyes had squatted down. Beyond her, the towers of the town were visible in the dawning light; far beyond them the horizon, red with travail, was about to give birth to the sun-urchin. There was a smell of swamp, of lost summer, of sleepy birdcall. Over on the right, a milling horde of rats was moving toward the Aare. The crones tittered.

Here the story of Charlott and the crimson bird approaches its conclusion. Charlott had just reached the tall alder, the point where the men's tracks forked right and left, when, less than a hundred and fifty meters away, Tscharland and the valet, with the three dogs, started their beating. The air was filled with barking, as if a strident madness had eaten into the dogs' brains. The sound of the hunting horn, the men's shouts as they beat the undergrowth with heavy cudgels, as they broke through the marsh shrubs, alerted the sleepy trees and bushes and whatever lived in them, down to the tiniest spider ant, to the threat of death. Off flew the night herons, the white-fronted geese, and the lapwings; noisy cries of complaint rose from the robins, the reed warblers, the crested larks, the buntings, the screech owls, the partridges and coots, the black scoters, the plovers and hoopoes; scolding loudly, the blackbirds flew off, as did the sandpipers, the curlews, the moorhens, and the snipe. And the kork-kok of the crimson pheasant could be heard as if calling out to Charlott, "Run! Run!" And just as Charlott reached the belt of trees and ran straight along the narrow path leading into it, the sound of shots reverberated ahead of her in the clearing.

Charlott knew little about hunting. And no doubt she wouldn't even have listened if someone had tried to explain to her the essential ingredient—apart from a true aim—in hunting wildfowl: patience. At the first sound of the horn, a hunter in the marshland raises his gun to waist level. Standing in his cover, legs wide apart, he makes sure he has a firm footing under his boots. He watches. He waits. He sees the pink dawn light swiftly brighten behind the trees and calmly looks on as the first flock of songbirds scatters into the sky in front of him. But in spite of his mounting feverish excitement, he knows from experience that the large birds will only leave their cover in the wake of those noisy, fleeing songbirds, and will emerge from the woods with a whir of flapping wings into the field of fire. He may even allow the partridges to fly past him, and the hen pheasants (protected by law) also need not fear that the experienced hunter will pull the trigger on their account. But now he quickly raises his gun to his shoulder, now at the sound of the indignant kork-kok and the sight of the cock pheasant shining, gold and crimson, in the first light of the sun above the still treetops; now he aims three lengths ahead and fires, emptying first his right barrel, then his left. He lowers his gun and, groping for two new cartridges to reload, watches the parabola of death performed by his booty before it hits the marshy ground. But even now his self-control does not desert him. However much the pride and certainty of having hit his objective in flight makes him breathe faster, he does not dash out into the open. His restraint is such that he stands poised for the next double shot, or until the horn announces the end of the hunt. The collecting of the downed birds is expertly taken care of by the dogs.

The three hunters in their stands could not believe their eyes when, from the left, a slight figure in knee-length skirt and windbreaker, hair flying, came running into the clearing, stumbled, stopped. Unmistakably a young woman. But women had no business here; this was men's work! By repeating the signal for "Hunt suspended!"—three short, two long notes on the horn—Tscharland the gamekeeper announced an unforeseen occurrence. And it was Ulrich Winter who recognized his daughter, leaned his gun against an alder tree, and began with measured but firm steps to walk toward her. Charlott was standing in the clearing about eighty meters from the trees.

"Charlott!" her father called. "Come here!" She did not move. He too looked toward the right at the dogs sniffing the ground as they ran back and forth across the clearing. He too saw, as Charlott saw, Dr. Von Sury's slim pointer carrying the motionless pheasant by the neck in its mouth, and, when Dr. Von Sury whistled, beginning to run, first a short distance toward the doctor's stand.

But then the dog turned and loped unhurriedly toward Charlott. Although Ulrich Winter was convinced that he, rather than either of his two companions, had brought down the bird, he had already decided to congratulate his guest from Parma on his marksmanship and, with a toast, relinquish the trophy to him. After all, generosity in small things had never been a bad business principle, as long as one didn't lose sight of the main issue. Now he could stay where he was and watch the dog run up to Charlott and, proudly wagging its tail, deposit the crimson pheasant at her feet.

Charlott crouched down. As if in a dream she patted the dog. She took the big, bloodied pheasant into her arms and stood up. Then she walked off toward the woods. Was the pheasant still alive? And would it one day fly around the house again, fly again? Charlott's red windbreaker was visible for a while in the undergrowth before it disappeared.

Father went on standing there in the clearing for some time. Then he must have realized that this was a matter not of uncontrolled emotions but of the success or failure of a hunt. He raised his arm toward Tscharland. Tscharland understood and put the horn to his lips. The notes resounded across the wide marshland, now bathed in sunlight. The hunt continued.

*   *   *

There certainly are people who can be described: Gret and Samuel, Charlott, perhaps even Aunt Esther, and Father too, and Mother. If someone wishes to tell who they were or are, and description is inadequate, their stories might serve. But in Uncle Ludwig's case it would be difficult. The stories about him were numerous and crazy, so much so that they contradicted one another, in fact canceled each other out. Add to this that they were told by Herminia differently from the way Mother or Aunt Esther or Charlott told them. Moreover, they were told in ever-new, expanded, and altered sequences: they were legends in the true sense, passed on orally in the house, as well as in town and at the factory, told and retold and embroidered. As a result, although Thom had a pretty clear memory of the tall, broad figure, he was left with a legendary character scintillating in too many images, hard to document in historical terms. Only those things could be told that could be compared.

When morning came, the night withdrew into the darkness of the barn, the attic, the beams of the washhouse. There it spent the day until it crept out again in the evening. Those Uncle Ludwig stories behaved in a similar way; only in the evening and the night did they wander like phantoms around the house and through the empty rooms.

Nevertheless, try again to give a picture of Uncle Ludwig. Who was he? To Thom it seemed as if Uncle Ludwig had always just arrived at the house or was on the point of leaving again. For an instant Thom heard his mother's voice: "Ludwig, what a restless creature you are!" Restless, yes, that was the word. What drove him? What fear?

Yes, this picture: Uncle Ludwig, carrying his dark-brown leather suitcase, coming down the stairs, laughing as he claps his great hand on Thom's shoulder in the hall, then disappears along the passage and out the front door. Or this: His uncle, again carrying his suitcase, coming along the passage, stopping, the winds of a world—unimaginable to Thom—full of excitement and secrets and mysterious experiments still in his face, laughing again and calling out, "Hello, I'm back!"

Then he looks at Thom who, aged about six, is standing shyly in the kitchen door. "By the way, did I ever finish painting you?"

Thom was sitting at the desk in the Blue Room. Once again he had been trying to jot down a few notes as to possible motives for the deed; but even as he wrote he realized yet again that his spurts of systematic procedure were really quite futile—more so today than at the start of this search nine days ago. Which of the men could have done it? Hadn't Aunt Esther also said, "Or, if you like, which of the women"? Possible motives. Persons known to have been in the house. Presumed time of the deed. He had a fleeting vision of his mother's pale face on the pillow, her eyes looking at him, worried, containing what question? And Charlott's voice, Charlott standing in the door to his room saying, "She's already dead."

Once again: Possible motives. Even underlining those two words yielded no fresh insight. He was moving, thinking, in circles. What in the world had made him take on this absurd search for a perpetrator? All because of that ridiculous entry of Aunt Esther's for which there were apparently neither supporting evidence nor reliable witnesses—all because of those two sentences in an old diary whose existence his aunt had obviously forgotten as she ceaselessly spun her tales? Had Samuel's and Herminia's icy expressions and Gret's strangely overwrought rebuff, when he told them about Aunt Esther's diary, reinforced his suspicion of the possible truth of those terrible words, to the point where he still couldn't rid himself of it?

And there was something else. There was this barely palpable idea, defying formulation—like an infinitely remote, long since faded memory, or like the trace of a suspicion that occasionally brushed him these days but that, as soon as he tried to grasp it, vanished again—the idea that somewhere, underneath all these stories, in the depths of their totality, a piece of evidence did after all exist.

As soon as he decided to get up, throw away his aunt's green diary, and pack his bags in order to join Lis in Saint-Rémy, leaving this dizzying vortex behind, it was this suspicion and the memory of it that undermined his departure—or his desire to escape? Suspicion of what? Again that feeling that what he was looking for lay within himself—but in a blocked area; he would merely have to remember in precise detail, and the barrier would fall. Some key word in his vocabulary must have been mislaid, or rather, banned, banned from his consciousness. But by whom, by what authority? And again that feeling: like an archeologist, he must search through all those layers of stories, clear them away, bring them one by one to the surface and translate them back into language; then he would find the word.

But Uncle Ludwig? What could the stories of that brilliant dreamer and brother of Thom's father, that painter of seascapes, researcher of myths and genes, inventor of rocket cars and hand grenades, space planner, confirmed bachelor, and chief ideologist of the Winter corporate philosophy: what could Uncle Ludwig contribute to the search? After all, he had died seven years earlier than Mother.

Thom stood up and began to pace up and down in front of his mother's bed. Uncle Ludwig, then.

Thom had no trouble recalling that morning when, at the age of six, he had stood on a dais upstairs in Uncle Ludwig's studio, he had stood on a dais made of two wooden drawers, one large, one smaller, to pose for his uncle. He had been wearing that sailor jersey and the matching long navy-blue pants that he only ever put on, and tearfully at that, in response to his mother's threat that he would be sent to bed before supper and without her goodnight kiss. There he had stood, not allowed to move, told to raise his head slightly to the right and look out the window at the big ash tree. This had gone on for three days for an hour every day, his uncle sitting at the easel. After the first hour Thom could see only the outlines on the stretched canvas, but he could already make out that his uncle, with his charcoal pencil, had placed him on one of his cliffs above the sea. After the third hour Thom was simply amazed: the painting, now in lurid oil colors, showed him to be unmistakably present, but not in his hated sailor suit—Thom, grasping a spear, stood as a young warrior on the cliff, his face raised defiantly toward the right, his eyes gazing into the distance; Thom not at his real age of six but already as old as Charlott, at least fourteen. He liked the painting. Yes, that was how he wanted to look one day, with that shining cuirass on his chest, the short kilted skirt, the shinguards, that spear in his right hand, and that bold look of the conqueror. The painting had also greatly pleased his parents and for years had hung outside in the gallery. When Thom thought of it now, he shuddered. What a strange conception of themselves and their descendants this family of the Winters had expressed in his uncle's painting!

Still wondering in which corner of the house the painting might now be gathering dust, Thom saw in his mind's eye the studio above his uncle's laboratory in the annex, himself standing in the doorway. On the dais, in a pale summer dress, his mother. Uncle Ludwig sat behind the easel. He asked Mother to move her left foot in its high-heeled shoe ten centimeters farther forward. "And your right hip, Lilly, a bit more prominently to the front, if you don't mind. And turn your shoulders just a shade more toward the window—good! Lift your chin a little to the left, a bit more, a bit more—that's it!"

At that moment Thom heard footsteps behind him on the spiral staircase leading up from the lab. Father—who ten minutes earlier had said goodbye to them—was back again. Thom moved aside. Carrying Mother's beaver coat over his arm, Father pushed his way in. He was laughing. "Now, Lilly," he cried, "we'll make you into a queen!" Under the fur coat, which he laid over the back of a chair, he had been carrying a long, formal evening gown. "Here!" And with a laugh to Uncle Ludwig, "That's what she must wear, right?"

Mother's face wore an uncertain smile. "Must I?" She hesitated a little, but Thom could tell that she didn't want to be a spoilsport. She stepped down and, walking past Thom, disappeared with the dress down the stairs. Uncle Ludwig uncorked a bottle. "You're right," he said, "quite right, brother, I'll make her into a queen—or how about into a saint? I'll paint her walking on a cloud: a saint, that's right, and distinguished, very distinguished." Mother returned. The long gown made her walk more erectly than usual. That day must have been a bright one, a bright spring or fall day. Thom had sat down at the desk again. Bright, yes, maybe a thunderstorm had passed over toward noon, then the sun had come out? As he scribbled down his notes on that scene in the studio, he suddenly felt tempted to describe his mother's dress in detail—she had now resumed her place on the dais—to describe the light from the windows, or how Father said this, Uncle Ludwig said that, and how they both laughed, and on Mother's face that mixture of coquettish smile and doubt, too, and that same hint of uncertainty. But did he really still remember all that? Wasn't it possible that his memory had now swept into one pile all those various scenes as he had witnessed them so long ago? How could he write, let alone claim, that the dress had had a bell skirt and a little stand-up collar—oh yes, the standup collar, he was sure of that, but otherwise: the color? Corn yellow? Did the dress really have short sleeves? A silky sheen?

But this much Thom could remember clearly: there had been some kind of ammonia smell coming up from the lab. Uncle Ludwig had risen from his chair behind the easel, and, with a light touch on Mother's hips, turned her slightly more to the left into the light from the window. Then he had bent down and moved her left foot a shade farther forward. At the same time Father had crossed to the dais and placed the fur coat around Mother's shoulders. Both men stepped back a few paces. Lovely! They nodded as they contemplated their handiwork. "But now," said Father, "for the crowning!" He put his hand in his coat pocket, and when he pulled it out and held it up, a sparkling piece of jewelry dangled from it. A necklace?

"Lilly, here—this is for you!" Turning up the dangling end, he joined the two ends to form a glistening band, its three strips widening in the middle to some six centimeters and narrowing toward the two ends. Father was relishing the surprise; he had meant to wait and give it to her on their wedding anniversary. A little diadem. "Look at it!", he said, as he handed it to her.

Thom's mother must have been radiant. Holding out the sparkling object in both hands, she looked at it, looked at Father, then at Thom and Uncle Ludwig and back at Father. Thom remembered her stepping down from the dais and putting her arms around Father. Perhaps—no, probably—Father had gently pressed the diadem onto her hair. Probably too, Mother had walked bemusedly to the mirror on the back wall and studied herself with the little sparkling crown in her hair. Uncle Ludwig lit a cigar. Coughing through clouds of smoke he said, "Diamonds! Must have cost a fortune!" Again he asked Mother to resume her pose for him. "Wearing the crown, of course!" he said. "Come!"

For a moment she remained standing, the mirror behind her. Thom had already been imagining how the whole procedure on the dais would now start all over again—higher, turn more to the right, a bit to the front. But it never came to that. His mother, advancing slowly, removed the diadem from her head.

She would love to wear it, some day—"for you, Ulrich. On our wedding anniversary." She smiled. But not in a portrait—suppose it were hung in the gallery and she would have to see herself every day like that—as a queen? Ridiculous. She was sure they'd understand. She put the diadem down on the corner table. Both Uncle Ludwig and Father looked like bridge players who find themselves holding new, unexpectedly bad cards. Even this evening gown, Mother said, was too much of a good thing—but all right, if that was what they wanted. She laid aside the fur coat too. Then she mounted the dais again. "And Ludwig, now you'll let me stand the way *I* like best, won't you?"

Without a word, Uncle Ludwig began to sketch. Father pushed Thom by the shoulder to the door and walked down the stairs behind him.

Three or four days later—Mother had been posing for an hour every day; everyone, including Father, was sitting around the long table after supper, and Herminia and Frieda were already clearing away the dishes—

Uncle Ludwig suddenly appeared in the door to the Paneled Room. He switched on the chandelier and proceeded to carry in the large painting in such a way that those around the table could at first see only the gilt frame and the light canvas backing. With his foot he pushed one of the armchairs next to Mother's seat by the window closer to the wall, turned the painting around and, resting its lower edge on the chair arms, propped it gently against the wall. "There!" was all he said, flushed with exertion. He stepped aside. And to Father: "A gift for you!"

In the middle of the picture the light from the chandelier was reflected on the fresh oil paint. Nevertheless Thom saw immediately: his uncle had painted Mother with the fur coat over her shoulders and, yes, with the diadem in her hair, walking on a cloud against a background of distant mountain peaks and a vitriolic-green sky. Thom darted a quick glance at his mother. Out of the corner of his eye he could also see his father groping for his spectacles and getting to his feet. At the same time he heard Aunt Esther calling out, "Bravo, Ludwig, bravo!" She clapped her hands: What a true artist her brother was! Gret and Herminia also applauded; Charlott, sitting beside Thom, said, "Really super!"

The left half of Mother's face began to twitch. Now she would jump to her feet. Thom could feel his throat tightening. Now? Or now! Oh yes, he could remember that down to the tiniest detail. Father's laugh, and the way he exclaimed: "Magnificent!" seemed to contain a note of guilty conscience. And Mother, the left corner of her mouth still twitching, seemed to reflect as she looked at the portrait. "Strange," she said. "Very well painted, Ludwig, there's no denying that." She looked slowly around the table, then, without getting up, looked at the portrait again. "So you all like it? The only thing is: that's not me. You have turned me into a figment of your imagination."

Thom was startled, and would gladly have taken back the words immediately, when he heard himself break the silence with: "But you look beautiful like that, Mother!" They all laughed, and he was relieved to hear his father exclaim, "Even little Thom—did you hear?"

"Don't begrudge us our pleasure, Lilly!"

"Just imagine the portrait hanging out there in the passage! Or in the gallery! And I walk past it seven times a day and have to see myself in that pose? Impossible! Ulrich!"

Once again there was a quarrel in the air. Well, Uncle Ludwig said, how about his turning the cloud under her feet into a mountain, a hill carpeted with flowers?

"And the little crown must go as well, that most of all. And the coat is also too much! But for the rest," Mother said with a shrug: if that was what they wanted . . .

Thom and all the others watched Father walk over to Mother and kiss her on the forehead.

So in the end everything had turned out all right.

Or hadn't it? An hour later Thom was in bed, the quilt drawn up to his chin. He felt a cool tear running down his cheek. Whyever did his mother refuse to be a queen?

In Those Days

NO, NO MEMORIES. JUST SOMETIMES IN THE SMALL HOURS AND ONLY THE long-distance truckers are still on the road, and under the quilt someone turns toward the wall. Bertha, if she is the one, but probably she is nameless, had at that time . . . but 1932 is too long ago, the Depression wasn't over by 1934, and anyway what did they imagine? How was she to feed her two kids, and her stupid sister too, without at least some work? She was standing in the office, and the bald-headed man with the glasses and the white shirt said, "Nothing yet, Bertha." Now she was standing in the lineup. In front of her someone said, "We're not going to starve— don't push." And someone else said, "That's what *you* say." When her turn came, the woman from the welfare office ladled two scoops of barley soup into her milk pitcher and gave her three slices of bread; she could go home now. We're not going to starve. In 1936 she had a job again, from six to eight sweeping the floors in the Winter administration building. Now she was at least

and in her dream turns under the quilt toward the wall. Sometimes she mutters in her sleep, but there is no one left to hear it.

Saga of Origin V

NEXT MORNING BRAN AND HIS FOLLOWERS ENTERED THE HOUSE OF DANA. She, the Great Mother, embraced him. She inflamed him with love for her. Thus she celebrated the wedding with her son. But Bran knew that in a year's time she would transform him into a ram, lure him into the Great Cave, and kill him with the double axe of the waxing and waning moon. Thus he would have to spend the winter in the underworld until Dana summoned him again.

Bran pondered. One night, when Dana lay asleep, he seized her weapon, the double axe. The following day at noon, Dana found her spouse on the throne, holding out the axe toward her and announcing, "Henceforward this is the law—I am the father, the son, and the spirit of all things. No one mounts the throne except through me. My name will be Bran in the West and Yahweh in the East."

The messengers of the Great Father proclaimed the New Law throughout the land. The priestesses of Dana were driven out of the temples; the images of the Great Mother were destroyed.

But Bran slew Dana with the double axe. One night he dreamed that the cave beast was once again seven-headed. He ordered his hunters to search for the monster. As they approached the Great Cave, one of them was devoured by the monster; the others took flight. But the vessel of abundance had disappeared.

Bran prepared to do battle. Accompanied by his warriors, he marched to the Great Cave. Once again there was a struggle between him and the beast from the depths. Once again he succeeded in cutting off six of its seven heads. Yet the heads grew back. Then, as the beast retreated into the cave, Bran caused the cave entrance to be blocked by huge boulders. In addition, seven warriors mounted guard outside the cave. Bran ordered his messengers to proclaim throughout the land: "Fear no more. The cave monster is dead!"

The people held celebrations in honor of the Great Father. But in their memory fear of the Great Mother's revenge lived on. And rumors that the cave monster continued to live on and on refused to die down. Moreover, young warriors from time to time still went out in search of the vessel of abundance.

*   *   *

When Aunt Esther leaned back and closed her eyes for a few moments, or simply stopped speaking, her face collapsed. She suddenly looked as though about to come to terms with the fact that even she was, after all, a member of this race of mortals. When she resumed with, "That's how it was and not otherwise," adding, "Now you know," or said, "What can you do: c'est la vie, Thom," or, with a sigh, "All the stories have been told, told seven times over, are stories of stories, are echoes of echoes of stories, and yet, Thom, until you have told them all, down to your very last one, there is no prospect whatever of dying, let alone of life after death"—when she lowered her clenched fist or just sat there, or laughed, or when she looked past Thom toward the fir trees and smiled as if she could already see the Promised Land: each time it was not, as might have been supposed, the end. Each time she would again launch into one of her sevenfold-retold stories.

What happened one time. And that one time must have been in the late forties. "One morning your father, God bless his memory, said to me. In those weeks after the great freeze of 1952. Now you have the picture, Thom. Just a few days after the equinox. You must know everything, you must have the picture, when one day someone comes to you and asks, What kind of a love was it that made your father keep that particular transaction a secret from the woman who was after all his wife?" (Aunt Esther pronounced it *transaction*, the French way.) Or she said, "By all means ask Herminia, the door to the pantry was ajar, she must have heard it all as she sat out there at the table pretending to study the newspaper advertisements for Sunday afternoon and evening dances in the area: by all means ask her if you don't believe what I'm saying." Or: "Do you want to know what possessed that woman who is your mother, less than a week after her husband's funeral, to go to the telephone and call the treasurer of the Winter Corporation?" Or: "What do you imagine, Thom, was going on here in town on August 6, 1950, the evening of the 6th?" Or simply: "Let us assume, Thom, that you have been on a business trip to Munich, you are sitting back, dead tired, in the black limousine as our Mr. Wenger drives you up the avenue, and you see the light burning over the front steps, and you realize that really is your wife pacing up and down on the flagstones—now, an hour before midnight?"

Once upon a time. Or simply: "You see, it happened like this." Then Thom knew what he must do to make her tell this story again, this one too. He got up, took the Green Glass, the Murano glass, from the back of the sideboard, as well as the silver tray and the bottle of sherry. After setting it all down, filling the glass, and resuming his place on the stool, he watched her light a cigarillo and take a sip, and he waited, waited full of fear and eagerness, for Aunt Esther to call upon him, *him*, to make up his mind about his mother and her behavior in this story of the end of the Winter family's power in the Winter enterprise. For Aunt Esther admitted that she had not been present herself, or only in a peripheral way. So she used variations of Who-knows?, of conjectures that may have been mere allegations prompted by her malice, such as: "Your mother must have been blinded by her arrogance. How else can you explain it?" cried Aunt Esther into the late, now golden afternoon— "blinded, how else, Thom?" And so it was up to him to cudgel his brains for possibilities other than the one Aunt Esther was so strongly implying, at least implying.

"And yet," she said, "the sound of the church bell tolling over your father's grave had scarcely died away"—her brother, that lawyer Theodor Schaub, hadn't even let a decent interval elapse before opening the will— "and there she stood, out in the passage one morning in August '52, demanding to speak to the treasurer of Winter's, Director Berger, a man of honor, as you know. And her manner, Thom! The very tone of her voice! After her husband's death, she said—incidentally as if that death of my dear brother had been no more than the result of a tragic accident— after his death, she said out there on the telephone, she considered it her duty, as one of the heirs and the administrator of the three children's legacies, to discuss the consequences with the gentlemen of the board. He, Mr. Berger, would please be kind enough to invite them in her name to a conference on the morning of the day after next, followed by luncheon in the General Wille Room at the Schweizerhof, and to put the following points on the agenda, unless he wished to bring up additional subjects. She spoke as if this were a hereditary monarchy and she were without question the successor to my dear brother, endowed, as president of the company and spokesman of the board, with the right to issue any orders she chose and to round up directors and board members for a conference.

"Faithful Mr. Berger must have been thunderstruck. No doubt he asked her whether all that were not somewhat precipitate. Moreover, he was doubtful whether the gentlemen would find the date and the agenda convenient; he would prefer to consult with them, at least with the members of the executive committee, but now her voice was to be heard outside again, and her pleasant laugh as she informed Mr. Berger that he should let her worry about who would or would not find it convenient, and with a curt 'Till Wednesday, then,' she hung up."

Aunt Esther had leaned forward and put down the empty Green Glass. Resting her head again on the chair back, her eyes closed, she looked, while Thom refilled her glass, as if she were listening to a chorus of voices from bygone years. Or as if she were trying to imagine Thom's mother, in August '52, in that black jacket dress clicking down the steps in her black high-heeled shoes that made her appear even taller than she was, and passing "our good Mr. Wenger" as he removed his cap and opened the car door for her, disappearing into the rear of the black limousine, where she sat with Ulrich Winter's brown briefcase on her knees while the car drove off with her down the avenue to that momentous conference.

"Not mad," said Aunt Esther softly. "Blinded, I think that's the word, Thom. Or, to be more precise, she will simply not have been prepared to acknowledge what had happened during the preceding months." Thom wondered about the meaning of that last sentence. While Aunt Esther went on to tell him how his mother had been received by Director Berger and ushered into the conference room by him; about the seven board members already waiting for her, those seven and, surprisingly enough, that bank director with the odd name of Schilling; and while she went on describing the exchange of greetings, and how his mother, without being invited to do so, had assumed the seat of the chairman or, in this case, chairwoman, Thom was trying to figure out what Aunt Esther could have meant by that sentence. Still listening to her, he mentally repeated: She will simply not have been prepared to acknowledge what had happened during the preceding months. As a sixteen- or seventeen-year-old monastery pupil he had no trouble parsing the sentence. What Aunt Esther must have said was that Thom's mother had not been prepared to accept something: specifically, something that had happened in the preceding months. What she had meant by things that had happened in the preceding months and probably even years was clear to him; he knew, not only from Aunt Esther but also from his mother, that before his death his father had recklessly plunged into risky financial ventures that had burdened him with extremely serious worries. Oh yes, his mother had told him about it herself, three years after Father's funeral, which meant she must have acknowledged it, at least at some point since then. So far so good. But why didn't Aunt Esther simply say, She was not prepared? Thom conjugated in his head: She is not prepared. She has not been prepared. She was not prepared, had not been prepared. She will not be prepared—yes, that's how it went, all the way to She will not have been prepared—not prepared to acknowledge what had happened.

A future tense? What had made Aunt Esther transpose into the future something that clearly lay three years and several months or even longer in the past? Or must he see or hear the sentence differently, and Aunt Esther had used "she will" in the sense of "She must have been blinded," as a form that, while implying the past, at the same time made it clear that Aunt Esther was merely surmising that his mother had not been prepared? Did it mean that Aunt Esther wished to emphasize how gingerly she handled the truth? Or did it mean that she accused Thom's mother—although only indirectly, by way of noncommittal conjecture— of being so arrogant, so confident in her striving for power that she was no longer able—or in Aunt Esther's words, prepared—to acknowledge what had happened during the time before Father's death?

When Thom asked Aunt Esther exactly what he was to make of "She will not have been prepared," she merely laughed, and her sudden surprised look made him wonder whether she had even understood his question. "But that's what one says, isn't it?" she said. And: "Go ahead and look for the answer yourself, or better still: Ask her, ask your mother how she can explain the fact that at that board meeting, after Mr. Schilling's brief statement, she had sat there as if she had been forced to swallow a toad.

"But we must go back to when those at the conference table had first sat down, then, at the request of faithful Mr. Berger, risen again in order to honor the memory of the deceased by one minute's silence. At least that was how Mr. Berger described it to me when I telephoned him to find out what had actually happened. For three days after the conference, he said, Thom's mother had had all her meals brought up to the Blue Room by Herminia, and during that time had probably done little more than walk up and down in her room or lie on the bed and calculate, mentally calculate—in short: after that minute of silence for my dear

departed brother"—Aunt Esther sipped some sherry—"Lilly Winter, according to Berger, as if taking it for granted that she was to preside, had
said, 'Gentlemen: I have been developing some ideas concerning the
long-range policy of the company.' The time had now come, she felt,
after this post-1938 phase of progress, of expansion, and the internation-
alizing of various branches of production since 1946, for management
to confront some fundamental questions. The first question she had noted
down"—Aunt Esther laughed, "and you must imagine her, before Mr.
Schilling had had a chance to reveal the true situation to her, sitting in
your father's big armchair at the head of the conference table, in her
black blouse, and presuming to discuss matters that are clearly a male
preserve—anyway, her first question was, Today's production: Production
of what? How much production? And: Production at whose expense and
for whose benefit? As a second point or second question—and in this
area too she had decided to accept the responsibility she had inherited—
a true challenge!—she wished to focus on the problem of corporate
structure. Here the question must be asked, in terms of humanization
and efficiency: How much central power, how much decentralization?
Or more bluntly: How much hierarchy is actually necessary, how much
can be dispensed with? She felt it was important to assure the company
employees of strong participation in the decision-making process. The
third set of questions to be discussed concerned social security: such items
as old age pensions, severance pay, maternity insurance, apprentice training were enough to start with. She requested the gentlemen to reflect on
these three major questions of corporate strategy before the next session
at the end of September. She herself hoped to be able to present them
with a detailed paper well ahead of time.

"Then, Thom, the silence around the table was broken by Dr.
Schilling clearing his throat." As always, at the approach of a dramatic
climax, Aunt Esther took a sip or lit a cigarillo or looked out the window
into the light of the setting sun or perhaps into the rain as it trickled
down the windowpane; she drank, she smoked, she leaned back again
and continued; you could tell from her dark voice and the occasional
abrupt laugh how she always enjoyed postponing the crucial moment.

This gave Thom time to remember how his mother, in answer to
his question, had made him come and sit beside her at the window in
the Paneled Room. She had gazed past him down the avenue and said,
very calmly, "As you know, Aunt Esther can't forgive me for being
different from her image of a sister-in-law. Probably she was so greatly

attached to her brother, your father, that she is bound to hate the woman who for many years was closer to him than she was. You can understand that, can't you? Regardless of how many lies Aunt Esther has the habit of inventing, in this respect at least," his mother had said, "Aunt Esther has told you nothing that was not true.

"It was a shock for me. Your father had actually told me nothing, heaven knows why. That's how it was." And in answer to Thom's questions she told him, so that he could gradually begin to understand. As a result of the expansion of business that began in the early forties, it had twice become necessary to increase the company's capital. The only way Thom's father, who with 55 percent was the main shareholder, could ensure his majority was by raising very considerable loans from the bank, for which he had to deposit his parcel of shares as security. This may be all right as long as business continues to expand. However, if the bank decides that the value of the shares—in this case, the equity and future development of the Winter Corporation—no longer offers sufficient security, it is free to dispose of those shares at any time. So the shares, including the new issues, had been deposited as security and for the time being everything went smoothly.

Once again his mother had looked obliquely along the avenue through the rain trickling down the windowpane. "Why did he keep all this from me, you may ask? Probably to spare me anxiety. I knew he had invested hundreds of thousands of francs in his brother Ludwig's experiments and lost most of it, also that the increasingly frequent phases in which he drowned his consciousness in alcohol were endangering his position in the company more and more. But as for mortgaging the shares—no, I knew nothing about that."

But that was not all. In fact, it was only at that board meeting that Dr. Schilling had told her the truth, that very bitter truth. Thom's father had felt under ever-increasing pressure. No doubt he had tried desperately to free himself from this dependence on the bank. Then, two years before his death, in the spring of 1950, the Winter Corporation was offered the patented invention of an Italian engineer called Edoardo Germi, a machine with electronic remote control, called a robot, and capable of receiving and executing wireless instructions—a bold innovation. He was fascinated by it. Convinced that the future of industrial production would belong to this robot, he did everything in his power to persuade the board to purchase the patent. However, the majority of the directors rejected the proposition.

Well, it was here that Thom's father—in financial straits as he already was—staked everything on this one card. In other words, he, in his private capacity, bought the license for the invention and began to finance the production of, initially, three prototypes in Monza, north of Milan; to finance this not with his own capital, which was already mortgaged, but again with a bank loan. Once again the bank loaned him money; once again it demanded securities. So Thom's father now also mortgaged the big farm in the Rychenwyl that he and Ludwig had inherited from Grandmother Helen, and he also mortgaged the property here, including the stables and the villa.

"You must know, Thom," his mother went on, "that the more ominous the financial situation appeared to your father, the more often he would turn to drink. And the more often he drank, the stronger became the forces among the shareholders and board members that demanded his resignation as president and spokesman."

"What would you, Thom," cried Aunt Esther in the dusk of that rainy afternoon, "what would you do or say, supposing you had sat down in the chairman's place, convinced that with the majority of shares you held the reins of power in the company, and made great speeches about strategy and perspectives, and now, in the silence that followed, this Dr. Schilling cleared his throat and, without mincing matters, proceeded to explain the situation? Ulrich Winter's towering entrepreneurial personality had always, of course, been a crucial security for the bank; but upon his death—with all due respect to Mrs. Winter and her co-heirs—a new situation had arisen. Moreover, the bank had recently had to take into account the present far-from-rosy business trend of the Winter Corporation as well as the following circumstances: the bank's representative had returned the day before from an inspection trip to Monza. The practical realization of the undoubtedly brilliant invention of a robot was threatening to turn into a venture that might continue to swallow up funds for many decades, apart from the approximately three million francs already invested. Might she, Mrs. Winter, be prepared to hold herself responsible to the bank, with corresponding new securities, for the amount of five and a half million francs?

"In the event of a negative response from Mrs. Winter, Dr. Schilling said he was able, after lengthy consultations, also with the present board members, to propose the following solution to these awkward problems. So what could you, Thom, have possibly done in that situation other than what she was forced to do: that is, sit there wide-eyed and silent, as if you had swallowed a bat? Yes, she will have remained silent for a long time." Aunt Esther laughed. "She will have listened to Dr. Schilling's proposal like someone listening to a judge passing sentence: twelve years' exile. Those scheming board members! That crafty Dr. Schilling! Of course they were all in cahoots. At last they saw a chance of taking over the Winter family shares. Whether the bank, the board members, or all together, working behind my dear brother's back, had actually encouraged the subcontractors in Monza to press their claims for payment immediately following the news of Ulrich Winter's death is a question that will, I suppose, remain their murky secret. In any event, at last they had a chance to get their hands on the family's shares. God knows they made the most of it. So Dr. Schilling proposed that the bank immediately make use of its right, take over the mortgaged shares and properties and dispose of them, and use the proceeds to cancel all debts, including the accumulated interest, seven percent at that time. In the unlikely event that a credit balance in favor of the heirs of the mortgagor should result, it was to be placed at the disposal of the rightful heirs in the form of cash.

"What can you do?" Aunt Esther blew smoke rings in the air. "Business is business, Thom. Your mother will have asked for three days to think it over. Then, as I told you before, those of us here in the house were aware of her walking up and down, up and down in her room, and Herminia had to take all her meals up to her. But no matter how much she added and subtracted, the accounting she had been presented with, along with copies of all the contracts, remained what it was. Nor did it help your mother that she decided to fight. And that is what she did. And spent night after night writing her letters."

Aunt Esther sighed. Thom poured her some more sherry. Thom's mother had fought. Aided by her brother Theodor, the lawyer, she had used all kinds of legal arguments and even gone to court in her efforts to get back the shares, in spite of everything, Thom. But the era of the Winter family's power over the Winter Corporation had come to an end.

Nevertheless, Aunt Esther continued, and outside the window the November storm of 1956 had now risen, the pattering of the rain increased, after two years Thom's mother—and Aunt Esther did not wish to belittle this—had extracted whatever was still to be had: a monthly pension for herself, the widow; the discharge of the lien on this property in exchange for a new mortgage of two hundred and eighty thousand francs; plus an undertaking by the corporation to provide for the education of the sole male heir, Thomas Winter, until his twentieth year.

For a while all was quiet, apart from the roar of the storm and the pattering against the window. Dusk filled the room, making it hard to see Aunt Esther's face and whether there was a smile on it. The dream was over, said Aunt Esther, the absurd dream of a woman who had believed that with her husband's death, which they knew was not an accident, her path to the chief executive's chair was open. To her, she said, the whole thing seemed to be something more than crafty Dr. Schilling, abetted by those other schemers, tightening his evil noose: no, it was as if Thom's father himself, from his grave, had wanted to teach his wife a lesson about what is a woman's place and what isn't.

But: "Will she have finally and truly learned that lesson? I know how stubborn she is," she said. "And you know that too."

"Will she have learned that lesson?" Another of those sentences. Another of those future tenses, but one that scarcely implied the future. What was it called?

Passages VI

OR HE HAD A FEVER, LYING THERE IN THE SEMIDARKNESS, HIS THOUGHTS flitting about like butterflies. Butterflies from the egg, from the caterpillar, from larva or chrysalis, tiger moth, swallowtail, peacock-eyed hawk moth or red-banded underwing, in the cardboard box on the windowsill caterpillars, larvae, through the peephole, feverishly coming and going and was there again at night with that heat and vinegar poultices and three times a day a spoonful of cough syrup and medicine before his mother tiptoed out of the room in the dark

He had a fever, and although the rocking sensation made the six-year-old boy's limbs go all limp, still sometimes the longing for it never to end because *she* was there now or at least kept coming back even at night and would sit on his bed, my little patient, open your mouth, that's right, and another ten drops in the spoon

Never end, being able to feel his mother quite close, to breathe in her scent of freshly laundered linen and of her skin and the faintly sweet perfume under her ears on her neck when he suddenly hugged her so that she had no choice but to hold him tightly in her arms, at least for a few moments and because he was sick. He wanted her, wanted her close, very close here on the edge of the bed, just there, just there for him, for once only for him and it would never end, this feeling her so close, and now that frenzied male voice shouting away on the radio, the Führer's voice would at least be far far away again and he wouldn't have to hear it at night in the dark, wouldn't have to think of the Führer and hear

"all world-historical events are merely the expression of the races' drive for self-preservation"

this or hear the voice cracking

"It is the Jews who are behind this campaign against Germany German people you will be strong when you are united"

wouldn't have to hear any more of that other, that foreign grownup language

"responsible for the fate of the German nation I as the German people's supreme judge"

and the voice echoing on and on through the house in the dark in dreams

"the result will be not the victory of Jewry but the extermination of the Jewish race"

so that he could only burrow even deeper into the warmth of the pillows and quilt, and the fever coming back and his thoughts flitting about like butterflies like caterpillars like larvae and turning into a chrysalis when that voice on and on

"But once Russia is destroyed, England's last hope will be extinguished"

and

"The Communist is not a comrade before and not a comrade after This is a war of annihilation"

on and on a voice shouting shouting

"to the east only to the east must our vital arteries extend with body and soul in its true battle for the sacred mission of my life the extermination of Bolshevism"

shouted no threatened, threatened deafeningly up through the house and he knew that Mother was sitting down there by the radio and Father was leaning against the tile stove beside his chair or pacing nervously up and down

war of annihilation and sacred mission and when Russia is destroyed and: Sieg—heil! Sieg heil! Sieg heil! Sieg heil! Sieg—

yet all he wanted to do or at least hear and see and smell was her sitting there and comforting him or stroking his hair my little patient, why are you scared, that's only the Führer of the German people, go to sleep now, and who knows, Thom? Maybe by morning the first little butterflies will show up outside?

Time
of the
Island

"Oh, Thom," said Aunt Esther, with her beloved *Figaro* before her. "When will I ever cease to be amazed? Here I am, soon to be joining the ninety-year-olds," she laughed, "the hundred-and-ninety-year-olds, and I still never cease to be amazed. The wheel of time. Do you remember how it almost stood still, seven or eight years ago at the end of the war? Here—look at these pictures: Berlin. Eight years later a divided city. Germany: a country divided in two. Who would have believed at that time, when there was still *one* Führer and *one* Reich, that there would ever be a Communist Germany? The wounds of war are slowly healing, but the limbs that were shot off will never come back."

She reflected. "But shouldn't this be exactly what we Swiss want?" Her face wore that sly look. "We small ones are only big when the big ones are small too. No no, the wheel does not stand still—it is turning, turning faster and faster again. Take this Marshall Plan"—and while she started to wax enthusiastic about the thirteen billion dollars and about progress, Thom

"Can you imagine all those technical miracles in store for us?"

felt he would have liked to tell her about what had happened a few days ago at the monastery school. He would have liked to ask her, "About the Jews, Aunt, and what happened to them—how do you feel?" But she was talking as if he hadn't been liberated only two days ago and out of a clear blue sky, liberated by Charlott from his prison behind the monastery walls. No, she wouldn't listen. The wheel of history. In Italy: de Gasperi as president—"a gentleman, Thom!"

Whatever she told him, whatever she conjured up, he heard her voice, but it remained outside him. Inside him was amazement that he was here again, at home. Never to have to pack his trunk again and go back behind those monastery walls! How had Charlott ever found the courage to say, "Very well. Then you'll come with me now!"

Never back to that cubicle? Four rows of twenty-five wooden cubicles, a hundred cubicles each in dormitories A and B. Thom's cubicle, including the door, had been 1.9 meters long and 1.8 meters wide. By stretching up, you could just reach the top edge of the partitions with your fingertips. Above that the cubicles were open to the ceiling, about forty centimeters higher, so at night you could hear the groans and snores, and sometimes the screams, of the sleeping pupils. Hanging by a hook on the door was the black habit. In the top drawer of the bedside table Thom kept his letters, letters from Charlott, from Mother, and the two letters from Father; in the small drawers below, his underwear. There was no closet in the cubicle, and no chair. His clothes were in his trunk and in the cardboard box under the bed. Cubicles with windows were reserved for pupils from the third class up, but only for those with good marks, especially in Diligence and Deportment. Even when he was in the third class, Thom was not given a cubicle with a window. He didn't mind. The mountains out there around the valley blocked most of the sky anyway and were usually wreathed in clouds.

How could he have made Aunt Esther understand what had just happened there? And what it meant in that closed male world, inaccessible to women, in that society made up exclusively of men in monk's garb? She didn't even know the stone staircase, where every whisper echoed, and every sandaled footstep, no matter how soft. Or the smell: everywhere in the rambling monastery and the school building with its vaulted corridors, the refectories, the washroom dormitory study room and the series of classrooms beyond and above one another: no, she didn't even know that combined smell of stale pea soup, floor wax, sweaty underwear, unwashed male bodies, and shoe polish; nor the smell of incense in the corridor outside the chapel or in the sacristy of the magnificent baroque church. The mumbling, the incessant whispering, murmuring; the stench from the toilets. How could he have made Aunt Esther see those looks or even told her about them? Those pairs of eyes in the pale, ageless, monkish faces—the eyes behind the thick glasses of Father Prefect; the eyes of the homeroom teacher, the eyes of supervision, the pairs of eyes behind balustrades and windows? The eyes, not visible, only sensed in the dark, above the cubicle partition, and coming closer and closer through the walls of the fortress of Aulis?

But happiness—he could have told Aunt Esther about happiness; also the story of how Christian had become his friend. More than two years before that, Father Placidus, the conductor of the church choir, had told Thom and Christian to stay behind after choir rehearsal. He had informed Christian—who was three years older than Thom and already in the fourth class—that, with his still unbroken alto voice, he was needed as a soloist in the monks' Matins choir; Thom, he said, would now also be singing with them at Vigil, as a soprano. At first Thom had assumed this to be a punishment. Although the appointment meant they had been chosen, at the same time it entailed additional instruction in Gregorian chant, as well as getting up at 5:30 every morning instead of 6:15.

So from then on Thom and Christian were wakened by a gentle knock on the cubicle door, instead of by the horrible clanging of the handbell from the dormitory door. They met on the staircase. Still half-asleep but already out of breath and always only just in time for Vigil, they entered the chancel by way of the sacristy. Side by side, in their black habits, they advanced to the high altar, made the Sign of the Cross, genuflected; then each walked toward one of the two choir stalls right and left of the altar and sat down in the front row. Here, separated by the width of the chancel, they knelt opposite one another, each with monks beside and behind him, two sixty-voice male choirs, as they chanted the Gregorian Matins service antiphonally—*a cappella* or accompanied only by the small organ.

Happiness, and the tremor of fear in his voice when Thom realized that, prompted by a slight nod from Father Placidus, he was singing, singing alone, the two monks' choirs having fallen silent, and Thom was suddenly aware of himself; that high singsong of the still unbroken boy's voice, yes: that was himself. The fear was gone. He forgot the square notes on the four staves in the manual before him; he knew them, had long known them by heart, and his voice echoing far back in the lofty church nave turned them into rising and falling cadences, choral singing, solo singing, antiphonally with the monks' choirs as they came in again in powerful unison—alternating not only with them but also with Christian's responding solo voice, and again Thom would take up the part and repeat a motif in response or sing it first. Never before in this prison had he felt such happiness. The music, both strange and familiar, allowed him to enter completely into the realm of something beautiful that seemed to offer him salvation from the torments of the earthly day in the monastery fortress; he became part of that unearthly beauty.

All the more grim was the everyday world in which he found himself once again each time the sounds of the last chorale had died away.

But then the scandal set off by Christian. Once each semester a movie was shown in the auditorium. On that occasion it was *The Island of Refuge*, announced for Wednesday afternoon. The previous Monday evening, at 6:15, after the Vigil chanting had died away, Christian and Thom were the last to file out of the church behind the long procession of Benedictine monks. Christian whispered to Thom, "Come with me!" From the sacristy, where the vestments glittered in the still open closets, they went into the adjoining room, past Brother Sacristan. Christian sat down on the table. Beside him stood a box encased in hammered silver, and behind that a number of golden chalices set with precious jewels, as well as several small silver wine carafes.

Christian picked up one of these and flipped open the lid. "Stop!" Thom's attempt to prevent Christian drinking came too late. Christian held him off with his left arm. "Don't get excited!" He took another sip. "Not bad! Have some!"

But he mustn't do that! Sacramental wine! That was wine that the holy transubstantiation during Mass had changed into the blood of Jesus Christ!

"Oh, come on," said Christian, "they just say that. This is wine—here, you can smell it."

Not blood? Thom was convinced that during Mass, after the transubstantiation, the priest at the altar drank blood, the true blood of our Lord. Gathering up the skirts of his habit, he sat down on the only chair in the room. No, he didn't dare drink any of it. Only the ordained, only priests, were allowed to do that!

Christian placed the silver box on his knee. The lid sprang open. He put his hand inside. Thom shuddered when he saw Christian raise a little pile of the sacramental wafers to his mouth and take a bite. Had he gone mad? The Eucharist! "This is my body"—weren't those the sacred words the priest murmured at the altar when he transformed the white Host into the body of our Lord and Savior? Christian went on chewing. Again he took a little pile of sacramental wafers out of the box as if it were filled with pretzels. At this point Thom said aloud, "*Hoc est enim corpus meum! My* body, Christian: *hoc est!*" With his mouth full,

Christian replied that whether the Eucharist *was* or *represented* Christ's body was something scholars had been arguing about since the sixth century. In his opinion, and he had been an altar boy for quite a while, these wafers were well baked yet as soft as Paris bread. "Don't look at me like that! Console yourself if you like with *these* words, which you'll also find in the text of the Mass: *Accipite et manducate ex hoc omnes!* Eat ye all of this! So what else am I doing?" He laughed.

Suddenly he said, "That movie, the day after tomorrow. I saw it last fall in Zurich, with my mother. She's Jewish, you know?"

Thom could only say, No, he didn't.

That movie showed, Christian said, how during the war Switzerland became a haven for refugees. But that fine-sounding claim represented maybe one-tenth of the truth. As for the remaining nine-tenths: this country had not, as Christian duty and old Swiss tradition demanded, accepted the refugees, but had had them taken back by police, sometimes even by soldiers, to the border—to their deaths. The reason given, by the way, was: the boat was full.

Christian went on. When France capitulated, his grandparents had fled secretly across the border from Annemasse. In Geneva they were met by Christian's mother. That same night a police checkup in the hotel revealed them to be Jews—they were called Rosenbaum and had fled from Pomerania to France—and, escorted by two soldiers, they were taken back to the border. In France they would be quite safe, they were told. Three weeks later they were arrested in Nevers. Both perished: murdered in Dachau. Thousands trying to get into Switzerland from France suffered the same fate.

Christian drew a deep breath. "The official directive of the Swiss government concerning refugee policy had included the sentence: 'Refugees for reasons solely of racial persecution are not to be regarded as political refugees,' in other words: are to be turned back at the border. Do you understand? From Italy, thousands of Jews tried to enter Switzerland; from Austria, thousands; from the German Reich, tens of thousands. At the beginning of the war only about eight thousand Jewish refugees were in Switzerland; in 1944 there were altogether 70,000 refugees, of which 22,000 were Jews: that was all." Christian gazed past Thom.

Thom listened silently. He felt as if these figures were accusing him, him personally. "Add to those 70,000 refugees, 80,000 interned military personnel—mainly Poles and Italians—so there may have been a total of about 150,000 refugees among a population in Switzerland of roughly five million: approximately three percent. What do you say to that?"

Christian's voice was calm. "Or to this: In the camps of the Third Reich, well over five million Jews—including women and children—were gassed, hanged, or shot.

"Or this, Thom: *Our* government, the Federal Council, succeeded by dogged negotiations in persuading the Reich Government to have the passports of all Jews within the Nazi German sphere of influence stamped with a large J, in order to distinguish the holders of such passports from other refugees, or, to put it bluntly: to be able to turn them back at the Swiss borders."

Could that be true? Only a few days ago, in a preparatory lesson for the upcoming movie, the padre who taught them history had told them: Yes, Jews, Communists, and gypsies had been driven out of Germany. "But here, in our beautiful country, they found a new home."

Christian looked down at the habit covering his knees. "My mother wrote hundreds of letters to the authorities. With the help of Father and her friends she hid Jewish men, women, families with children, sometimes for months on end, in cellars or attics, in order to protect them from deportation. Many Swiss men and women protested against the official policy. They fought for the refugees, took them in, looked after them. But," he said, "imagine an apple. You cut it open, and nine-tenths of it are wormy. So what is the truth about this apple? Is it sound or rotten? Your history teacher and this movie, they say it's sound."

Aunt Esther was still talking. "Don't you remember? Even you must remember how we used to sit around the radio in the evening, while I was trying to get the soldiers' program from Stuttgart, and at the sound of 'Lili Marlene'—even your father would be standing by the tile stove with tears in his eyes"—on and on she talked, and Thom wanted so much to tell her about Christian and the Jews and ask her how she felt about those extermination camps, and that Christian, in the little room next to the sacristy, had said he had a plan. Would Thom help him? Could Thom keep a secret?

Wednesday afternoon, 5:30. They filed into the auditorium two by two, class by class, first the pupils, then the monks. Short welcoming speech by Father Prefect. Then the lights in the hall went out. Against a musical background that evoked the roaring of the sea, the words *The Island of Refuge* flickered in large letters on the screen. Thom pulled one of the leaflets from his breast pocket. He tapped the boy in front of him on the shoulder and handed him the unfolded leaflet, whispering, "Read it and pass it on!" Five minutes later he also handed his neighbor a leaflet, saying it had come from "over there," pointing vaguely to the right across the aisle. Read it and pass it on. In the dimly lit darkness it was possible, by holding the leaflet close to the eyes, to make out just the title: "This movie is a lie," and underneath: "Pass it on!"

On Monday evening and again the evening before the performance, Thom and three other close friends of Christian's, sitting in their cubicles, had secretly copied out in block letters the text composed by Christian. Each of them circulated these leaflets during the showing, five copies each.

While the first reel was being changed—the lights had gone on again—groups of boys standing around and reading were already forming in the hall. "This movie is a lie," and underneath, point by point, line by line, the facts that Christian had assembled. "The truth looks quite different."

During the second intermission there were some disturbances. All over the hall, boys, especially from the higher classes, were engaged in what soon became noisy discussions. Padres intervened.

The movie came to an end; the closing music likewise proclaimed the triumph of Swiss humanitarianism. When the lights were turned on, Father Rector was standing in front of the screen, holding up two of the leaflets: "I assume that whoever wrote these leaflets will at least have the courage to stand up!" Thom could feel a blush flooding his cheeks. For a minute there was silence. "No one? Cowards!" Fortunately the evening meal could not be delayed. After supper teachers interrogated individual classes. The pupils' answers were all of the same kind: "When the lights went on, the leaflet was lying on my lap." Or: "Yes, it came from behind." "It came from over there on the right." "In the dark I couldn't see who passed it to me." "No, I saw nothing." The questioning continued for a nerve-racking day. They were also summoned individually. Gradually, as announced on Thursday evening by Father Prefect in the study room, the number of suspects was whittled down to ten. Christian murmured as he passed Thom, "We know nothing, right?"

On Friday morning Christian and Thom sang at Matins. Thom only just managed to get through his solo part. Christian's voice also sounded forced; twice he had to cough. When it came to Christian's seventh and last solo, there was a pause. Thom could sense the powerful presence of the sixty cowled men beside and behind him. Come on, Christian, sing! Sing, please! Jesus, give him the strength to sing!

At last Christian's voice. Suddenly there it was, clear, loud, a little too high perhaps: "I am half Jewish. My real name is Ismael. I was baptized at the age of eight. Yes, it was me: I wrote the leaflets. From now on I will profess my Jewishness. As of now I am leaving a church that is incapable of allowing the truth to be told about the failure of this Christian country! I wish to be called Ismael again."

On the small organ Father Placidus played a transition to the final chorale. At the door to the sacristy, Father Rector was already waiting for Thom and Christian. They followed him silently into the rectory, where the padre asked Christian whether he meant to abide by his decision. If so, he would telephone Christian's parents, shortly before eight o'clock. "As for you, Thomas, do you not also wish to tell the truth now?" Thom first stammered something unintelligible, blushing again to the roots of his hair. He nodded. "Yes," he said. And Christian quickly added, "I talked him into it"—Thom had helped him copy out the leaflets and also to distribute them.

At nine in the morning, while Thom was sitting in his classroom over his math, there was a knock at the door. Christian came in and walked over to Thom in the third row from the rear. He was wearing a sweater and knickerbockers. He said he was taking the 10:20 train, and "Thanks!" and "Take care!"; he left.

From then on Thom, instead of playing Ping-Pong, spent all his free time in the empty classroom. He had been told to copy out five times fifteen pages from the book *The Island of Refuge*, the chapter in which Jewish émigrés expressed their gratitude to the Swiss people for rescuing them from great peril. So there he sat, day after day, alone.

At three o'clock on the sixth day he was called out of the study hall: there was someone to see him. His sister was waiting for him in the visitors' room by the front entrance.

Charlott! His habit gathered up to his knees, Thom rushed down the stairs and along the corridors. There sat Charlott at the big table. She laughed. "How are you, little monk?" He hugged her, his eyes smarting as he felt her warm cheek against him. For a while he sat across from her without saying a word. How pretty she looked in her red jacket. "The only things missing," he said, and knew she understood: "the only things missing from it are the wild beasts!"

And slowly he began to tell her. He confessed that almost every night as he fell asleep—he had only to think of the pigeons at home—he cried into his pillow. "It's a terrible place," he said. "I'm sure if Father were still alive he would take me away from here!"

Charlott sat with her chin cupped in her hand. When he told her about Christian, she also listened quietly. She looked at him for a long time, as if lost in thought. "When I hear all that," she said. And after a long pause those words: "Very well. Then you'll come with me now."

Could Thom believe his ears? "Yes, but—what will Mother say?"

"Leave that to me. I think she'll understand."

In the Dovecote

SEPP'S BROTHER JONNY HAD ALWAYS BEEN A HOTHEAD. HE HAD BEEN DEAD for two years now. Sepp sorted Jonny's postcards, the photos, and the three letters from Spain, and now this other letter had arrived, yesterday, which Sepp wanted to read again, after which he intended to add it to Jonny's things. It was signed Emil and Hans.

Actually, it was about Jonny's gravestone. A week ago, late Wednesday afternoon, Emil and Hans had suddenly come up to the table in the Waadtländer Hall where Sepp was sitting and said, "They told us at the villa that you'd gone into town"—they used the familiar "Du"—"we're old comrades of Jonny's, we fought together in Spain." They had been to the cemetery, they said, and there was still no gravestone, and yesterday they had sent this letter; yesterday. They wrote: "After all, he was our comrade and we fought side by side." That's why they wanted Sepp to know that they would like to have Jonny's headstone carved with the words: "To the memory of the anti-Fascist fighter for freedom in Spain." If he agreed, they wanted to share in the cost by contributing six hundred francs. Emil's signature was legible; Hans's wasn't.

Sepp lay back on the mattress and read the letter again.

"We met your brother there in 1936. On the train between Figueras and Barcelona. On a small railway station we saw a lot of young Spanish men and women, with their big black anarchist flags, and our flags on the train were red. When the train stopped, the anarchists cheered us. Then through the window we saw a man at the rear of the train get out, a big fellow with a red flag, one of us, and walk over to those people. The Spaniards and he embraced. Suddenly he waved a black anarchist flag. He laughed, and all of a sudden the Spaniards had his red flag. Then red and black flags were exchanged through all the train windows. That was your brother Jonny. You can imagine the astonishment of the International Brigade committee when this train full of members of the Brigade arrived in Barcelona with the black flags of anarchy! No *pasarán!* We will never forget him.

"And want you to know our wish: 'In memory of the anti-Fascist fighter for freedom in Spain.' "

At this point Sepp had to take his glasses out of their case. Why not simply: "In memory of the fighter for freedom"?

If he agreed, a contribution of six hundred francs.

Sepp had already twice been out to Schär the stonecutter's on Lager-Strasse to discuss a memorial. But he hadn't been able to make up his mind yet. In marble, the headstone would cost thirty-eight hundred francs, with only a cross, name, and date of birth and death. In Jura limestone, thirty-one hundred francs. And to add to this the long additional line about the fighter in Spain would almost certainly add another four hundred francs. "In memory of the fighter for freedom" would be cheaper. If at least the "anti-Fascist" could be left out. For a moment Sepp was reminded of Mr. Oltramare and the National Front, of the thirteen people who had been killed, back in 1932, and in the Waadt-länder Hall they had called him, Sepp, a "Fascist pig." For a second he saw himself hitting out at the Socialists with his blackjack outside the Schweizerhof ballroom. Tempi passati. "Anti-Fascist": today no one knew what that meant anyway.

He had told Schär: In three to four weeks. It was now more than four weeks. Sepp closed his eyes. Jonny's cheerful face, and Jonny saying, "Why don't you come along, Sepp? If those fellows win in Spain we'll soon have dictatorships everywhere. Do you want a dictatorship?" Hm. Jonny had learned upholstering and paperhanging; then, from 1931 on, he had been unemployed. Later he worked as an antiquarian in Zurich.

Sepp was familiar with the contents of the three letters from Jonny, having reread them every few months since Jonny's death. The first was dated November 18, 1936.

"Dear Sepp: On November 7 we were the first international regiment, the 'Edgar André,' to march into Madrid, the first combat unit divided into battalions and platoons. We marched from the station through the whole city, and the crowds cheered us with an enthusiasm that was quite embarrassing, seeing that after all we hadn't done anything yet. But for the Spanish, the appearance of the International Brigades represents a totally unexpected act of solidarity in their struggle against Fascism.

"We then took up a position in the Parque del Oeste and set to work right away digging trenches. But the very next day the Fascists launched an attack to capture the Puente de los Franceses, and the following day, two days ago, we also sustained heavy losses in the fighting for the Ciudad Universitaria. If only we had better weapons! These old British ones from the 1914–18 war aren't much good, and we have to devise makeshift hand grenades."

It was true that Sepp hadn't much liked what he later read and heard about Hitler and those camps; but Jonny as he was in those days, and his enthusiasm for all that Leftist stuff—no, Sepp was still in favor of a certain neatness and order. After all, hadn't Mr. Ulrich himself said, "A new order has to be established, Sepp, in this pigsty of Europe?" And when he came back from Berlin in 1936, he had said, "Fantastic, Sepp, the things those fellows over there in the Reich have achieved," and for his thirtieth birthday the boss had given Sepp a book, *The Heroes of the Alcázar*, about the Franco loyalists and their heroic battle for control of the surrounded fortress against the superior strength of the Red tide. So when Jonny returned home from Spain and came to see Sepp, Sepp had to hide the book from his own brother. They had then gone off to the back room of the Terminus bar, and Sepp knew there would be another row between them. At first he had just listened, and there was nothing wrong with Jonny's tales of the battles in Albacete and along the Ebro, with Jonny representing the Swiss, and, as Sepp was ready to believe, with a certain amount of honor.

But then he had started off again, as in his letters: "Anarchism, Sepp, is society without domination, it's the ultimate," and Jonny had seen it working in Spain, where villages, whole areas, were anarchist. "With no master: that's anarchy—it's the taking over of businesses and factories, it's self-administration by the workers, self-administration by the communes, Sepp, and the abolition of the power of capital, do you understand? The eyes of the Spaniards would light up," Jonny went on, "and they would say, 'Now there are no more señores and señoras, they are all compañeros and compañeras. '*La dulce anarquía*,' the Spaniards would say: the state is the instrument of power of the ruling class, it must be abolished," until Sepp finally said, "Well, surely there must be *some* kind of order?" And at the thought of the Franco loyalists of the Alcázar, he found he really sided more with Franco. Franco was at least, like Hitler and Mussolini, an instrument of Providence, and a Catholic. Why, after all, were the anarchists executed even by the Communists? Somehow Sepp became fed up with all that ranting, but Jonny wouldn't stop, which was how they came to have another row that very first evening.

Later Jonny was tried for having served in a foreign armed force and weakening the defensive power of the Swiss Army: seven months' confinement in a fortress at Savatan, in the Canton of Valais. From there he wrote Sepp that the goal of anarchism is freedom, but not merely personal freedom, rather the freedom of all united in solidarity. In the margin at the bottom Jonny wrote: "The defeat of the idea of proletarian-republican freedom in Spain is the disaster of my life. *Dulce anarquía!* Terrible how quickly the freedom of a people can be destroyed!"

That was in 1939, in December. But Sepp was still hoping, even after El Alamein, even after Stalingrad, for the final German victory; and sometimes, when Mr. Ulrich and he were driving about the countryside and they were both drunk and stopped at an inn in Kappel or Kestenholz, they would sing the Horst Wessel song. The few people at the other tables would merely look and say nothing: everyone knew that was Mr. Ulrich Winter, who otherwise had a good heart and often stood them a round of drinks, and even the innkeepers chose not to say much, it being Mr. Ulrich after all.

What Sepp really wanted was simply to write to those two, Emil and Hans: "I would like the following to be carved on Jonny's headstone: Antiquarian, then the years of his birth and death." "To the memory of the anti-Fascist fighter for freedom in Spain" was simply too much. And the questions people would ask! On the other hand, Emil and Hans really had been comrades-in-arms of Jonny's, and if Sepp agreed they were willing to contribute six hundred francs.

After all, since Stalingrad Sepp had had absolutely nothing more to do with politics.

For a few moments those little pigeon feathers whirled about in the dovecote again. Sepp waited until they were gone, then placed the letter in the box with Jonny's things. Maybe it would be best if he wrote a short letter tomorrow to Emil and Hans: "Your letter acknowledged with thanks. Will be glad to accept your offer made as brothers-in-arms. Would you agree to the following inscription: 'To the memory of the fighter for freedom'? That's simpler. And nicer, too."

Or perhaps another way: just let the whole business of the headstone rest for a few days?

Jammers, July 4, 1982

Dear Lis:

No, no disaster has befallen me. On the contrary: something wonderful has happened to me—your express letter has arrived, this time shortly before noon. Thank you so much! For everything you said. The sermon, together with your "Come," has caught me in a mood of expectation (though there are no real grounds for it) that the distance between me and what I am searching for is becoming smaller and smaller.

Nevertheless, I am now setting a limit to myself and to this search. I hereby solemnly vow to you—your outburst of rage still ringing in my ears!—that on Tuesday morning I will take the nine o'clock train to Avignon—come what may! Surely that's something? As you see, you and my longing for you have convinced me.

My decision does not alter the fact that I am still in this strange state. Even though this morning at 8:30 I plunged, or one might say fled, into my draft about the General, and even though physically I don't feel in the least ill, that vague fear is still there, and with it that—what shall I call it: feverish?—feeling. I am without doubt here in the present, in the Blue Room. But at the same time, over and over again, for seconds, minutes, often for an hour—yes, at the same time I am utterly and totally in the past. Have you ever experienced anything like that? Obviously the result of my numerous Argonaut journeys—desired and staged by myself—down through the decades into my childhood. Staged regression, I suppose it might be labeled. The amazing thing about it really is this simultaneity: the way it mixes and mingles so that one can no longer— at least not always—distinguish: am I there, or am I here? And that in turn means that the fears of the past are also once again present.

Late yesterday. After an evening with André, I returned to the house, which was already dark, and sat for a while in the armchair by the open window in the Paneled Room. Hardly had I sat down when, although I was there, in the present, I was simultaneously dancing, being whirled around by my laughing mother. She was holding my hands and skipping about the room with me. A little waltz on the radio set the tempo that I, of course, aged about four, was quite unable to translate into dance steps. Even so, I was blissful! In our high spirits we both laughed so hard we almost fell over. Had I ever known Mother to show such gaiety, such outright exuberance?

Our gaiety didn't last long. Suddenly, and already out of breath, Mother stopped. She took a few steps over to one of the south windows and looked down onto the driveway. Sure enough: through the music from the radio she must have heard Father's red Fiat. And at that very moment the laughter, the high spirits, the joy in her face, vanished. From one second to the next, her face had once again assumed the cool, controlled expression that restored the everyday normal reserve between the two of us. That was how I learned, on the side as it were, that dancing and high spirits were taboo.

But above all: there it was again, that abrupt change from happiness to threat. Didn't that also have to mean for me: being happy is taboo, since happiness was invariably followed by the punishment of strict reserve? Oh yes, that abrupt change, that turnabout in the atmosphere of the house, was familiar to me from a hundred other occasions. Later my fear of this went so far that in my morning prayers I never failed to ask God to preserve me all day long from any kind of happiness, so as to make sure it wouldn't occur to anyone in Heaven to send me the punishment that was bound to follow upon happiness.

And it was precisely that fear, that child's fear, that pervaded me as I sat downstairs in the armchair: me, whom until then I had assumed to be a more or less adult person of forty-four! I actually did experience that fear.

But to bring all this to a conclusion—or your accusation that I am deceiving you by this excessively intense preoccupation with my mother will receive new impetus: After that, I had to ask myself once again what had happened to it—that love of life, that warm, sensuous presence of my mother as I had experienced it in our merry little dance?

So enough of all that. I'll call you Saturday evening and let you know my arrival time in Cavaillon. Eight o'clock? If I can't get through to you, please try to reach Jammers one hour later.

The thought that in three days we'll be falling into each other's arms! Looking forward to it more than I can say,

Forever yours!

Your call just came. Your voice, and your joyful anticipation—thank you!

By the way, I'll bring along the draft of my work—completed for the time being—as well as some other things I've written: stories and outlines of stories I want to tell you, now that we'll have plenty of time together.

From Class to Class

"BUT DON'T FORGET," AUNT ESTHER WOULD OFTEN SAY, "DON'T FORGET the power of imagination!" *That* was what Thom must develop. The best way to do that: to every story he must imagine a different ending.

She leaned back and closed her eyes. Or she didn't close them: while her right eye remained closed, she kept her left eye, wide open and quizzical, fixed on Thom. Or she drew on her cigarillo, wound a ball of wool, or angrily crumpled up her *Figaro*, threw it on the floor beside the little table, and spoke or whispered one of her Aunt Esther sentences: "So is madness Fate? And if it is: *what*, Thom, did my brother Ludwig do to deserve that fate?" Thom knew that, in quarreling with Fate, she was quarreling with God. Although she liked to cite God, she was not—unlike Thom's mother, in fact unlike his father too—conspicuous by her religious fervor. True, she had the vicar of Saint Mary's bring Holy Communion to her every two weeks, usually Thursday, as she sat in her wheelchair, and over coffee and cake or sherry she would often chat for hours with the clerical gentleman about spiritual matters; but she preferred to keep the Holy Catholic Church at arm's length as an authority over her conscience. She was the only person in the house to subscribe to the wisdom that God helps only those who help themselves, and often she was bold enough to state, like her mother Helen, that a man's will is his paradise.

Yet she seldom lost the thread. "Is madness Fate? Is it, must it be"—and she would quote Lombroso—"the price the man of genius must pay for his genius—inescapably, Thom? But in that case," she would exclaim, "what happens to freedom? The freedom of decision, which, after all, is what endows the individual with dignity?" And she would raise her small, bony fist above the part in her silvery hair so that even Thom had to wince and wonder: What indeed? God, if asked at all, or in His place Fate, remained silent. Through the open window, Charlott and her friends could be heard teasing Thom's cousin Rolf when his croquet ball missed the little iron hoop again; and from high above the fir trees, the kite or the falcon trilled as if the very question about human free will were part of human illusion.

But Aunt Esther had not heard the mocking trill. Resuming her conventional tone, she said, "It is true, Thom, that life led your Uncle Ludwig also—I say, also—into the depths of unfulfilled passions. It was not given to him—that is, if we disregard Ludwig's brief liaison with the Baroness von Scarpatetti, a lady of spirit from Merano—it was not given to him to meet the woman who would have been the equal of his genius. Should he, as this relation by marriage who is your mother demanded, spend his life as a *célibataire*" (pronouncing the word the French way and ignoring Thom's question)? "Are we, you and I, Thom, to reproach him for looking for playmates, whether in Munich, Lucerne, or Milan—dancers, loose women, perhaps even streetwalkers? If people in this house assume to this day that the terrible sexual disease that so often leads to dementia was the cause of his madness, that it was God's punishment for a dissolute life, this could only be, if not the intention to destroy his reputation, a case of sheer stupidity, a mentality that is simply incapable of grasping the breadth and depth of Ludwig's genius." Where genius penetrated the most profound mysteries of matter—that was where danger lurked, that was where the discoverer, like a polar explorer, must accept the risk of being swallowed up and destroyed by the object of his scientific obsession. Thom saw Uncle Ludwig striding through the storms and blizzards of polar nights, across frozen crevasses as he approached the Pole, and like an Amundsen, a Fridtjof Nansen, or a Scott, disappearing in the primordial mists illuminated by Northern Lights.

Or he saw him, heard him, in his dementia, having his presidential couch erected up there in the gallery—four covered mattresses in a big oblong. Sepp had placed slats under them and enclosed them in a wooden frame. From the four corners, tall bedposts reached up to support the deep blue canopy that Frieda, following Uncle Ludwig's instructions, had sewn, and Uncle Ludwig had personally fastened the white plumes to the top of each post.

Thom had not been present when the change in Uncle Ludwig took place. It was not until two weeks after it happened that he returned home, in mid-August 1945, from a vacation spent, when he was seven, with his godmother Aunt Elsa in Mümlis.

Now that Aunt Esther was talking about it, seven or eight years later, he remembered Uncle Ludwig's voice and, as he walked up the driveway carrying his suitcase, Uncle Ludwig himself, standing in the open second-floor window above the front door, wearing the gold-embroidered vestment of his great-great-uncle Aloys the provost, and gesticulating across the steps and beyond the park down toward the town's sea of roofs. Then, as Thom came to a halt, it dawned on him that Uncle Ludwig, as the President of the United States of Europe, was addressing his people.

"You remember, Thom," said Aunt Esther, "Hiroshima."

City in Japan, on the island of Hondo, population 460,000: Thom remembered. University, textile industry. On August 6, 1945, was hit by the first atomic bomb, dropped from an American bomber. 260,000 dead, 163,000 injured and missing. A 20-KT-type bomb.

Thom thought of the power of imagination he was supposed to test. "Might it be possible," he asked, "that Uncle Ludwig, while believing himself to have invented the atom bomb, in actual fact did not—might that be possible?"

Aunt Esther asked him not to use such stilted language. "Besides, we haven't nearly reached that point yet. On that August 6, 1945, we were about to gather around the supper table; even your father was already rising from his armchair." And she proceeded to tell Thom what he had already been told by her, by Charlott, and several times by Herminia; yet again, again, he wanted to hear how Uncle Ludwig, beaming from ear to ear, had stood in the door to the Paneled Room. And how he had looked at them all, and amazed at the world, the Americans, and himself, had murmured, "We have won!" But by "winning," he meant not so much the imminent capitulation of the military might of Japan; with that "we" he meant himself, and also with that "have won." As at least Aunt Esther had known for a long time, during the war years Uncle Ludwig had not only been engaged in the invention of weapons for the tactical battlefield, having considerably increased the firepower of the machine gun and the effective lethal radius of the offensive gas hand grenade: based on Niels Bohr's atom model of 1930, his inventive genius had revolved increasingly around a practical application of the explosive liberation of energy by splitting the atom.

"It was your Uncle Ludwig, Thom, who, as early as 1941 and in complete secrecy, was the first scientist in the world to discover the formula for the atom bomb and—theoretically—develop it to the stage of potential serial production.

"Needless to say, he knew he was strictly committed to the principle of neutrality as proclaimed by our Swiss state. So in December 1941 he called upon the ambassadors of the warring parties in Bern and personally handed each of them, in exchange for a receipt, a copy of his invention, bearing the code name 'Morning Star,' to be conveyed to the governments of the German Reich, Italy, the United States, and France. In the accompanying letter"—Aunt Esther smiled modestly—"of which I typed four copies with my own hands while preserving the utmost confidentiality, he pointed out that the contents of his paper were crucial to the outcome of the war. In this way he gave each of the combatants the same opportunity—not, mind you, without adding that a patent had been applied for at the appropriate office, and that simultaneously a sealed copy was being conveyed via the Swedish Embassy to the Royal Swedish Academy in Stockholm in return for written assurance that the seal would be broken only on receipt of his handwritten request: in the case of his death, his sister Esther Winter would represent him. Those were his precautions. Although each of the combatants now had an opportunity to utilize the epoch-making invention, the inventor's intellectual and material claims remained protected. By this means too, the Stockholm Academy was being given an opportunity eventually to award the inventor its Nobel Prize for physics. 'Eventually' meant as soon as the bomb, as predicted by Uncle Ludwig, had ended the war and simultaneously prevented any future war.

"You know, Thom, how your Uncle Ludwig waited, waited calmly in the knowledge of having entrusted his invention to men of honor in four nations. He never doubted that his fully fledged theory would lead to worldwide success at the hands of natural scientists and technologists like himself. He knew they were at work, racing against each other, against time and the war. Which of them would be the first secretly to detonate the test bomb? Which—the German Reich or the United States—would end the war in Europe with the first atom bomb? As you know, in the absence of my brother's help the war was carried on until the collapse of Germany, continuing only in the Far East against Japan. My brother had become very quiet. You remember? Had he been hoping in vain? Telephone calls from Rome and Berlin were no longer to be expected."

Aunt Esther fell silent. The first pools of the night, seeping in through the window, spread across the carpet. "He waited. No wonder he was now spending a lot of time beside the radio.

"And then, on August 6, 1945, that news. A city in Japan had been virtually wiped out. Ludwig's face shone with happiness over this triumph, so long and so ardently desired. You can imagine how the glasses were soon being gaily clinked across the table. Only your mother withdrew into a piqued silence, and soon went upstairs to the Blue Room. My brother sparkled with wit, telling amusing stories about inventors—about one of his correspondents, for instance, who had invented a helium-borne airship but had forgotten to apply for a patent; the news of the maiden flight of the *Graf Zeppelin* prompted him to throw himself off the tower of the minster"—she laughed—"of Bern Minster! At Ludwig's suggestion we also observed a minute's silence to honor the poor victims of Hiroshima—hasn't history always shown that the blood toll of the few is the price to be paid for the liberation of the many? Now blind Fate had chosen them. To them above all, Ludwig said, was due the gratitude of all those liberated from the scourge of war.

"You must," Aunt Esther went on, "understand our mood of elation. We had all observed my brother's patience, his waiting, his withdrawal into silence over the years. And on that memorable evening we couldn't know how much disappointment was in store for your Uncle Ludwig in the weeks to come.

"To be brief!" Aunt Esther exclaimed. "That very same night Uncle Ludwig wrote his letters, and two or three days later he dispatched telegrams to the White House in Washington. After that he began his attempts to speak to President Truman personally on the telephone. To no avail. Then one afternoon a few days later he came home from the post office in a mellow mood." While Aunt Esther suddenly dabbed with her handkerchief at her tears of emotion, Thom could imagine his uncle walking out to the tea party around the stone table and announcing, in High German on this occasion, that he had been awarded the Nobel Prize for physics. A friend had telephoned him from Stockholm. The family's delight was shared by the guests, among whom were Dr. and Mrs. Muralt, Father Zemp, and the relatives from Como.

Aunt Esther sobbed quietly. "I was happy, believe me, Thom: blissful! All the more terrible was the shock I suffered when the next day my brother—I was coming into the hall after breakfast—when he stood up there at the gallery balustrade making a speech to the peoples of the

United States of Europe. He was arrayed, as I noticed on my way up the stairs, in the brocade vestment of Uncle Aloys of blessed memory, the provost, that was always kept in the black attic closet. As soon as I saw the light in his eyes, I knew this wasn't some prank. When he finished his speech, he came up to me, kissed my hand, addressed me as 'Queen Mother,' and promised to call on me that afternoon so we might discuss certain pending matters. He needed my advice, he said. As for the rest," Aunt Esther sobbed, "you know that."

No, she was no longer prepared to test the power of Thom's imagination with him. And he had been so looking forward to telling her how differently the story might have turned out. Aunt Esther needed to relax now. But even while Thom was tiptoeing out of the room, past Frieda sitting by the window with her embroidery frame, his mind was still full of what his aunt had called "the rest." The sight of Uncle Ludwig, as Thom walked up the drive with his suitcase, standing up there at the window, arrayed in that vestment and addressing his peoples in a loud voice; or the next day, still wearing that vestment, reclining under the canopy on his presidential couch in the gallery, propped up with a few cushions, and dictating to his secretary at breakneck speed letter after letter to Pope Pius XII, to Stalin, to Churchill and a queen mother. Beside him was the little red telephone that had been given to Gret and Thom years before as a toy. Battery-powered, it rang if you pressed the button. It often rang now. Then Uncle Ludwig's voice was to be heard answering it with "Winter, Nobel Prize laureate, speaking," or simply, "This is the President." In order to prevent his brother from continuing to address his peoples twice a day, Thom's father told Sepp to wire shut the bolts of the second-floor windows, the ones overlooking the grounds and the town.

And this too, as Thom left the room, was vivid in his mind: the cries for help coming one night from Uncle Ludwig's room at the end of the upper corridor, next to the salon—cries that turned into screams. The whole family, including the servants, gathered in alarm in the gallery, the grownups in their dressing gowns or bathrobes. When Father opened the door, his brother leaped at him, clutched him tight; on and on he screamed, stammering and sobbing. "The Japs! They're coming!" Gret explained to Thom that Uncle Ludwig meant the Japanese: There must be thousands of them invading the town, little figures pouring into the grounds and through the house, even climbing up the façade outside and swarming into Uncle Ludwig's room. Led by men with harakiri swords who surrounded the bed of the Nobel laureate and inventor of the atom bomb; behind them the women, the old men, the children, two hundred sixty thousand of them, from Hiroshima. Dr. Muralt, summed by telephone at two A.M., gave Uncle Ludwig some injections that made him sleep until late in the day.

But the following night the terrible screams of the great genius again echoed through the house. Father's idea, supported by Dr. Muralt, at first prevailed over Mother's suggestion that Uncle Ludwig be placed in a mental hospital, and Father ordered some panels of steel bars to be made at the plant. Around eight P.M. Mr. Wenger drove up in a truck, and he and two men from the foundry carried the four panels, each three by two meters, up to Uncle Ludwig's room and placed them around the bed. A fifth item, an oblong grille, was laid as additional protection over the top of the panels, one of which contained a door also consisting of steel bars. Although the whole thing looked exactly like a cage, it was meant rather as a protection. Now the president could retire to bed; the door could be locked only from the inside. In this way he felt protected from his Oriental avengers.

So Uncle Ludwig, sedated as he was by tranquilizers, could spend his nights asleep.

However, it was not long before he began to refuse to leave the protection of the steel bars. His presidential couch in the gallery remained unoccupied even during the day. But he continued to talk on the phone to the White House, to his friend Harry, as by this time he was calling his fellow statesman Truman. And when Herminia got tired of bringing him his tea, his port wine, and his three meals a day, and so far forgot herself as to tell him that in her opinion it was time he stopped these antics, he coolly replied that complaints were to be submitted, in writing, to the chief of the presidential office. He no longer left the protected area. Sometimes, when Herminia or his mother went up to see him— Mother always planning to persuade him to ask to be sent to the hospital in Basel—Thom watched from the half-open door as his uncle, robed in his vestment and seated behind the steel bars, dictated letters to the empty chair beyond the bars.

Two or three more weeks, and the time had come. Two orderlies arrived to take Uncle Ludwig away in the black limousine that Thom recognized. Holding his grizzled head erect, waving at the crowds, he proceeded slowly down the stone steps in his brocade vestment—Ludwig Winter, Nobel Prize laureate and president, escorted by his bodyguards.

The General's Politics VIII

THE SUMMARY MUST CLEARLY SET FORTH:

There can be no doubt that in the virtually hopeless military and political situation existing between August 1939 and mid-1944, General Guisan did his utmost to fulfill his mandate to the extent that this was possible.

To characterize his politics on the basis of his three outstanding actions—the secret agreement with France, the Rütli address, and the Alpine redoubt—the following must be noted:

(a) With the secret agreement (1) he overstepped his authority; (2) by violating the principle of neutrality, he gave the government of the Third Reich a pretext for attacking Switzerland (and an opportunity to march through it toward central and southern France); and (3) he accepted the possibility of a French military occupation of large parts of Switzerland, leading, in the event of a German attack, to military and political chaos. All three factors are negative. In mitigation it may be noted that the mandate given the General by parliament and government was imprecisely formulated in terms of neutrality and alliance policy.

(b) With both the Rütli address and the concept of the Alpine redoubt, Guisan demonstrated a remarkable talent for staging community spirit and the will to self-preservation. He was able to mobilize the army and the population for his objective of "total" resistance consistent with his mandate. When the democratically elected government signaled an adjustment to the "new order" in Europe, or at least was vacillating, his decisions put it under pressure. Even those who, thinking in the patriotic context of those times, are prepared to support the idea of resistance through conventional warfare of army against army, must recognize elements of a coup in the way the General implemented his concept in the face of the government's attitude. What would probably have been inevitable in extremis had already taken place in anticipation: the priority of military over civil power.

(Marginal note: Given that I am confining myself to a perspective of constitutional law, how can I deal with my own conflict? I will do my best to understand my subject in its historical context; moreover, had I been an adult during the forties, I imagine I would have had no trouble being a patriotic supporter of the doctrine of total resistance. But 1982:

Military? Army? Soldierly ideals? Heroic resistance to the last man? Thinking from the viewpoint of national states? These terms have become alien, dubious, to me. Faced with seventeenfold atomic overkill, I can only plead for radical disarmament of that entire arsenal, real and conceptual. Once again: I must at least make clear that I am working with this fundamental reservation.)

(c) The concept of the Alpine redoubt, apart from the effect mentioned under (b), is evidence of political action that has detached itself from the actual situation and entered the realm of cloud-cuckoo-land. There is much to be said for the theory that this concept was the fruit of a military mentality created in the hothouse climate of a supreme command, a climate insulated for years from everyday reality. What this mentality brought forth as a decision was a stage manager's directions—utterly devoid of any relationship to contradictory reality—for an opera; the staging of a work of art, performed with real-life actors in an extremely realistic setting of rocks, eternal snow, and glaciers. It celebrated the heroic military spirit in honor solely of itself.

The bitter, indeed somewhat ironic circumstance that in the last analysis made this performance possible—Nazi Germany's willingness to provide it with the necessary raw-material basis—was deliberately disregarded, it being essential to the grand gesture of resistance to that self-same Germany.

Military historians agree that within a few days two-thirds of the poorly defended territory, including the men, women, and children, would have been overrun by generals à la Guderian, Rommel, etc., and their armored units. But what about the fortress constructed in those remote regions of snow and ice? Would it have withstood an assault? The General knew there was no victory to be won there. And he also knew with certainty: A war for the Alpine redoubt, estimated to last a year, would have cost the lives of approximately 500,000 soldiers on both sides. But he must also have known that a German export ban would have been enough for the redoubt eventually to fall into the hands of Nazi leaders without a struggle; and it is certain that a military siege would have forced the General and the Swiss Army either to starve to death or to capitulate from exhaustion.

In other words: It may be assumed that, although General Henri Guisan saw the obvious weaknesses of his concept, he chose to disregard them, as suggested under (c).

Or: he deliberately underestimated those weaknesses and overestimated the effect of the mobilization as well as the potential deterrent effect. In that case, one must conclude, he was betting—quite recklessly—on a self-perpetuating and electrifying Nibelung spirit of manly valor that blossoms in the very knowledge of being destined for a bloodbath and death. In this he would have proved himself, psychologically at least, to be a shrewd strategist.

In the final analysis, what he "preserved" and "maintained" was the idea of a Switzerland that would have endured as long as there was a single living soldier to carry the flag with the white cross on a blood-red field across the icy wastes of the Alpine wall.

That's how it may have been. Thom will have spent that afternoon in early July in a state of growing restlessness—the kind we experience when we sense that we are at last close to tracking down a long-forgotten, long-sought word. While Herminia was muttering away in the kitchen next door, he will have read the day's news over breakfast in the pantry. Perhaps he had already walked twice around the house in an early-morning light— misty, whitish—that held little promise. Probably too it was now— now?—that the front-door bell had rung, and Frieda with her worried look had announced that two men with a pole were outside. Thom had not reacted to the news.

However, the noise must have prompted him to go out into the hall. In the door to the kitchen, he paused. The two men, identifiable as carpenters by the folding rule each had in a thigh pocket, were busy jamming what Frieda had called a pole at an angle under the beam that supported the gallery—a post with the diameter of a telephone pole. With the blunt edge of an axe, one of the two men was driving the foot of the post, blow by blow, along the tiled floor toward the staircase until the post, when measured with a spirit level, was exactly perpendicular.

As the two men stepped back, Thom walked over to the post and touched the light raw wood. Just for something to say, he asked, "Maple?"

One of the men laughed; the other shook his head. "I bet you're not in the lumber business!" Now they were both laughing. The order was for oak. A waste of good wood. That"—he pointed at the post—"will still be standing long after the roof has collapsed and killed everyone in the house." Touching their nonexistent caps, they left.

Thom gazed at the fine coffered ceiling. Mentally he corrected:

"after the roof will have collapsed and killed everyone in the house."
Now that his eyes had become accustomed to the dim light in the hall,
he saw the cobwebs, gray with dust, hanging in the coffers that had once
been painted red.

From the hall closet Thom took one of the brooms and the dustpan.
While he was cleaning the coffers, starting from the far corner, he muttered phrases like: "Does everything really have to go to wrack and ruin
here? What a filthy mess! No one left? No one responsible any longer?"
But suddenly, quite loudly: "Goddammit!" A fat garden spider had let
itself down onto his bare forearm and was running up onto the back of
the hand that held the broom. He stared at it, petrified with fright, dropped the broom, slapped his hand against his thigh. The spider scuttled
across the red tiles toward the rear glass door and disappeared. The sweat
on his forehead made Thom suddenly aware of the chill in the hall.

Or did he really have a fever? He swept the few cobwebs he had
dislodged into the dustpan and carried the disgusting little pile to the
garbage pail in the closet under the sink. No, he had no wish for the job
of cleaning up this house.

Nevertheless, that restlessness. He must do something. He was aware
of the enormous effort it was to concentrate on a single thought. Hadn't
he felt like that once before? Restlessness, even in his limbs, as if he had
drunk ten cups of coffee in quick succession. For a second or two the
thought flared up in him like a warning signal: Is this how a bout of
psychosis begins? Maybe he should look for some shorts and running
shoes upstairs in Samuel's room and go for a long run through the woods
above the grounds.

Full of determination, he went up the stairs, entered the library,
and immediately started in on the heap of files and bundles of letters.
He would stack the personal and family papers under the rear window
and the business papers under the front window beside the radiator. After
that preliminary sorting would come the arranging of all these papers,
these contracts and letters, according to the people they had belonged to
or who might have written them; after that, the sorting according to years,
decades, and categories. Uncle Ludwig's writings, topped by his manu-
script "The Machine," would be stacked in front of one of the glass
cabinets, over to the right. He would collect what seemed to be very few
letters in his mother's or father's handwriting and put them on the round
table, where they would be ready for him to read.

For maybe an hour he stooped, knelt, peered at some of the documents, turned pages, formed little piles beside him, stood up, carried them over here, carried them over there; yes, this work, which was gradually becoming physically tiring too, did him good. He also made a separate pile of the numerous random photographs, which he intended to sort and carefully scrutinize. He was constantly tempted to linger over some of the papers. But first get them into some kind of order; for the time being that was more important.

Opening the largest of the tied boxes, he found it filled with mostly black-bordered letters—letters of condolence on Father's death, as well as telegrams, addressed to Mrs. Lilly Winter. Squatting on his heels, he slowly turned over the letters, looking only at the handwriting—Aunt Bertha; Councillor Obrecht; Othmar Spenger, foundryman; Machine Tool Factory Sulzer, Winterthur; Reinhardt, president of the administrative council—on and on.

Still squatting, Thom turned his head toward the door. He was right: there stood Gret.

Again wearing Mother's turquoise-blue housecoat with the white embroidered flowers. With Frieda's help she must have altered and widened it by half a width of material so it could encompass the whole of her ample matronly body. They looked at each other. At last Thom, trying to smile, managed to say, "Gret—what is it?"

Gret remained silent. From town came the sound of the bell from Saint Mary's: Thom counted eleven strokes. That pair of blue-brown eyes—and now it suddenly came back to Thom, the whole solemn scene at the cemetery, the open grave before him, Father's grave, the flowers, the wreaths, the hundreds of people in black. Across from Thom stood his mother, with Charlott beside her. Gret's eyes, that was the look, the look he recognized, directed at him across the open grave by his mother— now, across thirty years, in these five or seven seconds in the library while Thom and Gret looked at each other and Thom stood up, feeling Gret's eyes on him as he did so, and looked at Gret again. Why was Gret looking at him like that: Gret—or his mother across the years? "What is it?"

In a trembling voice, the chairman of the Swiss Industrial Association, standing at the graveside, paid tribute to the deceased and his good works, concluding with the words that it was up to all of them, the survivors, to carry on the work of the prematurely departed, all of them, and to support the heir—with a glance at Thom—the sole male descendant, should he one day follow worthily in the footsteps, etcetera. Thom had felt his mother beside him clasp his wrist and, without moving, press it hard as if she too wanted to imbue him with courage and enterprise. Again the priest blessed the grave, recited prayers. The coffin, held by two ropes, had been slowly lowered, ashes to ashes, dust to dust, and once again the priest had swung the censer over the grave; the silver whisk had sprinkled holy water over the grave, then walked to the far side, where, with her hand, as if stroking a wisp of hair back from her forehead, she lifted the black veil up over her eyes onto her hair. So now, from across the grave, that look. That moment.

Never before had Thom been struck, as now in the library, by the resemblance of Gret's eyes, just her eyes, with those of their mother. A quite ridiculous resemblance between the otherwise so markedly differing features—ridiculous, as if over the decades Mother's eyes had strayed into the now plump face with the dark, brown-tinged complexion of the alcoholic. Was there a smile passing over it? Thom couldn't have told either what he had been able to read in his mother's look across the grave or his own feelings as he had perceived them at the time. For six or seven seconds—what had the eyes wanted to tell him? And Thom: had he loved her, his mother? Had he still felt rejected by her and banished to his Isle of Aulis? And hated and loved and hated her, also because, in her elegant widow's weeds, she had been beautiful and almost a stranger? His queen, who yet had constantly disappointed him, chained him to herself, and apparently not been prepared to be his queen? Had he desired her? Was that why suddenly a wave of heat mounted to his cheeks, his forehead? Yes, again—ridiculous, at least as remembered now in these few seconds in the library: a queen? Nothing more than the daughter of a nouveau-riche comb baron who had eventually ended up in bankruptcy; a woman who, with her purity cult and her perhaps not altogether abstruse idea of a woman's independence and self-assertion, had tried repeatedly to transcend the limits set her by her class and—as André said—the phallocentric male half of the bourgeoisie.

No, of course not. At the time he had merely sensed, not known. True, she could send signals of love: for instance, when she would suddenly move close beside or behind him and briefly put her hand on his shoulder or, almost shyly, stroke the dark-blond hair back from his forehead. At the same time—and this too he began to suspect at the age of twelve or fourteen—she would try to draw him into her perpetual conflict with Father. Had that also flashed through his mind and soul at the graveside? For it had been she, not Father, who had considered him underdeveloped for his age; now the time had come for a tough training for his body too, and she had actually driven with Mr. Wenger in a company van, with Thom beside her on the front seat, to the Loosil sporting goods store, the principal one in town, and picked up the things she had ordered: gym equipment, a leather vaulting buck on four tall, adjustable legs, also some boxing gloves, a heavy leather punching bag, and two thick green mats. The buck was then set up on one of the mats on the rear terrace; to the right, in front of the window with the colored bottle-glass panes, the bag hung from the ceiling down to Thom's chest level, a partner for future boxing proficiency. For the first three weeks the young athletic coach Saladin was engaged; after that Mother, wearing a divided skirt, a light sweater, and gym shoes, personally took charge of the summer fitness program.

The coach had begun by emphasizing the value of gymnastics—hip bends, with and without twists, jumping on the spot, skipping rope, breathing exercises with arms raised, also such activities as eighty-meter sprints. With an almost sensual pleasure Thom learned to fly lengthwise, bent forward and legs straddled, over the buck and land, feet brought lightly forward, on the soft mat. When Mother took charge of the lessons, Thom discovered that her understanding of physical improvement was different from the coach's. As before, the lesson began at six A.M. sharp; now too, they started off with hip bends, twice to the left touching the toes of his gym shoes with his fingertips, twice swinging his arms up over his head, then twice—five six!—touching his toes to the right. But his mother didn't count a mere twelve times through the exercise, nor a mere twenty times—one two three four!—now he was ordered to do it fifty times and soon sixty, with the added command, "Faster, Thom, faster! Grit your teeth!"

When it came to boxing, Saladin had been concerned mainly with fancy footwork, with the correct positioning of the forearms in front of the face and the lightning punch from right or left from behind the cover, but what counted for Mother was the attack, the powerful direct blow. Once she gave the punching bag a push, but too violently, at the same time ordering Thom to advance and attack the bag as it swung back. "Hit it, knock it out!" Her command "Now!" came too early. Thom reached the two-hundred-pound bag when it was only halfway along its pendulum swing. Before he could put the heavy gloves up to his face, he and the swinging opponent collided. Thom, struck in the face and chest, was sent flying. It was a few seconds before he realized that he was lying on his back, dazed and in great pain. "Get up!" Mother's command sounded unmoved. "You're not going to give up, are you?" Staggering around, Thom had carried on under her eyes and orders for the remaining half hour until, streaming with sweat, his arms and legs leaden, he lurched over to the bench by the wall where he sat, bent double, gasping for air. When he looked up—"What's the matter, Thom? If you want to become an officer like your father . . ."—Mother was already standing by the door to the house. She gave him another brief glance, then left him to his own devices. There on the bench, and as he walked over to the well by the washhouse, it occurred to him for the first time that his mother's objective went beyond Thom and his physical improvement.

She is training me for a purpose.

The words suddenly appeared as if imprinted on his groping thoughts. What was going on? Whad did his mother intend to do with him?

Had it been like that? It could have, it must have, been like that. A week later Thom suddenly had the answer—a week later, just a few days before Father's death. Again in the chilly morning air, Mother in her white sweater, and the program called for vaulting over the buck. But now it was no longer a matter of an ecstatic straddle vault. The buck stood there in front of the mat, its legs adjusted so that it was higher than eye level. Thom was to take a running dive over the buck, as if over a horse's back, in such a way that he would roll over and up onto his feet on the far side.

At his mother's command, he took off. Yes, he was scared. He managed a powerful leap into the air and, arms outstretched in front of him, to fly over the buck and pull in his head before landing so he would be able to roll onto the mat in a somersault, but the somersault came too late. Instead of rolling up in a ball from which he could unroll onto his feet, Thom landed full length on his back. He lay there panting— no, gasping for air. For a few seconds he was sailing under water through a landscape of giant ferns. He called for help but knew that no sound issued from his lips. Then, vaguely, he saw his mother, there beside him, half crouching, pulling him up. As he sat, he let himself fall against her shoulder. Still no air; at last a searing intake of breath. Thom gasped, yet he could hear her, hear her low voice: "Silly boy—I said 'roll over!' " Then, as if to herself: "Why did I bring this son into the world—I *need* him—d'you hear?" Her arm was around his shoulder, shaking him. "I *need* you!"

Later, when Thom lay on his bed upstairs in his room, Mother brought him some tea with her own hands and pulled up the quilt before leaving the room. The words flared up in his mind again like an illuminated sign. Yes, she needed him. She was training him, no doubt for his own good, so that one day he could hold his own in battle in that male world he would soon be entering. But there was something else, yes, something else: she was training him to be her comrade-in-arms— or even the one who would someday avenge the injustice she had suffered from Father?

When he awoke—maybe an hour, maybe a day had passed—it was to find her face leaning over him, close to him, her eyes with the heavy lids. In that pensive gaze lay—well, what, actually? Pity? Anxiety? Doubt? And the question: Will you ever manage it—to be my bodyguard and if necessary my avenger, against him, against *him?* She was wearing the housecoat with the faint sheen on the greenish-blue background and the flower pattern.

So there was her gaze, those bluish-brown eyes looking at him in the library, Gret leaning against the doorpost, neither of them speaking: that was Mother's gaze as she leaned over him in his bedroom; and it was Mother's gaze directed at him across the open grave for a few seconds while the heat mounted in Thom's cheeks—an unfathomable gaze, anxiety, doubt

Thom gave a start, suddenly aware that the eyes of all those many people around him and around the open grave, including the eyes of the priest, were staring at him. He realized it was his turn; they were all waiting for him—the sole male descendant of our esteemed departed Ulrich Winter—to stand at the end of the grave and, the first after Mother, sprinkle holy water over the grave and the coffin—oh God, of course, the ritual required that. Mother's eyes were no longer there. As he stood facing the grave and, with a trembling hand, at last doing his duty, Thom heard the loud singing of the male choir behind him

and Gret—scarcely seven seconds could have passed—said from the door, "We two can't bring her to life again. What happened in the past, Thom, leave it in the past." She inhaled deeply, exhaled sharply. "All we can do is accept it, finally accept it, as part of ourselves—or," and her voice was bitter, "as our shadow."

She had lain awake half the night, she told him, in her mind's eye seeing him restlessly poking around, day after day. She couldn't take it any more, she felt. Even though she tried to shut out the sound of his footsteps wandering about the house and coming from the garden through the window—it was no use.

"What are you still digging for? The causes? And how it happened? Do you believe that everything can be explained? Somewhere there is the inexplicable in what we do—even you have to accept that, dear brother. Isn't that so?"

That was how it must or may have been, and Thom said, "For the causes, yes. I'm digging around here in search of the truth. If I don't find it, how am I to accept it all as part of ourselves, as a shadow? Who was it? Gret?"

She wasn't listening. She left.

Time
of the
Mirror

By this time, not much imagination is needed to picture Thom Winter roaming, still driven aimlessly—or so it seemed—through the much too large, dilapidated, and silently decaying house, opening a door here, turning a key there. Or is he once again sitting in the Blue Room over his notes on the stories of bygone days? Or the notes for his work? The breathless heat in the open window. Or a gust of wind suddenly blowing a window open and shut and open again—one of those squalls that come down in the evening from the sunlit Jura to set the scene for the end of a day or whatever else. Whatever story.

Or to set free a word containing the core of Thom's question, of his story and its outcome.

Hadn't Thom long since visited all the locked rooms in the house? The vaulted cellars, the salon on the second floor, the adjoining rooms? They were mostly empty; or swathed and bulging mattresses and dismantled bedsteads stood propped against the walls, and the light bulbs had long ago been removed from the broken sockets of the lamps and chandeliers. On the parquet floors among swollen wood blocks the rings of dried-up puddles; tattered wallpaper hung in loose strips from the walls; closet doors had split lengthwise and across from the harsh alternation of cold and heat; the gray-white dust covers were draped in mournful festoons between the now purposeless furniture they were supposed to protect from decay. Hadn't he opened up these rooms, from which all life, except for woodlice, woodworms, and spiders, fungus, and swarming microbes, had long vanished—opened them up, one after another, wandered through them, looked around them, and locked them up again?

Now, as he stood outside the locked door across from the Paneled Room, he recalled that quaint word "smoking-room," as they used to refer to it. The key was not in the lock.

Thom crossed the corridor to the sideboard under the Holy Family. Gret kept the keys in the left-hand top drawer. The Paneled Room and the study were, he remembered, the only rooms fitted with those elaborate brass locks, so he must look for a brass key. Thom unlocked the door. The drapes of one of the windows were drawn back.

No dust covers here. Everything seemed to be shining in former splendor: on the right, by the big bookcase, stood Father's massive desk. Over by the tall fireplace, the two little smoking tables, as well as the three dark-leather armchairs, the fourth, as always, against the wall. On the right of the fireplace General Wille looked down from World War I; on the left, General Guisan from World War II. Thom walked a few steps into the room: even the fine old Afghan rug with its red-and-blue patterns glowed as if Frieda or a maid had only yesterday carefully brushed the dust from its fibers. The wide gilt frame of the mirror on the wall above the dark, marble-topped cabinet used as a bar—everything, including glass and marble, seemed newly polished; the reddish wood of the furniture looked as if someone had that very morning gently rubbed linseed oil into the grain. Even the heavy drapes with their richly embroidered valances, even the stucco design of the ceiling and the five-branched chandelier—all intact. Splendid: that was the word for the study, only that the air no longer smelled of Father, of cigars, of the card players by the fireplace; it was slightly stuffy, as in the other uninhabited rooms in the house.

Thom sat down to the right of the fireplace, lifting and turning the armchair slightly so that he sat facing one of the three windows whose drapes were still drawn shut; Father's desk was behind him. Now, by turning his head to the left, he could see—indistinctly in the dim light—the three large paintings on the east wall beside the door: there they still hung, still a little too high, the three great personages of the Winter clan, the three entrepreneurs and personalities of public life, Theophil, Elsazar, and Ulrich, each in an unmistakable posture of power—at least that was how their portraitists, they themselves, and their era had wanted them to look: powerful pioneers gazing fearlessly out of their oval frames into the future, into progress. Men. Masters. There were no portraits of women in the study, if Thom disregarded the bronze beauty whose body—half nymph, half liberty, modestly veiled—reached up from the nearest of the two smoking tables toward the light she was holding aloft in the form of a two-branched candelabra.

Once again Thom was conscious of that restlessness in his limbs. He lit a cigarette. Even the two brass ashtrays shone as if just polished. Thom got up, walked over to the drapes, and groped for the cord. As he pulled, the drapes parted. Just as he was about to open the window, he saw Gret coming up the driveway with Urs. There was no mistaking: Gret was swaying slightly, her free right hand gesticulating in the air. Urs was leading or at least supporting his mother. As they reached the steps, Gret placed her arm around Urs's shoulder, and thus they walked up, step by step.

When Thom returned to his armchair he could see through the uncurtained window that the light was turning rosy; the sun must have already gone down. The brightness from the evening sky over the Jura was still shining on the shifting leaves of the single branch of the hickory oak that hung down outside the window. What he could hear was Gret and Urs coming through the front door and the porch into the passage. Gret was singing in a soft, high voice, singing, "Once again the roses bloom—ro-o-ses red."

Gret! The haunting thought drifted through Thom's mind.

He closed his eyes. While a no! was still forming in him he saw himself—again, again!—at the sick woman's bedside, looking across the bed straight into his sister's face. Gret stood up and asked him to lift their mother's head so she could push a fresh pillow under it. Thom bent over his mother and carefully raised her head, and again those eyes looked up at him for a few seconds with that mysterious gaze. Gret put the discarded pillow on the quilt between herself and Thom. Yes, and at that moment he had left the room—hadn't he? Left to go to his own room? Hadn't he seen Aunt Esther with her impassive face as he walked toward the door? She had merely stared past him at her sister-in-law. Again the image slid away, the image of Gret lifting the pillow from the quilt under Mother's chin, lifting it and—

No. No! Gret as the culprit—surely the thought, no matter how persuasive, was absurd. He stood up, walked a few steps on the carpet, stopped, tried once again to visualize the sequence. Again it slid away, and only by a great effort could he say under his breath: But that would be—matricide!

He walked over to the bronze figure and pressed the knob. One of the two bulbs under the parchment shade gave a bright light. He smoked another cigarette, sitting for quite a long time in the armchair, leaning his head back, his eyes closed.

As he stubbed out his cigarette he saw dusk falling beyond the window. He could feel a sudden slight trembling in both arms. The light in the leaves of the hickory oak had vanished. The dusky air grew darker. Yes, he was trembling: was that the answer—Gret?

As if to avoid having to explore still further within himself what had happened that evening twenty years ago up there in the Blue Room, he tried to take in through the window every detail of this transition from darkening day into night. As if to gain a last reprieve for himself by intense observation. Suddenly he saw the bright lamp in the windowpane. And when he crossed one leg over the knee of the other and leaned a little to the right in his chair, he noticed the movement of a pale patch reflected in the windowpane.

He closed his eyes. Now, all of a sudden, he felt he could visualize himself leaning over his mother, her head gently cupped in his hands as he waited for Gret to change the pillow. He carefully let his mother's head sink back onto the fresh pillow, then sat down, again facing Gret on the other side of the bed. She too had sat down. She was looking across at him.

And while Thomas Winter observed the patch under the lamp in the windowpane turning more and more clearly into his own face, he was slowly—at the same time as Gret—reaching out his hand. Simultaneously, always simultaneously, with his sister's hand he felt for and grasped the pillow on the quilt between them. They were looking above the pillow into each other's eyes. They did not look down as their hands raised the pillow and simultaneously placed it over the face of the sick woman.

What was that? Fragments of memory of something that had really happened, and that only now, here, he was allowing to surface? Or the memory of images arising from a wish that he could not allow himself to have, could not possibly have had: how they might have moved their hands, one from each side, toward one another? Their fingertips touched. Gret's hand slid over his. Their eyes met. Images of the wish to kill, they might both have let their hands on the pillow become heavier and heavier, they might have looked at one another—fascinated, yes: carry on with the monstrous deed? For ten more seconds? And ten more? Another surge of the wish to kill, and in Gret's eyes a spark as if she were asking: Which of us two, brother, can endure the killing the longest?

A shiver ran through Thom, as in a fever. No! Yet—could at least that murderous wishful fantasy be real: at least the fantasy?

He glanced up. In the windowpane, reflected by the night, he saw himself.

Myself, he thought, with Gret?

His face, brightly lit by the lamp, showed up clearly in the reflection: the eyes, mouth, nose, the hair, the shoulders, the blue shirt collar, open.

Myself?

Was his search over? He groped for the knob at the base of the lamp. When he pressed it the images disappeared. He sat in the dark.

Probably just a surmise. Who, apart possibly from Lisbeth Bronnen and probably Gret Winter too—provided she had managed to cut down on her drinking during those early days of July 1982—could claim that this was how it had been and not otherwise?

A surmise. But it is a fact that Samuel, coming in from the front steps about eleven that night, saw that the door to the study was ajar. He put his briefcase down on the sideboard in the passage and pushed open the door. When he turned the switch the single bulb of the candelabra went on. Thom was sitting in one of the four leather armchairs to the right of the fireplace, leaning back, his arms resting on the chair arms, his head slightly bowed.

Samuel described how he had asked Thom whether he would like to have a glass of white St. Saphorin with him at the stone table outside. The weather being so sultry, he had added.

He described how when Thom still didn't look up or make any reply, Samuel moved closer to him. "What is it—are you asleep?"

Thom did not move. Samuel had repeated his question, this time in a whisper, and laid his hand on Thom's shoulder. Thom looked up, staring first at the chandelier, then down at the floor again, as if studying the lines of the carpet's blue-and-red geometric design. No, Samuel said, he wasn't drunk.

Samuel suggested that Thom get up from the chair and go to bed.

For a short while nothing happened; then, as if Samuel's voice had only just reached him, Thom stood up. Moving stiffly like a sleepwalker, he crossed the study into the passage and from there into the hall. "I followed him. He had stopped. I stood in front of him and grasped him by the shoulders. 'Thom. Thom! What's happened?' I shook him gently. His gaze passed through me into a void. I led him to the staircase, and he slowly walked up ahead of me. At the top he walked on, still without a word, and entered the Blue Room. When I saw from the doorway that he was starting to unbutton his shirt, obviously still unaware of me, I said goodnight and closed the door."

Then, Samuel said, he went across to Gret's room, where light showed through the crack under the door. He knocked. After a while she opened the door, looking as if she had already fallen asleep, probably in her armchair, her smile slightly lopsided from the alcohol; it faded as she listened to Samuel. Together they went across to Thom's room. Thom was sitting up in bed, the pillow behind his back. Without looking at them, he stared at the ceiling. He did not react to their questions.

Gret did not think they should call the doctor. Leaving the door to the Blue Room open, she said she would leave her own door open too. She would set the alarm and look in on her brother every hour. "These things happen." When she wished her husband goodnight in the gallery, that lopsided smile was back on her face. She had seen Thom like this before, she said, in the days right after Mother died. The aftereffect of shock. Yes, she remembered: "A kind of stupor" was what the doctor had said; a torpor following an overwhelming, sudden experience of great importance to the victim of the stupor; the victim's psyche had not had enough time to digest that experience, that realization—something like that, Gret said. Would the torpor wear off after a few hours, or maybe even months, or not at all, she had wondered? On that earlier occasion, anyway, Thom had awakened from it. She had read up on the condition to find out whether the awakening was a normal stage in the illness, or— she hesitated, fell silent. With her fist at her mouth, she looked at Samuel, then turned toward her own room.

Next day Gret reported: On returning to Thom's room at five in the morning she did not turn on the light right away. In the dawn shining through the open window Thom was lying there only half covered by the sheet; he had pulled his tan raincoat over his head and shoulders— "yes," she shrugged, "his raincoat. Thom looked as if he was hiding under it. Going closer, I somehow felt that, although I could see only his bare legs, he wasn't asleep. He must have been lying there in a state of extreme tension, all his senses alert to picking up even the slightest sound. Suddenly, ripping the raincoat from his head, he sat up. His eyes wide with terror, he stared toward the desk. Then, as if trying to stop himself from screaming, he pressed a piece of the raincoat with both hands against his mouth. I sat down on the edge of the bed. 'What's the matter, Thom?' At that, he did become aware of me. 'Come on, lie down again!' It took me quite a while to persuade him to sink back on his pillow. 'Gret?' he asked, as if from very far away. And all of a sudden he started talking to himself, rapidly—incoherently: he would outsmart them, that much I began to gather, and there was something about flames, then, clearly: 'You know, with snakes in their hair, and scourges, they're lashing out with scourges!' "

She gave him some sleeping pills. Yes, now he was sleeping, still quietly sleeping.

Gret insisted on taking care of Thom; she didn't want anyone else to go and see him. Not even Barbara, not even Urs. "He is ill. What he needs is rest, lots of rest."

When Thom called for Lis that afternoon, Gret promised to phone her. She tried, without success. At seven that evening, Lis called back. And the following day—she must have taken the early bus to Cavaillon—Lis arrived by taxi late in the afternoon. Carrying her suitcase, she walked up the front steps and rang the bell; when nothing stirred in the house, she pushed the heavy door open with her shoulder. In the passage she stopped for a moment and softly called "Hello?" From the kitchen came the sound of water splashing noisily into the sink. Strange—there was a sudden smell of burning: no question, burning wood. She opened the study door. Standing in front of a blazing fire, wearing her blue housecoat and with her back to the door, was Gret. Lis approached. Gret was standing there quietly, apparently absorbed in the play of the flames. Then with both hands she crumpled some paper into a ball and threw it into the fire. It was only after they had exchanged greetings, Lis said later, that she noticed the big pile of loose, handwritten sheets lying on the table to Gret's left beside the fireplace. As if to shield them, Gret had unobtrusively moved in front of them.

"Surely you're not burning"—Lis broke off. "But that's Thom's handwriting!" Again Gret threw a hastily crumpled handful of paper into the fire. "Don't try to stop me," she said. "It's probably just as well that Thom got all these old stories off his chest. We know now it hasn't made him any happier. In any case, I think things have gone far enough. This stuff should be burned before it causes any more misery. Would you like to take a look upstairs? Thom's probably awake." And by the way, she went on, she had taken care to put his professional notes over there; perhaps it would be best if Lis were to take them upstairs right away. Gret handed Lis the other stack of papers.

And that was what caused Lis to make a scene. Which papers were to be destroyed and which weren't was a matter solely for Thom to decide, Lis ended by shouting. She had then appropriated both piles, left the room, and gone upstairs.

As for Thom: although when Lis entered he was sitting propped against his pillow, he did not look up. And even when she put her arms around him as she sat down beside him, he stared straight ahead at the quilt. When she stroked his forehead and cheek and kept repeating his name, he turned his face toward her. His gaze rested on her, but even when he murmured, "You're here?" she had a feeling that the message of her arrival was being blocked at some switch point in his brain between perception and consciousness. No smile. He continued to stare straight ahead. When she held the glass of fruit juice to his lips, he took a sip.

Downstairs in the pantry, Lis was told by Herminia that during these two days Thom had been keeping to his bed he had taken nothing but a little fruit juice, just like in the days right after Mrs. Winter's death.

Lis spent the evening in the Blue Room. Thom dozed; from time to time he would look up at the ceiling as if wondering how the crystal chandelier could be repaired. Lis told him about her phone conversation with Gret, about her last evening in Saint-Rémy, about her journey. Perhaps by talking she would succeed in gradually penetrating his consciousness? He did not react. What if he were to remain barricaded in this inaccessible zone of silence, forever? She refused even to contemplate that. At twilight she switched on the desk lamp. Hoping to find the root of his illness in the stack—still ten centimeters high—of sheets covered on both sides with Thom's writing, she began to read, although not quite sure whether the hope was enough to authorize her to do so. She went on reading until far into the night.

Just before two in the morning she lay down beside him, taking care not to waken him. In the darkness she held her arms around his shoulders. She could hear, could feel, his even breathing as he slept. She gave a sudden start: she must have fallen asleep. Thom groaned, tossing his head from side to side. Her hand felt cool perspiration on his forehead.

Through the open window came the sound of bells from the town: five o'clock. Dawn was breaking.

Lis, seized by something like combined rage and despair, sat up and suddenly called Thom's name, then grabbed him as he slept by both shoulders and shook him. "Thom, please wake up—please!"

A surmise, nothing more: that Thom sat up. In the gray dawn he stared at her in amazement: when he said, "Lis?" two or three times, "Lis?" they embraced.

As if still in a daze, Thom ran his hand through his hair, over his forehead. He got out of bed, walked to the window. And now, without turning around, he said, "Lis, I saw myself: me." And when he came back and sat down beside Lisbeth on the bed, he repeated: "Me."

"You?" Lis still could not understand.

So, haltingly, he began to tell her.

After that, Thom slept until late in the day.

Some Source Material

This novel is based in part on information drawn from the documentary and scholarly literature on the subject of Switzerland between 1933 and 1945, in particular from: Edgar Bonjour, *Geschichte der schweizerischen Neutralität I–VI*; Alfred Haesler, *Das Boot ist voll*; Mathias Knauer and Jürg Frischknecht, *Die unterbrochene Spur*; Werner Rings, *Schweiz im Krieg*; Oskar Felix Fritsch, *Geistige Landesverteidigung während des Zweiten Weltkrieges*; J. R. von Salis, *Chronik des Zweiten Weltkrieges, Radiokommentare*; Jakob Tanner, *Bundeshaushalt, Währung und Kriegswirtschaft*; and others.

The figure of Major-General (Ret.) Ulrich Lyss is also historically documented. Lyss has also written about the discovery of documents at La Charité-sur-Loire.

The story of Max Strub, who was beaten up during a National Front assembly in the Jammers auditorium while he sang the "Internationale," is also historically authentic. This actually took place not in Jammers but in Olten, Canton Solothurn. The author owes the description of events and persons to the work of Peter Heim ("Olten im Frontenfrühling," 1982, unpublished).

In one of the chapters titled "In the Dovecote," Sepp describes events in 1932 leading to thirteen demonstrators being shot to death by an army unit. The account is based on what happened in Geneva that same year. In Geneva the "Public Indictment of Mr. Nicole and Mr. Dicker" delivered by Georges Oltramare, leader of the Fascist Union Nationale, was the cause of and pretext for deploying the Army within the country against civilians. In other chapters titled "In the Dovecote," the author also ascribes to Sepp the recollection of historically documented events occurring at that time not in Jammers but elsewhere in Switzerland. Thus the Jewish cattle dealer Arthur Bloch was in fact murdered by a Fascist terrorist group in 1942 in the town of Payerne, Canton Vaud (Walter Matthias Diggelmann has given a moving description of that murder in a story "Der Jud Bloch"). Other recollections of Sepp refer to the mechanics' strike in Zurich (Helvetia-Platz) and the dyers' strike in Basel: protest actions that resulted in death and serious injuries among the strikers (cf. Irene Soltermann, *Die Blutnacht und der Monteurs Streik in Zürich 1932*, Bern, 1985). The story of Sepp's brother Jonny is based on Richard Dindo's documentary work on the Swiss who fought in the Spanish Civil War.

Mrs. Esther Winter's claim that an honorary doctorate was awarded Benito Mussolini by the University of Jammers must be emphatically denied. This is a claim made by a storyteller whose unreliability as a witness is notorious. The existing documents prove beyond a doubt that credit for having thus honored Mussolini in 1936 belongs to the University of Lausanne.

Meanwhile, Thomas Winter's work has been published: *The General's Politics. Between Mandate and Coup*, Basel-Zurich, 1984, Edgar Bonjour, historical emeritus, having advised Thomas Winter to write up the case of the documents found at La Charité and referred him to an American study in the journal *Documents on German Foreign Policy 1918–1945, Series D 12*, Washington, 1962. In his research the author has made use of the above-mentioned sources as well as the first description of the case by the Geneva journalist René-Henri Wüst, 1966; also the diary entries of Bernard Barbey. On General Guisan's orders, the secret documents relating to the military alliance in the possession of the Supreme Command of the Swiss Army were destroyed—entirely?—as early as the fall of 1940. In answer to Thomas Winter's inquiry, the sole survivor of the close circle of officers to whom Guisan had divulged the secret replied in writing: "Presumably your knowledge of the matter is not complete. I swore an oath of secrecy to the General from which he did not release me before his death. More than that I cannot say."